ARMINIUS

One man's greatest victory.
Rome's greatest defeat.

Robert Fabbri read Drama and Theatre at London University and has worked in film and TV for twenty-five years as an assistant director. He has worked on productions such as *Hornblower, Hellraiser, Patriot Games* and *Billy Elliot*. His lifelong passion for ancient history inspired him to write the Vespasian series. He lives in London and Berlin.

ARMINIUS

THE LIMITS OF EMPIRE

ROBERT
FABBRI

CORVUS

First published in hardback in Great Britain in 2017 by Corvus,
an imprint of Atlantic Books Ltd.
This edition published in paperback in 2017 by Corvus.

10 9 8 7 6 5 4 3 2 1

A CIP catalogue record for this book is available from the British Library.

Paperback ISBN: 978 1 78239 701 4
E-book ISBN: 978 1 78239 702 1

Printed and bound by CPI Group (UK) Ltd, Croydon, CR0 4YY

Corvus
An imprint of Atlantic Books Ltd
Ormond House
26–27 Boswell Street
London
WC1N 3JZ

www.corvus-books.co.uk

For Leo and Jodi Fabbri, wishing you a long and happy life together.

Welcome to the family, Jodi – and, of course, that bean, Carl!

PROLOGUE

�֍ �֍

RAVENNA, AD 37

'TO FACE SYNATOS the *retiarius*, I give you the *secutor*, Licus of Germania!'

The crowd's roar of approval drowned out the games-master's voice; but to Thumelicatz it was a muffled drone that just penetrated the bronze helmet encasing his head. He strode into the arena, raising his short sword to the ten-thousand-strong crowd as they chanted 'Licus! Licus!', the shortened form of his Latinised name: Thumelicus. Pumping his sword in the air in time to the chant and holding his semi-cylindrical rectangular shield, emblazoned with a boar's head, before him, he acknowledged all parts of the oval, sandstone arena.

Thumelicatz had learnt early on in his five years on the sand from his *lanista*, Orosius, his owner and trainer, to work the crowd, despite his feelings for them: a popular gladiator with the support of the mob had the edge in any fight and, if he was defeated, could expect their mercy. Orosius had a wealth of experience having been granted the wooden sword of freedom fifteen years previously, after fifty-three fights; today Thumelicatz would come to within one fight of that total, thanks mainly to his lanista's teaching. Thumelicatz held his sword towards his mentor sitting in the crowd; Orosius, once an object of fear and loathing but now one of grudging respect, inclined his head in acknowledgement.

Finally, shouting the prescribed words of a gladiator about to do mortal combat, Thumelicatz saluted the games' sponsor, seated beneath the only canopy around the arena. With a gracious gesture of one hand, the sponsor, the newly installed prefect of the small, provincial town of Ravenna, indicated his readiness to see blood spilt; he adjusted his white toga bordered by a thin purple stripe, indicating his equestrian rank, and held his palms out to accept the accolade of the crowd.

Sweat rolled down Thumelicatz's face from under the felt cap beneath his helmet; he blinked and turned his head, searching through the two small eye-holes in the blank face-guard for his opponent, the helmetless, net and trident wielding retiarius, Synatos. Finding his foe he kept his eyes firmly fixed on him, knowing that the lighter and more agile fighter would try to use his speed to unsight him. Weighed down with helmet, shield and wide leather belt securing his loincloth, along with thick padded linen guards on his right arm and lower right leg as well as a greave of boiled leather on his left, the secutor was comparatively slow; Thumelicatz knew from long experience that it was crucial to finish this fight quickly before exhaustion claimed him.

He touched the hammer amulet hanging around his neck. 'Donar, hone my blade, guide my hand and give me strength, Great Thunderer.'

The *rudis*, the wooden staff held by the referee, the *summa rudis*, flashed down between the two fighters; the crowd quietened. Thumelicatz's sharp breaths, amplified in his helmet, came fast as he tried to extract as much oxygen as possible from the stifling atmosphere that surrounded him. He stamped his left leg forward, pulling his sword arm back overarm so that the blade was angled down, level with his eyes, and presented his shield, staring over its rim at Synatos. The retiarius stared back, eyes squinting against the loose dust that matted his black curls; he crouched, leading with the left of his sculpted, oiled body, flicking his weighted net in front of him with his right hand, and probing with his trident in the left, protruding from the thick linen that protected that arm – a chainmail shoulder-guard above it completed his meagre protection.

The rudis remained between them; Thumelicatz held Synatos' gaze, trying to guess his first move; they had fought together many times in the *ludus*, the training school, and knew each other's styles well; they had also met once before in the arena. On that occasion, five months before, Thumelicatz had won after a hard fight, eventually disarming Synatos and giving him the puckered scar that ran down his right forearm; the crowd had shown their appreciation by granting the loser his life. Thumelicatz had been relieved. Despite a retiarius being looked down upon by all sword-wielding gladiators as not being a gladiator at all in the strictest sense of the word, Synatos was as close a friend as Thumelicatz would allow himself in the enclosed ludus where men were trained to take life indiscriminately.

He'll jump to his left and thrust his trident at my unprotected right thigh, Thumelicatz thought as he noticed a slight movement of the eyes to that part of his anatomy. *Then he'll flick his net at my hand as I block the blow, trying to dislodge my sword.*

With a barked command to fight, the summa rudis raised his staff; the crowd roared in anticipation of blood. Synatos leapt to his left and, with a lightning jab, powered his trident at Thumelicatz's right thigh. Already expecting the blow, Thumelicatz thrust his sword down, at an angle, between two of the barbed points of the trident; with a spray of sparks and a metallic rasp, the trident grated up his blade, coming to a clanging halt on the oval guard. Punching his shield out, he deflected the net aiming to ensnare his right hand. Pushing forward, Thumelicatz tried to close with his adversary, the retiarius having nothing but a *pugio*, a short dagger, for close-quarters work. Synatos saw the danger and jumped back leaving his net, like a circular shadow, on the ground in front of him to trip Thumelicatz should he try to follow up.

A trident jab to the throat forced Thumelicatz's shield up and he stepped back as the three evilly sharp barbed points skewered into the leather-covered wood, cracking the rim back to crash into his face-guard; his ears rang as the clang resounded around the helmet. He yanked his shield away, hoping that the trident was firmly embedded and that he could haul it from Synatos' grasp; it came free as the net landed over his head. Thumelicatz felt the draw-cord around the net's perimeter instantly begin to tighten, threatening to entrap him. The secutors' helmets, being completely smooth with no extraneous rims, fins or guards, were designed to avoid being caught in the retiarii's nets. Thumelicatz pulled his head back, slipping it from under the net, and raised his sword so that the blade seared through the twine. Backwards he jumped, blocking repeated trident thrusts, rending the net in two until he severed the draw-cord, rendering the weapon next to useless.

Again the trident slammed into his shield as Synatos attempted to cover his discarding the net and grabbing the long shaft with two hands. With the extra strength of a double grip the trident became a fearsome attacking weapon; to the crowd's raucous approval, Synatos thrust it down again and again towards Thumelicatz's unprotected bare feet forcing him into a dance of necessity and to bring his shield ever lower, hacking with his sword at the metal head and thick shaft as he waited for the inevitable.

When it came he was ready.

The triple spikes abruptly raised and flashed over his lowered shield towards the base of his throat; he ducked and heard the trident scrape over the crown of his helm as he pushed forward, punching his shield before him into the chest of his opponent. With an explosive exhalation, the wind was knocked from Synatos' lungs; he staggered but brought the shaft of his weapon cracking down onto Thumelicatz's shoulders as he, in turn, thrust his sword towards the retiarius's heart, jolting his aim so that the point punched harmlessly into Synatos' shoulder-guard. Both gladiators crashed to the ground, sand immediately sticking to their sweat-lathered bodies. The clamour of the crowd rose even further as they contemplated a to-the-death scramble to savour between two men who quite evidently had each other's demise in the forefronts of their minds.

With a bone-jarring crack, Synatos pulled the shaft of his trident, two-handed, down again across Thumelicatz's shoulder blades; grunting in pain, he slammed his sword-weighted fist into the side of the retiarius's unprotected head whilst pressing down with his shield on his already empty chest, denying him breath. He felt Synatos begin to change his grip on the trident behind him, bringing the points round to plunge into his spine; he exploded up onto his knees astride his prone opponent, knocking the weapon from his weakened grasp. A searing white light of agony flashed before Thumelicatz's eyes as Synatos brought his shin crunching up between his legs; disobeying every urge of his body to double over to protect that precious part of his anatomy, he flung himself backwards as the pain seared up through his lower abdomen like the repeated manic stabbing of a stiletto blade. His chest heaved and vomit squirted from his mouth over the inside of his face-guard.

Grabbing his pugio from its sheath, Synatos pushed himself up, jumped to his feet and threw himself at Thumelicatz. Still hyperventilating with pain, Thumelicatz just had the presence of mind to punch his shield up, deflecting first the blade and then the body wielding it; he rolled away to his left and struggled to his knees as Synatos hit the sand and, with the agility of a lizard, flicked himself back round to face his opponent. Using his sword as a stick, Thumelicatz forced himself to his feet; he was too weak to prevent Synatos scrambling to regain his trident. Now, with his principal weapon in his right hand and the dagger in his left, the retiarius squared up to Thumelicatz. The crowd's roar was deafening, penetrating even into Thumelicatz's bronze-encased ears, as they cheered the prospect of renewed hostilities with both gladiators back on even terms; and then the chant of 'Licus! Licus!' broke out above the wave of sound.

Still in pain and more weighed down by his equipment than his opponent, Thumelicatz knew that he had to finish it soon before he tired beyond the point of effective attack. He let his shield sag, sword arm drop and knees buckle slightly as if he had already reached that stage of exhaustion; with a snarl of triumph the retiarius lunged forward, thrusting his trident at chest height. With a fleet, violent motion, Thumelicatz smashed his shield across the path of the weapon knocking it aside and hacked his sword up at the dagger following it, sending it, with a resounding metallic ring, flying skywards as he continued his right arm's trajectory and slammed his fist, still gripping his sword, into Synatos' face, flattening his nose with a wet crunch of cartilage. The retiarius arced back, blood tracing his path through the air, trident flying from his loosened grip, to land with a lung-emptying jolt on the arena floor. Thumelicatz stood over his victim, who looked up at him and immediately raised his right index finger in submission; the summa rudis brought his staff across Thumelicatz's chest bringing the fight to a close. He breathed deeply of vomit-reeking air, in ragged bursts; sweat stung his eyes as he looked down at the man, who was almost a friend, lying defeated at his feet.

It was now up to the sponsor of the games to judge the mood of the crowd and decide upon Synatos' fate.

The chorus of 'Licus! Licus!' continued as he raised his sword to the sponsor in a gesture that all present understood to mean: life or death? The prefect got slowly to his feet, his right hand balled into a fist across his chest; he looked around the amphitheatre.

The tone of the mob changed; slowly at first but inexorably, the chant became: 'Death! Death!' Their memory was long and they were not prepared to spare a man defeated by the same opponent twice.

Synatos' face registered the call for his cold-blooded despatch and he turned his head slowly to the sponsor; their eyes met. Holding the gaze for a few moments as the crowd hushed, the prefect of Ravenna thrust his right arm forward, fist still clenched with the thumb held tight against it, in imitation of an undrawn sword. Pausing for dramatic effect as silence fell around the oval he inhaled deeply, savouring the power of life and death; abruptly his thumb flicked out, horizontally, from the fist in imitation of a drawn sword: the sign of death.

Synatos gave a faint smile of resignation to Thumelicatz and got to one knee.

The crowd howled their delight, many visibly excited beneath their tunics, toying with themselves – some frantically, some with unhurried relish – as they contemplated another life extinguished for their pleasure.

Thumelicatz held his sword aloft and slowly turned on the spot; the disgust he felt played freely on his face obscured by his helmet as his eyes took in every member of the crowd: bakers, clerks, petty magistrates, professional sycophants, shopkeepers, whore-boys, merchants and more, all equally as unmartial as the women they ploughed. The useless fat of empire – whose only justification for existence was the physical fact of their birth – baying for the life of a man who could end most of their miserable existences in less than ten heartbeats. Was this what the Romans had forged their empire for, so that the timid and the flabby could live their martial fantasies vicariously, spilling their seed as the blood of better men was spilt upon the sand?

Thumelicatz approached Synatos and stood before him.

The condemned retiarius took a firm grip of his right thigh and raised his head, staring straight into his executioner's eyes. 'Make it clean, my friend.'

'Do you not want a weapon in your hand?'

'No, I travel a different path to yours; mine leads to the Ferryman not Walhalla.'

Thumelicatz inclined his head, took his sword and placed it vertically between the base of Synatos' neck and collar-bone, just next to his shoulder-guard; his left hand clasped the top of the hilt over his right.

The noise of the crowd had reached almost impossible heights.

Synatos swallowed, looked briefly at the sun burning in a blue, cloudless sky and then nodded.

Using all the power in his shoulders, Thumelicatz drove the blade down through skin, flesh and lung until the point punched through the muscled wall of the organ now pumping at thrice its normal rate. Synatos' eyes rounded with pain, his chest heaved, exhaling a deep grunt that was violently curtailed by blood exploding into his gorge. Thumelicatz felt the dying man's grip on his thigh tighten, his fingernails breaking the skin; he took no notice, it always happened. With a twist of his wrists left then right he shredded the heart and then, gripping Synatos' right shoulder with his left hand, yanked the blade free with the liquid slurp of lessening suction.

Synatos remained upright for a few moments, blood seeping from his open mouth and nostrils, trailing in long strings down from his chin, eyes sightless, expression rigid: dead. The crowd let out a satiated moan, bestial in its rawness; the corpse collapsed back onto the sand.

Thumelicatz raised his sword in the air, saluting the objects of his contempt, wishing for death to visit every life deemed to be inadequate; which was most of them. Without a glance down to his victim he turned towards the gates; they began to open. Eight auxiliary archers filed in, four left and four right, arrows nocked but bows undrawn.

Thumelicatz stopped and threw down his sword.

Two silhouetted figures, one draped in a toga, followed the archers in.

Thumelicatz recognised the bulked-muscled outline of his lanista, Orosius; a quick glance up to where the sponsor of the games had been sitting confirmed the identity of the second. The prefect of Ravenna raised his arms as he strode out to the centre of the arena; Orosius remained in the gateway, watching.

The crowd cheered their prefect with the reserve of people lauding a man more known for his power than his popularity; if the prefect realised that, he gave no sign of it on his face. He approached Thumelicatz and gestured for quiet; the crowd was happy to oblige.

Although it shocked him, Thumelicatz could guess what was about to happen but could feel no excitement, no pride, no relief after five years of having to fight for his life on a regular basis. He had one thought and that was of his homeland, the land that he had never seen; the land he never thought he would see. It was a land he knew only from the tales his mother, betrayed to Rome whilst she had been pregnant with him, had told him in the brief years that he had lived with her before he had been taken away, at the age of eight, to train for a life in the arena, where, because of whose son he was, he had expected to die.

The prefect had begun to address the crowd but Thumelicatz could only hear his words, not concentrate on them. The mental image of the father he had never met burnt in his mind as he contemplated returning to the land that his father had liberated from Rome six years before Thumelicatz's birth: the land of Germania Magna. Over four days his father, Erminatz, known to the Romans by his Latinised name, Arminius, had destroyed Publius Quinctilius Varus' army of three legions and their auxiliaries in a series of running battles in the Teutoburg Wald; his mother had told him great stories of the massacre. Three Eagles had been captured and Rome had retreated across the Rhenus. Thumelicatz would go back to a land of free men; a land where a man's worth was judged by his prowess and where small-hearted men were of no account, no matter how much silver they held.

He felt a hand pulling at his elbow and his thoughts were jerked back to the present; he heard the prefect speak in a tone as if he were repeating himself. 'Remove your helmet, Licus of Germania.'

Thumelicatz slid his thumbs under the rim and pushed up; the bronze helmet slipped off and the air became easier to breathe. With pale blue eyes, squinting in deep sockets beneath thick, black eyebrows, he looked down at the prefect who winced. Thumelicatz wiped the back of his hand over his clean-shaven face, removing as much of the half-congealed vomit sticking to it as possible before pressing a finger to his long, sleek nose and clearing each nostril of acidic fluid.

The prefect looked at him in distaste. Thumelicatz wondered if he would go back on what he had planned but then realised that the prefect would lose face should he decide not to grant freedom to a gladiator just because he found his appearance after combat unsavoury; he hawked and spat a mixture of blood and phlegm on the sand.

The prefect rummaged in the fold of his toga; he brought out a wooden training sword, the type that Thumelicatz had used for years, day after day for hours on end, practising every prescribed move in every combination until they were as natural as breathing.

With a theatrical flourish the prefect held it aloft. 'I, Marcus Vibius Vibianus, prefect of the city of Ravenna, award the gladiator, Licus of Germania, his freedom after five years in the arena.' He presented the sword in both hands to Thumelicatz who took it without thanks.

Knowing that he could not afford to insult the mob, Thumelicatz punched the symbol of gladiatorial manumission in the air and rotated once, accepting the accolade of the citizens of Ravenna for what he hoped was the last time.

'You may become my client and bear my name,' Vibianus said with an air of self-importance.

Thumelicatz looked at the prefect as if he could not believe what he had just heard. 'I'd sooner become your bitch and bear your runtish whelps, Roman.' He barged past the prefect and walked towards the gates, ostentatiously peeling off the accoutrements of a secutor and discarding them to cheers, working the crowd in the knowledge that Vibianus would not be able to do anything against him while he enjoyed their support.

Vibianus followed him, trying to make the best out of the situation, head held high, the very picture of a haughty magistrate.

'I take it you and our esteemed prefect won't become regular dining companions,' Orosius commented, falling in step with Thumelicatz as he passed through the gates. He handed him a papyrus scroll. 'This is your certificate of manumission.'

Thumelicatz took it without reading it. 'Thank you, Orosius. How did this come about? I thought that I was destined to die in the arena.'

'You were but that's a fact that no one had bothered to acquaint our new prefect with before he took office. When he told me that he wished to buy the favour of the mob by freeing you, who was I, a mere lanista, to gainsay him?'

Thumelicatz's pace slowed as they negotiated their way through the torch-lit, fume-filled bowels of the amphitheatre, clogged with terrified, shackled prisoners awaiting the jaws of the wild beasts whose famished roars echoed around smoke-stained, brick-built arches. Water dripped from the ceiling into puddles, edged by green slime, on the worn paved floor. 'Why did you do this for me? You owe me nothing. Quite the opposite actually, I owe you everything for the personal training you gave me.'

Orosius smiled and looked sidelong at his companion. 'Would you believe that it was to stop you exceeding my tally and becoming the most renowned gladiator ever in Ravenna?'

'Bollocks; no one gives a fuck about being anything in this shithole.'

'That's where you're wrong; the prefect does. He wants to gain favour with the new Emperor, Gaius Caligula, by increasing the flow of tax from this city into the imperial coffers. He plans to do it by firstly buying the goodwill of the citizens and then making cuts, one of which was how much he pays me for my goods and services; the amount that he offered me in compensation for freeing you was derisory. I think when the Emperor finds out that Marcus Vibius Vibianus, in an effort to make himself popular, has freed the son of Arminius he'll be called back to Rome to explain this rather novel way of containing our enemies; at the very least he would be advised to forget any senatorial ambitions.'

'And things here will get back to normal for you?'

'That's all I ask; so you had better leave right now before someone tells him he's made rather a foolish mistake.'

'I need to go somewhere first.'

'No you don't, I've had your prize money brought from the ludus; you're a rich man, you could almost afford to buy yourself.'

'Keep it, it'll make up the shortfall in your compensation.'

'It'll do more than that.' Orosius signalled to two guards on the gates to the outside world to open them. 'What else is so important that it's going to delay your departure?'

Thumelicatz stepped out into the street, free for the first time to go wherever he wished. He nodded at the sheathed sword hanging from Orosius' belt. 'May I?'

Orosius unclipped the scabbard from his belt and handed it to Thumelicatz.

'Thank you, Orosius. I need to get my mother; she's a slave in the house of my uncle.'

Thumelicatz pounded on the door of a substantial villa on the wide and busy thoroughfare that linked Ravenna's forum with its citadel. After a few moments a viewing slot at head-height opened to reveal a dark, questioning eye.

'I have come to see Tiberius Claudius Flavus,' Thumelicatz announced, trying to suppress the tension in his voice.

'What name shall I give, master?'

'Tell him that it's his brother's son.'

The slot snapped shut.

Thumelicatz waited with growing impatience wondering if his uncle, Flavus, whom he knew as Chlodochar, would dare open the door to him after such a long absence.

The answer came with the grating of a bolt and the clack of a key.

The door swung back.

Placing his hand on the pommel of his sword hilt, Thumelicatz walked through the vestibule and on into the atrium of his uncle's house for the first time in fourteen years.

The atrium was that of a Roman, not of a Germanic warrior from the Cherusci tribe to which both Thumelicatz and his uncle belonged. A fine mosaic floor, depicting scenes from the *Aeneid*, surrounded the impluvium at the rectangular room's centre; the fountain within it was of Salacia, consort to Neptune, portrayed as a nymph crowned with seaweed. There were no weapons or other tools of war hanging on the walls, no boar tusks, no antlers, nothing that Thumelicatz's mother had told him decorated the walls of a nobleman's longhouse; there were no long wooden boards and benches at which his followers would feast and sing, just low, polished marble tables on ornate legs, littered with glass bowls and bronze statuettes of Roman gods. To Thumelicatz it looked like every other Roman house that he had been forced into to perform displays of swordsmanship for Ravenna's wealthy at their luxuriant and wasteful dinner parties; he spat on the floor.

'That's exactly the sort of behaviour I would expect from a slave and a gladiator,' came a voice from the far end of the room, oozing contempt. 'Why aren't you dead yet and how did you get permission to visit?'

Thumelicatz looked up to see a tall, portly man, wearing an equestrian toga, entering the room. His hair was short and greying blond; a livid scar where his right eye should have been disfigured a round and flabby, florid face.

Thumelicatz spat again, this time in contempt for the man he saw rather than the culture that he surrounded himself with. 'I'm not dead because I have the protection of Donar, a warrior's god; and I am here because I don't need permission to go anywhere being neither a slave nor a gladiator any more, *Uncle*.'

Flavus stopped; his expression changed from sneering aloofness to shocked concern almost before Thumelicatz had finished speaking. 'You're lying. Guards!'

Thumelicatz pulled the wooden sword from his belt and walked up the room as four substantial bodyguards entered behind Flavus; their swords were drawn. Thumelicatz paused to the left of the impluvium.

Flavus gestured to his men to stay back. 'Who gave you that?'

'*Your* prefect, not one hour ago.'

'Then I shall tell him to take it back.'

'He couldn't if he tried; my certificate of manumission makes me a freed citizen of Rome. I could appeal to the new Caesar and he would have to uphold my case.'

'Or he could just have you killed as Tiberius should have done years ago.'

It was now Thumelicatz's turn to sneer. 'You know perfectly well why Tiberius didn't have me killed. It was for the same reason that he refused the king of the Chatti, Adgandestrius', offer to poison my father; because he had some honour – a concept that you forgot about years ago. Now give me my mother and I will leave you to rot in the rancid fruits of your treachery.'

'She is not mine to give, she belongs to Rome; I just mind her.'

'She is your brother's wife; now that he is dead you have the right to dispose of her as you wish. Give her to me and I will leave thinking slightly better of you; I will forgo my father's vengeance that is now mine by right and you will never hear from me again.'

'And if I choose not to?'

'Then I will choose to take her; and my father's vengeance on you will be that of a man murdered by his brother.'

Flavus laughed, hollow and mirthless; he pointed a thumb over his shoulder. 'And you think that *they* will let you?'

Thumelicatz looked along the line of bodyguards, Germanic auxiliaries who had completed their service and had stayed in the employ of their commander, he supposed. 'If I was to think about them, I would think about them one at a time.' In his mind Thumelicatz marked the dark-haired man on their extreme right and the older man with a full blond beard next to him.

There was something in the casual tone of his nephew's reply that caused Flavus to hesitate for a moment before his one remaining eye hardened. He stepped aside. 'Kill him!'

The four bodyguards surged forward without hesitation and together, in one line. Thumelicatz knew they had made a serious mistake; he jumped right, onto the raised side of the impluvium, as the dark-haired man's sword slashed down where he had been an instant earlier. Sweeping his sword out of its scabbard, Thumelicatz continued the weapon's upwards motion into the man's jaw, severing it to sway loose – attached only by the thin skin of his cheeks – as the blond guard sliced a horizontal cut towards his thigh. With a rapid downwards jab of his left hand, Thumelicatz caught the blow with the practice sword, slowing and deflecting it, as it cleaved through the hard-ened wood, to slice into his calf with little momentum; riding the pain he flashed the wooden sword's splintered rump up, forcing it into the blond man's eye, sending him sprawling back with a desperate shriek. Jerking his dripping blade out of his first victim – who buckled, gurgling to the floor – Thumelicatz pointed it at the remaining two guards. They stopped, unsure of how to deal with a man who had just felled their two comrades in less than five heartbeats. Thumelicatz did not wait for them to come up with a plan; tossing the weapon from his right hand to his left, he accelerated the blade, backhand, towards the nearest man, in a blurred arc that terminated in the hollow, wet thud of a butcher's cleaver rending a joint of pork. The guard's head twisted with the velocity of the blow to slew to its right; anchored by a few unsevered ligaments, it perched on the shoulder, staring in horror at his comrade next to him as his heart gave two final, mighty beats, exploding blood into the air. The head toppled forward, pulling the body down behind it, as Thumelicatz's blade slammed into the open, incredulous mouth of the fourth bodyguard; its tip burst out of his neck. Before the surprise had even begun to register in the man's eyes, Thumelicatz turned and surveyed the room; his uncle was gone.

A woman's scream from the courtyard garden, at the rear of the house, rang around the atrium. Thumelicatz let gravity do the work of removing his sword from his final victim as the body crumpled to the blood-slick mosaic floor. With a quick glance around the room to check for other retainers intent upon defending their master, Thumelicatz ran towards the *tablinum*, at the far end of the atrium, and passed through it and on into the garden.

'Put down your sword and your mother will live!' Flavus stood between two of the columns supporting the portico at the far end of the garden; a woman in her sixties, tall with wild grey hair and pendulous breasts swaying beneath a thin knee-length tunic, struggled in his grip with a knife at her throat.

Her blue eyes widened in recognition. 'Thumelicatz!'

Thumelicatz raised a hand. 'Stay calm, Mother.'

Behind Flavus, another woman of similar age, but of squatter build, lurked in an open doorway; a dagger flashed in her hand, hate ate into her face. 'Kill the bitch anyway, Husband; and then we'll settle with her whelp over her corpse.'

'Silence, Gunda! Thumelicatz, drop your weapon.'

'And what happens if I don't?'

'I slit Thusnelda's throat.'

Thumelicatz carried on walking forward past a large fig tree that dominated the garden. 'And what happens then?'

'Then it will be your turn.'

Thumelicatz scoffed. 'You're an old man, Uncle; and you won't get to be one day older if my mother is harmed.' He stopped two paces from Flavus and Thusnelda; with ostentation he lowered his sword but kept a firm grip of it. 'So what's it to be, Uncle, death for you both or life?'

Flavus looked at his nephew from over Thusnelda's shoulder; uncertainty and fear played in his eyes.

Thumelicatz held his gaze; a flicker of amusement passed over his face. 'You were always too keen on life, Uncle; that's why you chose it over honour and murdered my father.'

'Erminatz would have had me killed; only one of us could live.'

'My husband loved you, Flavus!' Thusnelda shouted. 'You were his younger brother; he would have forgiven you had you returned to Germania and renounced Rome. That's why he met you and my father alone that night, he believed your lie that you were coming home to him and bringing me and my son with you; but you betrayed his trust and the bonds of blood, treacherously murdering him.'

'I did what was best for—'

A shrill scream accompanied by a flurry of skirts and hair brought Gunda diving out of the shadows, teeth bared, dagger raised over-arm, aimed above her husband's shoulder at the side of Thusnelda's neck.

Flavus spun round, exposing more of Thusnelda's body to the attack as a flash of burnished iron flicked up from below; Thumelicatz's sword parted the knife-wielding fist from Gunda's right arm. The look of horror on Flavus' face as he watched his wife's hand spin through the air, spiralling blood, was suddenly replaced by agonised surprise as Thusnelda's sharp teeth sank into the base of his thumb; with two savage shakes of her head she ripped the flesh and muscle from the bone, exposing the joint as the point of her elbow rammed into her brother-in-law's solar plexus. The dagger at her throat clattered to the ground, the noise drowned by Gunda's uncontrolled shrieks as her eyes swivelled constantly between her severed hand on the floor and the newly carved stump resting in her left hand, pumping bloody spurts.

Thusnelda kicked Flavus' knife away as she broke from his grasp and, stooping to sweep up Gunda's hand from the ground as she passed, stepped into the safe embrace of her son's left arm. She turned and looked down at her erstwhile gaolers now both sunk to their knees; working her jaw, she chewed hard before spitting a semi-masticated ball of flesh into Flavus' upturned face. 'Now it's my turn, Chlodochar; now you and that bitch-wife of yours will find out what I've been dreaming of for the last twenty-two years.' She smiled coldly at Gunda who whimpered softly, squeezing her wrist to stem the flow of blood. 'And don't worry, my dear, after you're gone you will always be remembered.' She held out the severed hand. 'Your finger bones will look charming woven into my hair.'

Thumelicatz hauled on a rope and then secured it to a lower branch of the fig tree; Flavus was suspended by his wrists, his feet just above the ground.

Thusnelda raised her head. 'Donar, hold your hands over me and my son as we travel through strange lands and grant that we return to Germania. Accept this gift of blood, the most precious gift that I can give you other than my own son: the blood of a kinswoman who has given birth.' Thusnelda lowered her eyes from the heavens and met those of Gunda, bound to the tree's trunk. 'The Great Thunderer will take you, bitch; you should thank me that I've given some worth to your miserable existence.'

Gunda spat in Thusnelda's face. 'Our son, Italicus, will avenge us.'

'Italicus! What sort of name is that for a son of Donar?' Thusnelda raised her knife and placed it to Gunda's throat. 'You've lost everything that you were born with; you even lost the ability to choose an honourable name for a son.' She jerked her arm; honed iron sliced through flesh.

Gunda's eyes widened, liquid bubbled in her throat and her body juddered against its restraints.

Thumelicatz walked forward, raising his sword to Flavus, dangling from the tree watching, with horror, the death-throes of his wife. 'Donar, bring us home and strike me down from above with thunder and lightning if I ever have anything to do with Rome or her people ever again. I want nothing from her, I am done with her; see that I keep my oath.' The tip of his blade slid into Flavus' lower belly, a gasp exploded from the suspended man. Bringing his left hand to reinforce his right, Thumelicatz pulled the blade upwards, sawing. Up it sliced, cleaving through muscle and gut, releasing noisome gases and fluids and causing pain that Flavus' screams could not do justice to. As the blade reached the ribcage, Thumelicatz withdrew it and walked behind his uncle. Putting his arms around the writhing body, he stuck his fingers into the wound and yanked it open. Grey steaming coils of slick innards flopped out, tumbling down Flavus' legs and piling up at his feet. His shrieks warmed Thumelicatz and Thusnelda's hearts.

They looked at each other and smiled.

'I've missed you, my son.'

'I know, Mother. Let's go home.'

CHAPTER 1

❧ ❧

GERMANIA MAGNA,
SPRING AD 41

THUMELICATZ WATCHED THREE mounted warriors approaching from the west, half a mile away across the valley. Picking their way along the edge of a ploughed and sown field, a *rode* cleared out of the surrounding forest by the sweated labour of generations gone by, the horsemen descended the hill and skirted an area of marshland fed by a river flowing into the reed-lined lake beyond. A gentle breeze rippled its surface; it glistered silver and gold in the westering sun in stark contrast to the conifer-swathed hills encircling it. The sweet scent of so many trees' resinous sap infused the warm air and gave the name to this high range of hills in the heart of Germania Magna: *Harzland* in the language of the Cherusci tribe – the Land of Sap.

The approach of armed men caused no consternation for Thumelicatz and his kin, as tied to the tips of their spears were branches of beech with freshly sprouted leaves, the sign of peaceful intent. Nonetheless, the dozen men living within the compound had retrieved their weapons from the longhouse at its centre and now stood on the walkway that ran the length of the palisade surrounding the small settlement. Only Thumelicatz remained unarmed, standing in the open gateway. Yet he was not unprotected; to either side of him stood two huge, shorthaired brindle hunting dogs; they growled deep in their throats, as the three horsemen drew nearer.

Thumelicatz tapped the muzzles of both dogs. 'Beisser, Reisser, stumm!' The dogs immediately ceased their noise and looked up to their master, ready to follow his lead in however he chose to react to the new arrivals.

Thumelicatz's eyes squinted in deep sockets against the lowering sun; he rubbed his beard, now grown so full that it climbed almost to his high cheekbones, and then ran a finger along thin, pale lips as he scrutinised the three warriors, now less than a hundred paces away. Looking up to the man nearest to him on the left-hand side of the palisade, he frowned. 'Chatti?'

The man grunted and then nodded his head. 'Yes, lord, they're all wearing iron collars; front rank infantry, the bravest of their warriors.'

'How long is it since Chatti have ventured into our lands, Aldhard?'

'Five years ago; the year before you returned, my lord. But they came with their swords unsheathed and the points of their spears bared; we stopped them as they tried to cross the Visurgis River. It was a hard fight and we lost a good few men that day; their blood-price has yet to be repaid.'

Thumelicatz nodded; he had heard the songs about the last Chatti raid into Cheruscian territory in the year before he had won the wooden sword. The year before he and his mother had endured the harsh crossing of the mountains, fleeing Italia for Germania.

The three warriors cantered the last part of the way across open ground and pulled up their mounts twenty paces short of Thumelicatz. They each presented their leaf-adorned spears, holding them high in the air so there could be no mistaking their intent.

Thumelicatz studied the men; all had long, flaxen hair, tied in a top-knot, and flowing, well-kept beards that partially obscured the iron collars, three fingers thick, around their necks. Two were his age, mid-twenties, but the blond of the central rider's beard was flecked with silver and his ice-blue eyes had weathered wrinkles in their corners; Thumelicatz addressed himself to him. 'What brings you so far from your homeland?'

'My name is Warinhari and I come from the Hall of Adgandestrius, the king of the Chatti; I am his son. My father sends his greetings to Thumelicatz, son of Erminatz; do I have the honour of addressing him?'

'I am who you seek.'

'It is a privilege to meet the son of Germania's greatest warrior; thirty-two years ago this autumn, when I had but sixteen summers, I fought with your father in the Teutoburg Wald.'

Thumelicatz smiled to himself; there was not one warrior in the north of Germania Magna over the age of forty-five who would not claim to having been present at the battle that stopped Rome's march eastwards and showed her the limits of empire. 'I'm told that the Chatti fought bravely – once they had charged.'

Warinhari inclined his head at the backhanded compliment, refusing to acknowledge the jibe: the Chatti had stood back for the first two days and had not committed their forces until the outcome was almost assured. 'The Chatti always fight bravely.'

'What does Adgandestrius want with me? The last time he wanted anything from my family it was my father's death.'

'That was a generation ago; he was protecting his position after the breakup of the alliance that your father had built. Now things are different and my father has a proposition for you concerning the safety of all the tribes of Germania; it is something that must be considered by the hearth, not in the open. I must discuss it with you soon for a decision needs to be made by tomorrow, two days before the full moon.'

Thumelicatz looked up to Aldhard who had listened to the

whole conversation; with a discreet nod of his head he showed his agreement. Thumelicatz turned back to the visitors. 'Very well, I accept the tokens of peace, you may enter. Bear your weapons with honour and cause no harm to any person within.'

Although the day was warm a fire burned in the round hearth in the exact centre of the longhouse; its fumes partially obscured the gabled, thatched roof as they struggled to get out through a hole in its apex. Hams and fish hung from the rafters, curing in the smoke. Apart from a scattering of tables and benches on its rush-strewn floor, the longhouse was bare. Thumelicatz led Warinhari to a plain wooden table next to the fire and bid him to be seated on a bench on one side. Sitting opposite him he clapped his hands; an old slave appeared from behind a leather curtain at the far end of the room; his thin grey hair was cut short, Roman style, but his beard was long and ragged.

The slave bowed. 'Yes, master.'

'Serve us beer, smoked meat and bread and send word to my mother to join us.'

'Yes, master.' The old slave turned to go, keeping his eyes fixed on the ground.

'And Aius.'

The slave stopped and turned to face his master.

'Take food and drink to this man's companions waiting outside and tell Tiburtius to rub down my guests' horses.'

'Yes, master.'

As Aius left, Thumelicatz turned to Warinhari. 'That slave and his comrade Tiburtius both served my father.'

'Roman?'

'Of course, part of Varus' army captured at Teutoburg.'

Warinhari furrowed his brow, quizzically.

'They swore by all their gods never to try to escape so my father spared them from the fires of our gods; they served him faithfully even after his death. When I returned I found them still at my father's longhouse, looking after his horses and hunting dogs, polishing his weapons and armour, cutting and spreading fresh rushes on the floor and keeping his hearth-fire burning. It was as if he hadn't been dead for fifteen years.'

'They must have loved him.'

'Loved him? I doubt it; you should know well that men didn't love my father. But all who knew him feared him for there was nothing that he would not dare do; no boundaries he would not break; no limits he would not exceed.'

Warinhari nodded, his eyes distant with reflection. 'He was a dangerous man – both for his friends as well as his enemies.'

'And for his kin,' a silhouetted woman said from the doorway; her hair fell wild about her, bones woven into its midst chinked as she moved.

Thumelicatz stood. 'Mother, this man's name is Warinhari; he comes under a branch of truce with a proposition from his father, King Adgandestrius. I wish you to listen to him with me.'

Thusnelda stared at Warinhari as he rose from the bench and bowed; her deep blue eyes became slits and her face creased into an age-lined scowl. 'Why should I listen to the messenger of the man who offered the Emperor Tiberius to kill my husband?'

'Because we are living in different times, Mother; and besides, Tiberius refused the offer.'

Thusnelda spat into the rushes. 'Because he had more honour, despite being a Roman, than that weasel of a Chatti king.'

'Mother, that is all in the past. Adgandestrius would not have sent his son here unless he wanted the proposition to be taken very seriously; we should listen to him.'

Thusnelda dipped her hand into a leather bag hanging from her belt and fiddled with something within; it seemed to calm her. 'Very well,' she conceded as Aius shuffled back in with a tray, 'but I warn you, Thumelicatz, this man will tempt you to break an oath – the bones have spoken.'

Thusnelda sat next to her son, glaring at the visitor while Aius poured them each a horn of beer and then left them with a plate of bread and cold meat between them on the table next to a sputtering tallow candle.

Thumelicatz took a deep draught of his ale and set down the horn. 'Well, Warinhari, what is your father's proposition that he feels is so important that he would risk a son to bring it to me?'

'It has to do with Rome.'

'Then you're wasting your time; Rome has torn my family apart.' Thumelicatz pulled out a hammer amulet, hanging around his neck under his tunic. 'I swore to Donar the Thunderer never to have anything to do with that ravenous beast of an empire again. I sealed the oath with the sacrifice of my treacherous uncle and his wife; and then, when the Thunderer had fulfilled his part of the bargain and brought my mother and me home, I confirmed it with three Roman merchants burned in wicker men in the same sacred grove that my grandfather, Siegimeri, was forced to hand over his two sons to the Roman general, Drusus, as a hostage.'

'The story is well known: at the age of nine your father and his younger brother were taken to Rome.'

Thusnelda leant forward, putting her arm around Thumelicatz. 'And I too was taken and Erminatz never saw his son; my disloyal father, Segestes, delivered me up to Germanicus, whilst I was with child. I was taken to Rome and gave birth there. Two years later my father watched as an honoured guest of the

Emperor as I and my son and brother were paraded through the streets in Germanicus' Triumph. His loyalty was more to Rome's riches and the power they could bring him rather than to his kin; to prove it finally he helped murder my husband with his own younger brother. We want nothing of Rome ever again; now go!'

Warinhari stared over the table at the mother and son, their faces set rigid; he drained his horn. 'I understand the strength of your feeling and believe me when I say that I and my father feel the same hatred of Rome. However, Rome is a reality; even here in Germania Magna we still feel her power. Which tribe between the Rhenus and the Albis rivers does not have treaties with Rome that force them to provide young men for her auxiliaries and pay tribute into her coffers? Every one; the Chatti, the Frisii, the Chauci, the Angrivarii, all of them, even you, the Cherusci.'

Thumelicatz slammed his palm down on the table causing the candle to gutter and spit. 'That proves nothing!'

'It proves that the arm of Rome is long and the tribes of Germania are too weak to resist it.'

'But we are still free, Warinhari, there is no Roman governor here; the towns Rome built before my father defeated her have crumbled and returned to the forest, and we enjoy our own laws. How much more freedom can we expect?'

'The freedom that comes from not living in fear every year of a fresh invasion.'

'Rome's expansion east has halted, my father saw to that.'

'Halted or faltered? Has it really stopped? Can you look into your heart and know for certain that Rome will not try again?'

Thumelicatz rubbed his beard with both hands, his elbows resting on the table, staring at the thin stream of smoke spiralling up from the freshly extinguished candle. 'No,' he said after a short while. 'No, I cannot; as Rome expands she makes more citizens who are eligible to serve in her legions. Unless there is a plague her manpower is always going to grow; soon the three legions that my father destroyed will be replaced and then Rome may well come again.'

'Exactly; so we must ensure that Rome is too busy elsewhere to be able to come.'

Thumelicatz raised his eyes and met Warinhari's gaze. 'How?'

'Two days ago some Romans arrived at my father's hall in Mattium; they were looking for you. They have a knife that belonged to your father which they hope to give you in return for you meeting with them.'

'My father's knife? How can they be sure?'

'It has "Erminatz" engraved in runic figures down the blade; I have seen it and it looks to be genuine.'

'How did they come to possess it?'

'Two of them claim to be the sons of the centurion who escorted your father from his people to the Rhenus and then on to Rome when he was taken hostage.'

'Erminatz gave the centurion his knife,' Thusnelda confirmed. 'He told me that he asked him to give it to his mother when he returned; he never did, though, the dishonest Roman pig. What makes you think that the sons of a thief are to be trusted?'

'My father, Adgandestrius, always speaks the truth and so can tell a lie; these men are genuine.'

'Why do they want to meet with me?' Thumelicatz asked, picking up the jug and filling Warinhari's horn.

'They want to know where the lost Eagle of the Seventeenth legion that your father took at Teutoburg can be found.'

Thumelicatz thumped the jug back down, beer slopping over its rim, as he broke into a mirthless laugh. 'They would exchange a knife for an Eagle? Even Erminatz would not put such a price upon his blade.'

Warinhari did not share the laughter. 'Whilst that Eagle remains on Germanic soil, Rome will always come looking for it. Germanicus came back five years after Teutoburg and again the following year and defeated your father three times. He came back not just for revenge but also to restore Roman pride; he came back to retrieve the three Eagles lost at Teutoburg. Do you think that he would have come back if it wasn't for the Eagles? However, he had only found those of the Eighteenth and Nineteenth legions before Tiberius, jealous and fearful of his accomplishments, recalled him to Rome.'

'And no one's been back since.'

'Until now.'

'A few Romans with a knife?'

'It's the start. Only your father knew which of the six tribes that took part in the battle received the Eagles. Germanicus found the Marsi's and the Bructeri's and we received the Capricorn emblem of the Nineteenth Legion; so that just leaves your tribe and the Chauci or the Sugambri. Do you know where this Eagle is?'

Thumelicatz hesitated and then nodded. 'Yes, I do.'

'Will you help these Romans to retrieve it?'

Thumelicatz grasped the hammer pendant around his neck. 'If I did, Donar would strike me with a bolt from above for breaking my oath.'

'Even if your actions secured his people's freedom for genera-tions to come?'

'How would the return of one Eagle stop Rome ever trying to spread her empire across the Rhenus again?'

Warinhari smiled and leant his face closer. 'Rome has a new Emperor, Claudius; a fool who drools, we are told. The men who benefit from his being in power naturally want to keep him there; to do this they need the army to love Claudius so that they'll gain a victory for him so large that it will secure his position with the people.'

'And this Eagle will gain Claudius the army's love?'

'Yes, Rome still feels shame at its loss. If Claudius is seen as being responsible for its retrieval then his legions may do what they didn't do for his predecessor, Caligula: they will embark on ships and invade Britannia.'

A smile of comprehension gradually spread over Thumelicatz's face. 'Four, maybe even five, legions and their auxiliaries.'

Warinhari nodded. 'Exactly; and every one drawn from either the Rhenus garrison or the Danuvius to our south. With that number of troops tied down across the Northern Sea we—'

'Will be safe from invasion for generations,' Thumelicatz said, finishing the sentence.

'Yes; safe for a hundred or two hundred years, by which time, perhaps, we will be stronger than Rome and can threaten her western provinces.'

'And beat her back to ensure a Germanic future for the west.'

'Perhaps.'

'Where are these Romans?'

Thusnelda grabbed her son's arm. 'What of your oath, my son?'

'Mother, the Thunderer will understand why I do this and forgive me this once; I will show these Romans to the Eagle and keep his people safe from conquest whilst they grow stronger.'

'You do the right thing, Thumelicatz,' Warinhari said. 'In three days' time at the full moon, the Romans will be at the Chalk Giant in the northern reaches of the Teutoburg Wald where, in its shadow in the Teutoburg Pass, Varus made his last stand on the fourth day of the battle.'

Thumelicatz held Warinhari's gaze for a few moments as the decision hardened within him. Slowly he nodded. 'I will be there, Warinhari, I swear. I will hear what the Romans have to say and then, if I deem them honourable, I will, whatever the cost, help them get their Eagle back.'

A strong breeze blew from the south, filling the leather sails of four fat-bellied longboats sailing with the current down the Visurgis River. That morning, Thumelicatz and his kin had loaded their baggage and horses into the boats, housed in a crumbling Roman river port, and sailed north. They had ridden down from the Harzland the day after Warinhari's arrival and crossed the lowlands to its west, arriving at the river by evening to camp on its banks. Aldhard had been sent on ahead the day before with four men, travelling at night, to prepare the meeting place in accordance with their lord's wishes.

Thumelicatz stood with his mother on the fighting platform at the bow of the lead boat; he inhaled deeply of the crisp, morning air as he watched water-fowl diving in the shallows. 'The air is getting cooler, the Ice Gods are close; no more than two or three days away, I should think.'

Thusnelda cursed under her breath.

'What is it, Mother?'

'The time of the Ice Gods is not auspicious for us. It was during the three days that they roam the earth, bringing frost in May, that your father was given up to Rome as a hostage. At the same time of year I was betrayed to Germanicus by my own father; and he and Chlodochar also killed Erminatz while there was ice on the lakes during the spring mornings.'

'That's just coincidence.'

'There is no such thing. The three Norns sit and weave the

threads of fate of every man's life; all is set out in advance.' Her
hand delved into the leather bag at her waist and brought out five
straight, carved, thin bones covered on all four sides in runes. 'If
it were not so, how could the Rune Bones predict the future?'

'When you cast them last night and this morning, what did
they say?'

Thusnelda looked at the bones in her hand and shook her
head slowly. 'I didn't cast them either last night or this morning,
nor will I cast them tonight.'

Thumelicatz frowned. 'Why not, Mother? You've always read
the bones at the rise of the sun and at its setting.'

'I'm afraid to see what I know in my heart they will say.'

'You think that Donar won't release me from my oath?'

'I know the Thunderer won't; an oath to him is binding for all
time.'

'Mother, if he does see fit to strike me down for helping to
secure the freedom of all his people then I will go to Walhalla
willingly. This act will reduce Rome's legions on our frontiers.
We can go back to fighting amongst ourselves and posing no
threat to Rome. A balance will be drawn along the Rhenus and
Danuvius; Rome won't have the legions to invade us because
they'd be busy in Britannia, but nor would they feel they needed
to do so because we would be disunited and pose no threat to
Gaul. And then we wait – maybe for generations – until disease,
soft living and years of peace take their toll on Rome, and then
we will pour across the Rhenus.'

'But you will be dead.'

'Of course I'll be dead, the wait will be long.'

'No, I mean you'll be dead if you do this thing.'

'Do you think so?'

'I'm sure of it.'

'Then cast the Rune Bones and let us see for sure whether Donar will release me from my oath on this one occasion.'

With a look of sorrow to her son, Thusnelda brought the bones to her mouth and breathed on them four times before shaking them in the palms of her hands. 'I call upon Air, the spirit of spring and of sunrise, the breath of new life and new growth. I call upon Fire, the spirit of summer and of the noonday sun, the heat of vitality and abundance. I call upon Water, the spirit of autumn and of twilight, of open seas, running streams and cleansing rain. I call upon Earth, the spirit of winter and of the night, deep roots, ancient stones and winter snows. I call on all these spirits, Air, Fire, Water and Earth, to come now and guide these bones.' She cast the five bones at Thumelicatz's feet; they clattered briefly along the deck and then were still.

Thusnelda knelt and passed her hands over the bones, examining them; they were intertwined but only one touched all the other four. Her face clouded. 'If you stay on this path all that you have said could come to pass. The bones tell me that you risk much, perhaps even death, but they cannot see into the mind of the Thunderer; it isn't clear whether he will release you from your oath. But what is clear is that one comes who will have the fate of Germania Magna in his hands one day; that man must leave with what he wants and feel no need ever to come back.'

Thumelicatz looked back along the boat, past Aius and Tiburtius tending the horses and on to the boar's head painted on the sail: the boar of the Cherusci, the emblem of the tribe that he loved as much as his life; the tribe that had existed for him only with Thusnelda's tales for all those years whilst he lived in the empire but now was a solid reality. 'What is my life against the survival of the Cherusci and the other tribes of our Fatherland? I will risk the Thunderer's wrath even though it is for his children that I break my oath. If my life is forfeit then so be it; I care not, Mother, because I have acted in the same way as my father would.'

Thusnelda smiled, thin, looking out at the endless procession of trees lining the bank. 'Of that there is no doubt.'

The horses' hooves crunched down onto green-tinted human bones of every variety. From the smallest finger to the pelvis, all were there strewn out along the path; all were there in abundance.

Thumelicatz glanced at the skulls nailed to tree trunks on either side of the path as it broke out from under the trees into a clearing, almost a mile long and three hundred paces across, surrounded by a low, wooded hill on one side and a reeking marsh on the other. The ground was mainly sand and would have been yellow had it not been for tens of thousands of bones; the bones of Varus' legionaries still lying on the field where they had been slaughtered on the final day of the battle. Germanicus had visited this place and spent days having his men bury the dead but, since his return, Thumelicatz had had many of them, at least half, dug up again and spread over the killing ground.

'That is a fitting memorial to your father,' Thusnelda declared as she surveyed the bleak carpet of death.

'I'm not sure Aius and Tiburtius would agree, Mother.'

Thusnelda looked over her shoulder at the two Roman slaves, their eyes streaming with tears as they looked upon their erstwhile comrades who had been allowed no dignity in defeat.

Although they were the remains of soldiers of the hated empire, Thumelicatz shivered at the sight of such mass loss of life; about seven thousand had died here in Varus' last stand.

Aldhard rode down the hill out of the trees and across the last desperate earthwork of Varus' legions: a low wall that stretched for almost the whole length of the clearing, facing the hill. It was broken down in many places as if trampled upon by hundreds of feet; the decomposed hoof of a dead mule protruded from one section.

'Is everything ready?' Thumelicatz called, pulling his horse to the left to face Aldhard.

'Yes, my lord, the tent is up and decorated and the appropriate sacrifice is being made.'

'Good. Have the keepers of the bones been rewarded and sent away?'

'Yes, they will leave after they have helped Odila make the sacrifice; they won't return for three days.' He gestured around at all the bones. 'Nature won't make much impact on all them in that time. It's just us and the priestess of the grove here.'

'Thank you, Aldhard, you've done well; have some men stay down here to lead the Romans up when they arrive.'

'Yes, my lord.'

'I shall go up the hill and wait.'

It was not a high hill, just three hundred and fifty feet; Thumelicatz led his mother and slaves swiftly up although it was thickly wooded. Towards the summit they came to a clearing with a grove of beech trees at its centre; a tethered white horse grazed peacefully within it near to an altar dripping with blood. A wild-haired woman, reciting rapidly to herself, was tying a freshly severed head by the hair to a branch at the clearing's edge. Two other heads, in different states of decomposition, hung close by; skulls with scraps of flesh and hair still clinging to them lay on the ground all around the perimeter. In the shadows of the trees beyond the clearing Thumelicatz just glimpsed two men dragging away a headless corpse.

'Odila has cleansed the hill,' Aldhard observed with an approving nod. 'All is set. Now we have to wait to see what the Norns have woven for you.'

'You knew my father well, Aldhard; did he believe that every man's destiny is set out in advance and inevitable?'

'Of course; that's why he dared do so much. He knew that if he saw an opportunity, however outrageous, however far-fetched, then he should follow it through because the very fact that he'd seen it meant that the Norns must have already woven it; it was therefore his fate to follow that path.'

'Destroying three legions, for example?'

'Exactly; and abducting your mother from her father's house on the day of her marriage.'

The slope eased and they reached the summit; it had been cleared of trees to leave a meadow, sprinkled with wild-flowers. Set in its midst was a ten-foot-high, fifty-foot-square, red-leather tent next to a solitary, ancient oak.

'You did well to set that up with only four men to help you, Aldhard,' Thumelicatz commented, swinging off his horse.

'It would have taken twenty slaves just two hours to set up Varus' command tent but it took the five of us most of yesterday. The leather is damp and musty as it hasn't been unpacked since your father captured Varus' baggage, thirty-two years ago, but we've washed it as best we could as well as clean the furniture and silver plate.'

'And his uniform?'

'His uniform is polished and ready, my lord; you'll find it laid out in the sleeping compartment.'

Thumelicatz looked at his reflection in a half-length bronze mirror as Aius and Tiburtius fastened his hobnailed sandals; he shuddered at the sight. Looking back from beneath the distorted surface was a Roman governor in full military uniform: muscled bronze breastplate inlaid in silver figures around the edges, representing the former owner's household gods as well as Mars Victorious; a crimson sash was tied high around the midriff and a cloak of the same colour hung from one shoulder and was swept back from the other. From a red-leather belt hung a pugio and a gladius – the sleek and deadly two-foot-long sword that eviscerated with ease. Thumelicatz completed the image by placing a burnished iron helmet with thick, articulated cheek-guards, inlaid with bronze, upon his head; crowned with a high horsehair plume, dyed red, he took on the appearance of a person he despised the most: a Roman of the officer class. Yet one thing was out of place: his full beard; that at least distinguished him from the hated enemy.

'You take this too far,' Thusnelda muttered, a worried frown set on her forehead.

'I do this so that these Romans will see the reality of their defeat all those years ago; their wounds must be opened again and salt applied.' He turned to Aius and Tiburtius standing to one side now that they had finished dressing their master. 'Is everything correct?'

The two slaves surveyed him for a few moments and then nodded dumbly, averting their eyes as soon as possible from the vivid reminder of their former lives.

'And the food?'

'Is ready, master,' Aius replied, 'as are we should you require a reading.'

'I haven't decided that yet.' Thumelicatz took one more look at himself in the mirror and then strode through the door into the main part of the tent. In the dim light seeping in through the few open flaps in the tent, bolstered by tallow candles flickering all about, he examined the elegant room furnished with couches, finely carved chairs and tables and decorated with small bronze statues in amongst ceramic or glass bowls and vessels. Wooden columns, painted to resemble marble, supported the ceiling; the floor was of waxed oak cut into three-foot squares for ease of transport. He made for a curule chair next to a sturdy wooden desk with scrolls arranged on it and sat down to wait.

Sleep had almost taken him and he slipped between rational thoughts and semi-conscious dreams of no substance when foot-steps entering the tent disturbed his peace.

Aldhard pushed his head between two flaps at the far end of the room. 'They're here, my lord.'

'How many?'

'Four who wish to see you; they're escorted by about five *turmae* of Batavian auxiliary cavalry, a hundred and fifty men or so.'

'Send the Romans in and make arrangements for their escort to camp in the clearing for the night.'

With a nod Aldhard disappeared. A few moments later came more footsteps and then the flaps opened again to reveal four Romans dressed in the chainmail tunics of auxiliary cavalry. Two brothers were easy to discern: both had the same round, sunburnt faces, dark eyes and similar large, almost bulbous noses. Of the two the younger had a more open and accommodating expression and, to Thumelicatz's surprise, seemed to be the leader as he preceded the party in. Of the other two men, one was young and unmistakeably patrician with a long, thin nose and a haughty look; the other, the oldest of the group, had a hard, battered face, cauliflower ears and quick searching eyes that would not miss a single detail: a street-fighter without a doubt. What strange company these officers keep, Thumelicatz thought, making no attempt to get up – although he was tempted to, just so that he could tower over these representatives of the stunted race that had brought so much misery to the world.

'Welcome, gentlemen, I am Thumelicatz, son of Erminatz.'

The leader opened his mouth to greet Thumelicatz but was halted by the raising of a hand. 'Do not tell me your names, Romans, I have no wish to know them; after I escaped from your empire I swore to Donar the Thunderer to strike me down with a lightning bolt from above if I ever have anything to do with Rome again. However, at the behest of my old enemy, Adgandestrius, I have asked the god to make an exception this one time for the sake of my tribe and Germania.' He indicated to the couches around the room. 'Sit down.' The Romans accepted the invitation and settled down on a couch each. 'Adgandestrius tells me that you wish for my help in finding the one remaining Eagle lost by your legions at my father's victory here in the Teutoburg Wald.'

'He is correct,' the younger brother replied, holding Thumelicatz's eye with a confident gaze.

'And why do you think that I would help you?'

'It would be in your interests to do so.'

'How can it be in my interests to help Rome? At the age of two I was paraded, with my mother, Thusnelda, in Germanicus' Triumph in Rome; a humiliation for my father. Then in another humiliation to him we were sent to Ravenna to live with his brother Flavus' wife; Flavus, who always fought for Rome even against his own people. Then, in a third humiliation, I was taken at the age of eight and trained to be a gladiator; the son of the liberator of Germania fighting on the arena sand for the gratification of the mob of some provincial town. I fought my first bout when I was sixteen and I won my wooden sword of freedom fifty-two fights later, four years ago, at the age of twenty. The first thing that I did once I was free was settle my score with my Uncle Flavus and his wife and then, with my mother, I came back here to my tribe. With all that Rome has done to me, how could my own interests and yours ever coincide?'

The young brother told him of the planned invasion of Britannia and Adgandestrius' strategic view of its consequences.

Thumelicatz listened and learnt nothing that he did not already know but was pleased to have it confirmed from the mouth of a Roman. 'And you can guarantee that Rome won't just raise three or four more legions and replace the ones in Britannia?' he asked. 'Of course not; Rome has the manpower for many more legions and that old man, Adgandestrius, should realise that. Unless the empire is hit by a terrible plague it will continue to grow in population. Citizenship is being awarded to more and more communities in every province. All the time, slaves are being freed and receiving citizenship; they aren't eligible to join the legions but their sons are. But I agree with Adgandestrius in the short term: an invasion of Britannia will very likely keep us safe for a few generations.' Thumelicatz removed the crested helmet and placed it on the desk, his hair falling to his shoulders. 'If it had not been for my father there would still be a Roman wearing this uniform even now in Germania; but because of him I can wear it now as I deal with the successors of the man to whom it belonged. I can also entertain them in his tent and serve them refreshments on his plate.' He gave a sharp double clap of his hands; Aius and Tiburtius shuffled in with trays covered with silver cups, jugs of beer and plates of food. As they padded around the room placing food and drink on tables, Thumelicatz noticed the shock on the Romans' faces as they registered the old slaves' Roman hair. 'Yes, Aius and Tiburtius were both captured in this place, thirty-two years ago. They have been slaves here ever since. They have not tried to run away; have you, Aius?'

'No, master.'

'Tell them why, Aius.'

'I cannot return to Rome.'

'Why not?'

'Shame, master.'

'Shame of what, Aius?'

Aius looked nervously at the younger Roman and then back to his master.

'You can tell them, Aius, they haven't come to take you back.'

'Shame of losing the Eagle, master.'

'Losing the Eagle?' Thumelicatz ruminated, turning his blue eyes onto the old soldier.

The years of servitude and shame came to tell in Aius and he hung his head and his chest heaved a couple of times with repressed sobs.

'And you, Tiburtius?' Thumelicatz asked, staring at his other slave. 'Do you still feel shame?'

Tiburtius just nodded dumbly and placed his last jar on the desk next to his master.

Thumelicatz was amused as he saw the shock turn to outrage on the face of the younger brother.

'Why haven't you done the honourable thing and killed your-selves?' the young man asked, barely concealing his disgust.

A smile played at the corners of Thumelicatz's mouth. 'You may answer him, Aius.'

'Erminatz gave us the choice of being sacrificed by burning in one of their wicker cages or swearing upon all our gods to stay alive for the task that he wanted us to perform. No one who has seen and heard a wicker sacrifice will face the fire; we chose what every man would.'

'I wouldn't argue with that, mate,' the street-fighter chipped in; Thumelicatz noticed a look of distant longing pass over Aius' face at the sound of street Latin. 'The idea of my balls roasting over the fire would be enough to make me swear to anything.'

Thumelicatz removed the lid from the jar. 'But they wouldn't have roasted; we always take care to remove the testicles first.'

'That's very considerate of you, I'm sure.'

'I can assure you that it's not out of consideration for the victim that we do this.' Dipping his fingers into the jar Thumelicatz pulled out a small off-white egg-shaped object and bit it in half. 'We believe that eating our enemies' testicles brings us strength and vigour.' He chewed loudly on it, pretending to savour its taste whilst relishing the look of horror on his guests' faces. He slipped the other half into his mouth and, with equal pretence of enjoyment, ate that while indicating to his slaves to take a seat on the far side of the desk.

He took a swig of beer to rid his mouth of the very masculine flavour. 'After the battle here and all the battles and actions that my father fought in our struggle for freedom, we had almost sixty thousand testicles pickled; my father shared them out amongst the tribes. This is the last jar left to the Cherusci; I keep it for special occasions. Perhaps we should think about refilling our jars again soon?'

'You'd be mad to try,' the elder brother said, 'you could never cross the Rhenus.'

Thumelicatz inclined his head in agreement. 'Not if we stay as disunited as we are now and even if we could you would use the resources of your empire to beat us back in time. But you still have the strength to cross the other way and that is why I am here talking to you against all my principles. One of you has something to show me, I believe.'

The younger brother took out a knife and passed it to Thumelicatz; he examined the blade and saw that it was indeed engraved with his father's name. 'How did you come to be in possession of this?'

'Our father was a junior centurion in the Twentieth Legion in Drusus' army. After Arminius ...' He paused as Thumelicatz gave him a scowling glare. 'I'm sorry, Erminatz. After Erminatz and his brother had been handed over as a hostage, the general, Drusus, detailed our father's century to escort them back to his household in Rome; he got to know Erminatz quite well in the two months that the journey took. The further they travelled west and then south the more Erminatz began to realise just how far he was being taken from home; he began to despair about seeing his parents again, especially his mother. The morning our father delivered him and his brother to Drusus' house, Erminatz gave him that knife and made him promise to give it to his mother. Our father promised, thinking that he would be rejoining his legion back in the east. However, Drusus had fallen from his horse three months after they'd left and he had died of the injuries a month later. My father met his funeral cortège on his way back and this legion was with it. They were then posted to Illyricum and, with Tiberius, campaigned in Germania Magna again a few years later; but this time they came in from the south to fight the Marcomanni and didn't reach your father's lands. Then later, during another campaign, he was almost gutted by a spear thrust and invalided out of the army; so he never had the chance to return to the Cherusci's lands and give the knife to Erminatz's mother.'

Thumelicatz continued staring at the runic engraving, thinking, and then nodded. 'You speak the truth; it is exactly how my father set it down in his memoirs.'

'He wrote his memoirs!' the younger brother exclaimed, unable to keep the incredulity out of his voice.

Thumelicatz suppressed the sudden anger that he felt at the Roman's patronising surprise. 'You forget he was brought up in Rome from the age of nine. He learnt to read and write, although not that well as it had to be beaten into him; we do not consider them to be manly practices. However, he had a better idea: he would dictate his memoirs to his crushed enemies and he would keep them alive so that they could read it out whenever it was necessary, and today it may be necessary. Mother, would you join us?'

Thusnelda entered; she looked at the Romans, contempt blatant on her face, before turning to her son.

'Mother, is it necessary to tell my father's story to these Romans? What do the bones say?'

Thusnelda pulled her Rune Bones from her bag, breathed on them and muttered her call upon Air, Fire, Water and Earth before casting them to the ground.

Stooping, she examined their fall for a few moments, pawing at them. 'My husband would wish his story told to these men; to understand you they must understand where you come from, my son.'

Thumelicatz nodded. 'Then so be it, Mother, we shall begin.'

As Aius and Tiburtius began to unroll the scrolls on the desk, the younger brother indicated to them and said, 'So he spared these two to write down his life and read it out?'

'Yes, who better to tell of the life of Arminius than the *aquilifers*, the Eagle-bearers, of the Seventeenth and Nineteenth Legions?'

CHAPTER II

'MY FATHER'S STORY begins almost fifty years ago to the day,' Thumelicatz informed the Romans, 'during the time that Drusus, Augustus' stepson, was attempting to complete the conquest of Germania Magna.' He nodded to Aius who spread a scroll out on the desk, cleared his throat and began to read.

It was at the time of the Ice Gods, in my ninth year, that my mother woke my brother Chlodochar and me early, before the dawn.

'You must both come quickly,' she said, stroking my forehead and gazing at me with a strange look that I had never seen before in her loving eyes, reflecting the fading glow of the fire.

I look back now and recognise it as a look of longing; longing for a life that would never be, a life in which she would bring up her two sons to become warriors of the Cherusci. At that moment she knew that she had lost that life for ever; I did not.

'What is it, Mother?' I asked, determined not to be frightened by her expression.

'Your father and your tribe have need of you both; you must be brave and know that what you are being asked to do is for the good of all of us.'

I remember the thrill of feeling that I was being called upon to be brave, brave as a warrior, brave as my father, Siegimeri, the king of the Cherusci. I crawled out of the bed of furs that I shared with my elder sister and younger brother in a corner of my father's longhouse; all around, men were stirring from their beds, talking softly to each other, lighting tallow candles, combing their hair and beards and pulling on their war gear. My childish sense of excitement grew as I stepped into my breeks and then pulled on my doe-skin boots: perhaps I was to accompany my father on a raid against the hated invaders of our land, the ironclad men of Rome. Then one look at the confused face of my seven-year-old brother, as my sister, Erminhild, helped him to dress, put an end to that fantasy. Intrigued nevertheless, I fastened my belt over my tunic and attached to it my prize possession: a knife, given to me by my father, with my name engraved in runes down one side of the blade.

Pulling my cloak around my shoulders and grabbing a sliver of smoked venison and a hunk of dry bread from a platter left on a table from the previous night's meal, I walked, chewing thoughtfully, out into the cold pre-dawn air; my breath immediately started steaming and my boots crunched on the frosted ground. The Ice Gods had passed in the night.

Slaves had saddled the men's horses and waited with them, in flickering torchlight, for their masters to emerge from the longhouse. I looked around the warriors as they mounted up and realised that their mood was sombre, lacking the sense of nervous excitement I had come to recognise as the prelude to combat. I had last seen the men in that mood half a moon previously on the final day of the muster of the Cherusci here in the high hills of our natural stronghold of the Harzland; that day my father led more than ten thousand warriors east towards the Albis River, shadowing a great force of Romans who had skirted around the Harzland to the north, in the hope of taking the invaders by surprise. What remained of the army of the Cherusci came back little by little over the next few days, defeated men, grim but defiant. My father eventually returned and for two days and nights he had sat taking counsel with the headmen of all the clans of the tribe; at the end of the moot each man renewed his oath to my father and he distributed gifts of silver before they dispersed to their lands.

When I asked my father why it had been necessary to renew the oaths that bound the tribe together for as long as this Middle-Earth existed he replied enigmatically: 'Things have changed.' Nothing more could I get out of him. However, the reported sighting, four days later, of more than a thousand shackled prisoners, once-proud sword-bearers of the Cherusci, being sent west into servitude confirmed the truth of that statement.

My father's men began to mount up, but of him there was no sign; until I had spoken with him I did not know what was expected of me. I waited, stamping my feet and flapping my arms across my chest to ward off the chill breath of the Ice Gods who revisit our land for three days every spring before returning to their halls of ice below the Middle-Earth to regain their strength whilst fairer gods hold sway. My cousin, Aldhard, who had been born in the same summer as me, appeared from the deep shadows by the latrine, shivering and fastening his breeks.

'What's happening?' he asked.

I shrugged.

He noticed my cloak. 'You're going with them?'

'Yes; at least I think so. My father has sent for me.'

There was a stir amongst the men and my father strode out of the longhouse dressed in his finest bear-fur cloak and with a thick golden torque around his neck. He lifted my brother up to my uncle, Inguiomer, placing him in the saddle in front of him, and then signalled to a couple of slaves concealed in the shadows. They stepped forward holding bundles of freshly sprouted beech branches and started distributing them amongst the men who tied them onto the tips of their spears; I knew then that there would be no fighting.

'We must be going to negotiate,' I observed to Aldhard.

'Then why's he taking you and your brother?'

'Perhaps he wants to teach us something.'

A wistful look spread over Aldhard's face and I cursed myself for being so tactless: his father, Vulferam, my mother's brother, had not returned from the battle and Aldhard did not know whether he was dead or enslaved; the Romans had had the captives burn the fallen on mass pyres so there was no way of knowing who was alive or dead. I knew, however, what Aldhard would wish, what we all would wish, in that terrible uncertainty: to die with honour, grasping a sword, with dead enemies at your feet or to live out a short, miserable life in the mines or arenas of Rome; between death or living-death, who would choose the latter?

My father mounted his horse and, catching my eye, signalled for me to join him. I clapped Aldhard on the shoulder and walked towards him, looking around for my mother and sister to say goodbye; there was no sign of them and I thought nothing of it as I clambered up into the saddle in front of my father, I would see her that evening or maybe tomorrow. He kicked the horse forward towards the gates; they slowly opened. I did not look back as we passed through; perhaps had I done so I would have glimpsed my mother in the doorway of the longhouse, weeping, with an arm around my sister. I do not know; but what I do know is that I did not see my mother again until I was a man, and my sister, never.

The negotiations were already over.

We rode in silence as the dawn came up before us, crisp and clear, following the path east through the frosted, wooded hills of the Harzland; the snorts and steady hoof-steps of our horses, the morning song of birds and the rushing gurgle of the upland stream to our left, whose route we followed, were the only sounds to break into my thoughts. My father had an arm tight around me and I sat enjoying the rare closeness as I waited for him to speak; it wasn't until the sun was two hands' breadths above the horizon and we were descending to the flat lands that lie between the Harzland and the Albis River that he chose to break his silence.

'There is a time, Erminatz,' he almost whispered in my ear, 'in every man's life when he must realise that to proceed with a course of action in unfavourable circumstances is folly. For me that time came as the flower of the Cherusci broke upon the regimented shields of Rome.'

I tried to turn to meet his eyes but he tightened his grip and would not let me. 'But you will fight again, Father, surely?'

'Of course, but not in the same manner as we did the other day, that's for sure. It would be folly to take Rome on again in open battle and alone; we cannot defeat the legions like that.'

My naïve faith in the prowess and bravery of our warriors clouded my youthful judgement and I felt a wave of anger towards my father for daring to say such a thing. 'But they are runts, half-formed men of no stature, you told me so yourself; our warriors tower over them.'

My father sensed the ire in my voice and raised his. 'What size a man may be individually counts only in single or dispersed combat, boy; but when you have thousands of individuals all acting as one then it does not matter how tall or short each one is if you can't break their shield wall and get amongst them to use your superior strength. My warriors died by the hundreds at the hands of men whose training and discipline far exceed our own and negate our physical advantage. I will not see more of them die in a useless cause; I will not risk the survival of the Cherusci. I will not enter Walhalla as the last king of our tribe; how would I face my forefathers with that shame hanging over my head?'

'How will you face them if you don't fight?'

I could not see the expression on my father's face but I sensed that it had become downturned with regret and perhaps sorrow; his voice remained resolute but was tinged with these emotions. 'I have fought and I fought well; however, we were defeated even so. But now, for the moment, the time for fighting is over; the Cherusci will not face Rome's legions again head on or unaided. I believe that now we must look to the long term and develop a strategy that will ensure Rome's eventual expulsion from our lands and the lands of all the tribes east of the Rhenus. And what I've learnt, my son, is that we Cherusci aren't powerful enough to achieve that on our own.'

Although this statement went right against everything about my tribe that I had been told and so, therefore, fervently believed, the timbre of my father's voice convinced me that he was speaking the truth and I accepted it as such. 'So you would form an alliance with whom? The Chatti? The Chauci? The Marsi? They're all our enemies, you've told me so.'

Again I felt my father's expression change, I assumed into a faint smile as I heard a touch of amusement in his voice. 'Yes, I told you that and, at the time, I was right to do so; but things have changed. You'll come to understand that your greatest enemies are always closest to hand until another foe, from further away, threatens you all; then, in order to survive, your greatest enemies become your most valuable allies. We now need the Chatti, Chauci, Marsi, and all the other tribes of Germania; only together can we rid ourselves of Rome. I intend to build an alliance against Rome, not just an alliance of tribes because that will fracture; it has to be deeper than that: it must be an alliance of All Men, united in our struggle against our Fatherland's common foe. In other words: a united Germania.'

We rode on in silence for a while as I contemplated what that would mean; I had no concept of how large an area Germania covered as I knew only the Harzland and the lands surrounding it. I had never travelled, although that was about to change.

'Who would lead this alliance of All Men?' I asked eventually.

My father laughed. 'They say that a child can see straight to the heart of an issue, Erminatz, and you have certainly proved that saying to be true. That will be the problem. It should be me as it is my idea but the reverse is also true: since it's my idea it cannot be me because the other chieftains will suspect that my overriding aim is to gain power over them. If one thing is as sure as the changes in the seasons it's that men will not relinquish their power willingly.'

'So therefore you must be the first to do so; you cannot be the leader.'

I remember this exchange vividly because it earned me the rare praise of my father. He squeezed my shoulder and hoomed in the back of his throat. 'You will be a deep thinker, Erminatz, I can see that and it gives me pride. Yes, I'll relinquish my claim to leadership and I hope that it'll encourage others to do the same in favour of the best man and not the most arrogant.'

It was my turn now to laugh and I did so in an easy companionship, way beyond my years, as if we were equals and not father and son. 'I cannot see that happening.'

'Whilst we're at war with Rome, then no; but in the years to come when Rome believes we have accepted her rule and are settling down to become like the three Gallic provinces, then we will have a chance.'

I was shocked by the implication. 'You will surrender?'

'Very few of the tribes remain openly hostile to Rome and I hope that my surrender of the Cherusci will hasten the end of the others' piecemeal resistance. Then, when we have peace and Rome starts to impose her taxes and laws upon us, resentment will grow and I'll be able to forge an alliance of mutual hatred, willing to rebel as one. We'll rise up together, united for the first time, not to take on Rome in open battle that we can never win, no, we will have to do it a different way; a way that I've not yet seen. But I will and when I do we will wipe out Rome's legions here in Germania Magna in one stroke with a victory so thorough that they will never return.'

'How long will this take to achieve, Father?'

'I will have to wait at least ten years, as will many other chieftains – some maybe more than that – but eventually they will all be free to act. But first we must have peace.'

'Is that where we're going; to negotiate peace with Rome?'

'We're going to meet with Drusus, the Emperor Augustus' stepson, the general of the Romans in Germania, a man of honour and my equal in the field of battle; a man to whom I am content to bow my head. But we don't go to negotiate, the terms have already been settled; we're going to deliver the surety that he needs.'

This hit me like a spear thrust to the heart. 'That's why you will have to wait at least ten years, isn't it?'

'Yes, my son. But you and your brother must put it to good use; you will learn their ways, befriend them, fight for them. You must gain their trust so that they believe that you have both become one of them. Only then will you be allowed to return and I will be finally free to act. Do you understand me, Erminatz?'

Despite the sudden, sickening emptiness in my stomach I managed to answer: 'Yes, Father; if you ask it of me then I will do it.'

I now understood why my mother had looked at me that morning in such a way and had entreated me to be brave for my father and my tribe: it was as much to herself that she was saying it as to me, her eldest son at whom she was gazing for the last time as a child; her eldest son who was about to become a hostage of Rome.

I had never seen a Roman, not even from a distance, but I had seen the helmets, armour, shields and weapons that our warriors had brought back as trophies from skirmishes, so I was prepared for their outlandish appearance. What I was not prepared for, however, was the regimented way in which they seemed to do everything. The legionaries would wait, all standing in exactly the same pose in regular lines the same distance apart. When they travelled they would, again, do so in lines, all holding their weapons and equipment in the same hand and walk – or march, as I found out they called it – in step. Every man seemed to know his place and where to move to, and how quickly to do so, on the orders of their centurions and optios.

Of course, this is completely unsurprising for anyone who has seen the legions of Rome as all people reading or listening to this will, no doubt, have done; however, to me as a nine-year-old boy used to seeing our war bands set off on a raid or return from one in, what I can only describe now as, a shambolic fashion, it was an education. Within an hour of rendezvousing at the Albis River, with the general, Drusus, and the cohort that escorted him, I understood what my father had been saying: it was hard to imagine our brave but chaotic warriors triumphing against what was evidently such a disciplined instrument of war.

Drusus was very respectful of my father; he had greeted him as an equal, dismounting when my father had done so and grasping his forearm rather than receiving the subservient bow of a defeated enemy. This behaviour, again, had surprised me – almost as much as Drusus' proficiency in our tongue: I had imagined that submitting to Rome would be an endless series of humiliations designed to fully unman the vanquished. But no tribute was exacted; my father and all his warriors were allowed to keep their weapons and Drusus confirmed my father in his crown.

There was only one humiliation to be borne and that was the swearing of an oath of allegiance in one of our sacred groves on the west bank of the Albis. This, my father explained to me as we led the Roman column there, was unavoidable as Drusus would only accept his oath if it was made before our gods in their place of worship. 'However,' he added with a sly grin, 'it won't be binding on me because the Romans abhor human sacrifice. I told Drusus that we would normally seal such an oath with the blood of one of the defeated warriors but he's forbidden it and demanded instead that we sacrifice two of our horses. Neither Wodan the All-Father nor Donar the Thunderer would hold me to such an insufficiently blooded oath so therefore I have nothing to worry about from the rest of the gods when I break it.' He looked at me solemnly. 'And break it I will, Erminatz, just as soon as you and your brother are back from Rome. Then I shall have a victory worthy of my name.'

I smiled because my father's name, Siegimeri, means 'famous victory' in our language.

The oath-swearing was conducted by the priestess of the grove on a granite altar under the ancient oaks planted by the gods beyond the mists of memory and gnarled by time. Whilst the complicated ritual was carried out with its many forms of words, I had the chance to observe Drusus from close up. He was taller than I had expected for a Roman – only half a head shorter than my father, who was tall even by our standards. With a rounded, cheerful face dominated by a prominent, straight nose and full lips that often broke into a smile, despite his dignified bearing, Nero Claudius Drusus was a man who exuded authority. I could tell by the way his officers conducted themselves in his presence that he was a man who was loved by his men; they would die for him if he called upon them to do so. Many already had during that campaign season, conquering the Mattiaci on his way through to subdue us, and many more would perish as he went on to defeat the Marcomanni. For me, though, it was interesting to see a foe that could obviously inspire men to the same extent as my father and yet here was my father submitting to him. I realised for the first time the obvious truth that leadership is not just about bravery, cunning and being loved by those who follow; there has to be more to it than that, but at that young stage of my life I could not identify the missing ingredient. When finally I did, some years later, the world opened up to me.

As the life twitched out of the second horse, its wasted blood flowing over the altar and collecting in a tin basin below it, the oath was as complete as Roman qualms would allow it to be and the ceremony was at an end. Drusus beckoned to me and my brother to come forward; we did so, I with my head held high, remembering that I was the eldest son of the king of the Cherusci, and my brother with the timidity of his few years.

'So what did you learn?' Drusus asked me. He saw the confusion on my face and smiled. 'You've been staring at me for the duration of the ceremony, you must have learnt something.'

I felt myself redden but was determined not to let my embarrassment hinder my answer. 'In you I saw Rome for the first time and I learnt that although there are many differences between our peoples in appearance and the way we fight, the qualities that a man needs for leadership are identical. Had you been my father and my father the Roman general, the result would still have been the same: I would still be going to Rome as a hostage.'

Drusus threw back his head and laughed with genuine amusement. 'Your son is wise for his years, Siegimeri.' He went to ruffle my hair, then stopped himself and gripped my shoulder instead. 'He shows promise to understand that just from observation.'

'He has the ability to think deeply,' my father confirmed.

Drusus looked me in the eye, assessing me for a few moments, and then turned back to my father. 'I will have a century of my men escort him to Rome where he will be delivered into my household, Siegimeri; I will ensure that he comes to no harm and is treated with the respect due to your rank. He will learn everything that a young Roman of noble birth is expected to learn and he will return home to be a credit to the Roman province of Germania Magna.'

My father bowed his thanks; I suspected that he could not trust himself with words.

Drusus looked down at Chlodochar and ruffled his blond hair. 'And as for his younger brother, my eldest son is about his age, they will be educated together; perhaps they will become great friends.'

And that was to prove true for my brother but not for me; in my case Chlodochar's greatest friend would also, in time, prove to be my most implacable enemy.

The business was done and Drusus wanted to move south against the Marcomanni without delay. He favoured swift action and bold moves so there was no time for the customary feast and drinking session with which the Cherusci would normally have concluded the swearing of an oath of allegiance; a fact that I'm sure pleased my father as he would have considered it to be another reason why his oath was invalid. His pleasure, however, did not show on his face as Drusus walked up to him with a centurion.

'This is Titus Flavius Sabinus, centurion of the fourth century, tenth cohort of the Twentieth Legion,' Drusus informed my father. 'He and his men will escort your sons to

Rome; I've chosen him because of all my junior centurions he speaks a little of your language.'

The centurion nodded curtly to my father and eyed my brother and me with little delight. He pointed over his shoulder to a column of men. 'We're ready, there.' With a salute to his general he turned smartly and marched back to his century.

'Keep faith with me, Siegimeri,' Drusus warned, his face now hard, 'and your sons will be safe. Break your word and I cannot answer for the actions of my stepfather, Augustus.'

'The Cherusci are now at peace with Rome; our young warriors will serve in your auxiliary cohorts and our taxes will swell your coffers.'

Drusus pointed across the Albis River, over a hundred paces wide at this point. 'See that they do and Rome will protect you from the tribes that range out east for distances beyond imagination and will also give you the benefit of her law.' He offered his forearm and my father grasped it firmly. 'I will come back this way in four months having dealt with the Marcomanni. At the full moon in September have the first two thousand of your warriors waiting here at this grove, half infantry and half cavalry; the best sixteen hundred will be trained up over the winter to form the first two Cheruscian auxiliary cohorts.'

'They'll be here, general.'

With a half-smile and a slight inclination of his head, Drusus released my father's grip and walked away.

My father put an arm around my shoulder and took my brother's hand and, as he walked us over to the waiting centurion, Sabinus, he looked down at me with a self-satisfied grin and said, 'Rome is going to train the very troops who'll form the backbone of the army that will free us from her; I call that a satisfactory conclusion to our business.'

We marched west with Centurion Sabinus' century. I found it no problem to keep up with the pace of the legionaries but Chlodochar suffered; after the first couple of days his feet were raw but he bore it without complaint or tears. On the third day he was forced to lean on me for support as he hobbled, but still not a word of protest passed his lips. I told him that our father would be proud of him and he smiled faintly, gritted his teeth and pressed on. As the midday break finished and the legionaries got to their feet, Centurion Sabinus gave an order to one of his men, pointing at Chlodochar; the man gave his pack-yoke to a comrade and lifted my brother onto his shoulders.

'Thank you,' I said to Centurion Sabinus.

He grunted and then said: 'He deserves the help, he showed spirit.'

We marched on for three days, with Chlodochar being passed around the men, following tracks through forests and across open land until we came to the Roman military road that was in the process of being constructed to link the Rhenus to the Albis; because of all the rivers that this road crossed it became known as the Road of the Long Bridges. Even though Chlodochar's feet were healed by this time the legionaries still carried him; it was as if he had become a lucky mascot. They could not pronounce his name so they just called him 'Flavus', which means 'Blondie', and taught him legionary Latin, laughing at his pronunciation of the choice swear words whose meanings he did not comprehend.

Happy that my brother was being taken care of, I spent my days at the front of the column, next to Centurion Sabinus, as a feeling of helplessness crept over me the further and further we travelled from my homeland and I began to realise that Germania was far larger than I ever had imagined. At first we did not talk much but, after a while, we began to have some halting conversations and I got to know a Roman for the first time.

He was a short, stocky, round-faced man with a nose that looked as if it had been fashioned with no consideration for the proportions of his visage and so consequently it looked large and misshapen. His eyes, however, were kindly enough and, although I could not warm to him because of his race, I enjoyed the conversations that we had and began to pick up some Latin.

'This is not far,' he told me on the seventh day, after I had expressed a fear of travelling so far west that I would never be able to return home. 'We've only travelled just over two hundred miles; the empire is ten times that amount across in every direction.'

'But how do people find their way?' I asked trying, but failing, to comprehend such large distances.

'They follow roads like this one.'

The road was straight and paved with stones that fitted exactly together, cambered so that water would not collect on their surface. On either side the forest had been cut back for fifty paces; a huge undertaking just in itself, never mind laying the road. 'There are roads that travel the distances that you've described?'

'Yes, scores.'

'But who built them?'

Sabinus shrugged. 'Slaves.'

It was then I realised two things about Rome and her empire: firstly her scale. This is something that I take for granted now but then, to a nine-year-old boy who thought that seven days' travel must have been almost enough to reach the ends of the world, it was a dizzying concept, far larger than my mind could take in. But far greater and more awe-inspiring than that was my first real glimpse at her power: how many slaves would it have taken to build all those roads so many miles long? How many conquered peoples were there that Rome could grow so huge?

An almost subliminal hiss, a quick succession of dull thumps and a couple of agonised cries from back down the column cut across my thoughts and I was about to learn another two things about Rome; this time about her armies.

'Shields!' Sabinus cried and then followed it up with another order that I did not understand. He pushed me back amongst the column of eighty men as they strove to turn from a column, four abreast, into the prescribed configuration whilst receiving another volley from the, as yet, unseen enemy. Unslinging their shields from their pack-yokes as they discarded them whilst keeping the two javelin-like *pila* that each man carried fisted in their right hands, they stepped over the few dead or wounded and, within twenty heartbeats, had changed from a travelling column into a fighting formation with a wall of shields to the front and the second rank holding theirs over their comrades' heads. As one they took ten paces forward, clearing the road and gaining the firmer grip of the verge. Apart from Sabinus' shouted order and the moans of the few wounded, no one had uttered a sound.

Hunching down, I ran, ten or so paces, along the back of the line to where my brother had been dumped and pulled him to his feet and then hauled him off the road. We pressed close to the rear rank as another volley of arrows clattered in with juddering thumps onto the shield wall. A few skitted off the roof, landing behind us, close to a legionary with a skewered calf trying to haul his more wounded, unconscious comrade to safety; blood pulsed around a shaft protruding from his thigh and trickled from a nasty gash on his forehead where it had struck the road.

'Stay close to the rear rank,' I told Chlodochar, pushing him down into a squatting position. I leapt towards the stricken legionaries, feeling a rush of wind close to my ear and seeing, an instant later, an arrow bounce off the road with a crack and a glitter of sparks.

The legionary grunted in Latin and pointed to his comrade's wrist as I skidded to a halt.

Doing as I had been told, I pulled on the limp limb with a boy's strength, but that was enough to make the difference; between us, using all the power in his one good leg and straining every muscle in my whole body, the legionary and I managed to heave the unconscious man off the road, leaving a streak of blood smeared over the smooth grey stone. As we reached my brother a massive shout erupted from the tree-line. I recognised it as Germanic and, with a jolt, I realised that I was aiding the enemies of our land against fellow countrymen who wished them gone for ever: if this wounded man survived because of my help how many Germanic children might he go on to orphan? I sensed that I should use this opportunity to try to escape, but then, where was I? How would I get home? And who were the tribe attacking us and what would they do to me and Chlodochar if they found out that we were Siegimeri's sons? I decided that the best course of action was to wait and see how the fight developed and take my chances with the victors – a trait that I have observed in other peoples, not just the Germanic tribes.

I dropped the unconscious man's arm – his comrade patted me on the shoulder and muttered what I assumed were his thanks – and took my brother by the hand, drawing my knife.

At another bellowed order from Sabinus, on the extreme right of the line, the second rank lowered their shields and flung their right arms back, hefting their pila in their hands; the butt of one nearly knocked my head off. I could hear the raucous cries of a charging war band coming ever closer and could feel the tension of legionaries as they watched it approach in silence. Terror began to rise from the pit of my stomach and I noticed my blade shaking; I steeled myself but still it shook. A few moments later I heard Sabinus roar again; as a man, the century's right arms were flung forward, propelling their pila at a low trajectory towards their onrushing foe. In an instant they had grabbed their second missiles, held in their left hands with their shield grip, and launched them in unison at an even lower flight. I only saw later what damage they did and it was a sight that has stayed with me all my life even though I've since witnessed far greater battles.

With their primary weapons still in the air the legionaries whipped their short swords from the scabbards at their right hip and, taking me by surprise, broke into a jog. I tugged Chlodochar's hand – he looked terrified, as I'm sure I did too – and moved to keep up with them; we didn't have far to go. I felt the shock of impact of the two sides colliding shudder through the thin legionary line as, for the first time in the action, the Romans yelled a brief deep-throated war cry.

And then the screaming started.

I had heard screams of intense agony before – the sound of a man being burnt alive in a wicker cage over the fires of the gods is a brutal noise to endure – but this was amplified tenfold and came from so many directions with such varied discordant changes of pitch and fiercely accompanied by the harsh, ringing metallic clash of iron and the hollow reverberating thump of wood as if Donar himself was pounding his hammer alternately on a mighty anvil and the solid gates of Walhalla. It was then that I realised that to survive I must pray for a Roman victory, because such was the intensity of the violence that if their line broke then anyone found behind it would be dismembered before the blood-lust abated.

But to whom amongst all the gods of my people could I pray for a Roman victory? I was not yet familiar with the concept of irony; had I been as I am now I think that I would have smiled mirthlessly and shaken my head at the ludicrousness of the situation. As it was, I took a politic course and clutched the Donar hammer amulet around my throat and prayed ambiguously for mine and my brother's survival.

Then the Roman line began to move forward and, brandishing my knife and holding my brother's hand, I followed.

The second rankers held their shields hard against the backs of their comrades in front of them, pushing them forward as their swords stabbed through the gaps between their shields at the vitals of the enemy, clearing a path. Little by little we advanced until I began to notice the second rankers stabbing their swords downwards and I realised that they were now stepping over the bodies of the fallen enemy and making sure of their despatch. Soon we had progressed far enough forward for me to come face to dead face with the first man that I had seen killed in battle; and it was a shock. Not because he was dead, that was a normal sight, but because although his sword arm was severed, his throat was punctured and his blond beard matted with blood, his eyes were wide open, registering surprise: he had not expected to die when he woke up that morning, he had not even expected to die when he charged a Roman formation, and yet there he was, dead. Like many others, both Germanic and Roman lying lifeless on the ground, he had been taken by surprise and I wondered that if he had expected this fate at this time in such a minor skirmish then what force of nature would have been able to drive him towards it when there was so little to be gained? Death is only acceptable for high ideals and these lives lost trying to wipe out a mere century of the invaders were lives truly wasted. My father had been right: piecemeal resistance was futile; Germania needed a bolder strategy with a great design where the battles would be epic and a man would expect death in return for a great victory. What I was witnessing now was pathetic.

I looked up from the man's face, disgusted, my fear forgotten for those few moments of contemplation; but then it rushed back as, with an abrupt escalation of the battle's cacophony, the Roman centre began to buckle.

Gradually it fell back, stretching the line, forcing some of the second rankers to fill the gaps as it became more and more concave.

And then, for an instant, it broke.

Before the line managed to reseal the gap, half a dozen warriors had surged through, just twenty paces from me and my brother, as what was left of the second rank turned to protect the line's rear. Finding themselves cut off from the war band and with a shield wall preventing them from fighting their way back through to their comrades, the warriors swerved and sprinted towards us in an attempt to get around the right of the Roman line. I was transfixed at the sight of these large, bloodied men bearing down on me, snarling, with their long swords or spears raised and dripping gore. I stood there, rigid, with an arm around Chlodochar, eyes wide with terror and my knife, waving at the oncoming bringers of death, in my trembling hand.

The air exploded from my lungs as I was punched to the ground and in my petrified state it took me a few moments to realise that I had gone forward, not back, and I was lying on top of Chlodochar. I heard harsh fighting over my head and hot blood splattered my neck and hair; the desolate screams of dying men in mortal pain filled my senses. I opened my eyes to see a severed hand, still grasping a long sword, and Roman military sandals; beyond them were bodies with beards and long hair. As I looked, another crashed, with a wail, to the ground. I came to my senses and pulled myself back, dragging my brother with me until we were clear of the legionaries' feet. I got to my knees as the last of the six warriors fell, spilling offal, and saw Centurion Sabinus urging the eight men with him to strengthen the centre; as they rushed to obey their orders, Sabinus turned to me. 'I thought we'd lost you.'

I was still shaking and, I am ashamed to say, I felt warm fluid in my breeks; I managed to control myself enough to croak: 'Thank you.'

Sabinus nodded. 'Stay there.' With that he sprinted after his men whose added weight had managed to straighten the Roman line; it was now going forward, again, as one.

The rest of the action was a blur; how long it lasted, I don't know, not long I should think, certainly not as long as it felt. Eventually I became aware that there was relative quiet; the screams of the dying had been replaced by the pitiful moans of the injured. I looked around and saw the legionaries walking amongst the dead and wounded, tending to their own and despatching the enemy's. I got to my feet, hauling Chlodochar up as well, and walked towards Sabinus who was supervising the retrieval of the Roman dead, about a dozen in all.

Sabinus looked us up and down. 'Neither of you are hurt, I hope.'

'No; thanks to you, centurion.'

He grinned. 'I promised my general to see you both safe to his house; you don't break a promise to Drusus. However, I'll admit that it was luck that I came when I did; luck or the will of the gods. Perhaps they're saving you for something.'

I have often thought about that conversation and can only assume that they evidently were because I had been no more than a hand's breadth from death. It makes me wonder whether Centurion Sabinus, if he lived to hear of my victory at Teutoburg, saw the irony in saving the life of the boy who would go on to be responsible for the deaths of so many of his countrymen.

'How many were there?' I asked, surveying the bodies littering the ground.

'About two or three times our number, I should think; we killed about half of them before the rest ran off. Almost a hundred of the buggers didn't make it into contact.' He pointed to a line of dead warriors, twenty paces away, lying in twisted heaps amongst scores of pila. Pierced by the long iron heads, some with their faces pulped by the lead ball at the shaft-end of the head that weighted the weapon and made it so deadly, most of the corpses looked like they had been thrown back many paces by the heavy impact. I saw then the effectiveness of the legionary's primary weapon and realised that, again, my father was right: soldiers with a weapon like this cannot be beaten head-on.

'The pila volleys took the weight out of their charge; without them we would have been overwhelmed without a doubt.' Sabinus shook his head and spat on the corpse of a gutted warrior. 'This area's supposed to be pacified; the Marsi have sworn oaths and given hostages. I wouldn't give much for their lives when I report this at Castra Vetera on the Rhenus.'

I shuddered, thinking of the fate that awaited the men and boys who found themselves in the same position as me, and then noticed something around the neck of the gutted warrior, almost obscured by his beard: a collar of iron, two thumb widths across. Looking around I could see that many of the warriors wore the same thing. 'They're not Marsi, centurion.'

'No? What makes you say that?'

'The iron collar is only worn by the Chatti, my father told me.'

'Chatti? This far north?' He looked down at a couple of the dead warriors and then nodded. 'You're right. Well, Erminatz, you might have saved some Marsi lives.'

'But condemned Chatti hostages.'

Sabinus looked at the Roman dead now being piled onto a pyre. 'I wouldn't worry about them; their people killed my men and for what? Nothing. They didn't deserve to die here.'

Perhaps they didn't but then again they should not have been here, I thought; but I kept that to myself.

With the pyre lit and the wounded loaded onto makeshift stretchers of cloaks and pila shafts we moved off and, within two days, were at Castra Vetera on the Rhenus. Here I encountered the first in a series of the biggest things I had ever seen and the rest of the journey was punctuated with them. I shall take them in order. I had always thought that the Albis was the widest river possible in the world and then I saw the Rhenus; it was so wide that people on the far bank could only just be made out by the most sharp-eyed. Five times wider than the Albis, its magnitude made the next thing I saw even more impressive: a bridge across it. A wooden bridge constructed of whole tree trunks somehow sunk into the riverbed to support a frame that carried a road wide enough for eight men to march abreast. My wonder was magnified tenfold by Sabinus telling me that it was only a temporary bridge built by Drusus to take his army across the river for the campaigning season and it would be destroyed on his return. What were these Romans that they could build such things and think nothing of their destruction after so little time? Later I came to realise that it was because they are a practical people and they measure a thing's worth not by the effort needed to construct it but by its usefulness.

This wonder of construction spanning a wonder of nature led to a third wonder: a town built of stone with more buildings than I had ever seen in my whole life put together and then filled with more people than I had ever seen in one place outside the mustering of the tribe. But the muster is only for a few days; here they lived side by side all year round. How could so many people be fed? All the land for miles around must be cultivated to achieve such an enormous feat; and, of course, it was.

We stayed in Castra Vetera for two days and nights; my brother and I slept in a room on top of another room to which you climbed by stairs, a sensation that I would have made more of had my head not already been full of new sights.

On the third day yet another marvel: a ship with two banks of oars and a deck enclosing the rowers to protect them from missile fire. This new wonder took us up the Rhenus for more miles than I thought it possible for a river to flow and, when Sabinus told me that we were not even halfway to Rome, I despaired of ever returning home.

We left the Rhenus and marched overland, past mountains so tall there was snow on their peaks even in the summer, to a port on the Rhodanus and took a ship there down to the greatest marvel so far: the sea. Never had I imagined anything so huge; it stretched further than the eye could see and, so Sabinus informed me, it would take seven days to cross north to south or thirty days to go east to west and then he staggered me by saying that Rome owned or took tribute from all the lands surrounding it.

All this made our embarking on a ship twice as long as the two we had already sailed in an event of little remark and I barely gawped as I walked up the gangplank. We sailed east and then south, following the coastline for four days, until we came, at the beginning of July, to a port that made Castra Vetera seem like a collection of the meanest hovels; but I won't waste time describing Ostia because, four hours after our arrival there, I entered Rome.

If I had felt a hatred of Rome before travelling up the Via Ostiensis it was as nothing compared to my feelings as I passed under the triple arches of the Porta Trigemina, in the shadow of the tree-speckled Aventine, past the crowds of beggars, and then on into the Forum Boarium. Rome was magnificent: to my right towered the Circus Maximus, above it loomed the newly built, marble-clad Palace of Augustus on the Palatine with the shining Temple of Apollo beyond it; ahead and slightly to my left the ancient temples on the Capitoline soared to the sky over the Forum Romanum as if Jupiter and Juno were presiding over the heart of their children's empire.

Of course I did not know the names and functions of all these buildings when I first beheld them that day; I did not need to in order to hate them for what they represented. As I gazed around, no doubt slack-jawed in amazement, all I could think was: why? Why, when they had all this, did they demand more? What could Rome possibly take from the Cherusci that would in any way embellish the magnificence of what surrounded me? It seemed to me that Rome had need of nothing other than an antidote to avarice; and from that moment on I have hated her for her unremitting greed.

Sabinus guided Chlodochar and me through the teeming streets; just two of his men, divested of their uniforms and dressed in simple tunics, accompanied us, the rest had camped outside the walls of the city as armed soldiers were not allowed within its boundaries. As we climbed the northern slope of the Palatine, Sabinus pointed out the other six hills of Rome and named some of the buildings standing on them; he spoke in Latin now as our proficiency in the language had developed during the course of our almost two-month journey; however, his words hardly registered with me, deep as I was in my own thoughts. Now that we had come to the end of our journey I felt so far from home and so lost in a city whose magnitude overwhelmed me that I now truly despaired of seeing the forests of my homeland again.

'Where will you go once you've delivered us to Drusus' house, Sabinus?' I asked as we reached the summit of the Palatine.

'I'll allow my men one night in the city and then we'll start back to Germania tomorrow.'

'Will you go to the Cherusci's lands?'

'I should think so; Drusus is meeting your father with his auxiliary recruits at the first full moon in September, we'll easily be back by then.'

'Would you take something back to my mother for me?' I detached my knife from my belt and handed it to him.

'Why do you want to part with this?'

'I'm not parting with it; I just want my mother to have it whilst I'm away. Tell her that I'm sorry that I didn't say goodbye and that I hope to reclaim the knife from her one day.'

Sabinus took the knife and hung it on his belt and smiled down at me. 'You'll get home.'

'Will I?'

'Your gods preserved you against the odds; why would they go to that effort just to have you die so far from them?'

I shrugged and shook my head, contemplating that, and I have to confess it heartened me. As we approached a large house, less ostentatious than its neighbours on the Palatine, I grasped the hammer amulet around my neck and pledged myself to Donar if he should bring me safely home.

We mounted the few steps up to the front door and Sabinus pulled on a chain; I heard the sound of a bell tinkling inside and then a viewing slot opened to reveal two eyes.

'Centurion Titus Flavius Sabinus, charged by Nero Claudius Drusus to bring two hostages of the Cherusci to his household.'

The door opened and we walked in leaving our escort outside. I found myself in a room that would have encompassed my father's longhouse and was full of more riches than belonged to the entire Cherusci tribe: gold and silver ornaments and bowls on low marble tables with legs carved in the shape of animals; statues painted so lifelike that for a few moments I thought they would suddenly move or talk; a floor made of tiny stones fitted together to form pictures of animals and men, surrounded by geometric designs. But most unbelievable was a statue that spouted water constantly from its mouth into a rectangular pool at the centre of the room. White marble columns at each corner rose up to the ceiling, which had been left seemingly unfinished so that the sun shone in, casting a thick shaft of golden light that cut through the calm atmosphere of the chamber and reflected off the many precious items with a dazzling array of colour.

As my eyes took in all these things an elderly man dressed in a fine tunic spoke briefly to Sabinus and we followed him out, into a high, wide corridor that remained cool despite the July heat outside, and on into a smaller room – although had I seen it first it would have been the largest that I had ever seen. It was furnished even more sumptuously and decorated with richly coloured frescoes. Its high ceiling had a mist floating beneath it as if it was so tall that thin clouds had been captured within the room and at any moment there might be a gentle summer rain; I soon realised that this was the fumes from the many oil lamps and candelabras that augmented the light from three windows on the far wall through which I could see a garden in full bloom. The elderly man left us, giving no indication that we should sit on one of the plumply upholstered couches that populated the room. I stood there with my arm around my brother's shoulders; his eyes were as round as slingshots as he struggled to make sense of the splendour of our surroundings. Sabinus stood to one side, in front of a pair of curtains in which were woven mysterious signs in silver thread; as I looked at the signs, trying to work out what they represented, the curtains twitched and a small eye peered through the gap. I held the gaze for a few moments wondering who was observing us until footsteps coming through the door caused it to hastily withdraw and the curtains to be resealed.

'Centurion,' a woman's voice said, at once soft and authoritative.

I turned to see a lady of outstanding beauty come through the door; so elegant was her movement that she seemed to glide.

'I am Antonia; my husband wrote to me of your impending arrival. Thank you for fulfilling your duty; you may leave now.'

Sabinus saluted – a sight that I found strange having never witnessed a man do such honour to a woman – and then with a curt nod and something nearing a smile to my brother and me, he marched out of the room. That was the last time that I saw him. I pray to the gods that he has a good excuse for never delivering my knife to my mother because I cannot believe that he wilfully stole it; it would have been worth nothing to him. Perhaps he died on the return journey.

Aius stopped reading and rolled up the scroll.

Thumelicatz examined the knife and then looked at the two brothers. 'So we know now why your father never delivered the knife to my grandmother; but why did he never return it to my father?'

The younger brother bristled visibly. 'He didn't steal it, if that's what you're implying. The campaign in which he got so badly wounded that he was invalided out of the army happened seven years after he'd met your father; by the time that he'd recovered from his wound and returned to Rome, the following year, Erminatz was serving as a tribune in an auxiliary cavalry *ala*. He did try to return it; he told us so when he gave the knife to us last month.'

Thumelicatz studied the younger brother's face, sensed the truth and then thought for a few moments. 'Very well, the timing fits; Erminatz did begin his military service for Rome at the age of seventeen. But we get ahead of ourselves.' He looked over to Tiburtius who had the second scroll unrolled. 'Begin.'

CHAPTER III

The Lady Antonia scrutinised my brother and me for a few moments; I felt her startling green eyes boring into mine and had I not reminded myself that I was the son of the king of the Cherusci, I would have bowed my head to her. My sexual feeling for women had not yet developed but I felt my pulse quicken at her beauty: pale skin, full lips stained an intimate shade of pink, high cheekbones and a mass of auburn hair intricately braided and piled high upon her head secured with bejewelled pins and partially covered by a long turquoise garment that fell around her shoulders, wound around her body and draped over one arm; beneath that she wore an ankle-length, pleated dress of deepest red that swayed gently from side to side as she moved forward. I was smitten. I had never seen such beauty and elegance; I felt my nostrils flare as I inhaled her scent that made me desire something that I could not comprehend – it was not until a few years later that I realised what power the sense of smell had over both men and women.

Antonia smiled beneficently and with a trace of humour, and I realised that I must have been letting my feelings play on my face; I immediately blanked my expression and stared at her defiantly.

'What are your names?' she asked, sitting on a couch and placing her hands in her lap.

'I'm Erminatz and this is my—'

'Let the boy answer for himself.' She looked at Chlodochar whose gaze fell to the floor.

'Chlodochar,' he whispered.

'Speak up, child.'

'Chlodochar!' It was almost a shout.

'Chlotgelar? No, no, that won't do, no one will ever remember it.'

My brother raised his eyes and looked at her with apprehension. 'The soldiers called me Flavus because of my blond hair.'

'How very sensible of them; Flavus it is then.' She turned back to me. 'Arminetz is far too vulgar, Arminus ... no, Arminius, yes, that will do, you will be Arminius in Rome.'

'Yes, Antonia.'

Her eyes flashed. 'You will always address me as domina.'

I nodded, dumb, aware of the power that those eyes had revealed and not wishing to incur her displeasure again.

'Good. My husband writes that he wishes you both to be educated here in this house and that shall be so; we shall smooth out the barbarian wrinkles and make you presentable. But be warned, if you don't apply yourselves to your studies or if you are unruly or disobedient, you will be punished and your status as guests will be reduced to hostages and you will find your freedom greatly curtailed and will be little better off than slaves. Do you understand me?'

To be honest I'm paraphrasing that speech as I had only understood the gist of what she had said but her tone and the words that I had understood were enough for me to nod again. 'I will explain it to Chlodochar.'

Antonia's eyes flashed again. 'To whom, Arminius?'

'Flavus, domina.'

'Good, you're learning.' Her eyes then moved behind me. 'I know you're in there, so come out!'

I turned to see the curtains, which screened off an alcove, part and a boy, not much older than Flavus, stepped from behind them. He walked up to Antonia, with a confidence beyond his years, grinning as he did, and placed a kiss on her proffered cheek.

'These two boys will be sharing your lessons,' Antonia informed him, affectionately ruffling his hair.

He looked at us and scowled with a humorous twinkle. 'They don't look very clean, Mother.'

And that was how I met one of Rome's greatest generals, Drusus and Antonia's eldest son, Tiberius Claudius Nero, who would later be known as Germanicus.

Roman education is a series of hard-won lessons, each more difficult than the last and, having never had a formal lesson in my life, the first came as a shock to me. I had seen writing before – I knew, for example, that the runes engraved on my blade said 'Erminatz' – but I never thought that I would have to learn to decipher it; we had slaves who would do that menial job. But, nevertheless, at the beginning of my first lesson I was presented with a list of signs that I was told by my *litterator* were letters and I had to learn to recognise each one and what sound it represented in a language that I barely knew. As if that were not bad enough, I was sitting alongside two boys, three years my junior, one of whom, Germanicus – I will refer to him as such, although he had not gained the name as yet – had almost mastered this seemingly magical art. He would laugh at my halting renditions of alphabetical sounds and my humiliation at this would make my efforts even more stuttering and unsure so that eventually the litterator would have no option but to apply the rod, and my humiliation would be compounded by being beaten in front of my juniors and also by Flavus' easy aptitude at what I found so elusive.

However, progress was made; the beatings died down and sitting on the hard wooden benches for hours at a time became bearable. As we improved we were rewarded with more masculine activities such as wrestling and sword handling; but as I was that much bigger than Flavus and Germanicus they were always paired together and I would be facing whomever was teaching us. The result was that I would never win at anything and Flavus and Germanicus became staunch friends. I began to feel very alone and that feeling grew as Germanicus asked his mother for Flavus to move out of the room that he shared with me and into his; which she acceded to and Flavus did with pleasure.

And so passed my first couple of months in Drusus' house; but I will not linger any longer on them because something happened in late September that changed much.

We were sitting in the *peristylium*, the courtyard garden at the rear of the house, trying to get to grips with arithmetic, when a messenger, still covered with the filth of the road, was ushered through and into a room at the far end of the garden that was Antonia's private domain. I thought nothing of it as the black lacquered door was opened to admit him. However, a very short time passed before Antonia appeared; she walked, strangely erect as if she was forcing herself not to collapse, over to our little group beneath a fully laden apple tree.

She looked at Germanicus, her eyes blank of emotion, and without preamble said: 'Your father has died from injuries inflicted falling from his horse in Germania. You are now head of this household and will be expected to perform those duties at his funeral when his body arrives in Rome next month. Do not let the family down.' With that she turned and walked as fast as she could, without losing her dignity, into the house. With hindsight I realise that it was to be alone with her profound grief as soon as possible; to have given way to it – or even have her eyes water – in public would have been unacceptable to her.

Flavus and I both looked at Germanicus; his face remained neutral. He placed his stylus and wax tablet on the stone bench beside him, stood and said to the litterator: 'You will, of course, excuse me.' He followed his mother, with the same poise, into the house and I had my first lesson in Roman reserve and self-control.

How Germanicus could keep his feelings about the death of his father so locked away at that young age amazed me; it was close to inhuman in my eyes. Flavus told me that, throughout the time that it took Drusus' funeral cortège to reach Rome, he never once heard him cry at night. During the days he carried on with his lessons as if nothing was the matter and the only difference that I detected was that he did not laugh at me when I made one of my many mistakes; in fact he did not laugh at all.

And then the day came when Drusus' body entered Rome.

In the few months that I had spent in the city I had not been allowed out of the house, but, on the day of Drusus' funeral, Flavus and I were expected to join the family in their grief as guests of the household and so we were woken well before dawn. The house was full of sombre activity, quiet and ordered, as the slaves prepared for the return of their master. Flavus and I were fed quickly and then placed by the house steward in the far corner of the atrium with orders to follow the family at a respectful distance.

As the sun crested the eastern horizon, the doors were opened to admit Drusus' clients, more than two hundred of them – although I found out later that these were only the most prestigious of the few thousand citizens who counted Drusus as their patron. Wearing dark grey togas – called, I soon found out, the *toga pulla* – they walked with almost theatrical solemnity into the atrium and took up position around the edge of the room. Then Germanicus appeared, leading his mother and sister, and I almost gasped in astonishment: Antonia was holding a baby. I had never heard of a third sibling, no one had ever mentioned it. My curiosity was short-lived; as we followed the family out into the cool morning, to wait for the cortège's arrival on the steps of the house, a sound floated up from the city below, a sound that I had never heard before: the sound of tens of thousands of voices raised in communal grief. Gradually it grew, coming nearer and nearer until eventually the head of the procession came into view and Drusus' body could be seen on a bier carried on the shoulders of six men. I looked over to Germanicus and Antonia; neither showed the slightest emotion as their dead father and husband was brought home for the last time.

The stench of decomposition preceded the bier but everyone affected not to notice; I had the presence of mind to push Flavus' hand back down when he attempted to hold his nose.

Antonia gave Germanicus a tap on the shoulder as the procession arrived before the house and halted; he moved forward, bowed his head then turned and preceded the bier up the steps. I had to suppress a smile at the ludicrousness of the sight: the two bearers at the front were so mismatched in size that the bier rocked dangerously with each step. The man on the left was tall, even by our standards, with broad shoulders and a powerful chest; his understandably gloomy features and age – early thirties – suggested that he was Drusus' brother. His partner on the right, however, was in his mid-fifties and far shorter and thinner; almost to the point that he could be described as spindly. As all the men were in grey mourning togas I had no way of judging the rank of the insignificant-looking man, but I sympathised with his fellow bearers as they struggled to keep the body on the bier.

Behind them came a woman, slightly younger than the spindly man; full cheeks, a prominent straight nose and large eyes that never for a moment left Drusus' corpse. She held herself erect but walked as if in a trance and I guessed that she must be Drusus' mother; but the identity of the younger woman following her, shepherding five children aged between twelve and three, shrouded by an air of sorrow, I could not begin to fathom.

The rest of the procession remained outside and Antonia led the family in with Flavus and me being the last people to pass over the threshold. I was not aware of it at the time but as the doors closed I was in the presence of the entire imperial family of Rome; I was at the very centre of Roman power.

The name of the deceased had been called many times by the mourners and the prayers had gone on for an age before a coin for the ferryman was finally placed in Drusus' mouth and we left the house to make our way to the Campus Martius, to the north of the city walls, where the funeral pyre had been built. Crowds of people followed us and lined the route, putting on theatrical shows of grief: women tore at their hair and clothes, wailing shrilly, whilst men were unafraid to cry openly. I soon realised that grief in Rome was a public commodity and not something to be indulged in privacy and I understood Germanicus' seeming lack of emotion over the death of his father. As we progressed, he allowed tears to flow freely, as did Antonia and all the other followers and bearers of the bier. An actor led us, wearing Drusus' death mask and dressed as him in full military uniform, followed by others with the death masks of his forebears; professional mourners whipped up the crowd with heated displays of almost self-flagellatory grief. The atmosphere grew darker and darker as we neared the pyre and the height of the buildings along the route seemed to encase the wails and howling, trapping them so they reverberated around, unable to rise to the heavens.

Such was the infectiousness of the mourning that by the time we reached our destination my mood was black, as if I had lost my own father, and tears were trickling down my cheeks for a man whom I hardly knew and who had defeated my people and taken me hostage. The bier was positioned atop the square pyre of regularly placed logs that looked like a building and the family mounted a large rostrum next to it; my brother and I remained at the foot of the steps. The professional mourners raised their volume to beyond what I thought possible and the wearers of the masks stood still in poses of grief whilst the tens of thousands that looked on howled as if it were their own deaths that they lamented.

As the noise grew to a pitch that left my ears ringing, the spindly man stepped forward and, with a single gesture, silenced the huge crowd in an instant. And then he started to speak and I realised, with a shock, who he was.

'Today we mourn a son of Rome; a man as dear to me as my adoptive sons, Gaius Julius Caesar and Lucius Julius Caesar, the natural sons of my daughter, Julia.'

The spindly man was the most powerful man in the world: Augustus, the Emperor of the Romans. He pointed to the two eldest boys of the family of five.

'I pray that when the time comes for their sons to speak their funeral orations that they will have achieved as much honour in Rome's name as Drusus, a man that I considered to be no less my heir than those two boys.'

It seemed amazing to me that a man so lacking in physical presence, a man who would not stand out in a crowd, a man easily overlooked, could rise to the pinnacle of this martial race; and, as Augustus carried on his eulogy for the next hour, I examined him, curious to find a clue to his power. Although short and slim, he was perfectly proportioned so that if you saw him on his own you would have no idea of his size and would naturally assume him far taller than he really was; he was evidently aware of his stunted stature as I noticed his shoes had thick soles and heels, adding at least two thumb breadths to his height. At home a man would have been mocked for such vanity. His complexion was pale, his hair untidy, sandy curls and his nose Roman, crowned by eyebrows that met at its bridge. I saw nothing in him that could make me believe that he could master men, until his eyes turned in the direction in which I was standing and for a moment they met mine; and then I understood: they were bright and clear and so blue as to be almost grey. They were the eyes of a man of tremendous will, they shone with such intensity that it was almost impossible to endure their gaze for more than a few moments. With eyes like those a man could command others to do whatever he wished.

Augustus gestured to Antonia and to Drusus' mother and brother to step forward; he presented them to his audience who remained spellbound. 'I ask you, fellow citizens, to share the grief of Antonia, his wife, and their three children; share the grief of a mother, Livia Drusilla, my wife; and share the grief of a brother, Tiberius Claudius Nero.' All three held out their hands, beseeching the people of Rome to join in their grief, which they did without reserve.

Augustus allowed the lamentations to go on for a good while before once again gesturing for silence, which was immediate. He looked over to a group of some five hundred men standing on the steps of a building on the other side of the pyre – I later found out that this was Pompey's Theatre. 'Conscript Fathers of the Senate, help to assuage our grief, honour Drusus in death in the way that I should have begged you to honour him in life. The fault is mine for not petitioning you to award him the title that he deserves; I take the blame, Conscript Fathers, and I feel the guilt of inaction. For his victories in Germania Magna and the peace treaties that he forged there, the proof of which stands before me.' He looked directly at Flavus and me and then pointed at us. 'The sons of Germanic chieftains are here in Rome, not only as hostages to the good behaviour of their fathers but also to make Romans out of them. Drusus has forged for us a new province, securing our borders far to the east; I implore you, Conscript Fathers, honour him and his descendants with the name that he has surely earned: confer on him posthumously the name Germanicus, and let his eldest son be known as such in memory of his father.'

Such was the emotion in his voice and such was the fervour of his request that the Senate, almost as one, shouted: 'Germanicus!' The cry was taken up by the people of Rome and, as the chant grew, Augustus walked across to the pyre and took a flaming torch from a slave and thrust it into the oil-soaked wood. The flames leapt high, licking at the bier, sending dark smoke and a shimmering heat-haze skywards. Next to the pyre, men with togas pulled over their heads, covering their hair, sacrificed an ox, ram and boar, removing their hearts to throw into the fire. As the heat intensified, crackling the wood and sizzling the dead flesh, so did the chant, until it must have been audible to every god, both Roman and Germanic.

The Senate and the people of Rome did not stop honouring their beloved son until the fire began to die down and the body was nothing but charred bones; only then did they start to disperse and begin an official period of mourning that would close with the funeral games nine days later.

We returned to the Palatine and life carried on as normal with two exceptions: we were now occasionally allowed out under supervision to join the other boys doing gymnastics, wrestling and training in arms and on horses on the Campus Martius. The second thing was far less enjoyable: although I have referred to Germanicus by that name throughout my story so far to avoid confusion, it was only now that we had to call him that rather than Nero. So every time I spoke his name I was reminded of the defeat of my tribe and, although he did nothing to wrong me, I began to hate him just because of his name.

Rome became my life over the next few years and, although I was never comfortable with being taught in the Roman way, I began to excel in the physical training and managed to achieve adequacy in the schoolroom. My thighs, chest and shoulders developed and I could read and write Latin and Greek as well as speak both languages with little trace of an accent. By the time I was past puberty I was, to all appearances, no different from the boys with whom I trained on the Campus Martius: in short, I was becoming a Roman. My hair was cut regularly, my wispy beard was shaved every day and I had not donned a pair of breeks for five years. I understood the workings of government, the rigidly hierarchical social system and knew the command structure and drills of the legions. But, despite all this, I still kept hidden in my heart a deep love of the Cherusci and a fierce hatred for the people who had forced me to abandon their ways.

This was not true for Flavus; his friendship with Germanicus had grown to the point that the two were inseparable and his love of all things Roman had come to dominate his life to the extent that, even when we were alone, he refused to speak our mother tongue with me. His memory of our homeland grew dim and he began to be contemptuous of the Cherusci's 'rustic' way of life, as he put it, and berated me for not seeing the magnificence that surrounded me or understanding the power that it represented. He became truly Romanised: worshipping their gods, enjoying their spectacles in the arenas or the Circus Maximus and taking pleasure in their food.

We argued much in those days, often coming to blows; being older and larger, I would always give him a severe beating – for which I was usually punished – and this drove him further away from me and closer to Germanicus, whom he considered to be more of a brother than me, his blood.

With no one with whom to share memories of a lost childhood I felt more and more isolated and my bitterness burnt away inside me. This manifested itself in bouts of extreme violence and I became feared on the wrestling sand; my temper would flare if I began to lose, and my respect for the rules and etiquette of the sport would evaporate in an instant and I would have to be hauled off my bloodied opponent by the wrestling-master and given a thrashing.

After one such incident a youth, about my age, pushed through the crowd jeering at me as I received some harsh strokes of the rod.

'Leave him!' he ordered my flagellator. 'I'll give him a lesson in Roman behaviour on the sand.'

The wrestling-master let me go; I stood up and looked at my challenger. He seemed familiar but I could not place him; I certainly had not seen him training on the Campus Martius before – but then I was only allowed down every so often, so it was quite possible that our paths had never crossed. He was not strongly built for a youth of fourteen or so and slightly shorter than me. Large blue eyes, a full-lipped mouth and light brown hair, he looked more like a pleasure-boy, the sort that I had seen roaming some of the less-salubrious streets of Rome that I would occasionally explore when I managed to slip the attentions of my chaperone.

He stepped forward onto the sand, rolling his shoulders and fixing me with a determined glare. He was, like me, naked. Sand from a previous bout stuck in patches on his oiled skin and there was bruising up his arms and on his chest as if he had been recently bested.

I strode forward, the welts of my beating smarted but I did not let that show; I looked at him with the confidence of someone who makes judgements based solely upon what the eye can see. 'I look forward to my lesson with relish.'

'That's good because I can assure you that you won't look back on it with the same feeling.'

'I'm sure I'll savour it more.'

'Arrogant barbarians need to be put in their place.' He

crouched facing me and I copied his stance, circling around him, changing direction, as he slapped my shoulders and upper arms trying to get a firm grip on oiled skin.

I responded in kind and also slammed my forearms left and right, blocking his attempts to grapple me. Moving my feet with irregular steps was a trick that I had learnt; it made it harder for your opponent to predict the direction of your next move, yet it did not seem to confuse this youth at all. Round we went, left then right, slapping at each other with open palms, landing stinging blows that could not quite be converted into a firm hold. A smack around the side of my head made my ears ring and earned my opponent a cheer from the growing crowd. I forced my right arm up, crunching his away before he could convert the blow into a grip around the back of my neck, then countered with a feint to my left and followed with a sharp move forward with my right foot in an attempt to hook around the back of his knee. He read it easily and, as my leg flashed forward, he jumped back and reached down with his left hand, grabbing my calf; he jerked it up as his right hand went for my foot, twisting it towards him with a sudden, brutal motion that forced my body to roll with it rather than have the tendons in my ankle stretched beyond endurance. In an instant I spun in the air as he tightened his hold on my foot; as I rolled over he powered forward, forcing my leg to bend so that my heel almost rammed into my buttock, sending me crashing down, face first, in an explosion of sand accompanied by the jeers and laughter of the spectators. Rough grit scraped the skin from my chin, the tip of my nose and forehead and clung to my watering eyes. I rolled onto my back, blinking incessantly, my vision blurred with sand, and I felt my temper rise as my humiliation grew.

I rubbed my eyes clear and could see the youth standing over me, sneering and beckoning me to stand up; the crowd clapped their hands in slow time and my temper broke.

Pushing back with my hands, I propelled my aching body forward and leapt at him with a high-pitched cry of rage and, with no thought for the rules, went at him with my fists clenched. I felt my knuckles crunch into his chin and then crack onto the side of his head. He made no reply but just stood, leering at me. I lashed out with a flurry of wild punches, roaring incoherently, and then something happened that changed my outlook on life for ever: with lightning-swift motion, the youth caught both my fists in the palms of his hands, clamping them firm and then slowly forcing them down.

'What's the point in cheating just a little bit?' he hissed between clenched teeth, twisting my wrists outwards. 'You either play by the rules or break them to such an extent that your opponent is completely taken unawares and everyone fears you for daring to go so far.'

The pressure mounted and I collapsed to my knees, grimacing with pain. Suddenly he released my left fist and pushed the right one out; grabbing my elbow with his free hand he crunched my arm down onto his rising knee. A white flash of pain seared through my head as I heard my forearm snap like dead wood and I must have screamed, although I have no memory of it.

'That's how to cheat; anything less is pitiful and demeans both you and your opponent.'

I fell to the ground, clutching my shattered limb, tears of pain streaming down my agonised face and coagulating the sand stuck to it into a sticky mud.

After a few moments writhing in agony I became aware that

there was absolute silence surrounding me; I opened my eyes to see the crowd looking in open-mouthed astonishment at my vanquisher.

He stepped forward and hauled me up. 'It's a clean break; it'll set well. I'll have my father's physician come to your house to set it.' He put an arm around my shoulder and guided me through the crowd of spectators; they parted for us without a word. My chaperone, an elderly slave from the household, slipped my tunic over my head, collected my sandals and loincloth and then followed us back to the Palatine.

The youth dropped me at Antonia's house with a promise that the physician would attend to me imminently.

He arrived sooner than I expected and, as he examined my broken arm, I asked him the name of the youth.

He looked at me in astonishment as if everyone should know the boy's name. 'He's my master's youngest adopted son.'

And then, of course, I knew why his face had been so familiar: I had seen him before at Drusus' funeral; he was Lucius Julius Caesar.

Lucius called on me the next day and to my great astonishment and confusion seemed very amicably disposed towards me.

'How does it feel?' he asked, coming into my room unannounced.

I looked at him in surprise. 'It throbs,' I blurted.

'I suppose it will for a few days.' He sat on a stool in the corner of the room, leant back against the wall and put his feet on the low table next to my bed. For a while he surveyed me in silence.

At first I did not know what to make of it and then it started to annoy me. 'What are you looking at?'

'That's a stupid question.'

I grunted, vaguely acknowledging the truth of that observation, and then held his gaze. 'Why did you purposely break my arm and then come and see if I was all right?'

'That's a better one.' He smiled, not at me but to himself. 'Well?'

'I suppose I was bored.'

'Bored?'

'Yes, bored; you know: my mind insufficiently occupied because of the repetitiveness of life.'

'I know what bored means!'

'Then why did you ask?'

'I didn't ask what it meant, I asked ... I asked ... well, why?'

'I wanted to see how you'd take it.'

'Badly.'

'No, remarkably well; at least I thought so. And I wanted to see whether you'd learn from it.'

I narrowed my eyes. 'Oh, I've learnt from it and it was a very painful lesson.'

'All the best ones are.'

'That's not true.'

Lucius thought for a moment. 'No, I suppose that was rubbish; I had a very enjoyable, pain-free lesson only last night.'

I managed a half-smile.

'So?'

'So, what?'

'So, what did you learn?'

'I learnt that next time I wrestle with you I'm going to wrench your balls off and then break both your arms and say that anything less is pitiful and would demean both of us.'

'Ha!' He clapped his hands. 'I knew you'd understand; you'll be perfect.'

'Perfect for what?'

'Perfect for me now that my brother seems to spend most of his life playing at politics. A sixteen-year-old sitting in the Senate! What bollocks.'

'But he's Augustus' heir.'

'So am I; but he's welcome to it. I want to have some fun before I'm forced to grow up and behave like a gout-ridden ex-consul. I can't get too friendly with the boys of my class because I'm not stupid; they'll use that friendship for their own gain in the future or the friendship will cloud my judgement. So I have to look elsewhere for companionship.'

'And a barbarian suits you just fine?'

'Absolutely.'

'Because I'll never play a part in your empire's politics?'

'Precisely.'

'And therefore I'll have nothing to gain from our friendship.'

'Exactly.'

'So you'll feel that I'm a genuine friend and not a syco-phant?'

'True; but more to the point, my adopted father will think that and won't object to you being my companion.'

'Why should he care?'

'Because, obviously, you'll have to move into the palace; how else can we be educated together?'

'And do I have any say in this?'

'Of course.'

'And what if I say no?'

'Oh, I don't think you'd do that.'

'Why not?'

'Because you'd be missing out on a lot of fun. I'm the Emperor's adopted son; I can do almost anything I want.'

And so I moved into Augustus' house and became the friend of the joint heir to the imperial purple.

Tiburtius rolled up the scroll.

Thumelicatz smiled, without warmth, at the Romans. 'I find it a very pleasing irony that the person who showed my father that life must be lived to the extreme and the man who dares to go furthest will always win, was at one point destined to become your emperor.'

The younger brother waved a dismissive hand. 'Lucius would never have become emperor; his elder brother Gaius was being groomed for that.'

'Nevertheless, he was Augustus' co-heir whilst he lived and had he not died two years before his brother who knows how history would have changed.'

Thusnelda pointed a finger at the Romans. 'One thing is for sure and that's Lucius was a great influence on my husband. He accepted no boundaries either in pleasure, violence, vengeance or daring. Erminatz told me many stories of their escapades: street fights, sexual excesses, arson, sacrilege, just about anything. Nothing was sacred, nothing was off-limits and nobody was too exalted to escape their schemes.'

'Except for the Emperor and his wife, Livia,' Thumelicatz interjected.

'Yes, except those two. Lucius was very clever; in front of them he behaved impeccably, always the perfect-mannered youth of great promise. Anytime one of his exploits was brought to Augustus' attention Lucius would always deny it with wide-eyed outrage, insisting that he couldn't possibly have been responsible for whatever he had been accused of as he had been learning Virgil, or whatever, by heart with Erminatz; and then to prove it he would recite hundreds of lines perfectly and beautifully and Augustus would believe him. Livia, however, wouldn't; she hated Lucius and his brother as she saw them as obstacles to her only surviving son, Tiberius, becoming emperor. At this time Tiberius had left Rome and retired to Rhodos; people said it was because he couldn't stand the lewd behaviour of his wife, Julia, Augustus' daughter and the mother of Lucius and Gaius. Livia knew that the removal of Julia and her sons would leave the way clear for Tiberius to return and become Augustus' heir; so that's what she plotted to do. Augustus would not believe anything bad about his family – which is why Lucius would always get away with his antics – but Livia gently dripped poison into his ears until eventually he had Julia exiled to a barren island and her marriage to Tiberius annulled. And once that happened the lives of the two boys were in great danger.'

Thumelicatz held the palm of one hand towards her. 'Mother, you are leaping ahead; first we listen to the one example that Erminatz gives of his and Lucius' behaviour and we'll see how Lucius' way of solving problems deeply influenced my father when he came to deciding how to defeat Varus. Aius, read on.'

CHAPTER IIII

Being Lucius' friend could not be described as dull but what would be dull is to list all the outrages we perpetrated. I shall describe just one as it illustrates perfectly the large scale in which Lucius' mind worked, and also it concerns someone already mentioned in my narrative.

I had been living in Augustus' house with Lucius for almost two years and I had been thoroughly enjoying myself. Lucius left a trail of destruction wherever he went and I loved following in his wake; I felt as if I was in some way having my vengeance on the city that held me captive by helping Lucius wreak havoc on its streets and population. And, if I'm truthful, I had begun to feel at ease in my captivity in that I no longer felt held against my will; perhaps, despite myself, I was becoming Roman.

A particular favourite pastime of Lucius' was to attend the gladiatorial games whenever they were on. He used to take a perverse pleasure in calling for the opposite decision to the crowd, so if they wanted to spare a defeated gladiator he would loudly demand his death and the other way around. Being the adoptive son of Augustus, the games' sponsors would want to please him so they would often go against the popular wish just to ingratiate themselves with the possible future emperor. He used to enjoy seeing how far he could push the sponsor; one time he pushed so far that it caused a riot in the amphitheatre in which over a hundred people were crushed to death.

Obviously he would never indulge in this sort of behaviour if Augustus was present as he never did anything to tarnish his reputation in Augustus' eyes; he was far too clever for that.

We were at a huge, temporary wooden arena, constructed on the Campus Martius for the plebeian games that year, and had been watching a fight between a *murmillo* and a Thracian. The fight had been lacklustre and the murmillo had soon tired; he seemed rather old and not destined to be long for this world. The Thracian soon overcame him and had him lying on his back with the tip of his sword to his throat whilst the crowd hissed and booed and began to chant for his death.

'This'll piss them off,' Lucius said with the wicked grin that always presaged an act of calculated mischief. 'Life! Life!' he bellowed at the praetor who had sponsored the games and had the final word on the fate of the downed man. 'Life! Life!'

The praetor looked around nervously, assessing the crowd's mood as they bayed for the man's death.

Lucius chanted against them. 'Life! Life!' He pounded his fist into his hand with the beat and incessantly bellowed at the praetor.

The sponsor got to his feet and held out his arm with his fist clenched. The crowd stared at him, waiting for him to stick out his thumb in mimicry of an unsheathed sword, the sign for death. He stood there, motionless, his thumb firmly clenched. The crowd began to throw things at him but he did not change the signal and Lucius carried on his chant. The summa rudis acted on the call and moved the Thracian away, allowing the murmillo to get to his feet. The crowd went wild, screaming abuse at the sponsor as the murmillo walked off the sand. Just before he got to the gate he took off his helmet and I gasped.

'What is it?' Lucius asked through his laughter.

I stared at the retreating gladiator in disbelief. 'I know him.'

'Well, he's a lucky man; who is he?'

I stared harder to make sure that I was not mistaken but despite his lack of beard and his hair cut short, Roman style, I knew it was him. 'He's my mother's brother, Vulferam, my Cousin Aldhard's father; we didn't know whether he had died in our last battle with your people or had been taken prisoner.'

Lucius' countenance became suddenly solemn. 'Family, eh? Then it's your duty to free him and, as your friend, it's my duty to help you.'

'That's the only way in and out,' Lucius said as we completed a circuit of the gladiatorial school to which Vulferam belonged. It was a two-storey complex outside the city walls, on the Campus Martius, on the opposite side of the Flamian Way to the mausoleum that Augustus was then in the process of building for himself and his family. 'And although we could quite easily be allowed in there's no way that we would be allowed to walk out with one of their possessions.'

I looked at the iron-grille gates standing firmly closed and guarded by four bulky ex-inmates of the establishment, more to prevent egress rather than ingress. 'I still think that we should just make the lanista an offer and purchase his freedom. It would be so much simpler.'

Lucius turned to me with his brow furrowed in a pained expression. 'Where's the fun in simple? Simple is what you do if there's no time for the grand gesture, the extravagant, the outrageous. We have plenty of time, Arminius; your uncle won't fight again for at least a month or two and it won't take that long to work out how to burn this place down.'

'Burn it down?'

Lucius grinned. 'Of course; what better way to get the gates open? We'll get your uncle away in the chaos and it'll just be assumed that he's one of the poor unfortunates lying as a charred corpse in the ruins.'

'Let's hope that he's not and that we don't end up sharing the same fate.'

'Which is the risk that'll make this seriously good fun.'

I remember being unable to stop myself from smiling as I caught the desire for danger and adventure in his eyes. 'And what about all the others who may not be as lucky as us?'

'What difference does it make to them whether they end up dead in a fire or dead on the sand of the arena?'

'But they might be destined to live into old age.'

'Then that's what they'll do. Only the ones who are destined to die in the fire will do so; and that fire is destined to happen because I can see it.'

And, of course, that fire did happen; but what resulted from it was not quite as we had planned.

It had been easy for Lucius to get us into the school; the lanista, Cassianus Crispus, had been honoured that an adoptive son of the Emperor should take such an interest in his gladiators and so he allowed us to come and watch the training any time that we pleased. This had two obvious benefits: firstly, we were able to explore the complex. Secondly, I was able to see Vulferam and although I did not have the chance to speak to him I was able, by means of a bribed slave, to find out which cell was his and to get a message to him. He knew that I was coming for him.

It was some ten so nights after we had first looked at the buildings that we approached them in the dead of night in a covered wagon. Even at that time the Campus Martius was not deserted – there are very few areas of Rome that ever manage to achieve calm, even on the coldest of nights, because of the daytime injunction on wheeled transport within the city walls – but this suited our purpose as we could pass unremarked as if we were just returning from a night-time delivery. We pulled the wagon up next to the wall at the back of the complex, furthest away from the gates, shrouded in shadow thrown by a quarter moon, then unharnessed the horse and shooed it away.

'You hold it steady, Arminius,' Lucius whispered as we raised up a ladder that reached to within a couple of feet of the top of the wall. Within moments he was up on the roof and had lowered a rope, smelling of the oil in which it had been soaked for two days, to which I attached the first of four sacks containing our gear. As the last one was hauled up I followed up the ladder.

The complex was built around a central, rectangular court-yard in which the gladiators trained. The ground and first floors of the two long sides contained their cells whilst either side of the gate was devoted to smithies, armouries and other work-shops and storerooms. The side that we had chosen had the kitchens, eating area, infirmary and the slaves' accommodation; in short: the most combustible.

I threw the rope back down, taking care that it landed on the wagon's cover, which had also benefitted from a good dousing in oil, and then joined Lucius at the far edge of the gently rising roof above what we had worked out was the medical supply storeroom. Here Lucius had removed a dozen tiles and was now feeding a second rope into the gap and attaching it to the exposed rafter.

Lucius disappeared down through the hole. 'Perfect,' he muttered as he touched the ground. 'It's full of bandaging, blankets and rags just begging for a flame.'

I passed the sacks down after him, keeping only an unlit pitch-soaked torch and the wherewithal to ignite it, and waited, listening to the sound of Lucius dousing the storeroom with an amphora of oil.

'I'll whistle three rising notes once I've done the walkway outside,' he whispered as he pulled another couple of amphorae out of a bag. The room brightened a fraction as Lucius opened the door and stepped out onto the wooden walkway that ran around the entire length of the first floor, giving access to all the gladiators' cells.

My heart thumped in my chest and, despite the chill, my hands felt clammy as I waited for what seemed to be an interminable while but was probably, in reality, no more than the time it takes to empty one's bladder after a good night out. The signal came and, scratching flint against iron, I soon had sparks in my tinder, which I coaxed into a flame. As the torch flared up, I slid back down the roof and touched it to the oil-soaked rope. It caught immediately with a blue-red flame that rippled down its length at a leisurely speed, which increased the pace of my heart, until eventually it touched the covering of the wagon, igniting it with a sudden flash. I peered down, watching the fire grow until the wood had caught and the covering had burnt away exposing the stacks of amphorae within, each plugged with oiled rags; they too began to burn.

I sprinted back up the roof and slipped down the rope into the storeroom, holding the torch aloft.

Lucius stood silhouetted in the doorway. 'It's burning?'

I grinned by way of reply.

'Come on then.' He disappeared to the right. I threw the torch into a pile of bandages; they burst into bright golden flame that quickly spread to the left and right as well as down into the puddle of oil on the floor. As that too caught fire I ran out, following Lucius with a tongue of flame chasing me along the oil-drenched wooden walkway.

Within a few moments the first shouts had started and, as we ran to the steps leading down to the training area, a flash lit up the sky above us; the wagon-load of amphorae had exploded, spreading burning oil all over the outside wall, lighting up the darkness with a fierce orange glow.

We took the steps two at a time, Lucius with the three remaining sacks slung over his shoulder and me with flames licking my ankles. Hitting the sand, we darted to the right, into the deep shadow below the walkway, as dark figures began to run towards us from the gate on the other side of the courtyard. Skidding to a halt outside of a locked door, Lucius pulled a crowbar from one of the sacks and wedged it into the door-jamb. 'Three, two, one!' We both threw the weight of our bodies against the bar and, with a crack of splintering wood, the door burst open and we tumbled into the kitchens.

'Get the buckets!' Lucius shouted, pointing to the storeroom to the left of the great central cooking area, where we knew, from our exploration of the complex, the kitchen equipment was kept.

Grabbing as many buckets as I could, I ran back through the kitchen as Lucius lay two of the last sacks on the grill above the still glowing charcoal; they immediately began to smoulder.

'Over here!' I shouted, dashing out into the courtyard waving the buckets at the men sprinting towards the fire from the gates.

The closest one swerved over to me; throwing him a bucket, I ran to the nearest of the drinking water butts, placed around the courtyard to slake the gladiators' thirst during training, shouting at the rest of the men to follow me, and within a few moments I had a bucket-chain fighting the fire now spreading down the steps.

Lucius sprinted out with another half-dozen buckets as more men appeared to help fight the fire; we set up another chain before rushing back to collect yet more buckets for the ever-growing effort. In the kitchens the sacks were now flaming, heating the amphorae contained within; Lucius retrieved the final sack from next to the door as we ran out of the kitchen for the last time.

No one questioned us because, ostensibly, we were helping tackle the mutual threat: the fire. No one noticed that we did not belong there because, for the same reason, we fitted in. No one even paid us the slightest heed because we were striving for the common good. We were the enemy within and yet we were invisible; inside I was laughing fit to burst.

All around now the gladiators had started to beat on their locked doors, shouting to be let out as the flames spread despite the efforts of our fire-fighting teams; their noise rose over the shouts of the bucket-chains and of the inmates of the infirmary on the first floor as those who could walk helped those who could not to safety before the walkway was completely engulfed in flame. Rising above everything were the screams from the slaves' quarters as the conflagration threatened their bolted doors.

Lucius and I scurried around, shouting encouragement but not doing anything constructive, taking care to keep well away from the door to the kitchen. The din grew with the fire as did the desperation of the gladiators and the screams of the slaves as their quarters began to burn. Then, with a whoosh of heated air, a flare shot through the kitchen door as the remaining amphorae exploded; the hair of a couple of the men closest to the door ignited, sending them pelting, screaming, to the nearest butt to douse themselves. Flames raged in the kitchen and, above, the roof burnt freely.

'Release the gladiators! Release the gladiators!' a voice bellowed over the pandemonium – Lucius.

I joined in the cry, pushing men towards the cell doors to begin unbolting them.

'And the ones on the first floor!' Lucius shouted, pointing to the stairways, as yet untouched by flame, halfway down the courtyard on either side. Hauling a couple of men with me, I sprinted towards the left-hand one, following Lucius; we took the stairs two by two.

As I reached the top I pointed to the left and shouted at the two men: 'Take that end! We'll go right.' To the right was Vulferam's cell. As we went we pulled back the bolts on the outside of the doors, releasing the gladiators – many of whom had women for company. They streamed down the walkway, clad only in loincloths or completely naked, as we worked our way along until I pulled back a door to reveal Vulferam. He had a woman with him; she had her tunic on but he was just in his loincloth. I pulled her out of the cell and propelled her down the walkway.

Lucius threw the sack at Vulferam. 'Get dressed!'

My uncle tipped out its contents on the low bed: a tunic, a cloak, a belt and a pair of sandals. I carried on opening the cell doors along the rest of the way and then returned to find my uncle dressed.

'How did you find me?' he asked in our language.

'Luck; I saw you fight – and lose.'

'We don't have time for whatever you're discussing,' Lucius shouted in Latin, running out of the cell into the chaos on the walkway.

'Keep your head down,' I hissed at Vulferam as we followed.

Barging and pushing, we made our way down onto the training area and joined the surge towards the main gates that remained locked. Behind us the fire had spread down both sides of the walkway so that the first few of the gladiators' cells were now cut off and, no doubt, aflame. Heat seared around the complex and men sweated in the burning glow. All attempts at fighting the fire had now ceased and the only people left close to it were those unfortunate enough to have been trapped in its path; they now lay smouldering, either dead or, had they been very unlucky, rolling in scorched agony as the sand aggravated hideous burns.

The clamour at the gates grew but still they remained locked, fuelling the gladiators' indignation at being left to burn.

'I can't unlock the gate until Cassianus Crispus gives me his permission to release his property,' the head guard shouted at an angry deputation of incensed inmates.

'And where is the lanista?' came the heated reply from the group's leader, a taut-muscled Thracian.

'In his house on the Quirinal; we've sent him a message, he'll be here soon.'

The Thracian looked over his shoulder as the first sections of the walkway collapsed with a rush of searing wind, intensifying the blaze.

'By which time we'll all be running around like two-legged torches – you included.'

'I can't let you go!'

'Bollocks you can't!'

The guards were set upon, quickly disarmed and under very extreme duress revealed the whereabouts of the gate key as well as that of the armoury. The guardroom door was broken down, the keys recovered and, once the armoury had been looted, the gates were unlocked as a couple of centuries from one of the newly formed Urban Cohorts formed up on the Flamian Way, directly outside, to try and contain what had now become a mass breakout by over a hundred freshly armed professional killers.

Lucius and I held back with Vulferam as the gates swung open and the gladiators streamed out, brandishing the tools of their trade, heading directly for the shield wall that stood between them and freedom.

Lucius grinned at me and Vulferam as the surge gained unstoppable momentum. 'Straight through the gates and then dart sharp left and leave the fighting to the professionals?'

'Sounds like the sensible option.'

'Where do we head to?' Vulferam shouted as we joined the stampede to escape the flames.

'The Salus Gate is the nearest,' Lucius replied as the metallic ringing of clashing blades suddenly broke over the dissonance of bellowed curses and threats.

As the first screams of pain added to the mayhem we cleared the gate and hugged the wall to our left. Ahead, the Urban Cohort centuries had buckled under the pressure of the explosion through the gates of scores of men at the peak of physical condition both bodily and martially.

We pushed on towards the extreme right flank of the centuries' line along with a dozen or so gladiators more intent on a clean escape than on fighting their way out. The buckle at the line's centre had pulled the edges back but there was still less than two paces between the wall and the last soldiers who had, as yet, not been engaged. Seeing us approach, they brought their shields to bear and stared fixedly over the rims, left feet planted forward and right arms back ready to stab their weapons through the gaps in the wall.

Lucius pulled back and let a few bodies get between the soldiers and us; Vulferam and I pressed close to him, edging forward cautiously in his wake as all around the efforts of the gladiators, more used to individual combat, failed to break the unified discipline of men trained to fight as a unit. Slowly the escapees were giving ground and I could see that unless we broke out we would be crushed against the wall and butchered or worse: captured and exposed.

To my right a gladiator went down to an underarm thrust of a honed gladius blade; blood slopped black and glistening, faintly orange in the firelight, to the ground. His sword clattered on the paving; I stooped to retrieve it.

'Give that to me,' Vulferam demanded, grabbing my wrist. He took the weapon, judging the weight of it in his hand. 'Go!' he shouted, pushing me into Lucius' back.

Without questioning the order, we sprinted forward, keeping tight to the wall as the line's flank moved forward to close the gap. Vulferam accelerated beside me, bellowing a war cry of our people that I had not heard in years. The old but familiar sound lent strength to my legs and they powered me on as Vulferam barrelled towards the extreme right soldier, the tip of his blade aimed directly between the man's eyes. He immediately raised his shield and thrust it forward and up in an attempt to deflect Vulferam's blow; his distraction was enough for Lucius and me to clear the gap as Vulferam heaved his shoulder into the man's shield and brought his blade clanging down on his sword flashing out towards my thigh. Without the support of a comrade to his right the soldier crashed to the ground, entangling the feet of the man to his rear as he tried to step into the gap. Lucius and I pelted forward as Vulferam hurdled the downed man and the three of us sprinted for our lives down the tomb-lined Flamian Way into the deepening night away from the inferno and the blood-bath that we had caused to free one man.

I had been shown the meaning of the grand gesture and I loved it. More than that, I had learnt a crucial lesson: the most important ingredient of leadership is vision.

After a couple of hundred paces we slowed, seeing as there was no pursuit, and slipped through the tombs to our left, and, crossing Agrippa's Field, headed for the Salus Gate.

'Once we're in the city,' Lucius said, breathing deeply with the exertion and, no doubt, the exhilaration, 'we'll head across the Quirinal down into the Forum Romanum and then onto the Palatine. We can smuggle your uncle into the palace; no one would dare to search my apartments even if they did suspect us of having anything to do with such a despicable incident.'

'Why did you have anything to do with it?' Vulferam asked. 'I know who you are; I've fought in front of you three or four times.'

Lucius looked at Vulferam as we approached the torch-lit gate. 'If you know who I am then you will understand when I tell you that I did it because I could.'

'All those lives just to free one man.'

'Yes; just think how valuable that now makes your life, so don't waste it. Now pull your cloak tight around you and act as our bodyguard whilst we go through the gate.'

The soldiers on duty at the Salus Gate stepped out of the way as Lucius announced his name and we passed under the arch as another party hurried in the opposite direction. As we passed each other in the torchlight their leader glanced in our direction and suddenly stopped. 'Lucius Julius Caesar, forgive me for not showing you more respect but I am on urgent business.'

'Think nothing of it, Cassianus Crispus; please do not let me detain you.'

The lanista nodded to me and then glanced at Vulferam who tried to keep his face in shadow. With a hint of a double-take and a frown, Cassianus Crispus hurried off towards his ruined livelihood.

Lucius watched him go and slapped his hand against the wall. 'Shit!'

Two days later found Lucius and me sitting on a stone bench in the garden at the heart of Augustus' palace. We had been waiting for three hours since dawn when the summons had come to attend the Emperor at his convenience; we were in no doubt what it was about.

'I'll deny everything, obviously,' Lucius said for at least the tenth time, 'as will you.'

'Crispus saw us and he recognised Vulferam; how many times must we go through this? Deny it as much as you like, your adoptive father won't believe you.'

'Of course he will; he wouldn't believe anything bad of me because as far as he's concerned my behaviour has always been impeccable.'

'Don't be so sure, Lucius,' a female voice interrupted, surprising us.

We both looked over our shoulders; Livia, Augustus' wife, stood, beautiful, severe, remote, half shielded by a column in the covered walkway that surrounded the garden. I had never had any personal dealings with this elegant woman whom, if rumour was to be believed, played much more of a part in Roman politics than just the role of Augustus' wife.

'Augustus sees much more than you might think and hears even more than that; he is well aware of some of your unpleasant little hobbies, Lucius. He's been indulgent with you and your behaviour because, so far, it has not cost him any money. But now he's got a very popular lanista claiming that his son burnt down his premises and caused the death or escape of over half of his stock and the necessity to punish the remainder. I think that if you try to lie your way out of it then you'll only end up increasing his anger – which I can assure you is already considerable.' She smiled as if the thought of the Emperor's anger excited her, although her eyes retained the cold stare with which she had transfixed Lucius. They then flashed onto me for an instant and I shivered at the strength of her will. 'As for the barbarian, I suggest you keep away from him in future, Lucius; he doesn't seem to me to be a very nice companion. There's too much of the forest in him and that is something that no amount of civilising can ever eradicate. You can remove the barbarian from the wild but never the wild from the barbarian.'

Without even glancing at me again she turned and walked away, leaving us in no doubt as to the severity of our position; however, I felt oddly grateful that she had saved us from making it worse.

Lucius swallowed as he watched her go; gone was his innate patrician confidence and for the first time I saw uncertainty in his expression.

'What will you do?' I asked.

'Do? I don't know; I need to think about it.'

We sat in silence for another half an hour or so, contemplating Livia's advice until our uneasy peace was interrupted by the arrival of the First Man in Rome. He arrived unaccompanied, dressed in a simple tunic; in his hand he held a pruning knife.

I had grown considerably since I had last seen him and now, at the age of sixteen, I was taller than this most powerful of men, even though he was wearing shoes with thick soles and heels two thumb widths high. But height meant nothing when talking to Augustus; authority radiated from his small frame in the ease that he held himself. It was as if he had supreme confidence in his every movement; even the slight twitch of a little finger was executed in such a way that it seemed to have been planned well in advance and utilised at this time because it was exactly the right sort of twitch to emphasise his thoughts. 'What do I say to this man, Lucius?' he asked without any preamble – small-talk was an irrelevance to him, unless, of course, he was using it to unsettle his interlocutor.

I looked at Lucius out of the corner of my eye and was shocked; his face was now a mask of innocence. He was calling Livia's bluff. 'What man, Father?'

Augustus smiled at his adoptive son and grandson and held his eye for a good few moments; Lucius did not flinch, his face maintaining a casual puzzled interest.

Augustus reached out and squeezed his shoulder. 'I hoped that would be your reaction, my boy; in fact I was positive that it would be. Livia seemed to think that you had committed the outrage.'

'What outrage, Father?'

Augustus then gave a brief account of the fire at the school, which was remarkably accurate apart from missing out our involvement.

'So Crispus thinks that we did this just because we passed him in the Salus Gate last night.'

'He says that you were accompanied by one of his gladiators.'

'No, Father; I was with Arminius. Another man went through the gate just in front of us. I'd never seen him before; he'd been running and overtook us just before we passed the guards. I paid him no mind, but thinking about it now there is no reason why he couldn't have been one of the escaped gladiators; he ran off very fast up the Quirinal once he was through.'

Augustus turned his attention to a shrubbery and began pruning dead twigs and leaves from it. 'And just what were you two doing out on the Campus Martius at that time of the night?'

'We were on our way back from the Temple of Flora; we'd been making a dedication to her as her festival begins in a few days.'

Augustus concentrated on his gardening for a few moments. 'Yes, the Floralia is at the end of April; since when have you had an interest in her?'

'I always sacrifice to her at the beginning of spring.'

'In the middle of the night?'

Lucius shrugged. 'We weren't tired so we thought that we'd—'

'Liar!' Livia snarled, coming up behind Augustus.

Augustus carried on his pruning without looking at her. 'My dearest, there's no need to be so aggressive.'

'And there is no need for you to be so gullible.'

'Gullible?'

'Yes, gullible.' Livia pointed a finger at Lucius. 'You believe everything that he told you, don't you?'

'I certainly don't believe that he set fire to a ludus and caused the deaths of more than a score of gladiators and facilitated the escape of many more. Why should he want to do that?'

Livia looked at her husband incredulously and tore into him for being so easily duped by a manipulative youth. Augustus let the tirade blow over him and he continued his pruning as if he were relaxing alone. Lucius cast me a sidelong glance and I saw the triumph in his eyes as Livia, furious that her lies had failed to deceive him into admitting his guilt to Augustus, gave vent to her feelings – to no avail.

I understood, then, the value of mistrust and how it can keep you safe.

'Have you finished yet, woman?' Augustus asked placidly as Livia took a short pause for breath. 'Because I suggest that you do before I lose my patience.'

The underlying tone in his voice was one of menace; cold, cold menace.

Livia opened her mouth and then thought better of continuing; she cast Lucius a glare of pure malice and then looked pityingly at her husband before walking, with surprising dignity considering her temper, from the garden.

Augustus chuckled. 'Women, eh, boys? Such suspicious beasts; always prepared to jump and think the worst of people as quick as boiled asparagus.'

Lucius bent down and began to collect up all the loose trimmings. 'Indeed, Father; even when it's illogical. What could I possibly gain from burning down a gladiator school?'

Augustus contemplated the question for a few moments. 'That's what I wondered; it makes no sense.' He paused in thought, clearly oblivious to the fact that the deed had been done to facilitate the release of my uncle who had been smuggled out of Rome and was now on his way back to Germania so that he could not be used as evidence against us. 'Anyway, you seem to have annoyed Livia in some way, so I think it would probably be best for me to get you out of her sight for a while. Your brother, Gaius, is about to set off to the East to conclude a treaty with King Phraates of Parthia who seems to be under the impression that if he interferes in Armenia then I'll execute his four half-brothers and rivals to his throne that we hold here as hostages. I've told Gaius to take two legions and threaten Parthia's western provinces. Meanwhile, I've sent messengers to Phraates telling him that I certainly will not execute his rivals if he interferes with Armenia, even though they are hostages to Parthia's good behaviour; however, I would consider doing so if he and Gaius can come up with a suitable treaty that guarantees Rome's interests in Armenia. You're sixteen now so I think that it would be only right for you to accompany your brother. We'll have you in uniform getting military and diplomatic experience. What do you say?'

'But, Father, I would prefer to stay in Rome.'

'So that you can be accused of yet more mischief?' He chuckled again and slapped Lucius' shoulder. 'Look, my boy; I don't believe that you did it but that doesn't mean that you didn't. There is no smoke without fire – if you would excuse the pun – and you've been accused of many other escapades and misdemeanours that you have always denied and come up with very good reasons why you weren't even there in the first place. This time, however, a witness and your admission put you near the scene of the crime.

'A man should always have an eye to his possible failings: perhaps I am a doting old father and allow myself to be duped by you. So for all our sakes you will join your brother on his mission to the East; it'll be good for you. Besides, how can you be my joint heir if you don't know the waters in which I swim?' He looked at me. 'Arminius will go with you so he can see the extent of Rome's empire; you can both serve as military tribunes on Gaius' staff.'

Lucius and I shared a look and a grin: we had got away with arson and murder and now, as a reward, we were to see the East.

CHAPTER V

THUMELICATZ CAST HIS eye over his four Roman guests as Aius rolled up the scroll and Tiburtius prepared to read from the next instalment. 'Another dose of irony, I would think you'd agree, gentlemen: the Empress of Rome, through her malice, showing my father the importance of mistrust and the necessity to hold your nerve against anybody with a proven record of lying; and that's just about anyone who's manoeuvred their way to power.'

The younger brother stirred himself, snapping out of some reverie. 'It was a calculated risk on Lucius' part to deny everything to Augustus; he had nothing to lose. I would have done the same had I been in his position.'

Thumelicatz raised his eyebrows. 'Nothing to lose? He was Augustus' joint heir.'

'Yes, but he must have been aware, even then, of the ambition that Livia had for her sons. She had persuaded Augustus to make Drusus the foremost general in the empire and, with the glory he'd already won, had he survived he, rather than his dour elder brother, Tiberius, would have been the obvious heir to Augustus if Lucius and Gaius somehow disappeared. But with Drusus now dead and Tiberius in self-imposed exile in Rhodos, she had started to plot Gaius and Lucius' removal so that Augustus would be forced to fall back on Tiberius. Lucius calculated that if she was lying in order to frighten him into admitting his guilt to Augustus, thereby making all his other denials suspect and greatly losing favour with his adoptive father, then Augustus would believe him if he denied the accusation. However, if she wasn't lying and Augustus knew for certain that he had been responsible for the arson then he might as well still deny it at first and then admit it later under duress as the result would be exactly the same: all his past misdeeds would be exposed and he would be less in Augustus' eyes.'

'So you believe that Lucius thought that Livia was trying to undermine him?'

'Of course she was and most people suspect that it was her who was eventually responsible for both of the brothers' deaths.'

Thumelicatz offered round his jar of pickled testicles; there were no takers. 'My father points to that later in his narrative but he never had any evidence other than circumstantial.'

'But that evidence is interesting,' the street-fighter observed. 'Who became emperor after Augustus? Livia's elder son Tiberius because Gaius and Lucius both died young; and if half the rumours about Livia are true then I'd say that was more than circumstantial, if you take my meaning?'

'I do,' Thumelicatz agreed, 'but the truth will never be known for sure. However, once again we get ahead of ourselves, Erminatz deals with those deaths later. But first we have the mission to Parthia. Tiburtius, skip the journey out there as it is mainly a description of the sites along the route; the only points of interest are the repeated arguments between Lucius and Gaius. They took a passage across to Greece and then down to Athens and from there by ship again to Antioch in Syria where they were met by two legions and their auxiliaries. From there they marched to Thapscum on the Euphrates, the border between Rome and Parthia; close to the city is an island in the middle of the river.' He took the next scroll from Tiburtius' hands and quickly scanned it. 'Take it from this line: "Gaius' folly had grown in conjunction with his authority."'

'Yes, master.' The old slave took the scroll back and quickly found the place.

Even though he was only Augustus' representative and not the Emperor himself, Gaius insisted that he would not cross to the island before Phraates; a Roman should never be forced to wait for a barbarian, he reasoned. Obviously Phraates had the completely opposite opinion and with more justification as he was a king – the King of many Kings to be precise.

'We'll be stuck here for ever if you don't give in!' Lucius shouted at Gaius as he once more refused his brother's plea to cross to the island where the pavilions were already set up for the meeting. Gaius' staff, arranged around the *praetorium* tent, the command post at the centre of the camp, looked embarrassed at witnessing such a public row between the brothers.

But Gaius was adamant. 'I will not start negotiations from a position of weakness.'

'The negotiations have already happened, you idiot; you're just here to finalise them and sign the treaty in Augustus' name so that Armenia returns to our sphere of influence. Who gives a fuck who arrives on that island first.'

'I do.' Gaius turned to the senior military tribune on his staff, the son of the newly appointed prefect of the Praetorian Guard. 'Sejanus, see my brother and ...' He looked at me and sneered. '... his pet, out.'

Lucius Aelius Sejanus ushered Lucius and me from the tent with much courtesy and many apologies; he was ever anxious to ingratiate himself with people of status. Lucius, fuming at his brother's intransigence, shook off Sejanus' guiding arm and stormed from the tent.

I think that it was at this point when Lucius realised that he was the more flexible and pragmatic character of the two and, although I could never say he came to hate Gaius, in the short life that he had left he certainly began to dislike him and stopped looking up to him as an elder brother. He became open to me in his criticism of Gaius and I believe that the enemies of Rome have much to regret from the brothers' deaths: had they both lived I think their mutual antipathy, sparked at this moment, would have grown and if they had remained Augustus' joint heirs then that would have been a cause of civil war upon his death. But that was not to be.

For two days Gaius and Phraates stared at each other across the river surrounded by their armies. The Parthians with ten thousand horse archers and half as many heavy cataphract cavalry, a riot of colour with the gay caparison of the horses, the flags and banners and then the garish dress of the Parthians themselves, all camped in a haphazard manner, contrasted with the regimented lines and dull colours of a Roman camp and its occupants. Immediately my sympathy lay with the Parthians as I beheld a people of colour, irregularity and pride. I was reminded of my own people and their free, unordered life where a man was able to display his wealth and prowess in his dress rather than all wearing the same colourless toga or the same russet tunic of the legionaries. There, across the river, I saw individuals, the first I'd seen since coming to Rome, and my yearning to go home grew more intense. Not that Romans aren't individuals, they just manifest it in different ways so that, to an outsider, they all seem very similar. And, as I stood looking at the Parthians, a quarter of a mile away across the river, I got to the core of the

Roman character: their soldiers look the same; their elite in the senatorial and equestrian classes dress the same and follow the same career path, and although there is intense rivalry between them for status and position they all want the same for Rome and will put aside personal differences and strive together for that. So, I reasoned, if that were true then surely they could all be predicted to act in the same way given a certain set of circumstances that threatened Rome and therefore, by extension, themselves and their families; their strength in their unity and ability to act as one, the strength that makes the legions invincible if taken head on, could also be their weakness. If I could force them into a predictable course of action then I would not need to take them head-on because I could make them come to me, to a place of my choosing, to a place where they would not expect me to be. And it was with that germ of a thought, the way that had so far eluded my father on how we might be able to rid Germania of intruders, going around my head that I joined Lucius in his next piece of extravagance.

There were many boats in Thapscum, mostly belonging to fishermen, so it was with ease that we managed to cross the river to the Parthian camp. In order that there could be no doubt that we were Roman military tribunes and not spies we both wore our bronze, muscled breastplates, greaves, military cloaks and helmets – mine was a beautiful cavalry helm with a removable lifelike mask that had been Lucius' gift to me when we had kitted ourselves out in Rome; he had found it amusing to give me the mask, saying that it made me look more Roman because it hid my barbarian features.

'My name is Lucius Julius Caesar,' Lucius informed, in Greek, the Parthian guards on the jetty as our fisherman brought us gently alongside, 'and I wish to see King Phraates.'

Ever since Alexander's conquest, Greek has been the common language of the better-born men of the East – indeed, it is said that a man can travel all the way to far-off India and still be able to make himself understood with just the use of Greek.

The officer commanding the guards firstly looked astounded at Lucius as he jumped out of the boat and then he burst into laughter. 'There is only one Roman the Great King wishes to meet and I can assure you, young lad, that you are not he.'

Lucius had little patience with underlings and even less with underlings whom he considered ill-mannered and patronising. With no care for the fact that he was within the enemy camp, he stepped up to the Parthian officer, who was twice his age, and, grabbing him by the beard, pulled him close so that their noses almost touched. 'You evidently are not aware to whom you're talking so I shall make this easy for you. I believe that your master, Phraates, is extremely fond of impaling people who displease him; when he finds out that you did not pass on the fact that the younger son of the Emperor of the Romans wanted to speak to him I think that'll displease him immensely. Have you ever tried having anything bigger than a cock up your arse?'

The startled officer evidently had not and was not of the inclination to start experimenting with larger objects now; uncertainty played on his face as he stared at the sixteen-year-old youth who had bearded him, and calculated whether he was who he claimed to be. His men stepped forward, drawing their swords; the officer signalled for them to move back. He took Lucius' hand and pulled it from his beard, his mind made up to cooperate with the arrogant Roman youth, despite his shattered dignity. 'My most humble apologies, noble sir; you will understand that I had no way of knowing that you really were whom you claimed to be.'

'I will understand no such thing; the only thing that I will understand is: "will you please follow me; I will take you to the Great King's tent and inform his steward that you have requested an audience".'

The officer gave a wan smile, completely defeated. 'Noble sir, please follow me.'

'What if he detains you and holds you hostage?' I asked Lucius as we waited to be called into the Great King's presence, sipping a frothy drink that made our tongues tingle but was remarkably refreshing.

'And why would Phraates do that?'

'To put more pressure on Gaius to travel to the island first.'

'And thoroughly annoy Augustus at the same time? He'd be mad to, just as he's finally got a settlement with him that should hold for a generation or so and may even have secured the execution of his four half-brothers. No, Phraates will just listen to what I have to say and then he'll take my advice and soon we can all leave here very happy, with the exception of that pompous arsehole, my brother Gaius. You will tell me, won't you, if I start acting like one of those fifty-year-old men who have never led an army and never made the consulship and then puff themselves up within their dignity to disguise their lack of achievement in life?'

'You can't blame Gaius; it's not his fault that Augustus gave him the power and position that no eighteen year old has ever had before.'

'But it is his fault that he's trading off relative dignities with the Great King of Parthia.' He indicated to the vastness of the tent in which we were waiting – it was twice as large as any used by the Romans and served only as a waiting area before admission to the main audience tent. 'What Gaius doesn't understand is that the Parthians do things very differently to us. Look at this unnecessary extravagance; does Phraates really need such a large tent for us to wait and take refreshments in? Of course not; but he probably doesn't even know that he's got it. It's his courtiers who do such things because the greater they make their king the more important they feel themselves to be. It's about pride and pride is not going to let them allow their Great King to look inferior to an eighteen-year-old Roman no matter that he is the adopted son of the Emperor. Phraates knows that and so, therefore, won't countenance going to the island first because to do so would be to show weakness, and weakness in a Parthian king is punishable by death at the hands of a usurper. Gaius, however, doesn't have those constraints and should just be pragmatic and get on with it. No one here is going to laugh at him for waiting for Phraates. Rome's power won't be diminished because little Gaius had to hang around on an island for an hour of two; Augustus isn't going to admonish him just because he blinked first. No one in Rome gives a fuck.'

A chamberlain entered, softly clearing his throat as he pushed the curtains aside and glided in. 'The King of Kings, the Light of the Sun, Lord of East and West and Terror of the North has deigned to admit you into his presence.'

'How gracious of him,' Lucius said without a hint of irony before adding, under his breath so that only I could hear: 'And now I shall deign to show the proud bastard a way to save his bearded face.'

There was a general murmur of disapproval as neither Lucius nor myself even so much as bowed our heads let alone made the full prostration on our bellies before Phraates as protocol dictated. The chamberlain who, whilst escorting us into the royal presence, had insisted that we made the *proskynesis* looked up at us aghast as we stood before the king, next to his prone form, no doubt terrified that he would get the blame for such uncouth manners. Lucius might have complained about Gaius' standing too much on his dignity but he was not about to grovel before an Easterner, whatever the cost, especially one who was only a couple of years older than him. Phraates, however, seemed unconcerned about the lack of protocol; in fact he seemed unconcerned about anything as he sat on his high throne staring with dull eyes and a vacant expression into the middle distance somewhere above our heads. His beard, its sparseness betraying his youth – he was eighteen at the time – had been dyed purple and his shoulder-length, ringletted hair was held in place by a golden kingly diadem encrusted with rubies and pearls. Nothing about his countenance gave any indication that he had noticed our arrival in a pavilion that more than did justice to the size of the antechamber. Its sides were raised to allow a cooling breeze to waft between the many carved wooden poles that supported the lofty roof; all over the floor carpets were strewn of such intricate weave and variance of colour that each one seemed to be a work of art in itself. And within its expanse, having all performed the full proskyneses, stood the nobility of Parthia.

Standing next to the throne was a man of very advanced years; he was leaning on a staff, his back bent by time that had also thinned his beard and hair and reddened his eyes. 'What brings you across the river, Lucius Julius Caesar? Why do you disturb the Light of the Sun's peace?'

Lucius stood erect and looked directly at the king as he responded to the king's mouthpiece. 'We hope that we do not inconvenience the Light of the Sun; on the contrary, we have crossed the river to offer a solution to a problem and help ease his mind.'

There was a flicker of interest in the otherwise immobile face of the Great King.

'Then speak,' the mouthpiece ordered, 'so that the Light of the Sun may judge your words.'

Lucius paused for a few moments, looking down at his hands clasped before him, as if considering how best to frame his words to the Great King. 'There are times when for the sake of appearances, appearances need to be changed. The Light of the Sun will not travel to the island before my brother Gaius who, in turn, will not travel to the island before the Light of the Sun. Now, whatever the rights and wrongs of this situation may be, it leaves us with an impasse that will result in the treaty negotiated between our two great powers not being signed whilst we sit here in the sweltering heat achieving nothing. I therefore have a proposal: Gaius will travel to the island if the Light of the Sun *appears* to have already arrived on it. All that has to happen is that the Great King's entourage and banners cross the river; when Gaius sees that he will think he has won the standoff and will sail over, at which point the Light of the Sun can embark and arrive after him.' Lucius spread his hands and raised his eyebrows to emphasise the simplicity of the plan and all eyes turned to Phraates for his reaction.

It was slow in coming and was surprising when it did finally arrive: Phraates looked at his mouthpiece and asked his opinion.

The mouthpiece stepped forward. 'I cannot countenance this; it would mean that I and all of your obedient servants would have to be parted from your presence and wait for the arrival of a puppy of a Roman—'

'Your dignity is not the issue here, old man!' Lucius pointed a finger at the mouthpiece. 'The Light of the Sun asked you what you thought of my suggestion, not whether you found it personally convenient.'

The mouthpiece recoiled at the harshness of the rebuke from one so young and looked imploringly at his master; Phraates remained staring blankly ahead, focusing on nothing.

Lucius pressed him. 'Answer, old man: would you have your master take my advice at the expense of some personal inconvenience to yourself or would you have him keep your dignity intact and walk away from this place to be known as the Great King who was bested by an eighteen-year-old Roman?' The sudden, communal intake of breath at the implication that the Great King was anything other than infallible almost whistled in my ears and all eyes went to Phraates to gauge his reaction.

Phraates gave an almost imperceptible nod as the corners of his mouth twitched into what could be deemed to be a smile. 'Go, son of Augustus, and have your men watch the river soon after dawn tomorrow.'

Again, against all protocol, we turned our backs on the Great King to go.

'But your friend stays here as surety. If I arrive on the island to find Gaius not there I will depart immediately leaving him behind, alone and impaled.'

I felt Lucius tense beside me and cast me a sidelong glance before he turned back to face Phraates. 'If you wish someone to stay then let it be me, Light of the Sun.'

'If I was to force you, a son of Augustus, upon a sharpened stake then we would return to war. However, who would mourn a relative nobody from the dark northern forests – except you, perhaps, Lucius Julius Caesar, seeing as you have been companions now for five years or so. Now go!'

Stunned by the accuracy of the Great King's information, Lucius opened his mouth to speak and then, thinking the better of it, turned and left the pavilion, leaving me astounded by Phraates knowing who I was.

'You will dine with my mother and me at my table this evening, Erminatz,' he said as he rose from his throne, compounding my astonishment by using my Germanic name. Everyone within the pavilion abased themselves before the erect Great King; in my confusion I found myself upon my belly.

We had eaten in near silence for the best part of an hour, entertained by discordant – to my ears, at least – music, created by a variety of pipes, odd-shaped harps and softly struck drums that could change in pitch. I remember feeling a little uncomfortable as, having brought no other clothes, I was still in uniform. The one thing that I had found strange was that his mother was not present as he had claimed she would be; indeed, the company – a dozen, including the mouthpiece – was solely male, but then I reasoned that was only natural as the Parthians are even more assiduous at keeping their women hidden from view than the Greeks. However, the food was sumptuous as one would expect at the table of the King of all the Kings of the Parthian empire. Small white grains that I had never seen before, light in texture, mixed with dried apricots and raisins and nuts, green in hue, served with roasted lamb so tender that the first taste caused me to salivate liberally; there were also stews of chickpeas with …

'I think we can skip all this, Tiburtius,' Thumelicatz said, interrupting the old slave; none of his four Roman guests seemed to object. 'I think you'll agree, gentlemen, that listing the menu and then giving descriptions of Parthian table manners and dinner dress is irrelevant to our purposes.' He took the scroll and scanned down it. 'The one thing of interest is that my father describes how Augustus had given a Greek concubine of outstanding beauty to Phraates' father, another Phraates, the fourth of that name, as part of the negotiations over the return of the Eagles lost by Crassus at Carrhae. This woman, Musa, soon became Phraates' favoured wife and he made her son his heir. Musa then persuaded Phraates to send his other sons to Rome as hostages required by a further treaty, seventeen years later. Once all the possible rivals to her son were in Roman hands she poisoned the Great King and put her son on the throne to become the fifth king named Phraates. That in itself is not very interesting or remarkable; what is of interest is what had happened after.' He handed the scroll back to Tiburtius, pointing to a line. 'Start from here.'

Phraates wiped his fingers and then put his hand to his chest and gave a huge belch, which in Parthia signals contentment and repletion; all the other diners followed his lead, almost drowning out the music as slaves moved solemnly around removing the remnants of the meal.

Once due appreciation of the meal had been shown, Phraates noticed me for the first time that evening. 'I know, Erminatz, a surprising amount about the various hostages currently in Rome; my half-brothers, you see, are part of that community and I have agents constantly watching them and they report back to me not only on their doings but also on the others. I'm aware that you and Lucius cause mayhem in Rome and Augustus does nothing to stop you; nor indeed does he even believe the reports of your behaviour. I know that you are the son of Siegimeri, the king of the Cherusci, and that if you manage to return to your homeland you will be king after him. I know, also, that you and your younger brother, Chlodochar, are no longer on speaking terms because you consider him to be too Romanised and therefore conclude that you do not consider yourself to be so. I therefore think it safe to assume that you are, despite your friendship with Lucius Julius Caesar, no friend of Rome's. Am I right?'

Astounded by the perception of this youthful monarch, I hesitated a good few moments before giving my answer, judging that my position would be more secure if I told him the truth; he would be less likely to have me perching atop an impaling stake should Gaius not get to the island first if I was Rome's enemy. However, I answered cautiously. 'If I come into my rightful inheritance, Light of the Sun, then my duty will be to my people.'

Phraates smiled and lifted his bejewelled goblet in a toast to me. 'That is the answer of a man who suspects that Augustus has ears everywhere; even in this tent. But, although I can assure you that nothing said here will go any further, I won't press you on the matter. Suffice it to say that I feel that we could be friends.' With a fractional twitch of his right hand he dismissed the other guests who, bowing low, backed away from the royal presence; only the mouthpiece stayed.

Once the guests had left the tent, a curtain behind Phraates was pulled aside; a woman entered and I almost exclaimed aloud at the sight of her beauty. It was quite literally breath-taking. Her long, silken robes disguised any movement in the lower half of her body, making her seem to glide. Her head was lowered and she did not raise her cosmetically outlined eyes but I could see enough of her face to desire her fervently even though she was more than twice my age. Her skin was pale as the dawn on the first day of the coming of the Ice Gods in May. Her mouth, petite but with full lips, contrasted with her cheeks as an early blooming rose with the Ice Gods' frost; it had a petulant set to it as if defying you to deny her slightest whim. But it was her hair, piled high and bound by a band of silk with the fringes woven intricately back through that band to make a coiffured diadem around her head, that, despite the beauty of her face, drew the eye: golden-red as the rising sun over a frozen lake; gold but mixed with copper and burnished to a brilliance that I felt that to touch it would be to touch the most precious thing in this Middle-Earth.

And I was not the only man in the room to be entranced. As she approached, Phraates, for all his aloofness, staring into space, could not keep his eyes from her. He rose from his couch and held out his hands for her to take as she drew near. He looked down at her and sighed as if amazed by a beauty that he beheld for the first time; her eyes rose to meet his and they were filled with love and desire that made them warm despite their ice blue paleness. He stroked her cheek and bent to kiss her, their lips touched and parted and I had to tear my gaze away for fear of the jealousy rising in me for this king's possession of such a woman. I looked, instead, at the mouthpiece, old and wrinkled and smiling at me as if he knew what I was feeling and was revelling in it because those urges came no longer to his withered loins.

'Mother, have you spent the day well?'

My head whipped round to see who had spoken those words; but there were only the four of us present.

'Yes, my son,' the woman said. 'But I have been counting the hours until this moment.'

I hoped the horror could not show on my face as the truth of the matter hit me.

'Erminatz,' Phraates said while still gazing into her eyes, 'this is my mother, Musa. When she heard that you were accompanying Lucius she requested that she meet you if you seemed to be suitable for our purposes.'

'I am honoured,' I replied, my voice hoarse.

Musa left her son's arms and reclined on a couch; she indicated that I should do likewise as Phraates made himself comfortable next to her. The mouthpiece's smile had disappeared and he was once more a picture of courtly solemnity.

Musa studied me for a few moments, as if weighing my character; I felt uncomfortable under her gaze as I tried not to imagine the acts that she and her son indulged themselves in. 'You know what it's like to be taken from your home and forced to live elsewhere, do you not, Erminatz?'

'I do, er … my lady.' I was unsure how to address an incestuous queen.

Musa did not seem overly concerned about the exactness of her title. 'I was taken from my home in Corinth twenty years ago by Augustus. I was freeborn and, despite my youth, the most successful *hetaira* in my city, charging a small fortune for an evening of my company. My mother had been a celebrated hetaira and had brought me up well in the art of pleasing men. But beauty is Janus-faced and when rumour of mine reached the Emperor's ears he took possession of me, despite my freeborn status, and gave me away to a foreign king to secure a deal as if I were no more than a vulgarly painted ornament or a performing monkey.' She paused and stroked her son's beard, whilst smiling at me. 'I suppose you're wondering what complaints I could possibly have: I'm the mother of the Great King and we rule jointly; I have more power and wealth than I could ever have hoped to gain back in Corinth.'

In more ways than one, I thought.

Musa's eyes hardened. 'My pride was stolen. Control over my body was taken from me. Rather than live in a world full of men whom I could pick and choose at will, a different one every night, sometimes returning to a few favourites whether for their sexual performance or their conversation – a hetaira is not just a prostitute, you know?'

I did not but nodded anyway.

'The skills of our profession are in the whole span of the evening's entertainment: refined conversation, music-making, dancing as well as the sensual acts that make men part with their money in a way that I've always found amusing. But what use are these skills if one is suddenly thrust into a world of women, into the realm of the harem? A world that revolves around only one man, where all the women compete jealously for his attention, his favour and just one night to be given the chance to become pregnant and bring a boy-child into the world; a child who will be your tool to rise above the other women. And I took my chance and became pregnant and over the years wormed my way up the hierarchy using my son as my weapon until I disposed of all my rivals, all other possible heirs and then even of the Great King himself. But there is still one thing that I haven't disposed of and that is the cause of my loss of pride: Rome. Rome that traded me for her own self-interest in order to get back the Eagles lost at Carrhae. And now she has had them returned I want to take them back again.'

I was stunned by her vehemence that had built as she spoke but understood her resentment, her hatred. She was right: I knew what it was like to have your pride ripped away and control taken from your life and be placed against your will in an environment that was not natural for you. I knew that only too well; and there she was, an incestuous, husband-murdering queen, and I sympathised with her. 'I would love to see you do that, my lady.'

She threw her head back and gave a short laugh. 'So would I, my strong young Germanic warrior, so would I. But I'm afraid that I never will. Not even the Romans are stupid enough not to have learnt from Carrhae; they will never put themselves out in the open desert at the mercy of our massed cavalry again. We will only fight little wars with them now, skirmishes compared to the Carrhae campaign. But you, on the other hand, have legions roaming around your land; legions with Eagles; legions with Eagles waiting to fall. You could do what I cannot now; you could take back Rome's Eagles and help me restore my pride.'

I looked at her, this murderess, this lover of her own son, this beauty filled with cold hatred, this Ice Queen and I knew that, regardless of all that she was, I could not, would not, refuse her request. Even if I'd had no desire to humble Rome in the way she wanted, I would have done it for her, no matter the cost, but how I should do it was beyond me. 'What makes you think that I'd be able to do such a thing, my lady?'

Musa smiled and it pierced my heart. 'Already you are trusted by Rome; you are Lucius' companion and Augustus himself sent you out here to accompany him. You are a favoured hostage and because Roman arrogance is unbounded, they assume that if you become like one of them then you will always be that way; they cannot conceive of the possibility of a man having tasted the fruits and comforts of Rome wanting to turn his back on her. Your path will not be the Cursus Honorum, the succession of offices both military and magisterial that high-born Romans follow; yours will be purely military. You will be given command and responsibility, not in the legions but in the auxiliaries.'

And then I remembered the last thing that my father had said to me before I left for Rome with Centurion Sabinus almost eight years previously: *Rome is going to train the very troops who'll form the backbone of the army that will free us from her; I call that a satisfactory conclusion to our business.* The germ of a thought that I'd already had now sprouted: it dawned on me just how I could defeat Rome and the path I must take to do so; it was with growing certainty that I said: 'I'll serve Rome well in her auxiliaries and then when I have nothing but the Emperor's trust and respect I shall beg to be allowed to lead my own men.' I looked down at the masked cavalry helmet that I had placed on the floor next to me. 'Lucius' gift to me shall come of use; I shall get the Emperor to make me the prefect of the Cheruscian auxiliary cavalry ala.'

Musa smiled again and I had to supress a desire to grab her and hold her, to possess her. 'Exactly, my brave Germanic warrior; the Romans still persist in the dangerous folly of allowing their auxiliaries to serve in their own provinces. The Cherusci, Chatti, the Frisii all have treaties with Rome that oblige them to provide men for the auxiliary cohorts and many of these cohorts serve in Germania Magna protecting the legions based there.'

It was my turn to smile. 'It would be so simple once it was planned.'

'Wouldn't it just? At the moment there are three legions stationed in Germania Magna; all you would have to do is find some way to manoeuvre the Governor into bringing one of them into a vulnerable position.'

'He would have to be a certain sort of man; one who acts in a predictably Roman way,' I said. I considered my theory as to whether Romans could all be predicted to act in the same way given a certain set of circumstances that immediately threatened Rome. 'But given time I'm sure that I could manufacture the circumstances to get the Governor somewhere at a place of my choosing where there's enough of a threat to make it prudent for even the most unmartial of men to have the auxiliary cohorts scouting on the flanks.'

'And then destroy that legion with the very troops that have been trained by them to protect them.'

'The grand gesture would be to destroy the other two legions as they come to their comrades' aid.'

Musa looked quizzical. 'I'm sorry?'

'The grand gesture: it's what Lucius taught me. If you do something, do it in a way that is so monumental that it can't be undone. That's what this will be. I've always dreamt of leading my people in revolt against Rome but that would be nothing compared to this. This way, if I could make alliances with the auxiliaries from other tribes as well as get the tribesmen themselves behind me, I could destroy Rome's presence east of the Rhenus and north of the Danuvius with just three blows.'

She reached out her hand to me and I took it with pleasure. 'I knew you would understand. Now concentrate on that objective and that objective only. Take back their Eagles and restore yours and my pride.'

And so it was that the course of my life was set.

The following day we ...

Thumelicatz raised his hand, stopping Tiburtius. 'I don't think we need to know the tiresome details of how Phraates fooled Gaius into crossing the river. Gaius was furious and tried to leave but Lucius persuaded him that his dignity would be even more impinged upon if he was seen not only to have been tricked by an Easterner but then compounded the matter by running away from him as well. And the treaty, as I'm sure you Romans know, was signed.'

The patrician stood and stretched his legs. 'What happened to Phraates?'

'My father mentions a little later that he married his mother a few years after and tried to make her queen. That was too much even for the Parthian nobility and they killed him. As for Musa, well, she died at the same time and probably, knowing the Parthians, with more between her legs than she had ever had before. But there is no need to feel any pity for her after the murders she had instigated; neither is there any need for the next scroll as it is concerned only with my father's last couple of years back in Rome. We shall pick up the story nearly three years later with my father having already convinced Augustus of his complete loyalty. Aius, that scroll, please.'

CHAPTER VI

Chlodochar looked at me, his hatred undisguised. 'Never, Arminius, never. I'll not ride with you and your filthy Cherusci.'

His reply had been in Latin to the question that I'd put to him in our tongue; it illustrated perfectly just how far we were apart. I tried a different approach, hoping to change his mind at the very last moment for our ship sailed for Massalia at noon. 'If you come with me and serve in the auxiliaries we'll eventually get home; we'll see our parents again, our sister, our homeland ...'

Chlodochar spat. 'All that is dead to me. I'm not a savage and nor am I stupid: Augustus may trust you enough to put you in command of the Cherusci cavalry ala but I know you'll turn and bite his hand as soon as you can and I'll not be a part of it; I'll not suffer for your treachery. Rome is everything I need.'

'If I did that you'd die, because if you remain here you remain a hostage.'

'I'm a friend of Germanicus; I'm a Roman of the equestrian class. I'm no hostage to the good behaviour of a barbarian father or brother.'

I stared at him, our eyes locked, unblinking, and I saw that he was completely lost to me and my tribe; there was nothing else to say. I turned on my heel and left the house of Antonia for the last time to begin a journey that I hoped would take me home. With my heart by turns heavy from the loss of a brother and light at the thought of finally leaving Rome, I joined Lucius and his small group of staff officers for the short ride to Ostia, the port of Rome, for our paths were the same for a little while.

It was not normal for the road to Ostia to have so many crosses lining it but as we rode through the gates and then on past the granaries, leaving Rome behind us, I was struck by the number of executions of non-citizens there had been recently. Rome was showing all who arrived at her gates the fate in store for anyone who opposed her.

'There was a small revolt by the public slaves in Ostia,' Lucius explained as he noticed me shaking my head at the scale of the executions.

Sejanus, who had been seconded to Lucius' staff now that Gaius was spending all his time in the Senate, hawked, sending a globule of phlegm to splatter on the bloodied, broken legs of a victim, now on the point of death. 'The Emperor told my father to show them no mercy so he divided the prisoners in half.' He grinned. 'These are the lucky ones.'

'And the others?' I asked.

'The marble quarries up at Carrara; they'll take two years to die rather than two days.' He laughed; the others joined him.

I pretended to join in with the laughter, but as I did a mark on one of the corpses caught my eye; on the chest, over the heart, visible beneath the sheen of blood, was a tattoo that I recognised immediately for I had seen it many times before in my childhood and I hoped that one day I would bear such a symbol: it was a wolf; the wolf of the Cherusci.

The false laughter died in my throat as I looked at the once-valiant warrior passing from this Middle-Earth without a weapon in his hand; how would he find Walhalla now?

Rome had much to pay for.

*

The port of Massalia is a mixed city, founded by the Greeks in the area of Gaul that is now called Narbonensis, which the Romans just refer to as the Province as their dominion over it is so old; it has for generations been the hub of all Gallo-Romano trade and consequently has a population made up mainly of merchants and thieves – the two professions being interchangeable in my experience.

Augustus had given me no firm orders as to how I should reach Oppidum Ubiorum, the provincial capital of Germania Inferior, on the Rhenus, so long as I was there by mid-June in order to make the rendezvous with the Cheruscian cavalry ala that was to be my new command; I had, therefore, decided to accompany Lucius as our road was shared until we reached Lugudunum. I had realised that this was probably going to be the last opportunity to spend time with him before our military service divided us, he to the legions and me to the auxiliaries. And once I had further proved my loyalty by killing Rome's enemies for her with my new command of Cheruscian cavalry I was determined to take them back to Germania and then ... well, and then I knew that I would not be coming back and Lucius and I would become enemies.

But in the end I was saved that.

As soon as we disembarked in Massalia's military port I could feel that there was something wrong with Lucius; his energy had lessened and that was not due to the six days at sea from Ostia. Having made a half-dozen or so voyages with him, I knew that he was never affected by the sickness they could induce. Normally when we sailed into a new city he would suggest a drinking session of bacchanalian proportions that would last for a couple of very enjoyable days and leave a trail of debris, debt and dead. In Massalia, however, Lucius just busied himself with following Augustus' instructions, mustering the four cohorts of legionary recruits that had been waiting for him there. He spent a couple of days watching them manoeuvre, satisfying himself that their training was adequate, whilst the rest of the officers on his staff terrorised the quarter-masters into emptying the contents of their warehouses – which, after a couple of summary executions, they consented to.

'The bastards need to be taught a lesson,' Lucius informed his staff in his evening briefing at the garrison prefect's sumptuous residence on our third day in Massalia. 'Sejanus, organise some surprise inspections; if you find any evidence of another quarter-master hoarding equipment for his own profit then have his head off too. The fact that it is common practice is not an excuse as far as I'm concerned. I'll not have my men march five hundred miles without sufficient tents, spare boots, tunics and cloaks, along with adequate rations and enough weaponry to kill the enemy when we get there and, of course, the mules and carts to transport it all.' He glared around at his officers, his eyes hard with indignation; sweat on his forehead glistening in the lamplight. 'Once we've finally got everything we need have the rest of the quarter-masters broken down to the ranks; they can come with us and be reminded of the importance of replacement equipment.'

'Even the honest ones, sir?' a young thin-stripe tribune asked.

'I've never heard of an honest quarter-master, so yes; then perhaps next time I arrive somewhere needing supplies I'll be treated with a little more respect.'

'Or they'll hide their stock better before you arrive,' Oppius, the prefect of the small Massalia garrison, pointed out. 'They're very devious and I should know; they consider everything in their warehouses as their own personal property and hate losing it.'

'You shouldn't have let it get to this state in the first place; how much do they pay you to turn a blind eye?' Lucius gestured with his wine cup around the marble and bronze busts, the expensively crafted glass, silverware and furniture that made up the lavish décor of the room; he took a sip. 'And your wine seems to be of the finest quality; proper Italian Falernian, not that Gallic imitation muck.' He pointed over to two amphorae standing in the corner. 'And plenty of it too.'

'I resent the inference, Caesar; I'm scrupulous in overseeing the supply line through here and then on up to the Rhenus frontier.'

'Then why were my officers forced to summarily execute two of the quarter masters?'

'Because they were being *too* greedy.'

Lucius turned on him, his face paling with what we all assumed was anger at the man's obvious lackadaisical attitude to the theft of military property, until he choked and then spluttered, suddenly fighting for breath. I, along with a few others, rushed to catch him as his legs started to buckle and his eyes bulged. We eased him onto a couch; his chest was heaving as he managed to suck in small amounts of air. 'Get back, give him room,' I shouted, automatically taking charge as it was my friend who was suffering. I opened Lucius' mouth and seeing no obvious constriction in his throat stuck a finger in deep, turning his head to one side. He convulsed and then, with a massive effort, vomited, spraying the feet of those around him. With another heave, he emitted a further gush and then began to pant, short sharp breaths; he closed his eyes and then after a few moments gained control of his breathing.

'Get out,' he murmured, 'all of you.'

After a moment of indecision we began to withdraw; Lucius grabbed my arm. 'Not you, Arminius; I need someone that I can trust to get me something to drink.'

'Trust?'

'Yes, trust; someone I know who would not work for Livia.'

I poured him a cup of water from the jug on Oppius' desk.

Lucius shook his head. 'No, Arminius, not from there; throw that away. Get me some wine from one of those sealed amphorae that were already here; not one that we brought with us.'

I emptied the water onto the floor, took one of the amphorae from the corner, breaking its wax seal and pulling out the stopper, and refilled the jug. 'What makes you suspect that Livia is trying to poison you?' I filled his cup and passed it to his shaking hand.

'If she gets rid of me then Augustus will only have Gaius left to inherit; every wise ruler should at least have a spare. But if Gaius should also die young?'

I understood immediately. 'Then he'll be forced to recall Tiberius from Rhodos?'

Lucius took a sip, spilling a good deal down his chin. 'And Livia gets her son back and can pretty much name her terms. I realised that this was what she planned as I began to feel weaker and weaker on the voyage here; someone was poisoning me and I couldn't work out how as we all shared food and drink. But I worked out why.'

'And you're sure that it's Livia?'

'Who else would gain from my death?'

I filled his cup again and this time he drank more steadily, his breathing calming. 'How can we stop her?'

Lucius shook his head. 'I think it's too late; somehow she's managed to administer a lethal dose of a slow-acting poison before we left. I have not eaten or drunk anything that wasn't shared between us all and I've been very careful as to which cups or plates I've used, always swapping them with someone else on some pretext or another. And yet I've been getting progressively worse so that I'm finding it hard to breathe sometimes and my vision keeps blurring. I've written to Gaius to warn him that he's next, but you know what he's like, he won't believe me. Livia will win.'

I got to my feet. 'I'm going to call for a doctor.'

Lucius laughed; it was thin and full of regret. 'Don't bother, my friend; I'm beyond doctors. Livia wouldn't be foolish enough to use anything that had a possible remedy; she's far too good for that.'

'Then what can we do?'

'Do? Nothing; but I need you to make me a promise for the sake of the friendship that we have had.'

'If I can I will.'

'What might stop you being able to?'

'I don't know; it's just …' I trailed off unable to give him the reason which I knew to be that I planned never to go back to Rome. 'What is it you want me to do?'

'Just this: avenge me.'

We sent Lucius' body back to Rome the following morning; he had died at midnight. My grief was countered by my concern as to how to make good my promise to my dying friend because I hoped never to go back to Rome. But the fate that the Norns weave for us is always full of twists and turns and we are blind to their purpose.

I had not been at Oppidum Ubiorum for more than eighteen months when what Lucius had predicted came true: Gaius died suddenly in Armenia and Tiberius was recalled from Rhodos; the price that Livia exacted from Augustus was that he be given military command – a huge one: the overall military commander in Germania Magna. The objective of this command was to subdue and bring within the empire the southern marches of Germania bordering the Danuvius, which was to involve defeating the Marcomanni in Bojohaemum where they had recently migrated to, displacing the pro-Roman Celtic tribe, the Boii, from that *haemat* or homeland, hence the name of the region. To this end Augustus ordered one of the largest concentrations of troops since the civil wars that had brought him to power. To the province of Raetia were ordered ten legions and their equivalent in auxiliaries and my Cheruscian ala was one of them. It was a task that I was very enthusiastic about, seeing as it would put my objective closer within reach: should Tiberius be successful – and there was no reason to suppose that he would not be, considering the size of his army – then we would have proved our loyalty to Rome by partaking in a great victory against a Germanic tribe thus making it more likely that we would be allowed to serve closer to our homeland.

With that happy thought in mind, I led my ala south the following year, along the Rhenus and then east into Raetia to Tiberius' camp at Augusta Vindelicorum. My men were all from my tribe and, indeed, many of them were known to me from the reputation of their fathers that I remembered from my childhood. Although they had all volunteered to serve as auxiliaries in Rome's army, they were still very much Cherusci in themselves and considered me – even though they respected my father who still lived – to be more Roman than Cherusci, even after I had been in command for almost three years and had the Cherusci wolf tattooed on my chest. How could I dissuade them of that with words? I, who had been in Rome for all those years and had received equestrian rank from the Emperor himself? I, who spoke Latin with a fluency greater than I now spoke my own mother tongue? I, who had been placed in command over them by Rome? It was only my uncle, Vulferam, and my cousin, Aldhard, who had both come to serve as a debt of gratitude to me and now acted as my senior decurions, who knew my true character. To the rest I was, in short, a foreigner to my own people.

But that was to change shortly after our arrival in Augusta Vindelicorum.

Tiberius looked even more morose than I remembered him as I entered his praetorium soon after our arrival.

He looked at me, his eyes sorrowful as if he had recently received bad news. 'So you're the son of Siegmarius; I remember seeing you a few times in Rome.'

'Indeed, general, although we have never met formally.'

'No, I don't suppose we have.' He sighed as if the weight of his burden was such that he could barely stand it for much longer. 'Perhaps we will get to know one another better in the coming campaign.'

'It would be my greatest wish.' I was adept in the art of flattery, a subject that I had studied closely under Lucius.

Tiberius, however, being no flatterer himself, saw it for what it was. 'This is a military camp not some dinner party on the Palatine, Arminius. Here I expect men to behave as men, not as sycophants. It's soldiers I need not courtiers.'

I have to admit I liked him immediately. 'My apologies, general; I have been too long in Rome.'

'And I have been too long away from it to wish it to follow me here. Your ala has been assigned its quarters?'

'Yes, general.'

'Good; settle them in and then join me and the rest of my staff for a working dinner this evening. You will be busy here, prefect, cavalry are my eyes and ears and my sight and hearing both need to be sharp at a very long range.'

'We march in two days and will cross the Danuvius at Sorviodurum,' Tiberius announced to a packed triclinium, ripping off a hunk from the hard regulation loaf and then passing it to his neighbour; there was no luxury on his campaign dining table. 'From there it's around two hundred miles to Maroboden, the Marcomanni capital. My intelligence tells me that Maroboduus, their king, will be there for the coming month, ample time to get there and force them to battle. Defeat them and, preferably, kill the king at the same time and then you have the tribe by the balls.' He looked around the faces of the legates and auxiliary prefects; they nodded with sage agreement in the flicker of the few lamps that Tiberius allowed himself. Satisfied that his subordinates were behind him he turned to me. 'Arminius, your Cherusci and the Batavian alae will be ferried over in transports two nights before the main force begins its crossing, so you will march tomorrow. Ten miles from the river there is a high range of hills thirty miles deep; through it is one pass that goes to the north. To either side of the pass is the most inhospitable forest, the sort of terrain that your Cherusci are used to, I believe.'

I grinned and raised my cup. 'They will feel quite at home there, general.'

Any attempt at levity was lost on Tiberius. 'That's what I thought. I want reports from the entire length of the pass by the time the rest of the army has crossed the river two days later. The Batavians will act as your support, one ala in the pass and the other at its entrance for you to fall back on should there be enemy in substantial numbers in the vicinity.' He took a handful of garlic cloves from a bowl on the table and chewed one whole, turning to his neighbour. 'Varus, you will have overall command of the column and will take with you the legionary cavalry of the Ninth Hispana as your escort and to act as messengers. I'm sure Legate Bibaculus won't mind lending them to you.'

A corpulent man on the other side of the table from me raised a chicken leg. 'For the greater good, general, the greater good.'

Publius Quinctilius Varus puffed out his chest, evidently pleased at receiving personal command of the advance column. 'I shall keep you well informed, general.'

'See that you do, Varus; and remember my stepfather's promise.'

'How could I forget?'

I turned, with a questioning look, to the prefect of one of the Batavian alae, reclining next to me.

'He's been promised the governorship of Germania Magna, once it becomes an official province rather than a military command,' the prefect informed me.

'Has he now?' I looked over to the man destined to have the power of life and death over my people and decided that he was someone to cultivate to find out whether he was the right type of Roman for what I had in mind.

And so it was that the next day I began my acquaintance with Publius Quinctilius Varus as we rode east to the Danuvius.

'Of course, it was a great honour being made consul in conjunction with Tiberius,' Varus informed me with the sort of condescension that was only possible for the son of a patrician family of great lineage. 'But not surprising seeing as we were both married to Agrippa's daughters at the time. I can't deny that it did my prospects the power of good and have never looked back since, which is only right for the eldest living member of the Quinctilii. I'm now Augustus' favourite governor.' Inexplicably, he seemed to find this comment singularly amusing and compromised his patrician dignity by dissolving into a fit of what I can only describe as rather feminine giggles. Eventually he mastered himself. 'You see, this will be my third appointment as governor since leaving the consulship. Syria, Africa and now Germania Magna; all military provinces with legions, which shows just how much trust the Emperor places in my abilities.' He patted his horse in an encouraging sort of way as if he were reassuring the beast that it was just about qualified to be carrying so great a personage. 'I expect Germania will be the toughest posting yet as it's a barbaric place from all accounts; wouldn't you say so, Arminius?'

'It was when I left, sixteen years ago; barely a stone building between the Rhenus and the Albis.'

'Then that's one of the first things that I shall address if I'm confirmed in the governorship. We must have civic buildings sufficiently big enough to overawe the locals; only then can we begin to administer Roman justice with any sort of authority.'

'Indeed, Varus,' I said, not understanding at all what he was trying to say; but, as with all men who have an overinflated view of their worth, if you want to ingratiate yourself with them then all you must do is agree with them. 'And I'm sure that the Emperor is bound to confirm you in the position.'

'It's not whether or not I am to be governor that's in the balance; that fact is a given. No, it's whether or not Germania will need a governor yet, for if it is not declared to be a pacified area then it will continue as a military zone and not a province. There's the dispute: is Germania Magna fit for civil administration?'

'Well, governor,' I said with no trace of irony, 'let's you and I make sure that it is.'

Varus looked at me, guffawed and reached over to slap my back. 'I can see that we're going to get on famously, Arminius.'

And we did; I made sure of that.

'So now we get to see just how far ahead my father was planning,' Thumelicatz interrupted. 'And it wasn't hard for him to gain the total trust of the man he had now planned to betray.' He nodded to the slave. 'Skip to the river crossing.'

A night crossing of a river is always a risky affair, especially one as wide as the Danuvius; but to attempt it without first sending scouts across to check whether the far bank was being held against us was the act of a fool. Those abilities that Varus had boasted of and that the Emperor apparently placed such high value on were, evidently, much exaggerated. Fortunately there was no large force waiting for us; however, we did not cross without being observed, something that a few scouts might have prevented. It was a mistake that would cost many lives and from it I judged that Varus was the right man for my purpose: he was a typical Roman who could be made to react how I wanted him to. My heart sang; now it would be just a matter of getting my own people to act according to my will. And that, I knew, would be no easy affair.

The far side of the Danuvius is cultivated, rich land and looks no different from the imperial side: farmsteads, neat orchards and cattle grazing in lush pasture; easy terrain to pass through quickly, even in the dark. It is not until you get to the hills that the wild forest, which Romans fear so much, takes a grip on the land. As dawn outlined the craggy peaks of the hill range ahead of us, we started to climb up to the pass that bisected it.

Although none of us had had any sleep, the exhilaration of commencing a campaign wiped away any tiredness and it was with a clear head that Varus summoned me as we approached the entrance of the pass.

'You can begin your sweep of the hills, Arminius,' he said as I pulled up my horse next to his and raised the facemask on my helm. 'Half your ala to the north and the other half to the south; a couple of miles into either side should be enough to root out anything that could threaten an ambush. I'll bring both the Batavian alae at a slow pace east so that you can fall back on them should you find yourself in trouble.'

That took me by surprise. 'Both?'

'Of course.'

'But what about covering our rear? Surely one of the alae should stay here at the entrance of the pass in case the enemy should try to box us in.'

Varus laughed; again, it was quite feminine. 'They wouldn't dare do that with the main bulk of the army getting ready to cross the river, even if they were here, which I very much doubt as we have seen no evidence of them.'

'That's because it's only just getting light.'

He looked at me with an expression bordering on outrage that I should be questioning his decisions.

'You're right, sir,' I affirmed quickly, 'ten legions should be plenty enough to guard our rear.'

The levity brightened Varus' countenance. 'Quite; after all, they'll be starting to arrive on the west bank in the next day or so.'

I saluted him, wondering how he had survived out in Syria with such a cavalier attitude to the safety of his command. However, in my stomach I thought that he was probably right: surely no enemy force would try to take us from behind, knowing that there were ten legions steadily advancing on their rear. And so I split my force and, taking the southern command, led eight turmae of thirty-two men into the hills whilst Vulferam took the same amount north.

Scouting in enemy territory is always an activity to be taken cautiously and it was with methodical thoroughness that we moved forward. I organised my turmae so that each had a half mile frontage to sweep whilst I remained in the rear with four reserve turmae ready to charge to the aid of any of my units that got into trouble. Slowly we moved forward, always keeping in contact with Varus' main force travelling up the pass so that it did not outpace us. I didn't even bother to check whether Varus was sending scouts out in front of him as it was such a basic thing to do that it didn't occur to me that he would neglect even this rudimentary precaution. On we went and by the tenth hour we were almost halfway through the thirty-mile pass and had seen nothing of the enemy; my messengers came and went at regular intervals and reported nothing amiss with the main column and also that Vulferam's command in the north was progressing at the same speed as ourselves and had not come across anyone either. In short, the exercise was going to plan and that knowledge must have encouraged an already lackadaisical Varus into even more negligence. We camped with the main body in the pass that night and it was remarkable in that we built no palisade and set few sentries; Varus was convinced that the Marcomanni were far too scared of the main army behind us to pose any threat. And that night he was proved to be correct; we woke to nothing more than the news of three desertions and a death from the injuries sustained in a fall the day before.

So we breakfasted and then returned to our posts to press on towards the end of the pass that we hoped to reach by evening, at which time the crossing of the Danuvius would have begun in earnest.

It was just one scream at first that began it, high and piercing; a scream of pure, slow drawn-out agony rather than the scream of a man wounded in combat, and it came from behind us. One scream was not going to make me call in my men and rush to the protection of Varus; after all there could have been a number of explanations for it – admittedly none of them pleasant for the man emitting it. The second scream, every bit as harrowing as the first, was more worrying, and then the third, which acted as an accompaniment to the second, really became a cause for concern. Just then the latest messenger returning from Varus' command position came in; he had nothing new to report and said that he had set out before the first scream, although he did say that it had sounded to him as if all three screams had come from the same direction. And then I made the connection: three different screams, three desertions during the night; what if they hadn't been desertions but, rather, abductions? If that were the case then this was a statement of intent: we were not alone and those three men had just been sacrificed to ensure a victory; it's what any Germanic tribe would have done. But it was as this thought formulated that it was proved correct by the unmistakeable sound of a Germanic charge: horns and war cries echoed around the hills so that it was impossible, or so I thought, to tell from which direction they came, forward or behind. What was sure was that Varus' command was under attack. I sent out riders to bring in the outlying turmae with orders to follow my path north and set off with the four units I had, north to where the messenger claimed Varus' last position to be.

On we rushed, as fast as the density of the wood allowed us. The sound of fighting escalated at the same rate as my conviction that the sheer size of the force required to take on two Batavian alae and have a chance of winning would mean that the arrival of two hundred and fifty men would make very little difference to the outcome, unless, perhaps, Vulferam's men arrived from the opposite direction at the same time.

Breaking through the trees, I came to within sight of the pass; the Batavians, a hundred feet below us, were sorely pressed from both the east and the west. Varus had made the classic mistake of an aristocratic Roman commander who believes that ability is a birth-right: he had not scouted ahead and had not covered his rear and so consequently had managed to let himself be surrounded; he would be perfect for me. About a couple of hundred Marcomanni foot warriors had crept up to take him in the rear as a similar amount had charged straight up the pass at him. His cavalry had been unable to deploy from column due to the narrowness of the pass and so their numbers were neutralised as no more than

ten could fight to the front or rear at any one time. The rest
were trying to keep their mounts calm in the slowly confining
space within the column as the steep sides of the pass were
infested with Marcomanni, penning them in. It was chaos and
within the hour most of Varus' command would be dead or
captured.

There was no option other than to come to his aid and
thereby win his gratitude and trust.

'Dismount!' I shouted, my heartrate quickening at the
thought of leading my men into combat for the first time.
Now they would get the chance to see my mettle, although I
wasn't without trepidation as, apart from a couple of very minor
skirmishes, this was my first taste of battle.

The decurions relayed my orders and, within a few moments,
the half ala had become infantry far more suited to charging
down the steep sides of the pass and into the, as yet, unsus-
pecting backs of the Marcomanni to the west of Varus. If I
could get them to disperse then Varus could lead his men back
to the river and rejoin the bulk of Tiberius' army.

There was no time for any tactical planning and I knew that
had Lucius been present he would have just advocated hitting
them fast and hard; and that's exactly what we did.

Bawling the war cry of my people for the first time in anger,
I lowered my facemask, drew my *spatha* and waved it above
my head as I pounded forward. Down the steep slope we
raced, some tumbling and rolling as they lost their footing, in
a headlong charge aimed at the flank of the warriors between
Varus and Tiberius.

So intent were the Marcomanni on pulling the trapped and
immobile cavalrymen down from their mounts for slaughter
and so raucous was the din of the combat that our charge

remained unnoticed until I sliced my blade into the bare head of a young warrior. I took the crown from his skull like the top of a macabre hard-boiled egg filled with grey, rather than yellow, yolk that sprayed over his comrades, alerting them to our contact. But a surprise flank attack is very hard to recover from as the momentum of the impact sends men sprawling sideways and very quickly cohesion is lost and the formation is penetrated. Through their mass we went, reaping limbs and lives with bloody swipes of our swords and stabs of our spears, slowing the further we went as the Marcomanni were pushed together before us; but the mounted soldiers of the Batavians, seeing us arriving to their aid, renewed their struggles. Taking advantage of their foe's disorder they reared their horses so that their front hoofs flailed, cracking open heads and breaking collar-bones. Within a very few heartbeats the Marcomanni were being pushed back in two directions leaving grim corpses and howling wounded in their wake. Smeared with gore, I worked my sword with growing joy, not so much as a result of the success of the attack but more because these Marcomanni had just showed me how a small force of tribal warriors could negate a more numerous and better-disciplined Roman force. If we had not come to the rescue from the flank Varus would have perished. So, I pondered as the warriors turned and fled whence they had come and we followed them up with as much cruelty as we could summon, what would have happened if we had been on the Marcomanni's side? If the troops that protected the flank of a Roman column could be turned against their charge then that column would be surrounded, and the truth of my father's last words struck me full and hard: *Rome is going to train the very troops who'll form the backbone of the army that will free us from her.* I now saw proof of Musa's vision of how a legion could be destroyed and completely understood the direction of my father's thought: if my Cherusci ala and all the other Germanic auxiliary units protecting a marching column should turn on the legionaries that they were supposed to protect and if they were then joined by warriors from the tribes, it would be only a matter of time, if the terrain and conditions were right, before that column was destroyed.

And then Lucius' influence came unbidden to my mind: why stop at just a column? Why not an army? A whole army, the army of Germania Magna; the army that the man who disdained to scout ahead or cover his rear, the man whose life I had just saved, would soon be in command of. That would be the grandest of gestures: the annihilation of every Roman serviceman on Germania Magna's soil.

As these thoughts filled my mind, Varus approached, jumped from his horse and embraced me. 'My friend, we all owe you a great debt; with just a few men you saved us from a very unpleasant situation and I shall never forget that.'

I bowed my head. 'It was just my duty, sir.'

'A duty that only a Roman can understand: to save the lives of his comrades in peril rather than run and ensure his own safety; I see now that your time in Rome has been the making of you, Arminius.'

I did nothing to dissuade him of that view as a messenger from the main army arrived now that he was finally able to make his way through.

'Well?' Varus asked the man. 'How's the crossing going?'

'It's not, sir. It has been abandoned.'

'Abandoned?'

'Yes, sir. I've been sent to recall you to the west bank. Just after you crossed a courier arrived from the Emperor; there has been a huge uprising in Pannonia that's spreading. Augustus has ordered Tiberius to take his army south and suppress it with all necessary force. The advance units have already left.'

'And so began the Pannonian revolt,' Thumelicatz said, 'but that is of little interest to us, as my father served with distinction and ruthlessness leading punishment raids, burning villages, ambushing raiding parties and the like in what was a dirty war of attrition. But despite the Marcomanni remaining nominally unsubdued, Varus was confirmed as the Governor of Germania Magna and took up his position the following year. Two years after that, with the rebellion in Pannonia now under control, my father's ala was posted north; he was finally going home and it was a homecoming that he had by now long planned. Read on, Aius.'

CHAPTER VII

We crossed the Rhenus at Castra Vetera, the Eighteenth Legion's winter quarters, and then followed the Road of the Long Bridges east along the River Lupia, the border between the lands of the Marsi to its south and the Bructeri on the northern bank. Although the memory of my forefathers' country had faded in the sixteen years that I had been away, little seemed to have changed: the settlements and farmsteads were still organised in a familiar way around the central longhouse of the senior family; the fields around them were still divided into small areas rather than the vast, slave-worked fields of Roman farms; and the people toiling in them still wore Germanic dress. The only difference was the military road that we were following, which led right into the heart of Germania so that Rome's legions could penetrate her at will and with impunity.

If my men were happy at the prospect of returning home after six years' service then it can only be imagined how I was feeling after my long exile. But here I was now, returning home a Roman citizen with equestrian rank leading four hundred auxiliary cavalry, proud men of my tribe, the Cherusci, trained by Rome to fight for her; but now they had been delivered into my hands they would become one of the tools of Rome's demise in Germania.

My orders were to report to the Governor, my old acquaintance, Publius Quinctilius Varus. The fact that he was still in my debt from Raetia meant, I hoped, that it would be easy to ingratiate myself with him; if I was to bring the man down then it was vital that I should have his complete trust. I had been told by the prefect of the camp at Castra Vetera that Varus had headed east at the beginning of the campaigning season with the intention of marching through Germania with three legions, the Seventeenth, Eighteenth and Nineteenth, to assert Rome's authority over the new province and to bring the people a taste of her law. A more inept politician, jurist and soldier could not have been chosen for such a delicate task.

'He expected us to see justice in Roman law and fairness in her taxes,' Mallovendatz, the young king of the Marsi, complained to me as we sat in his hall, drinking. It was the fourth night of my journey east. 'He takes no account of the ways of our people when making his judgements, often outraging both the plaintiff and the defendant.' Mallovendatz waved a dismissive hand at my auxiliary prefect's uniform. 'What's more, he's taxing us to the extreme in order to raise money for Roman expansion onto the east bank of the Albis. But I suppose that you will defend his actions as you are now one of them.'

I bridled at the insult but managed to keep my face neutral by taking a large swig of ale; it would not suit my purposes to fall out with this young, proud king. Indeed, it would not suit my purposes to fall out with any of the leaders of the Germanic tribes this side of the Albis. 'How many men do you have serving in Rome's army?'

Mallovendatz's pale blue eyes smiled at me, calculating, over the rim of his drinking horn. 'My men are free to take Rome's silver.'

'So that you don't have to provide them with yours?'

The Marsi king slammed his horn down, spilling foaming beer over the board; conversation around us died and the dozen of my men who had accompanied me looked nervous, counting the Marsi warriors seated at long rows of benches throughout the smoke-hazed hall. 'You dare to impugn my generosity to my men in my own hall, Erminatz? You who've lived off Rome's scraps for the best part of your life? You who have no men following you other than those that Rome gave you?'

I raised my palms to him and inclined my head to one side to show that I conceded the point and wished to take the argument no further. 'I apologise.'

He grunted and held his horn out for a thrall to fill; the warriors surrounding us got back to their conversations satisfied that their lord was not in a dispute that would lead to violence.

I leant closer to him across the table. 'But seriously, Mallovendatz, how many men from your tribe do serve Rome?'

He eyed me suspiciously but saw no guile on my face as it was a genuine question and not meant to trap him. 'There are eight hundred infantry, give or take, serving with the First Marsian cohort under their own officers and not Roman imports.'

'Even the prefect?'

'Yes, he's my cousin, Egino.'

I grinned, amused by the arrogance and stupidity of Rome. 'Well, that's just perfect.'

The Marsian king looked quizzical. 'Is it? In what way?'

'You can still control them. How many others of your men take Roman silver?'

'Another four hundred serving with the Fourth Germanic cohort; the other half are Bructeri.'

'I imagine that the tension is quite high in that cohort.'

Mallovendatz shook his head, ruefully. 'That's what I mean: they take no notice of our ways and force my men to serve alongside our neighbours with whom, if we weren't occupied by Rome, we would normally be at war.'

I, along with everyone in Germania Magna and the two Germanic Roman provinces west of the Rhenus, was well aware of the antipathy between the Marsi and their neighbours to the north of the Lupia. I lowered my voice. 'But we are occupied by Rome and so for once you're not at war with the Bructeri, which means that they could be regarded as …?'

He wiped the froth from his long, blond beard and cocked a quizzical eyebrow. 'As not quite enemies at the moment?' He chuckled, enjoying his weak joke.

'If that's how you want to term them, then yes. The point is that you have over a thousand fully trained and armed men within the Roman occupation force …'

'Plus an ala of cavalry.'

'Twelve hundred infantry and almost five hundred cavalry; and what do the Bructeri have?'

He thought for a few moments. 'About the same in infantry and twice the number in cavalry.'

I knew that I had his attention now as it would have taken a great effort for him to swallow his pride and admit that the Bructeri outdid the Marsi at anything, even in serving Rome. 'And between you, how many warriors could you call to arms?'

He drank deep of his ale as he did the calculation in his head. 'Between us we could raise eight thousand well-armed men and another five thousand dregs plus five hundred or so cavalry each.'

'Put those warriors together with the auxiliaries and what would you have?'

He grinned at the thought. 'I can see what you're getting at, my friend; but that force would not be enough to stop three legions.'

'I agree,' I said, conceding the point, 'it wouldn't be enough to stop three legions in formation; but us combined with four other tribes in an alliance with no one tribe supreme, an alliance of All Men, and against three legions stretched out on the march?'

He stared at me in shock. 'How would you get three legions into a position that you could ambush them like that?'

'You leave that to me, Mallovendatz; the point is, if I do then would you stand, together with your ancestral enemies, and fight the common foe?' I fixed him with hard eyes, grabbed his left wrist and lowered my voice to a harsh whisper. 'If you want the freedom to fight against your enemies again, whenever you want, then first you have to stand together with them, behind me. I intend to free this land in a way that it stays free, and to do that means that we have to kill every last Roman soldier here so that they will be too afraid to come back.'

His eyes narrowed. 'Why should you be the leader? You're not even a king.'

'That's exactly why, Mallovendatz: I'm not a king; and, as you so rightly and delicately pointed out, I have been living off Rome's scraps for the best part of my life and I have no men other than what Rome has given me. My father, Siegimeri, still lives and is still king of the Cherusci so I have no position in Germania other than what Rome has given me: prefect of the Cheruscian auxiliary ala. I can expect to be trusted by Varus because he will see me as more Roman than Germanic; that trust will only come to me and me alone and that trust will be his downfall. Join me and I will get a confederation of the tribes together; all equal in the alliance of All Men.'

Mallovendatz contemplated this for a few swigs of ale as his men and mine broke into a raucous drinking song thumping their horns on the table in time and slapping their thighs. 'I cannot give you my word that I will join you, yet; but what I can say is that I will not work against you. I will repeat nothing of what you've said this evening and I will be ready to aid you if it looks as though you will succeed.'

'In other words you won't risk being on the losing side?'

He shrugged. 'I'm on the losing side at the moment, why make it worse for myself?'

I knew that was the best that I would get from him and, in fact, it was a reasonable position to take; after all, who would be mad enough to commit themselves to taking on three Roman legions?

And it was with a similar reaction that Engilram, the elderly king of the Bructeri, greeted my proposal when I visited him, two nights later, in his hall just to the north of Aliso, the largest Roman fort on the road. I had left most of my ala camped outside the walls of Aliso, crossed the Lupia and ridden, with a dozen companions, the twenty miles to the Bructeri's chief town situated on the fringe of the Teutoburg Wald, the great forest of the north. Here I was received with courtesy, taken on a boar hunt into the forest, given meat and ale of the highest quality, listened to with polite attentiveness and then bidden farewell with vague statements of support should the circumstances look opportune and the time seem right and other such platitudes. Again I could not blame Engilram for his hesitancy; he was, after all, long in years and had not survived to that age by behaving rashly. Nor could I find fault with Adgandestrius, the young king of the Chatti, who seemed intent in copying Engilram's longevity by also refusing to give me his unqualified support despite the fact that I had ridden almost sixty miles out of my way to visit him in his hall at Mattium, the Chatti's main stronghold.

'My people will only follow me against Rome if they are certain of victory,' Adgandestrius informed me as we talked in private in one corner of his great hall. 'In my father's time we lost too many lives in reprisal raids for attacks on Rome that failed. Now that he feasts in Walhalla I'm determined not to give him the company of any more of my warriors needlessly. Three legions will be hard to destroy even if you do manage to lure them somewhere they can't manoeuvre; what made you choose the Teutoburg Wald?'

'I was there a few days ago speaking with Engilram—'

Adgandestrius spat his disgust at the name. 'You don't expect that snake to support you, do you?'

'At the moment I don't expect anyone to support me because everyone seems to be more concerned for their life than their honour.'

Adgandestrius' eyes flashed with anger but he remained outwardly calm. 'It's not good manners to insult your host.'

'I didn't mean it as an insult; just as a plain statement of fact.' I put my hand up to stop his reply. 'Everyone that I've spoken to so far loves the idea of freeing Germania Magna from Rome but no one is prepared to strike the first blow just in case it goes wide of the mark. To do this thing I must know that the tribes will follow. What good would it do if I manage to trick Varus into taking his army into the Teutoburg Wald and I only have three or four cohorts of auxiliaries to turn on him with? There have to be thousands of warriors ready to descend upon his column from both sides once he realises that his own auxiliaries have played him false. We must hit him hard, with as many warriors as possible whilst he's still surprised, if we are to annihilate him; if we let him slip away then it will become a running battle over days and we might never manage to finish him off.' I slammed my fist into my palm and looked, cold-eyed, at the young Chatti king. 'In the Teutoburg Wald we can hide enough men to stop Rome once and for all; but those men will not be there if their kings don't lead them there.'

Although he was roughly the same age as me, Adgandestrius laughed at me as if I were a small child making some big and unobtainable boast. 'Do you really think that you can do it? You? Unite enough tribes to destroy three legions? Everyone will just see you as Rome's stooge strutting about in a uniform that they gave you when you denied your own kind and took Rome's citizenship.'

It was my turn to get angry but I knew that to pick a fight with this haughty young king would in no way hasten the defeat of Rome, so I bit my tongue and tried to calm my breathing. 'That's just the point; are you so obtuse that you cannot see that this uniform is the key to our victory? If every Germanic warrior in the uniform of Rome turned on her at one time when she doesn't expect it then that element of surprise would double their numbers. But there must be reinforcements; you, Engilram, Mallovendatz, the kings of the Chauci, the Sugambri as well as my own tribe, the Cherusci, must bring their men to the Teutoburg Wald at a time of my choosing. Think, Adgandestrius, think of the army that we could have; think what that army could do if it surprised three legions in column.'

Adgandestrius twirled his beard with a finger, contemplating the mental image. 'When will this be?'

I felt a relief pass through me. 'Not this year, this year I have to gain Varus' trust. It will be next year as he marches west along the Road of the Long Bridges at the end of the campaigning season. If I manufacture a rebellion to the north he will divert there to suppress it. It's about the timing; I need to get him to turn north so that he will pass through the Teutoburg Wald. With our auxiliaries acting as his guides we will be able to lead him to a killing ground and there we can finish it.'

The Chatti king smiled to himself. 'Very well, Erminatz. I will await your word, but I will bring my warriors to your ambush. However, there is one condition.'

'Name it.'

'That if the first action does not go well we will not join in.'

'So if the initial attack fails you would run and leave us to die.'

Adgandestrius shrugged. 'My father told me that one of the greatest rules of war is never to reinforce failure.'

I left him knowing that I would get no firmer commitment from him. However, his men would be there and he would be absolutely right to obey his father's advice. I would just have to ensure that the initial attack would not be a failure.

That problem occupied my mind as we travelled through the dark Becanis Forest and then crossed the Visurgis River to come finally once more into the lands of the Cherusci. The plan had been forming in my mind since seeing the dense magnitude of the Teutoburg Wald whilst hunting with Engilram: the forest was hilly, thickly wooded and studded with ravines, and if an army was rash enough to enter it then its progress through it would be dangerously slow.

However, that was not the forest's main advantage; what really got me thinking was its positioning just to the north of the Road of the Long Bridges. For over a hundred miles the road skirted the forest's southern flank and it was along that road every autumn that Rome's legions marched back to their winter bases on the Rhenus. If I were to bring Varus news of a fictional rebellion to the north when he was a quarter of the way across then he would be left with three choices: go back and around, go forward and then around, or just turn north and navigate the forest. That third choice would seem like the quickest to him because he would be travelling in a straight line. With his Germanic auxiliaries guiding him he would feel safe enough – until they turned on him, that is; which they would do with ease because they were serving under their own officers.

But to make this work I would already have needed to have hidden at least twenty thousand men in the forest; and that would be the challenge: how would I move twenty thousand fully armed warriors from all over the land to a single location without the Romans noticing? And once that had been achieved how would I be able to keep them supplied for as long as it would take to lead Varus and his legions to them?

So I pondered the logistical problem as we traversed the lush farmland of the Cherusci with the massif of the Harzland, crowned by its highest hill, the Brocken, growing ever larger before us. And by the time we trailed up the winding track that led to my father's hall I had got nearer to solving it; the answer seemed obvious. But then the sight of the home that I had not seen for sixteen years drove it from my mind as the joy of returning to my family washed through me and I kicked my horse forward to gallop the last quarter of a mile.

My reunion with my father and mother was as bitter as it was sweet; my sister had died in the time of the Ice Gods in May of that year, exactly the sixteenth anniversary of my brother and me leaving for Rome. Tears wetted my father's beard as he gave me the news and told me how she had lived her life bereft of her two brothers, her sadness making her unable to conceive so there were no grandchildren.

'And what news of Chlodochar?' my father asked as we sat next to the open fire in his hall, drinking deep in memory of the woman who, as a young girl, was but a hazy memory for me.

I wiped the ale from my lips with the back of my hand and put my drinking horn down. 'He's lost to us, Father; he loves all thing Roman and has no memory of his life here.'

My father's face darkened. 'How did you allow that to happen? It was you that was to keep him safe.'

'There was nothing that I could do, Father. He became the special friend of Germanicus, one of the Princes of Rome, and refused to talk our language with me. I doubt that he could remember more than a dozen words of it; he said it was a language for savages. He refused to serve with me in the Cherusci ala, staying instead with Germanicus. I saw him last when we served together in Pannonia, two years ago; he refused to speak to me, even in Latin.'

My father ruminated upon my words for a few moments. 'This Germanicus, is he the son of Drusus?'

'Yes, Father.'

'Then he will probably become as great a general as Drusus was and Chlodochar will serve him.'

'He will, in fact he already is becoming such; which means that Chlodochar and I will face each other across the battlefield one day when Germanicus comes looking for me for what I've done.'

'What have you done, my son?'

'I've dared to dream. Do you remember the last thing you said to me?'

'It was a long time ago.'

'But it stayed in my head. You told me that "Rome is going to train the very troops who'll form the backbone of the army that will free us from her". That thought has stayed with me and now I've worked out how to use those troops that Rome has so kindly given us.' I outlined my plan for the destruction of Varus and the problems that I foresaw while my father just stared at me, dumbfounded.

'In one strike you plan to kill every legionary in Germania Magna?'

'Yes, Father; a grand gesture.'

'Very grand indeed.'

'And taught to me by a Roman.' I smiled at the memory of Lucius and wondered what he would have thought of my plan; no doubt he would have approved of the concept if not the objective. 'I'll time it so that the garrisons that have been left behind will be massacred as soon as we make contact with Varus' army. Then we hold the Road of the Long Bridges against any contingents trying to escape in good order and scour the countryside for stragglers; there'll be no quarter. A few will get back across the Rhenus but that is to our good; they will tell of the wrath of Germania Magna and their comrades will fear to come back and avenge the dead. But they will eventually come back for vengeance and that is when we must draw them into the heart of the country; we will not face them by the Rhenus, let them come; we will face them on the Albis, far from their bases. We will harry their supply lines and make them fear to be cut off so far from home, lost in our forests. In short, Father, we will make them see that there is no future for Rome here and they would do better to let us run our own affairs. Our men will still serve in the auxiliary cohorts, our merchants will still trade with the empire, but their tax-farmers, their laws and their language will stay on the other side of the Rhenus. Germanic culture will survive untouched by Latin influence but our people will still benefit from Rome's silver.'

My father shook his head, more in wonder than disbelief. 'It was my dream too to use the troops that Rome trained against her. In the years that you've been away, my son, I have searched and waited for an opportunity to do the very thing that you have outlined, but just for the Cherusci and just against one legion, in the hope that our victory would encourage other tribes to deal with the rest as they came to revenge themselves upon us.'

'But you know, Father, deep down, that the other tribes would do nothing; they would watch you be ripped apart by Rome and cheer as it happened. That's the reality of Germanic unity.'

'I'm afraid that you're right, Erminatz; I haven't been able to get one king to support the idea of joint action.'

'Because you're a king yourself and what king would want to make himself subservient to another?'

'Exactly.' Then he paused and looked at me, the idea slowly dawning. 'But you're no king. You're just a man with a dream, a Germanic dream that kings could hold onto without losing their dignity to another. How will you get them together?'

'I've spoken to Adgandestrius, Engilram, Mallovendatz and now you.'

'Who else will you approach?'

'Just the Chauci and the Sugambri.'

'All the tribes around the Teutoburg Wald. What about Maroboduus of the Marcomanni in the south? If they took our cause it would be a major boost; they number many.'

'No, Father, it must be just those six. To have big groups of warriors travel too far will attract the attention of Rome's spies and Varus will become suspicious. For this to succeed I have to start mustering men in the forest at least a month before the attack, taking a few hundred in every day from different tribes.'

'They will all have to be fed.'

'I know; the game, wild berries and mushrooms in the forest will provide some sustenance but it won't be enough, so this year I'm going to start organising grain dumps and stores of salted meat.'

'That's a massive undertaking.'

'This is not a thing that can be attempted without forward planning; everything must be in order.'

'Where will you get the food from?'

'All three of the kings that I've spoken to so far have said that they will be willing to support me if the first blow is a success; they will lead their men into the forest but not against Rome unless our people and the auxiliaries strike at the column decisively.' I put a hand up to still my father's outrage. 'I know what you think, Father, I think the same. However, you can't blame them; if this goes wrong then the vengeance taken upon us will be long and bloody. Nevertheless, they are prepared to have their men waiting and watching. So I shall charge them for this privilege: they will donate the grain and livestock. If they want the chance of glory then it has to be on my terms.'

'And what about our people?'

'Our people are taking the greatest risk; we donate nothing but it will be us who make the forest store depots. We should have our men cut down a few rode now so that we can sow grass for grazing.'

My father grinned; he could see exactly what I planned. 'So only we will know the location of the depots.'

'And we'll only divulge their whereabouts as and when necessary.'

'So we can keep any surplus and ensure our people a well-supplied winter if the attack goes wrong and we find ourselves under siege in the Harzland.'

'Precisely; but it won't go wrong, Father. I intend to make sure that everything is thought of. But firstly I need to find Varus and report to him.'

'I'll take you to him tomorrow; he's on the banks of the Albis holding court and dispensing Roman justice.'

And that was where we found him, a day's ride away, sitting on a curule chair in a pavilion on the west bank of the Albis, in the lands of the Suevi.

'They look to be in excellent condition,' Varus commented, slapping me on the back as he inspected my ala after having adjourned his court for the day. 'Have they seen much action since I saw them last?'

'Punishment raids in Pannonia, mopping up rebels, but nothing like the affair against the Marcomanni in Bojohaemum,' I replied, exaggerating the incident considerably thus ensuring that I reminded Varus that he had me and my men to thank for his life. I felt my father look at me, frowning.

Varus slapped me on the back again. 'That was a bloody day; how they came upon us so quickly I will never understand.'

Due to your unprofessional lack of scouting, was the thought that I did not share with him.

'Still, your lads saw them off; it's good to see them again and you, Arminius. I welcome talented young officers onto my staff.'

His tone was patronising and aloof but I smiled my thanks at his welcome and gladly accepted his invitation to dine with him, an invitation that he did not extend to my father.

As we watched him walk away my father spat on the ground. 'Why did you save his life?'

'All things considered, I'd say that it's lucky I did.'

'This year I intend to make a few probes across the Albis and test the mettle of the Semnones,' Varus announced once his guests had taken their places reclining at table. 'I think it's time we taught them that Rome is here to stay on this side of the river and we won't tolerate any raiding by the even less washed barbarians on the other side.'

This remark raised a few sniggers from his officers.

'Do we intend to make a permanent presence over there?' asked Vala Numonius, prefect of one of the auxiliary Gallic cavalry alae.

'No, Vala; the Emperor has ordered me only to secure our eastern border along the Albis but to exact tribute and recruit auxiliaries from the tribes between it and the next large river, the Viadua. I believe that his long-term policy is to civilise them somewhat through contact and trade and their young warriors serving in our army, learning our language and getting a taste for our silver. Once that has been achieved he will incorporate those lands within the empire as the new province of Germania Ultima with the Viadua River as the frontier.'

Vala looked impressed. 'What next?'

'I don't know. Traders have reported another river called the Vistula a couple of hundred miles further east of the Viadua, but whether Augustus would wish to extend so far is debatable; for a start I'm told the tribes out there, the Gotones, the Vandalli and the Burgundi, are even wilder than the Semnones and have truly dreadful personal hygiene rather than just dreadful.'

There was a round of sycophantic laughter and a few tart remarks about Germanic cleanliness without anyone looking at me, embarrassed, and I realised that I had fitted right in: my short hair and my apparel, tunic and slippers, made me seem Roman and my faultless Latin made me sound so. It was like the night of the fire when we rescued Vulferam: because I seemed to be right, no one suspected that I was wrong. It did not occur to them that I was Germanic in my heart so I joined in the laughter and jesting in order that my real allegiance would remain hidden.

'But seriously, gentlemen,' Varus continued as the seam of humour began to run dry, 'our objective this year is to begin the pacification of the eastern bank of the Albis but not to occupy it yet. Augustus has told me to teach them to wash before we do that!'

That brought another flood of mirth and jokes, which I joined in as loud as the others as the first course, the *gustatio*, was brought in. With eyes moist from laughter I looked at the variety of platters being spread out on the table and, although they were elegantly presented and were a refined blend of ingredients, I despised them for their fussiness and had a yearning for a haunch of venison over an open fire in a clearing deep in a forest rather than being here sharing my enemy's cuisine whilst laughing at his jokes at my own people's expense.

'And so there he was,' Thumelicatz said, bringing the reading to an end with a sweep of his hand, 'an officer on Varus' staff. Accepted by his fellows as one of them; no different from those of Latin blood or Gallic blood or Hispanic blood because he had a Roman name, a Roman uniform and a Roman accent. How could he be anything other than a Roman? Why would he want to be anything other than a Roman? You just can't fathom how anyone who has been given your *precious* gift of citizenship could possibly want to reject it, can you?'

He paused and smiled as his Roman guests shifted uneasily in their seats, knowing that what he had said was the truth. 'Oh, Rome, you are your own worst enemy: because you think that you are so perfect you can't comprehend that anyone should find fault with you. And so through that arrogance, that blindness, that smug self-satisfaction, Varus let the man who had saved his life into his circle, oblivious to the fact that all his life he had secretly rejected Rome; oblivious to the fact that this man, Erminatz, planned to kill every Roman soldier in Germania Magna.'

CHAPTER VIII

'THAT'S FEELING MUCH better,' the street-fighter said, re-entering the tent, adjusting his dress with a pleased look on his face. 'That ale you're all so keen on here goes straight through me.' He looked at Aius and Tiburtius and grinned. 'I don't know how you boys cope with it; you have to piss three or four times before you even start to feel its effects.'

The old slaves looked at Thumelicatz who nodded giving them permission to speak.

It was Aius who answered. 'The master allows us wine from time to time. Now that the vineyards that you Romans planted—'

'*We* Romans,' the street-fighter corrected, sitting back down.

Aius shook his head, slow and sad. 'No, *you* Romans; we lost the right to call ourselves that when we lost our Eagles.'

'Have it your own way, mate.'

'Now that the vineyards that you Romans planted in the Gallic and two Germanic provinces have matured, the wine from those areas has become plentiful and cheap.'

The street-fighter poured himself some more ale. 'But is it any good?'

'It's good enough for slaves.'

'I don't believe it's a kindness, buying them wine,' Thumelicatz said. 'If anything I would have thought it's a torment for them to be reminded of home having sworn never to go back; but that's the price of marching into our land and then choosing not to burn in our fires after being captured. However, I buy it

186

and they drink it with gratitude and perhaps it salves some part of the raw misery in which they have chosen to live for they have never requested that I don't buy it for them.' He looked at the two ancient Eagle-bearers who both lowered their gaze to the scrolls on the desk in front of them. 'But who can say what goes on in those prideless minds; and ultimately, who cares? They're here to perform a function so let's not worry ourselves unduly about them.'

He picked up the next scroll and scanned through it quickly. 'So my father worked with Varus, helping him to carry out his orders from Augustus to begin the pacification of the eastern bank of the Albis. He took his cavalry ala across on numerous occasions to punish tribes that had raided our side; he took prisoners, seized chieftains and burnt villages. Neither he nor any of his men complained for they were fighting tribes that had in the past done the Cherusci harm and now he could avenge that harm and be seen as doing Rome's will. Varus took it all at face value, but there was one person who somehow saw through him and that man was not a Roman, he was Germanic and from the same tribe as Erminatz. In fact he was his kinsman, Siegimeri's cousin, Segestes. Whether he had a deep love of Rome or whether it was because he despised Erminatz for reasons that will become clear, Segestes did his best to convince Varus of my father's perfidy.' He handed the scroll back to Aius. 'Read from this point.'

The old slave squinted in the lamplight and then began.

I had never seen the like of her; she outshone Musa and cast every female around her into a deep shade. Her beauty was young and fresh as a sapling in spring and she burst with vigour and the joy of life, like a lamb gambling on a sun-rich morn. Hair so blonde it was worth more than its weight in gold, skin

so smooth and pale as to be almost reflective and eyes that …
Well, eyes in which a man could lose himself for eternity: blue
and deep as the sea on a summer's day, they could strip you
of your certainties and leave you a quivering wreck with one
glance, enthralled by them. I saw her, Thusnelda, for the first
time as the snow melted and the kings and sub-chieftains of the
six tribes gathered at my father's hall, and I knew that I had to
have her. However, she was still considered to be one summer
too young to be taken to wife and, anyway, there was also a
major obstacle to any plans I had in that direction: her father,
Segestes, my father's cousin; he hated Siegimeri because he felt
that he should lead the Cherusci and so, as the son of the object
of his jealousy, I was hated too. Yet I gazed upon her, as she rode
into my father's compound as a part of Segestes' retinue, as a
parched man would at a cool stream; wanting to feel her wash
all over me and then to drink her in. But even if there had not
been that impediment and the way would have been clear for
me to possess her that day, I would not have; not at that point.
For by the first occasion that I set eyes on her, my plans were
well advanced and I knew that I would have no time for the
joys of a young wife until they had come to a successful fruition.

I had spent the first winter back in Germania visiting, initially,
the kings of the Chauci and the Sugambri who both gave me
the exact same answers as the others: they would lead their
men to the Teutoburg Wald but would not commit until they
felt sure of victory. I left these two great men in their halls with
words of thanks and praise for their courage and vision in even
contemplating the idea that they may be part of an army that
would free our land from the people who had seized it by force.
I did, however, manage to extract one hard promise from each
of them: they would provide supplies. So it was with my men

of the Cherusci collecting sacks of grain and fodder and driving cattle and sheep into the forest and penning them in the dozen or so rode that we had cleared over the last year that I revisited the other three kings.

'So,' Adgandestrius mused as he contemplated my words next to the roaring fire in the centre of his hall, 'you wish to charge us for the honour of being present to watch your first attack; is that it?'

I did my best to hide my exasperation at the man's deliberate obtuseness. 'You know full well that is not the case, Adgandestrius. I am merely planning ahead. If you are good to your word ...'

'And there is no reason to suppose that I won't be; the Chatti always keep their word.'

'Indeed. When you fulfil your promise and bring your warriors to Teutoburg then they must eat; some of them may be hidden there for a moon.'

'A moon?'

'Yes, a whole moon. We have to get Varus to march to us; we have to be waiting and to do that we have to be there in advance, well in advance.'

'And what if I decide not to bring my warriors in advance – *well* in advance?'

'Then you will not have the opportunity to share the honour of Rome's defeat.' I held his gaze, my eyes hardening. 'And you would not have kept your word, and when we are victorious every tribe in Germania will know who was there and who had promised to be there but failed to arrive and no man will want to share his board with you and your warriors. You will all be accounted of little worth both by the other tribes as well as by your own women.'

And that produced the reaction that I had intended: with an explosive slamming of his fist on the table, Adgandestrius leapt to his feet, hurling his bench back to crash down onto the rush-strewn floor. His men all jerked their heads around in reaction to their lord's outburst as he went for his dagger and slammed the point down into the board and left the weapon quivering in front of me. I remained motionless, still holding his gaze.

'You would dare belittle me and the Chatti, you, you son of a friend of Rome; a man who's stood back and let Rome tax his people to penury and played lickspittle to Varus whilst he tramples all over his lands. A man who's—'

'Been practical, Adgandestrius; practical! As you all have been. Your father may have got a better treaty with Rome; he may not have had to send his sons as hostages, but that was because he had not just tried to defeat Rome in battle. My father negotiated with Drusus having lost a great battle in which the flower of the Cherusci were cut down; my father could not choose his terms; but now I'm choosing mine and you can be part of it or not. Let your honour decide.' I placed both palms on the table and pushed myself up, never once taking my eyes from his. 'How do you want your women to feel about you, Adgandestrius? How do you want the Chatti to be perceived? Think on that because only you can decide this matter.'

I turned and walked away knowing that I had made an enemy for life.

Nevertheless, the vision I had painted of a future in which the Chatti had no honour stirred Adgandestrius and he began to send supplies to Teutoburg, although he did it in such a way as to imply that it was his idea and I had been a fool not to have thought of it myself. Engilram of the Bructeri and

Mallovendatz of the Marsi needed less persuasion; the former, with the wisdom of age, saw the obvious necessity, and the latter's hatred of Rome meant that he would acquiesce to anything that would make her defeat more likely despite it being someone else's idea.

And so, using the cover of winter when the legions were back in their winter quarters and the garrisons left in Germania rarely ventured further than the frozen rivers to break the ice to refill their water-skins, we stocked our supply bases little by little; by the spring thaw there was enough to provision twenty thousand warriors for a month. This news was met with various degrees of congratulation when I informed the kings and their sub-chieftains, gathered around a great table in my father's, hearth- and torch-lit hall in the Harzland. It was the final few days before Rome stirred herself from her winter slumber and her legions marched east from the Rhenus to reassert their dominance over Germania for what, I hoped, would be the last time.

'And why should you be guarding the supplies, Siegimeri?' Adgandestrius asked my father, wafting smoke away from his face and looking in annoyance at the central hearth; the logs were damp with snow-melt.

'It is not for me to answer, Adgandestrius; Erminatz commands here as you well know, so that no one king should dominate another.'

My uncle, Inguiomer, nodded in agreement. 'It is a logical thing.'

Segestes, my kinsman, spat on the rushes. 'So it's logical to be dominated by a boy instead.'

It was the first time that I had let the sub-chieftains of the tribes into the plan, having previously only taken counsel with the kings, and many, Segestes especially, had felt insulted that they had been kept in the dark.

'What does this *boy* have that makes him think he can defeat three legions?' Segestes continued, his voice oozing contempt; his eyes flashed angrily in the flicker of the torchlight.

'I have the vision, Segestes; I have the vision, the will, the hatred and the plan but, most of all, I have the trust of Varus. I alone here wear the uniform of Rome. Yes, you fight alongside Rome, but as Germanic allies, not as I do, as a prefect of an auxiliary cohort. I am seen to be Roman and therefore can be trusted; you are considered barely couth barbarians and about as trustworthy as a Parthian.'

Segestes was incensed. 'We keep our word!'

'So do Parthians but Romans choose not to believe that they do. It's a matter of perception: in me they see a clean-shaven, shorthaired soldier, wearing a cuirass, a tunic and a red cloak and speaking fluent Latin with a patrician accent. Tell me, what do they see when they look at you?'

My kinsman looked around the gathered kings and chieftains, their hair top-knotted, their beards long and clad in trousers with swirling tattoos visible on exposed flesh. 'Will you take this insult from a puppy? A whelp of Rome!'

'I did not mean it as an insult; it's an observation to help answer your question of why I think that I can defeat three legions. I can defeat them because I can get at them from within; you on the other hand, you of all, you can only take them from the outside, head-on. We all know what happens when you take on Rome head-on.'

Segestes hawked and spat once more. 'I'll not listen to this runt any longer.' He pushed his chair back and stalked from the hall.

I watched him go with deep regret; not because he would not join our cause, which irked, but because it had been that morning, when he had arrived with his retinue and family, that I had beheld Thusnelda for the first time; now I wondered how I would ever get his permission to marry his daughter. But that worry was soon driven from my mind by my father.

'I'll make sure that he does nothing rash,' Inguiomer murmured in my ear as the assembled company broke out into rumbling conversation about the rights and wrongs of what they had just witnessed.

I looked at my uncle, shocked. 'You mean he would betray us?'

He shrugged.

My father leant forward keeping his voice low. 'He is a proud but resentful younger kinsman; he has never been more than the chieftain of a sub-tribe of the Cherusci. Now he sees you, returning after years in exile, positioning yourself to win more glory than he has ever dreamt possible with kings and other chieftains doing your will and he finds it intolerable; he would rather see you fail and condemn Germania to slavery than be remembered as just a kinsman of the great Erminatz.'

'What if he were to be remembered as my father-in-law?' I whispered.

My father frowned, looking at me from beneath bushy brows, as he worked out just what I meant. 'You would marry Thusnelda?'

'Why not? She's beautiful, she'll be of an age next spring and it would give Segestes a closer tie to me.'

He shook his head. 'All that you say is true, and even if Segestes could be persuaded to allow his daughter to marry you he would still be unable to allow the marriage to happen unless he broke an oath to Adgandestrius.'

'Adgandestrius?'

'Yes, Thusnelda is betrothed to him.'

I looked across the table to where the king of the Chatti sat and swore to myself by the Great Thunderer that such vitality and beauty should never be soiled by the man who had made himself my enemy. Choking down the bitterness that I felt I called the company back to order and waited for quiet, which eventually manifested.

'So now that we have the supplies ready we wait until September. In the meantime we do nothing to arouse Varus' suspicions. We do his bidding and pay Rome's taxes. If he asks for your warriors to supplement his legions and auxiliaries fighting to the east of the Albis, you send them or, better still, you lead them to his aid yourselves. We are the most compliant subjects; we welcome Rome and totally agree with Augustus' plan for Varus to prepare for the annexation of the eastern bank of the Albis. We look forward to the creation of Germania Ultima and will do everything within our power to keep Varus busy this year along the Albis. There will be no trouble anywhere else in Germania, nothing to draw him away from the east so that come the equinox in September, and it's time for him to return to his winter quarters, he will take the Road of the Long Bridges back west; and that is when I shall come to him with news of a fictitious rebellion of the Ampsivarii to the north of the Teutoburg Wald.'

I paused and looked around the men listening to me; all were concentrating on my words and not even Adgandestrius seemed to be in disagreement. So I considered it safe to issue my first order. 'The full moon will be early in September; that is when we will start amassing our strength in the Wald. When the moon starts to wane begin sending your warriors in groups of not more than a hundred at a time; try if possible to have them travel at night so that the mass movement is less noticeable. We will meet at the Grove of Donar, the southern one, that is, not the northern, on the day after the equinox and there we will wait for my father to send word of Varus' departure for the west. And then, my friends, we shall have him and we shall strike a blow that will echo down the ages.'

'And what about the auxiliaries?' Engilram asked.

'They will be told nearer the time. Send word to your headmen serving in the cohorts telling them to obey my word as if it came from their king when the time comes. This will be the moment that will decide all: if I can lead the auxiliary cohorts scouting ahead and to either side of the legionary column against it, then, along with my Cherusci warriors, we will be able to split the column into two or three. If we do that, my friends, the gods will be on our side and we can destroy the legions piecemeal. That would be the moment that I would ask you to lead your warriors to our aid; that would be the moment that we have to press our advantage and seize the victory. If we let them regroup they will build a defensive position; we do not have the discipline to conduct a siege and our men will melt away. So we must finish the thing on the first day.' I thumped my fist down hard on the board. 'The first day, my friends; the first day or we would have failed. You must make your decisions to join with me by noon on the first day.'

Adgandestrius smiled without warmth. 'And should we decide against sending in our warriors, what then? Our men serving in the auxiliary cohorts will have already turned against

Rome, there will be no denying it. Varus will assume that we ordered them to do it and will punish us as well as them.'

I looked at him and wondered how such a gift as Thusnelda could be bestowed upon a man with so little backbone. 'Varus can't crucify every man in Germania Magna. He will first come for the Cherusci. We are the tribe with the most to lose; we will suffer at his hands if we fail. You, on the other hand, can send hostages to him, beg for forgiveness, say that you were unaware that the villain, Erminatz, had poisoned the minds of your men. Or you can wheedle out of it any other way that you like, Adgandestrius; but remember this: should you decide not to lead your tribe in then we would have lost the chance to free our Fatherland for ever. I say let Varus do as he likes with us if we fail; what can he do that is worse than stealing our land and making us look weak before our mothers, wives and daughters?'

It was quiet at first, just a singular tap of the board; and then it was echoed from another corner of the table. Then a third joined in and the beats came in time, building, slow and steady. My father slammed his palm down, joining in the beat and causing my drinking horn to jump. I looked up and down the table: every man bar one was hitting it in time; every man was applauding my plan; every man save Adgandestrius. I smiled at him in triumph and he scowled back before joining in the beat with exaggerated mannerisms.

But I did not deign to notice his sarcasm because I knew then that I had won over the Chauci, the Marsi, the Bructeri and the Sugambri; with all those warriors allied to my father's Cherusci then surely this thing would be possible, no matter what the Chatti did. Adgandestrius would not prove false; he would not dare to lose face by slinking away with his tail between his legs. He would not want to be the only king without the stones to help annihilate three legions. His warriors would add their weight to the struggle and they would earn their glory despite their king's hesitation.

As the rhythm grew more frenetic my father signalled to his steward to admit the warriors waiting outside and to begin bringing in the roasted boars and deer and the barrels of ale so that the feast could begin. The men filed in through all three of the doors, cheering, not knowing wherefore but because their lords were doing so and I watched them with a smile on my face. But the smile was not solely because of the satisfaction that I was feeling at having been given approval of my plan, although that was good; no, the smile was given warmth by a separate thought because I had just conceived of how to humiliate Adgandestrius and at the same time get what I craved. It was a sweet thought, made sweeter still by the grandness of the gesture. Lucius would have been proud of me.

CHAPTER VIIII

THUMELICATZ FLEXED HIS shoulders and cracked his knuckles, smiling at his Roman guests as Aius rolled up his scroll. 'That was the point at which my father became the leader of the confederation of tribes that was responsible for keeping Germania Germanic. And it was also at that moment when my father sealed his fate and consigned himself to an early death. Unlike you Romans, it is not within our culture to let one man dominate us all.'

'A hundred and fifty years ago the same could have been said of us,' the younger brother said. 'When we were still a republic it was not possible for one man to dominate the city.'

Thumelicatz scratched at his beard. 'Until Gaius Marius changed the terms of military service and made your army professional: paid and with the promise of land on discharge rather than the duty of all property-owning citizens because they are considered to have a stake in society worth defending. I know your history and its consequences: as soon as soldiers became the clients of their generals who awarded them their plots after twenty-five years' service it was only a matter of time before individuals would amass the power to be able to exert their will on all others; first Marius then Sulla, Cinna, Pompeius, Antonius, Caesar, and look where that has led you to: now you have an emperor.' Pulling a louse from his beard, he inspected it before crushing it between his fingers. 'We, on the other hand, because we're tribal, could never accept a Caesar; the kings and the chieftains are too proud to allow domination and my father knew that when he became the leader of the confederation. But he also knew that he would have to continue to exert his influence in order to keep the confederation together to repel any attempt by Rome to retake Germania. I'm convinced that he understood then how that would end but nevertheless he carried on until … but I get ahead of myself.'

He took a draught of ale as the old slaves busied themselves with their scrolls. Putting the drinking horn down, he surveyed his guests who sat, expressionless, waiting for the next part of the tale. 'So Varus came back at the head of three legions and eight auxiliary cohorts, five of which were Germanic. That campaign season he followed Augustus' orders and probed the eastern bank of the Albis, testing the will of the leaders of the Saxones and the Semnones, bestowing and receiving gifts and threats in equal measure but doing nothing that could be construed as a cause for war. Chieftains from even further east sent emissaries pledging friendship and pleading poverty in the hope that Rome would not venture that far or, if she did, that they would be treated with leniency.

'And so the summer passed, the equinox drew closer and my father put into place the first part of his plan: because of all the contact with the eastern tribes, he had each of the kings of the confederation approach Varus and ask for garrisons to be left on their land to guard against the possible threat of those tribes making a pre-emptive strike into the west during the winter when the Albis was frozen and easy to cross. This, of course, was most unlikely but my father had the Governor's ear and had often expressed his concern that the eastern tribes could not be trusted and were very likely to raid Germania Magna for its riches, pointing out that they themselves had expressed just how poor they were. So when the kings, each in turn, made their requests, Varus took them seriously and left twelve half-cohort garrisons around the province, thus reducing his strength by almost three thousand men.'

Thumelicatz took the scroll that Tiburtius was preparing to read and glanced through it before handing it back to the slave and pointing to a line. 'From there.' He looked back at his guests. 'So, the time had come for Varus to head back to the west. He felt pleased with his summer's work and the garrisons that had been left behind added to his sense of wellbeing and security. He gave permission for his legions' legates, most of his tribunes and quite a few of his senior centurions to travel back to Rome for the winter, and so it was that at the feast to mark the conclusion of a successful season, shortly before he departed, there were hardly any Romans present, just the kings and sub-chieftains of the confederation. Tiburtius.'

It was a small gathering but the food was good, not the finicky little dishes that the Romans usually served but, rather, roasted meats, salted cabbage, carp, perch, bread and cheese – Germanic food; but this was, I suppose, because Varus was the only Roman present as he had sent most of his officers either back to Rome or posted them to one of the garrisons that he had been fooled into leaving behind. However, he seemed oblivious to the danger that he had placed himself in and drank deeply all evening of his Roman wine whilst we Germans, me, my father, Segestes, Engilram of the Bructeri and a couple of his sub-chieftains, guzzled ale until the fronts of our tunics were soaked and our bladders strained.

'To the success of our venture next year,' Varus announced, raising his wine cup in the air so that red liquid slopped down his wrist. 'May the gods of our peoples hold their hands over us as we venture further east.'

'To the East!' my father shouted before draining his drinking horn in one gullet-opening draft to the cheers of almost all present.

Only Segestes scowled, frowning into his horn, clasped in both hands; he had been brooding for the duration of the feast. He had made a point of sitting on his couch rather than reclining Roman style; the rest of the company had by now become used to the strange position the Romans adopt when eating and although it felt alien to us we had taken it on as part of our professed Romanisation.

Varus held out his cup for a thrall to refill. 'I fully expect the Emperor to order the complete annexation of the eastern bank next season.'

'Tactically that makes sense,' Engilram observed, his grey beard dripping with ale. 'The Marcomanni in Bojohaemum would be far more inclined to come to a negotiated settlement if they found themselves surrounded rather than hold out against the inevitable.'

Varus nodded his agreement. 'The punishment raids from Raetia and Noricum seemed to have only hardened Maroboduus' resolve; since Tiberius was forced to abort his invasion in order to suppress the Pannonian revolt three years ago he sees the smaller raids as a sign of weakness. But when we move across the Albis then he'll find Rome all around him and he'll have a simple choice: submit and become a client king of Rome or face an invasion of his hilly realm from north, south, east and west. That should focus his mind.'

This was greeted by enthusiastic rumblings of agreement, another chorus of toasts and draining of drinking horns.

'And then,' Varus continued, 'with that final part of Germania Magna subdued and Germania Ultima pacified I'll be able to return to Rome and enjoy the favour of Augustus and the benefits that will follow for bringing the whole of Germania under Rome's sway.' He looked around, smiling smugly as our rumblings of agreement changed to those of congratulations, our faces hiding the contempt that we felt for his boastful dismissal of Germanic pride.

All of us, that was, except one.

Segestes threw his horn down onto the table, cracking it open and exploding ale onto all of us gathered around it. 'You think that it's all so easy; that we will just roll over and bare our throats like beaten bitches! You're walking through this with your eyes shut; blind you are! Everyone in this room wishes for your death, everyone, that is, except for me.' He raised his finger and pointed it directly at me. 'And it's him; he is the one who has planned it: Erminatz. Erminatz, who pretends such loyalty, who is always willing to do your bidding and lead his *loyal* auxiliaries wherever you ask; he will see you dead within the month!'

All the Germanic guests stared in disbelief at Segestes who had risen to his feet and was swaying to and fro with alcohol; mouths fell open and eyes hardened at such treachery. I was on the verge of denying his accusation when, from my left, came the amused nasal guffaw that I was used to from the elite of Rome. Varus was laughing. I bit back the words of denial – which would have probably sounded weak, condemning me further – and joined in with his mirth; my father quickly followed my lead and so did, one by one, the rest of the guests until Segestes stood surrounded by open mockery.

'And why,' Varus asked, between bouts of laughter, 'would the man who saved my life want to kill me now? He could have saved himself the trouble and let me go down beneath the blades of the Marcomanni in Bojohaemum three years ago.'

'Yes, Segestes,' I shouted over the rising hilarity that masked the relief we all felt, 'tell me why I should kill the man who owes me such a debt? The man who, as Governor of Germania Magna, can show me favour.'

My father made a show of controlling his amusement. 'Indeed, tell us, Cousin, what Erminatz would have to gain by our governor's death?'

'Yes, tell us,' Inguiomer urged, scorn in his voice.

Segestes rounded on my father and uncle. 'You know perfectly well that it's not just Varus' death but also the death of every legionary in Germania.'

'Every legionary in Germania!' Varus burst out. 'And just how would you contrive to do that? Take us head on? No matter how many warriors you put against us, you would be crushed.'

'Of course not, you fool, he plans to lead you into an ambush.'

Varus leapt to his feet. 'Fool? Fool! You call me a fool? You, you hairy-arsed barbarian, dare to call a member of the patrician Quinctilii a fool? In public? I should have you put in chains until you learn some—'

'Then put me in chains,' Segestes roared across him, 'fool! But make sure you do the same to Erminatz; in fact arrest everyone here and take us back to your winter quarters with you. Mark my words, Varus, only that will save your life.'

Varus opened his mouth to shout at Segestes but then paused, thinking. 'Why do you tell me this? If a plot really did exist to rid Germania of me and my legions then, surely, you would support it or, at least, not betray it and be seen as a traitor to your own countrymen?'

'What loyalty do I have to them? Always the younger cousin; always looked down upon and given the bare semblance of honour.' He glanced at me; eyes brim with hatred. 'And now that runt would outdo me: he would become the saviour of Germania Magna and he is not even yet a king, as his father still lives; whereas the best I can hope for is to marry my daughter to a king and be able to boast a king as my grandson.' He shook his head slowly whilst we all stared at him, transfixed, as these words of long-harboured rancour tumbled from him. 'No, Varus, I have no loyalty to a people that consigns me to being a man of little or no import. A man with no respect.' He spat upon the table. 'No, I have made up my mind and I will support Rome because through her I can change my fortune; through her I can raise myself to the status that I deserve. But Rome will not exist in Germania unless you stop trusting him.'

The finger he pointed at me was steady despite his earlier drink-induced rolling; it was decisive and accusatory. All eyes turned to Varus to see whether he was swayed by it.

'Get – out – of my sight!'

It took a few moments for everyone to realise that Varus meant Segestes, not me. The surprise that registered on my kinsman's face quickly changed to incredulity before he turned and walked from the room leaving us all in stunned silence.

My father recovered first. 'My cousin has not been the same since my elder son came back home,' he explained to Varus. 'I believe that he harboured hopes of neither of them ever returning and my younger brother dying early; then he would have been my heir.'

Varus shook his head, pursing his lips, as if he understood only too well. 'So he's trying to discredit him with false accusations?'

'Precisely.'

'Just give me a chance to prove my loyalty,' I asked, most earnestly, my Latin as precise and elegant as Varus' own. I held out a cup for a slave to fill with wine to emphasise my attachment to Rome.

Varus smiled and reclined back on his couch. 'You'll get the chance, Arminius; I'll make sure of that. And when it's done then I'll have that kinsman of yours executed for his ill-manners.'

'I beg you not to do that.' I felt my stomach churn in disgust as I realised that I was almost simpering. 'It was just jealousy that motivated him. Not only am I the heir to the Cherusci crown but I also hold the rank of prefect and equestrian status and that he can't abide.'

'Perhaps I should recommend to the Emperor, in my next despatch, that he should raise Segestes to the equestrian order in the hopes of improving his manners?' He laughed at his own feeble wit and downed the rest of the wine in his cup.

We joined in, sycophantically slapping our thighs with mirth and suggesting that perhaps Segestes would only be happy once he was a consul and his family had been given patrician status.

'But then,' I quipped in my most-clipped tone, 'his Latin would have to improve quite dramatically!'

This sent Varus into a fresh burst of laughter and as the others and I joined in, I looked around their faces and those whose eyes I caught were laughing only with their mouths; their eyes, however, betrayed their amazement at Varus' credulity.

The air was chill and patched with wisps of pre-dawn mist glowing orange in the light of hundreds of torches sputtering around the camp. And the camp was enormous, built to house three legions and their auxiliaries, almost twenty thousand men; and that was not including the ancillary personnel. It had been the main base for the summer's campaign and, as such, had only held all three legions at the very beginning and now at the end as they mustered to begin the long march back west.

I stood, along with the other auxiliary prefects, next to Varus, on the steps of the praetorium, one of the few permanent buildings amongst a sea of tents, watching the legionaries form up in the eight-man *contubernia* and then ten of these coming together, with the aid of the harsh voices of centurions and their optios, to parade as a century. All through the camp, iron-nailed boots stamped, equipment clinked and jangled, breath steamed, burnished metal glinted, commands bellowed, *bucinae* sounded and standards were held aloft as the might of Rome in Germania Magna assembled, bleary-eyed and chewing on the last of their breakfast, into the order of march decreed by their general. In the background, hundreds of slaves began to pull down the newly vacated tents and extinguish cooking fires in clouds of steam, whilst others harnessed mules to carts and loaded others with provisions.

The first legion behind the auxiliary vanguard was to be the Seventeenth and it was its legionaries, their pack-yokes over their right shoulders and shields slung on their backs, that I was watching form up on the *principia*, the square at the camp's centre, and along the Via Principalis that ran east to west through the camp. And it was with a cold heart that I surveyed them; there could be no pity as, if I was to carry out my plan, every man of them would have to die. It was at this moment that doubt clouded my resolve; my vision faltered as I contemplated the sheer magnitude of the task as just one legion paraded before me. Despite the chill, I began to sweat.

With the blare of horns and the roars of the centuriate and their optios the men saluted their general who waited for the crash to die away before addressing them.

'Men of the Seventeenth Legion, you have served your Emperor well this year and have earned your winter's repose. For a good many of you this was your last year under the Eagle of the Seventeenth and you will be discharged upon your arrival on the Rhenus. I thank you for your loyal service and wish you long life and joy of many sons on the land you will receive. Rome salutes you.'

Varus slammed his right fist across his chest; a command bawled out from somewhere in the gloom. The aquilifer raised his Eagle standard and those of the cohorts dipped; as one, the legion crashed a right turn and then began to march westward, through the Left Gate and out onto the military road that traversed so many bridges on its two-hundred-mile journey back to the Rhenus. The auxiliary cohorts had already formed up outside the camp ready to fall into their position of march in the van and to either side of the legion as it passed.

As, almost half an hour later, the tail of the Seventeenth Legion disappeared through the gate, the legionaries of the Eighteenth began to take their place along the Via Principalis and soon Varus was repeating his speech to them. The light steadily grew and by the time the Nineteenth had paraded before Varus the men's faces were clearly visible and betraying the pleasure they felt at returning to their winter quarters and the relative peace and comfort that was associated with them.

Behind them, in the smoke-wreathed body of the camp, slaves continued to dismantle the empty tents, loading them onto each contubernium's mule and then filling each century's wagon with their millstones, the centurion's tent, sacks of grain and chickpeas and the unit's carroballista as well as any other equipment not carried by the legionaries and too heavy for the pack mules.

The tumult of the departure carried on all about us as the baggage train formed up and the camp-followers – in the main whores and merchants – tagged themselves on at the end of the column, the head of which had by now disappeared into the distance along the dead-straight road. The newly risen sun washed the backs of the men's packs and their helms with warm morning light so the column glowed like a luminous spear cast west across the flat heartlands of Germania.

'Fifteen miles a day, gentlemen,' Varus said to us prefects as he mounted his horse held steady by a stable-slave. 'We shall construct rudimentary camps – just a ditch, something to keep the men occupied at the end of each march – as there is no great threat to us on the journey. With luck we'll be back in Castra Vetera in fourteen days or so. Don't bother too much with scouting to either side; just send out a few patrols now and again but in the main keep your lads in the column. As to forward reconnaissance, all we need do is send small cavalry detachments ahead just for form's sake and to check that the bridges haven't been damaged by floods and such. Arminius, that'll be your duty; report to me every dawn, noon and dusk. Rejoin your cohorts, gentlemen.' With a curt nod, he kicked his mount on to race up the column and take his place between the Seventeenth and Eighteenth legions. As my fellow prefects made to follow I held two of them back, both commanding infantry cohorts: Egino of the Marsi and Gernot of the Bructeri.

'Have you had any word from your kings?' I asked, as we slowly made our way up the column; the legions had now burst into a raucous marching song and I had to raise my voice to make myself heard.

Gernot looked at me askance. 'In what way, Erminatz?'

'Concerning the value of my words.'

They looked at each other before both nodding to me.

'We are to treat them as if they come from our lords themselves,' Egino confirmed.

I smiled. 'Good. Then if, in a few days' time, the column veers off the road and begins to march northwest heading into the Teutoburg Wald, warn Varus of the dangers of ambush travelling through the Wald and ask that your two cohorts and the other couple of Germanic infantry cohorts should screen the march to the left and the right; he will see the wisdom of that precaution as he will think that he's heading towards a revolt. Once you're in position to his flank, listen out for my voice; I shall be speaking for your kings.'

The prefects both assured me that they would comply in every aspect of my request and I accelerated my horse away to talk to the prefects of the other two Germanic cohorts. Having received the same assurances from them I rejoined my ala and settled down to wait.

And I waited for two days, the tension growing within me all the time as I could not check whether everything was in place within the Teutoburg Wald. Had the warriors arrived? Were they being fed and watered so that they were not tempted to leave? Had the kings and chieftains managed to control their followers so that no tensions existed between the tribes and fights were kept to a minimum? These worries and more went through my head throughout the time I waited to see the sight that I knew would set in motion a series of events that would lead to the deaths of thousands of men; but whether they would be Germanic or Roman depended on what would happen in the next few days. And doubt still assailed me as every day I saw the length of the column; how could all those men be killed? How would it be possible?

On the evening of the second day, as we were halfway between the Albis and Visurgis rivers, skirting to the north of the Harzland, the sight that I had been looking for came into view: Vulferam and a small party of Cheruscian auxiliary cavalrymen galloped out of the north making for the command post between the first two legions where Varus rode. I immediately sped forward to join them although I had no need to hear what they had to say as it was I who had put the words into their mouths.

'What is it, sir?' I asked Varus as I pulled my horse up next to him.

Vulferam and his comrades had withdrawn to a respectful distance, their message delivered.

Varus chewed on his bottom lip before replying. 'It seems that the Ampsivarii to the north have taken this opportunity to rebel against us and murder all the tax-farmers and merchants in their tribal lands.' He pointed to Vulferam. 'Do you know this man, Arminius?'

I replied that I did and that he was an uncle of mine, my mother's brother, and my senior decurion and he could be trusted.

'I should divert north and deal with it on the way back; it can't be more than four or five days out of the way and the weather's set fair for at least that.'

And now I had him. 'Let me go with my ala; we can be there in half the time and if it's just a localised revolt then I'll have sufficient men to quell it.'

Varus looked at me, assessing me. 'A chance to prove your loyalty, Arminius; very well, go. But if it's too much for one ala, send me word; I don't want to march west with this smouldering behind my back. Fire tends to catch if it's left unattended.'

'Don't worry, sir; I won't be afraid to send for help if it's got out of hand. But I'm sure that we'll be able to manage; you can trust me.'

Varus nodded. 'I know I can.' Then he added with a grin: 'With my life.'

'Yes, sir; with your life.' I saluted him for the last time, spun my mount about and, signalling to Vulferam and his comrades to follow me, sped back down the column to collect my ala. After sending out messengers, recalling the patrol that had been sent up ahead, I led my men into the north. It was now a matter of timing: I had to wait until Varus had crossed the Visurgis and reached the southern limits of the Teutoburg Wald. Then I would send my distress message and then I would know whether he was as big a trusting fool as I thought he was. Then I would see if he would bring three legions into dense country to come to the aid of the man who had saved his life and help put down a fictitious rebellion.

Then I would see if he would come of his own volition to the killing ground.

CHAPTER X

'Will he come?' my father asked as I rode, the following day, with Vulferam and his men into the skull-lined Grove of Donar, in the south of the Teutoburg Wald.

Dismounting, I ignored the question as the answer would only be speculation; my father did not press the point as he too realised that it was a foolish thing to ask. 'Are all the tribes here?'

'The Chatti were the last to arrive two days ago.' He pointed to freshly severed heads hanging from the branches of many of the sacred grove's trees. 'The appropriate sacrifices have been made and the priestesses have declared the time auspicious for our enterprise.'

I hid my relief at that news; it went some way to relieving my growing concern about the magnitude of the killing that had to occur. 'Then we shall take counsel with the kings and sub-chieftains at dusk this evening.' I turned back to Vulferam. 'Have messengers sent to all the tribes: I shall hold a council of war here, by this grove, at the setting of the sun.'

To the west the sun sank behind the hills of the Teutoburg Wald, casting the valleys and ravines into gloom. Great fires had been lit in and around the Grove of Donar, washing the underside of the overhanging branches with flickering, golden light and casting ghastly shadows on the grisly fruit that hung from them. I'd had tables set up in a square, around one of the fires, in order that no man, least of all me, may say that he sat at its head; all must be seen to be given equal honour if this fragile alliance was to be kept together. Adgandestrius still managed to find that his dignity had been slighted because the bench that he and his followers were sitting on seemed to be lower than the rest of them, but after I had swapped mine for his there could be no more argument and the council could begin.

We drank three full horns of ale in a toast to our gods, our forefathers and our women and then I stood and looked around the bearded faces glowing in the firelight; all of them, young and old, had looks of barely concealed expectation, like children on the eve of the winter solstice. Even Adgandestrius looked eager.

I welcomed each in turn. 'I would know our strength; I will go around the table and ask each tribe how many warriors they have brought into the Wald. Please do not exaggerate the numbers; it's enough that you are here, it doesn't matter whether you have brought more or fewer men than your neighbour.'

Siegimeri spoke first, claiming eight thousand Cherusci and earning a disbelieving look from Adgandestrius as he stated that he had arrived with five thousand and then tried to claim that five thousand Chatti would be a match for eight thousand Cherusci. I gripped my father's shoulder, restraining him as he tried to stand and rebut the assertion, which would have led, as day follows night, to a fight.

'We will get nowhere if we constantly bicker and try to goad each other and outdo one another with boasts,' I said in as calm and quiet a voice as could be heard over the crackle of the fire in our midst. 'Thank you for your five thousand, Adgandestrius, may they fight well.'

'They will fight like gods of war.'

'I'm sure they will, when and if you let them,' I pointed out truthfully, silencing the arrogant king of the Chatti.

The other four kings gave their strengths and I tallied the entire total at a little over thirty thousand warriors. 'And with my four hundred and eighty cavalry and the three thousand two hundred auxiliaries in the four Germanic cohorts we can claim a muster of just shy of thirty-five thousand. That, my friends, should be enough if we can get them all into action at the same time.' I paused and looked at each king in turn. 'But to do that you must have faith in our victory; you must believe that, when the auxiliaries turn on the column along with my father's eight thousand Cherusci, we will prevail and the column will be cut into three. If you don't give your tribes the order to charge at that point then we risk losing everything that we have gained and Varus will have a chance to regroup and build a defensive position that we will be unable to shift him from. Retribution will follow and we will never be trusted by Rome again. Germania will be lost and the west will be forever Latin. That is something that our children's children's children will curse us for; and trust me when I say that they will not be cursing us in our tongue but, rather, the tongue of our enemy.'

There was silence around the table as my bleak words were digested; perhaps I had exaggerated for added effect but no man could accuse me of having done so, for fear of being charged himself with underestimating the threat to our culture. Gradually, low conversations sprung up as the various kings took counsel with their followers; we of the Cherusci sat in silence as our path was clear: we would be leading the attack.

Eventually Engilram of the Bructeri stood and thumped the board with his fist and soon all eyes were turned upon him. 'The Bructeri will not stand by while the Cherusci fight;

we will join with the first attack and I shall personally lead my warriors and be the first of my tribe to draw Roman blood.' His thanes cheered the old king as he sat back down while the rest of the company scowled and muttered amongst themselves until Adgandestrius stood and pointed a finger at me. 'You trust this whelp's leadership, Engilram? Would you risk your people's lives in a—'

'Enough!' I shouted with such force that I shocked even myself. 'Do not try to influence another man's decision, Adgandestrius; the Bructeri will fight alongside the Cherusci, so let that be. You have said that you will wait to see how the day goes before deciding whether to commit the Chatti or to slip away in order to avoid Rome's wrath if we look to be unsuccessful. I am pleased that you are at least here; let us leave it at that.' I slowly got to my feet and lowered my voice. 'Let each man here do what he deems best for the folk in his care; but let none try to foist their opinions on another. Let us have peace between us.' There was a smattering of mumbled agreement from around the table. 'My scouts tell me that Varus is now directly to the south of the Teutoburg Wald so tomorrow I will send messages to him begging his assistance in the north. Not to arouse his suspicions I shall ask only for him to send a legion and then, my friends, we shall see if he brings everything.'

Adgandestrius spat in disgust. 'He can't even guarantee that we will be in a position to ambush Varus.'

Hrodulf of the Chauci hit the table. 'No, he can't, Adgandestrius, but at least he will give us a chance to; so let us be grateful for that and pray to the gods of this land that Varus' Roman arrogance brings him blundering into this forest. The Chauci will fight alongside Erminatz as well.'

With that third tribe promising to join the beginning of the ambush my hopes of success rose. 'Thank you, Hrodulf; may the Thunderer hold his hands over you and your folk.' I sat back down and took a deep breath for we were about to reach the point of no return. 'The messenger will leave at midday tomorrow, which should mean that, if he comes with all three legions, then he should be around this point in three days' time. Three days, my friends, three days more in which to live as slaves.'

Adgandestrius went to add something to that sentence but my look made him think again and then keep his mouth shut. However, I could guess what he would have said and he would have been right: or three days more to live at all.

Egino told me after the event that Varus did not hesitate when he received my first message; he halted the column and began deploying a new order of march to traverse the Teutoburg Wald, despite protests from the few remaining Roman officers present. However, he would not be dissuaded and, I'm sorry to say, cited my friendship as his primary reason for taking the whole column through the forest. I'm sorry because, however just the cause, it is demeaning to trick someone by using a false friendship. Nevertheless, he turned north but not just with the legions and auxiliary cohorts: the fool brought the entire baggage train along with all the camp-followers; a massive encumbrance at the best of times travelling along a straight and well-made road, but in hilly terrain thick with trees and undergrowth the carts and the women would slow the column down to under ten miles a day. Not only that but also the slow-moving train would stretch the column from what was already nearly three miles long to almost four, thus thinning it and making it far more likely that I would be able to achieve the two breaks in it that would enable us to destroy the force bit by bit.

And so I sent messages to the four auxiliary prefects who had, good to their word, persuaded Varus of the value of having them scout to the east and west of the advance: they were to keep me informed of the route that Varus was taking whilst Engilram, Hrodulf and I manoeuvred our warriors into a position on either side of a heavily wooded vale that seemed to be directly in the Romans' path. There we waited, receiving reports every few hours or so of the rate of progress of the slow-moving column. Quite sensibly, rather than lose formation and therefore cohesion, Varus had sent out pioneers before him to cut a wide path through the trees, felling many in the way so the column could march straight through in close formation. This, however, was a lengthy process and he was forced to stop for two hours in every three as the men ahead sweated with axes and saws making a way wide enough to take an eight-man-broad column.

It took them two days to reach the site that I had chosen for the attack and all the while I had been sending more urgent messages, urging him to make haste. But finally, on a day of thunder and rain, the fourth to last of the month the Romans call September, the first cavalry scouts appeared through the downpour and behind them, in the distance, could be heard the axe blows and saw cuts of the pioneers. Varus had, of his own volition, brought his army to the killing ground.

'Hold it there, Tiburtius,' Thumelicatz interrupted, 'and perhaps you can give my guests an insight into what it was like in the column on your slow progress through the Wald; as the Eagle-bearer of the Nineteenth Legion you would have been towards the rear.'

The old slave looked at his master, his rheumy eyes blinking quickly a couple of times before laying down the scroll and then looking into the middle distance, recalling a time long gone and long forgotten.

All were silent in the tent as they waited for the old man to trawl through deeply buried memories, sifting out the ones that his master had ordered him to recollect.

'We didn't trust the general's judgement,' Tiburtius began, his voice gaining confidence with every word. 'Of course we had to go to help suppress the revolt, no one could fault him for that but anyone with the slightest military knowledge could see that ploughing through rolling terrain, which was more forested than it was cultivated, with the baggage train in tow was, at best, foolish. My legion was to the rear of the column, just in front of the rear-guard.' He suppressed a smile that crept over his face as recalled his legion. 'We had waited in the order of march, outside the previous night's camp, for two hours that morning as the head of the column moved off before we could even take one pace forward. The lads were nervous, they knew enough about the forests of Germania to be afraid of the spirits that dwell in them and no one wanted to stay for a moment longer than necessary in that haunted place. To add to their sense of unease a lot of the most senior officers weren't present having been given leave to return to Rome for the winter.' He shook his head regretfully. 'I think that was one of the major factors that contributed to the disaster.'

'Victory,' Thumelicatz corrected him, although not too harshly.

'Yes, master, victory, indeed. It was the lack of men of rank and experience that unsettled the lads as they waited that morning for the rear of the column to start moving. With our legate and the prefect of the camp gone back to Rome we were led by Marcellus Acilius, the thick-stripe military tribune. As you can guess he was a young man, not quite twenty, of patrician rank and no military experience who had been with the legion solely for that summer.'

'About as much use as a Vestal in a cock-sucking competition,' the street-fighter commented knowledgably.

Tiburtius paused and then coughed out a couple of raw bouts of laughter as if he had not laughed for a very long time. 'Exactly; even less use, actually, for he thought he knew everything there was to know about the army because his father, grandfather and every sort of forefather you could mention had served under the Eagles, so therefore with the arrogance of pampered youth he was probably worse than not having someone in command of the legion at all.'

'Worse than a man short.'

'Too right; that's just what we all thought. Anyway, we entered a valley, about two-thirds of a mile wide, with slopes wooded with beech and pine and, as we did, the sky darkened and we all began to feel the oppression of the landscape. The centurions and the optios did their best to reassure the lads but you know what a superstitious bunch soldiers are, and by the time we were on the move every century had managed to spook itself; men were spitting and clutching their thumbs between their fingers to avert the evil-eye and casting long looks to the side and behind. The senior centurion – the primus pilus was back in Rome – tried to get a few songs going but it was lacklustre and they all petered out after a few verses. And then it began to rain; not much at first but enough to make us all very damp and miserable, but after an hour or so it started to fall as if all the gods above were pissing on us and then thunder cracked as if they had all farted in unison. So we tramped on sullenly; stopping every half a mile or so when the column concertinaed to a rolling halt as more trees were felled up the front or a stream was bridged. On we went treading in the shit and piss of the baggage train that slithered along ahead of us, occasionally passing abandoned carts, their axles snapped by tree roots sticking out of the ground, or lame mules left to fend for themselves. Looking back I suppose you could say that those mules were lucky. All day we stumbled along, struggling to keep our eight-man-wide formation whilst slipping on the deepening mud which had been churned to a glutinous mess by the passage of thousands of our comrades and all the pack animals before us. Even if the column had moved at a quicker speed we would not have been able to as our legs began to ache with every step we took in that morass, and as the sixth hour came we were exhausted. Then the first javelins hit us.'

Thumelicatz raised a hand. 'That's enough, Tiburtius; you get ahead of my father's story. Read on.'

The old slave picked up his scroll, squinting at it in the dimming light.

There through the trees, down in the valley, small with the distance, were the first of Varus' men and I knew that the next hour had the potential to change history for ever. I kicked my horse to the right to where the first scouts of the auxiliary cohorts advanced in dispersed order and found Egino just behind them in front of the main body of his men. 'Stop your men here, Egino; we'll let the column carry on until the second cohort of the leading legion is level with you, then you'll hit them. Send a runner back to Gernot and tell him to position himself so that he hits the second cohort of the third legion.

Hrodulf and Engilram are giving the same orders to the two cohorts on the opposite hill.'

'And where are your warriors?' Egino asked, looking back up the hill to its brow fifty paces away.

'Hidden just over the crest are eight thousand Cherusci and on the other side there are eight thousand Chauci and Bructeri combined. My cavalry ala is a mile ahead ready to deal with the legionary scouting cavalry. Then the Marsi and the Chatti are behind the Cherusci warriors waiting to see the outcome and the Sugambri are over there, behind the Chauci.' I pointed to the opposite hill just over a half mile distant, praying that what I said was true and that none of the tribes had had last-moment doubts and just walked away. 'The rain is in our favour.'

Egino nodded, looking grim, as well he might before the attempted destruction of three legions; he halted his cohort and ordered one of his junior officers back with the message for Gernot. As the cohort formed up, four ranks deep, facing down the hill, I pushed my horse on up to the brow where I found my father, resplendent in his war gear: a bronze helmet sporting two boar tusks, a chainmail tunic, silver arm-rings, leather breeks and with a long sword in a finely decorated scabbard hanging at his side along with a great war horn. He raised his spear and oval shield, decorated with the Cherusci wolf, to greet me as I approached, water dripping from his helm onto his greying beard; he mimed the roar that he would have liked to have given had secrecy not been paramount. My heart leapt with the joy of it all; after all these years we were finally going to have our revenge. Behind him, bound to a tree, was Segestes, blood running rain-washed from swollen and cut lips, with my uncle watching over him.

'You will let him go once it is done?' I asked, dismounting next to my father.

'Of course; I would not be my cousin's murderer.'

'He would be yours if he could run to Varus now.'

'But he can't and I will let him live. Is Varus in sight?'

I nodded and took my father in an embrace, our chainmail rubbing together. 'This is for the time they stole from us, Father, and the grief that my mother feels at not watching her boys grow up and what my sister felt at having her brothers taken from her.'

He slapped my back and then held me at arms' length by the shoulders, looking at me as if it was for the last time. 'We'll meet over Varus' corpse.'

'We will, Father.'

Turning, he waved to Vulferam, in the trees a hundred paces away; he punched his drawn sword in the air and suddenly, behind him, thousands of warriors rose from the undergrowth stretching all the way to my right, rippling up in the direction of the rear of the Roman column, as far as I could see. Silent they were as they moved forward; the richer ones armed with swords and spears and helmeted, armoured and shielded; the poorer with their top-knots bare and no more protection than a leather jerkin and a rough, wickerwork shield and armed only with a spear and some rough-hewn javelins. But whatever inequality there might have been in their accoutrements of war they all had equal desire to avenge the defeat inflicted on them by Drusus, all those years ago, that ended with my father handing over his sons as hostages to Rome and Cherusci pride being buried beneath Roman taxes.

Together, my father and I led our warriors up to the crest of the hill, my heartbeat increasing with every step and me praying with every beat that on the opposite side of the valley Engilram and Hrodulf were bringing their warriors forward to support the auxiliaries over there, and if they were, would they heed my orders?

But those worries were driven from my mind as I crested the hill and looked down into the valley. Through the rain and the trees the first cohort of the Seventeenth Legion was visible; it was the elite unit of the legion and thus the one that I wanted to isolate and destroy first.

Now was the time; I knew it with certainty that now we must strike, now as the gap between the first and second cohorts came into view. I lowered my facemask and signalled to my father who lifted his war horn to his lips and blew a mighty note that rumbled through the trees.

And the Cherusci cheered as they surged forward, brandishing their throwing weapons that they unleashed as they drew level with the two cohorts of auxiliaries who loosed their first volley of one thousand six hundred javelins. In the opening moments of the ambush almost ten thousand lethal projectiles rained down towards the unshielded legionaries; although many thwacked, juddering, into trees, a goodly part of them flew true into their target, followed a few moments later by another volley almost as large, reaping bloody death and mayhem in the quickly disordered column. Hurling a javelin, I screamed the war cry of our forefathers and hurtled down the hill, flashing my sword from its scabbard as I went. All along the Roman line of march men writhed on the ground felled by the lethal downpour that intermingled with the natural rain that, along with the freshly spilt blood, turned the path into a quagmire.

But many more legionaries remained on their feet than went down and, being troops of the highest order, it was but a few moments before most of them had retrieved their shields, slung on their backs, and had begun to present a united front. The eight-man-wide column turned to face us as an eight-rank-deep line; and that was the moment I had told Hrodulf and Engilram to wait for.

And they did.

As we pelted down the hill, teeth bared, howling hatred, beards buffeted by the wind of our haste and eyes wide with fear and battle-joy, the volley that I hoped would break Roman cohesion thumped into the rear of their line, skewering unprotected necks and unshielded limbs and spreading terror through the rear ranks as they registered that they were under attack from both directions. But their discipline remained, despite the shock of a second ambush. Another hail of death slammed into them as their back ranks made to turn their shields to face this new threat, mowing down scores and creating gaps that they struggled to fill as we closed with them.

It was now that they began to see their opponents and the shock registered on many of their faces as they discerned not only Germanic tribesmen but the familiar uniforms and shield patterns of their auxiliaries. Formed to protect the legions and to give their cheaply rated lives in place of those of the more valuable citizens in the legions, the auxiliaries were now doing something unthinkable: they had turned on their betters. With a piercing clang of ringing iron that almost drowned out the rage of war cries and the desperate screams of the wounded, Egino's men cracked into the Seventeenth Legion, centred dead-on the fissure between the first and second cohorts. An instant later my Cherusci warriors threw themselves onto the rest of that legion and the Eighteenth behind it as a third volley from Hrodulf and Engilram's men thumped into the newly presented shield wall facing them. As I pummelled my shield boss into the rectangular shield of the legionary before me, thrusting the tip of my blade, overarm, at his ducking head, denting his helmet, I felt a shudder run through the Roman ranks as they were hit from behind, compressing their eight lines together, squeezing the men up so that sword work became restricted.

Sensing their opponents' difficulties, my Cherusci cheered as they hammered at shields with their swords and jabbed through the wide gaps between them with their spears, piercing and slicing flesh, cracking bone and causing grievous harm with the joy of men so long kept in the chains of occupation and now released to vent the pent-up rage that humiliation brings.

And they slew and they maimed so that the blood flowed so fast that the rain had not time to dilute it before it slopped to the ground; feet became clogged with cloying mud so glutinous that movement slowed for both legionary and warrior alike. It would have turned into a slogging match had it not been for one crucial factor: legionaries fight as a cohesive unit but my warriors fought as a collection of individuals. So the one-on-one combats lessened as the legionaries, knowing that not to do so would mean annihilation, pushed forward, closing up shoulder to shoulder, straightening their lines, and forming a wall of leather-reinforced wood. The blades of the Roman killing machine, which we all feared from haunted dreams, began to do their deadly work, hissing, lightning fast through the now narrowed gaps between the shields; they punctured our flesh like the stings of a hornet swarm. My warriors, enraged by the defiance, drew back and then hurled themselves against the wall, barging with shoulder-reinforced shields or flying one-booted kicks, not in unison but when each man had worked up the courage to try once more after the last attempt at making a breach had been thwarted by Roman teamwork. And, despite fighting to the fore and rear, the legion cohered.

I pulled back from the fray, passing beyond the more timid of our men who preferred to show their prowess by hurling insults and making false charges at the enemy, and ran a few paces back up the hill; my father joined me. From this vantage point I could see that the Seventeenth Legion, despite overwhelming odds, held firm; Only Egino's auxiliaries, to my right, had made any progress: between them and the auxiliary cohort that had descended from the opposite hill they had severed the legion's first cohort; but the head of the legion, despite being cut off, still had life in it and it fought like a wolf with slavering jaws.

It was at that point that I knew we would not manage to break them – this time – but perhaps we could vanquish that severed head.

'Enough, Tiburtius,' Thumelicatz interjected, jolting his guests back to the present. He turned to the second slave. 'Aius, you were part of that head; give us your recollections.'

The eyes of the once-proud Eagle-bearer of the Seventeenth misted over as he cast himself back to the last memories of his previous life. 'It was sudden and from the east; there was no warning, but then how could there be when it was the very units that were meant to alert us that were attacking us? Auxiliary javelins hissed all around, a couple cracked against the haft of the Eagle I held aloft causing it to sway and I stumbled in my efforts to keep it upright – for it to fall would have been the worst of omens. Horns blared and centurions roared orders. I went down on one knee to regain balance and that movement saved my life as, next to me, Pompilius, the *cornicern*, gave a strangled note on his horn and keeled over sideways with a javelin in his temple and surprise in his eyes. In front of us, the pioneers who had been clearing the way came pelting back down the path towards us as another volley clattered about my head. And then I saw it was our auxiliaries, the Marsian cohort, if my memory serves, as their forms came out of the trees, cloaked by rain, to manifest as our worst nightmare: allies bent on treachery. I felt my comrades pull me into their midst to protect our bird, as we liked to call the Eagle, and then the shock of impact shuddered through our ranks. They had hit the rear half of the cohort but we still felt it in the front ranks, and as we strove to turn and support our comrades behind us another shower of projectiles punched in on us but this time from the west. Fabius, the primus pilus, had gone back to Rome on leave and so the next most senior had taken over; cracking heads with the flat of his blade, he turned his century to the west to face the new threat as they were flayed yet again by another volley. The pioneers now joined us, shouting of enemy cavalry up ahead that had despatched the hundred-and-twenty-strong force of legionary horse that had been the advance guard; the trap must have been excellent if none of them had managed to escape it.

'Then the second blow came in from the west; more auxiliaries, but this time they hit the front of our cohort, slewing us round so that I could see all down the column from my position and the sight took my breath: thousands of barbar... thousands of Germanic warriors had sprung from the hill, covering our legion – which was the standard one thousand and two hundred paces long – and no doubt the Eighteenth behind us and maybe on into the baggage and the Nineteenth. Mates fell in sprays of blood, curses rang in my ears as I stood, immobile, holding our bird aloft with the standard-bearer of the first cohort next to me, giving our lads something to form on. And form they did, slowly;

getting over the shock and terror of surprise, they fell back on the innate discipline that is drilled into every legionary and is just second nature to the veterans of the first cohort. Shields came up and shoulders touched, the men of the second, third and fourth ranks facing in either direction made a roof, not that there were many missiles raining down on us as the combat was now hand to hand. And that was where we had the better of the auxiliaries who fight in a more dispersed order than us so that they can wield their longer spathae and negotiate on more rugged ground. But we closed up so there were three legionaries to each two auxiliaries and, although they had managed to separate us from the column, we locked ourselves down and soaked up all they could give us, never once letting them within our ranks.' Aius smiled at the memory. 'They might just as well have been attacking the camp's bathhouse.

'And then a voice, barely audible over the tumult of the battle and rain, could be heard: "Forward! Forward! On, men of the Seventeenth! On! Stay here and you'll die." The shout was taken up by our centurions and optios and we started to crab forward, pace by pace as the outside ranks held off the enemy taking deadened blows on their shield and flicking out their blades at our attackers, more in hope than expectation. How long we progressed like this I can't remember but after some while there was cheering from behind me, Roman cheering, and soon the word travelled up the cohort that we were no longer isolated: the second cohort had caught up with us, the column was once again intact and the general had made it to the front. Varus was with us, urging us forward to somewhere where we could build a camp. The very idea inspired us with hope and I dipped the Eagle to signal the legion's advance as if we were just on a route-march and not slogging through a forested vale beset on both sides.'

'And that is the brilliance of the famed discipline of the Roman legionary,' Thumelicatz said, cutting off Aius' monologue. 'By acting as one they could fend off many. Which general was it who said that he thought odds of seven to one were not unreasonable? No matter. Aius, the next scroll and start it from the point where I stopped you as Varus gets to the front of the column.'

CHAPTER XI

I could have wept with the frustration of it: seeing them, this enemy encased in a seemingly unbreakable wall of leather and wood, slowly moving forward whilst fending off the unco-ordinated attacks of my men, and there was nothing that I could do. How I wished then for artillery; but that was just a waste of thought.

Now I had to work out how to unravel the column's defence, to unpick it and eat at it from within and without. One thing was certain – throwing away the lives of my warriors by allowing them to carry on hurling themselves at the wall, for no better reason than to prove themselves braver than the next man, was not going to help. My father was of the same opinion as he and Vulferam found me gazing impotently at the three legions struggling on in the downpour; with a mighty breath he blew three blasts on his horn that echoed up and down the valley and was repeated by other thanes and gradually the warriors and auxiliaries disengaged and pulled back up the hill to either side. The column lumbered on heading ever northwest in the direction that my messengers had said the revolt was.

And that was it; the idea came to me. 'Father, we will let them go forward; have our men harry them with hit and run raids, keeping them nervous. They'll stop as soon as they find a suitable place to build a camp.'

My father looked at me sceptically. 'And how will we prise them out of that once it's built? You said yourself that our people don't have the discipline or mentality to conduct a siege.'

'We won't need to; I'll make sure he keeps moving northwest tomorrow and we'll wear him down slowly and then force him to a place of our choosing. I need to speak to Engilram.'

'So you failed and now the Cherusci's lives will be forfeit,' that unpleasant voice crowed from behind me.

I did not need to turn around to know that Adgandestrius was coming down the slope. 'No, we haven't failed, Adgandestrius; we just haven't succeeded yet.'

'You said that you had to defeat them on the first attack, break their formation and get amongst them.' He pointed down to the column that moved ponderously on, our men jeering at it from a safe distance. 'What's that, Erminatz? That is an intact Roman formation.'

I rounded on him, grabbing the collar of his tunic. 'Defeatism is the refuge of the timid, Adgandestrius, and I will not listen to it. You're right: the Cherusci's lives will be forfeit if Varus survives and someone tells him who was responsible for this; and I'm sure *someone* will. So therefore we have no choice but to keep on and make sure that Varus doesn't survive. So we keep at them; with this weather their progress will be slow so we'll hound them and whittle them down. You leave if you want to and take your warriors back to the taunting of their women; but the Cherusci stay here and hopefully so will the Chauci and the Bructeri.'

'And the Marsi will join them.'

I looked beyond Adgandestrius to see Mallovendatz, the young king of the Marsi, standing a few paces away, dripping with rain, listening to our confrontation.

'Perhaps five thousand more warriors would have made the

difference.' Mallovendatz paused and looked me in the eye; he seemed uncomfortable as his mouth searched for words. Eventually he found them: 'I have not been as worthy as Engilram or Hrodulf and I have heard mumblings amongst my thanes as we watched the attack; they wanted to be a part of it. I know if I order them away now that will be the last order I give. I have learnt much this last hour. The Marsi stay and I will fight in their front rank and regain the respect of my people.'

I let go of Adgandestrius, took off my helmet and felt under-cap, and let the rain wash away the sweat. 'You won't regret it, Mallovendatz; whether you live or die your name will be held in glory by your tribe and all the tribes in this place.' I looked pointedly at Adgandestrius.

'I never said we were leaving,' the Chatti king hissed.

'Nor have you said that you're fighting.' I turned to Vulferam. 'Send messages to our auxiliaries: they're to keep in position on either flank of the column just within sight of it; that should keep the bastards nervous.' I addressed Mallovendatz as Vulferam disappeared into the foul weather: 'The tribes will take it in turns to attack various points of the column and try to split it in half, so it …' I trailed off leaving him the opportunity to regain some respect in front of his thanes.

Mallovendatz understood what I was offering. 'It would be the Marsi's honour to make the first of those attacks.'

'And it would be my pleasure to watch you do so.'

And so the first day proceeded as the sun descended into the west, unseen behind clouds laden with rain and battered by wind, with each tribe making an attack at some point of the column and always being rebuffed. The casualties trailed behind the line of march, covered in slops of mud, the wounded tribesmen were taken to shelter and the legionaries despatched with various degrees of mercy depending on the number of comrades the warrior wielding the knife had lost in the day. On we went, Varus sending out cavalry sorties, using the two Gallic cavalry alae that had remained loyal to him, trying to catch our infantry unsupported, picking off a few here and there but never doing us enough damage for me to become concerned.

Night fell and the rain did not lessen, nor did Varus ease up on his men; they remained in column, unable to build a camp in such wooded conditions, edging blindly on as there was very little point in staying still. In the complete darkness of the night we could not see enough to mount any meaningful attacks, so we contented ourselves with hurling missiles and shooting arrows into what we thought was their formation. The occasional cry of pain gave us heart but the exercise was not so much to kill the odd legionary but more to keep every one of them on his guard, shields up and wary as fatigue began to eat away at their morale.

Our warriors were rested by rota, but whether they managed to get much rest in the sodden conditions I doubt. However, by the time the sun turned the night sky into dark grey our men were eager to throw themselves again at the column.

And in they went in the wake of javelin volleys hurled over their heads timed to strike the column moments before the charges hit home. The legionaries struggled to keep order on muddied ground that had already been churned by the passing of thousands of hobnailed military sandals. Pain and death was dealt out to the men encased in their iron armour and hiding behind their semi-cylindrical shields, but always they gave back as much as they got, and no matter where we struck we could not force a split in the column. For they had distributed the baggage train evenly within it and the legionaries marched in four files on either side of it so there were no natural gaps. Cohort segued onto cohort and legion melded into legion so that the formation had become one long shielded line of heavily armoured men; and not just men, but the best soldiers in the world. We had to break them up, but how?

As the second day came to a close and the Romans finally broke out from under the eaves of the trees and into some more open country within the Wald, cultivated to a certain extent and rich with pasture, I knew that this night they would be able, despite the continuing rain, to construct a camp of some sort. I decided to summon the kings and their thanes for it was time to take counsel together.

'They have started to build their camp on some land cleared for grazing, a couple of miles from here,' my father told the assembled kings and thanes, sitting on logs around a fire pit over which two spitted boars roasted. A leather awning had been rigged over us with a hole for the smoke to escape. All bar the Chatti had fought and we were now committed. Below us the path of the legions was illumined by the blaze of many oil-fuelled pyres on which our dead were consumed; their light danced on the stripped and dripping corpses of a couple of thousand legionaries marking the legions' passing and attesting to the very real damage we had inflicted that day and the previous one. 'The Nineteenth Legion has formed up facing us with the two loyal auxiliary cavalry ala, one on either flank, whilst the other two legions do the construction. We're trying to disrupt the work as far as possible but the fatigue parties are well protected. They'll have their perimeter secure by nightfall.'

There was a general disappointed mumbling but no one looked accusingly at me. The aroma of the sizzling meat wafted around the circle reminding us of our hunger.

I shrugged. 'We can't stop them from hiding in their camp but we can prevent them from sleeping too much in it; we'll launch a fire attack at the fourth hour of the night.'

'Why not as soon as it's dark?' Engilram asked. 'That would stop them getting any rest whatsoever.'

'Because I need a pause in order to get a messenger through the lines to Varus.' This statement was greeted with complete bemusement from all present but I did nothing to clarify what I was about. 'Engilram, you know the Wald better than any of us here; if Varus keeps travelling towards the supposed revolt in the lands of the Ampsivarii, will he pass a place where we could pen him in and kill him?'

The old king stoked his beard, his eyes glinting in the firelight, as he mentally went over the geography of the great forest that he had known all his life. 'There is a place on the edge of the Teutoburg Wald,' he said eventually. 'It's a pass that would suit our purpose very well. Just over a day's march from here, to the northwest, there's a huge area of marshland; there's a track that passes between its western side and a range of hills. A lot of the land between the marsh and the hills has been cleared for agriculture in a strip about half a mile wide that narrows. If Varus were to move in that direction, it would be the obvious way to go as it leads out of the Wald to more open countryside beyond. At one point the hills come very close to the marsh, so that there is little more than a hundred paces of open ground.'

I saw immediately what he was getting at. 'Easy to block off, you mean?'

'Yes. The whole area is about a mile long; it's called the Teutoburg Pass and it's overlooked by a hill that we call the Chalk Giant in our dialect.'

'Kalk Riese?'

'Exactly. It's wooded but has hardly any undergrowth so it's very easy to move through but at the same time it provides cover. At its summit the trees have been cleared for pasture; we could easily have every warrior we have with us concealed on that hill waiting for Varus. But how could we guarantee that he would travel in that direction when the obvious thing for him to do is stay safely behind the walls of his camp, send messengers out and wait for relief?'

'Not if he thinks that the whole of northern Germania is in revolt and today's attack was a coordinated attempt at stopping him from coming to my aid in crushing it.'

My father smiled slow and with pride in his eyes as he looked at me. 'Of course, Erminatz, that is deep thinking and worthy of my son: make him believe that the leaders of the revolt want him to stay in his camp and wait for help and he'll be minded to do the exact opposite. But how to get him to consider that?'

I looked at Vulferam, seated next to him. 'Would you be willing to act as a false messenger and slip into the Roman camp after dark?'

'If it was not for you I would still be fighting on the sand of the arena, Erminatz; or, more likely, dead. I can deny you nothing.'

There was much nodding of heads, hooming and rumbles of approval at that sentiment.

'Thank you,' I said, hoping that I was not sending the man to a very unpleasant death. 'At the second hour of the night, slip into the Roman camp; demand to see Varus, saying that you've come with a message from me. He'll recognise you and, with luck, believe you when you tell him that I'm tied down fighting overwhelming odds and desperately need his assistance if the revolt is not to spread. Tell him that the attack on him today was an attempt to stop him coming to my aid and that the rebels plan either to destroy him or to keep him penned up in his camp for as long as possible in the hope of raising the whole of the north against Rome.'

'Why will he believe me?'

'Because you will also warn him that the rebels plan to attack the camp at the fourth hour of the night.'

Vulferam gave a broken-toothed smile. 'Which you will and that will convince him that I am loyal to Rome.'

'Exactly.' My mind again went back to the night of the fire when Lucius and I freed him. 'He won't notice that you're wrong because he will think that you are fighting the mutual threat.'

'But it'll also mean that he's ready for our attack,' Adgandestrius said, clearly disgusted. 'And we'll lose more men than we would if it was a surprise.'

'I didn't think you were going to lose any men seeing as you still haven't committed to the fight; but you're right: those that have committed their warriors will most likely lose more men than they would have otherwise. But I consider that a fair exchange for Varus believing Vulferam and deciding to move off tomorrow, out into the open and towards the Kalk Riese Hill. My friends, do I have your agreement?'

'The Marsi will play their part,' Mallovendatz stated; his thanes, to either side of him, growled their agreement into their beards, not concealing their pleasure at their king deciding to fight. One by one all the other kings assented and Adgandestrius was left isolated as Vulferam was sent on his way.

All that I could do as we assembled the warriors for the night attack was pray to Loki, the god of cunning and deceit, that Varus would believe Vulferam. I was told later by one of the slaves to whom I'm dictating this that he ...

'Wait,' Thumelicatz interrupted, 'that was you was it not, Aius?'

'It was, master; I was in the praetorium when Vulferam was shown into Varus' presence.'

'Well? Speak.'

Aius bowed his head in acknowledgement of his master's will. 'Vulferam greeted Varus as if he were so relieved at finally finding him. "General," Vulferam said, his breath laboured as if he had just undergone great exertion, "thank the gods of our two lands that I've found you. Arminius sent me to beg urgently that you come to his aid; the Ampsivarii have risen and the Frisii will join them if they are not soon crushed."

'I remember Varus looking at him oddly, as if he could not quite understand what he was seeing and hearing. "How did you get in here? We're surrounded by Germani." "I know, they're trying to prevent you from moving forward. But I am Germanic; nobody stopped me slipping through the enemy's lines, and anyway they're busy forming up for an attack. It looks like they're going to try a fire attack in the next hour or so."

'That caused the general to issue a stream of orders sending cohorts to man the ramparts and to have others standing by in reserve should there be a breach. Once he had done this he took Vulferam aside and questioned him closely as to the situation in the north and exactly where he could find Arminius; it was then that his fate was sealed.

'Vulferam said: "When I left him he was falling back in the face of a huge war band that was threatening to overwhelm him;

thankfully they were mostly infantry so Arminius could outpace them. He's northwest of here, on the edge of the Teutoburg Wald at the northern end of a large area of marshland. He said that he would wait there for you for four days and if you didn't come then he would try his best to deal with the rebels with the resources that he had."

'Varus was full of concern. "How long ago was this?"

'Vulferam replied: "That was dawn this morning; I rode hard to get here. You could be there in two days, general; it's not too late if you leave tomorrow."

"'And I could have the rebellion quashed by the end of the month." Varus thought for a few moments and then gave the answer that destroyed three legions. "Very well, ride back, to him and tell him I'll be there in two days' time despite all the efforts the rebels are making to stop me."

'Vulferam bowed and left as I carried on supervising the fatigue party that was polishing the birds and the other standards in their sacred place in the praetorium.'

Thumelicatz turned to his guests. 'So it was not stupidity that led Varus on, it was loyalty and honour. Loyalty to his supposed friend, my father and the honour of Rome which was in his hands as the Governor of Germania Magna. Read on, Aius, from the night attack.'

It took the Eagle-bearer a few moments to pull himself out from the memories that he had just been ordered to share and it was with moisture in his eyes that he tore himself away from the image of the sacred standard that he had lost.

Fire is a double-edged weapon: whilst its destructive power is immense and its ability to instil the very real terror of an agonised death into even the most stout-hearted enemy is undeniable, it also has the major disadvantage of giving away the position of the men wielding it. With the benefit of prior warning an enemy may wreak havoc upon a fire attack; but we pressed ahead with it anyway. We had to. For two reasons: firstly Varus had to see Vulferam as truthful and reliable, and secondly it was the obvious way for us to attack a fortified camp seeing as we did not have the engines or the ability with which to conduct a siege.

And so our men perished by the score as we pelted across the open ground to the ditch and breastwork surrounding the Roman camp, carrying blazing torches, pitch-soaked faggots and skins of oil. With surprise not the issue we roared the battle cries of our forefathers and invoked the protection of our gods and the love of our women as fire-arrows left trails above our heads and then thwacked into the camp's wooden palisade. Ballista bolts, unseen in the dark, hissed past to disintegrate heads and to thump, hollow and wet, into chests heaving with exertion, picking warriors up, screaming, to slam into the men behind, coupling them with bloodied iron and leaving them writhing together on the ground.

From all sides we came and on all sides they defended. Our archers kept up volley after volley of fire-arrows, blazing across the night sky like plagues of shooting stars, but that did not keep the defenders down behind the parapet, and as we came within pilum range the weighted missiles hurtled down onto us, crunching into once-fearless faces, pinning shields to chests, bending on impact, the hafts gouging into the earth to trip the impaled warrior and send him, shrieking, tumbling down to bleed out in pain-wracked gasps for breath. But still we came on and hurled our skins of oil so that they burst upon the defences, throwing the torches after them, igniting the soaked wood and then, with the bravery of men who saw no difference between feasting with our forefathers in Walhalla or with kith and kin in this life, we scrambled down into the ditch, mostly avoiding the fire-hardened stakes, and tried to lodge the faggots at the base of the walls to add to the growing conflagration, as missiles continued to rain down upon us. Thrice we charged and thrice we fell back, leaving our dead and maimed behind us, the defences aflame and the defenders desperately dousing them with whatever non-flammable liquids they could find so that by the time we fell back for the third time, around the eighth hour of the night, the air was thick with pungent woodsmoke and urine-heavy steam; but fire burnt unrestrained within their camp even if they had managed to control the flames on the palisade.

'Bring all the warriors back to the southern side of the camp,' I ordered as we regrouped beneath the trees that skirted the farmland after the third and final attack. 'Varus will be thinking about leaving soon and we wouldn't want to prevent him.'

'Never disturb your enemy when he's making a mistake,' my father said, quoting a maxim that I knew had come down the generations of Cherusci kings, 'it's impolite.'

I grinned, blinking the rain from my eyes, and as I did so the gates to the north of the camp opened and out galloped the advance guard of two alae of Gallic cavalry. They drew up, their shadowy forms lit by the flicker of the fires raging within the camp, to fashion a screen for the legions that began to emerge from the camp to the blare of their horns. Rank upon rank came out, silhouetted in the pre-dawn light to march to the aid of the man who watched them go; the man who was not ahead of them but behind them. And I felt moved by Varus' loyalty and trust but not so that I suffered the pangs of pity; I just respected his honour, for all the good it would do him.

CHAPTER XII

'ENOUGH FOR THE moment, Aius,' Thumelicatz said, holding up a hand and casting his eye over his four guests and smiling. 'So, Romans, here we have a fine thing: Varus' sense of loyalty was to prove to be the death of almost all of his men. He left the relative safety of his fortified camp to march to the aid of a man he considered to be his friend even though Segestes had tried to impress upon him just how mistaken he was in that assumption. Yet still he went, blinded to reality by the belief, instilled by Rome's outrageous arrogance, that once a man has received citizenship it is inconceivable that he should ever turn his back on what is obviously the only civilisation of any worth in this Middle-Earth. With admirable motivation, Varus set out to come to the aid of the very man who had put him in such peril by conjuring a rebellion in the north; a rebellion that was all too easy for him to believe in as he well knew the extent of the enmity that bubbled beneath the surface of the newly seized province.'

'It wasn't just his misplaced loyalty to Arminius that made him go,' the younger brother said, a touch of petulance in his voice. 'In fact, I would suggest that was the secondary factor: his and Rome's honour were both at stake as far as he was concerned. According to the false message that Vulferam had delivered, Arminius was going to wait for four days by the swamp so it wouldn't have sounded to Varus as if he was in any imminent danger. You should be able to understand this,

Thumelicus, with your experience of Rome: yes, you are right when you assert that we have such strong certainty in the Idea of Rome that we find it hard to understand why a man would wish to turn from that ideal, but what makes that concept so strong in our minds is that fusion of one's personal and family honour with the honour of the empire itself. The two concepts are inseparable and with the possibility, fictional, granted, of the revolt spreading to the Frisii in the far north it would have seemed to Varus that Rome's honour was being threatened and therefore, by implication, so was his and his family's. Should he leave the rebellion unchecked and hide behind his palisade awaiting another man of noble birth to lead an expedition to extract him and his legions whilst the province disintegrated about him, his shame would have been insufferable and there would have been no option left to him other than to fall upon his sword. He had to go, whether he considered Arminius his friend or not. Each one of his officers and men would have understood why staying put was not an option.'

Thumelicatz took a swig of his drink as he pondered this asser-tion for a few moments, before turning his attention back to Aius. 'What say you, slave? When you still held your honour intact would you have defended it, and that of Rome's, even though it would have meant a hazardous journey towards a supposed rebellion under attack all the time by tribesmen and some of your own auxiliaries who, as far as you understood, were trying to prevent you from reaching the rebel area?'

For the first time, Aius met his master's eye and there was a slight hardening in his look as if the years of slavery were starting to shed and dignity was reasserting itself once more. 'That was the only option open to us; every man in those legions would have made the same decision as our general and they would also have left the camp in the same condition as he did, knowing all too well the greed of uncivilised tribesmen.' His eyes lowered back to the scroll in his hand.

Thumelicatz tensed, his fist clenching, as if he was about to strike his slave for answering the question with candour. After a couple of heartbeats he relaxed and gave a grim chuckle. 'So you still have your balls in place after all these years, slave; but mind how they affect your speech, else you may well see them being added to this jar. But you are right, I cannot deny it; the way Varus left his camp did make a difference: it bought him another day, or so he thought, but did not, ultimately, affect the result. It did, however, bring shame upon my father's alliance and showed the Germanic nature not in the best light. Read on, Aius, I'm sure this is a passage that you secretly enjoy.'

Whether or not his master's assumption was correct did not show on the old slave's face, now veiled again with subservience, as he scanned the scroll and began to read.

The sun had risen high behind the heavy, leaden clouds and the fires still burning within the camp had died down by the time the rearguard had passed through the gate and the auxiliary cohorts facing us, protecting the column's flank, withdrew. In all that time we did not show ourselves, keeping our men under the cover of the forest, hidden from the open ground and the Roman camp, resting and feeding, building their strength back up for what would come. As the last footfall of more than ten thousand surviving marching men faded into the distance I had the tribes muster, ready to harass the Roman advance: the Chauci and the Marsi to their right, the Cherusci and the Bructeri to their left with the Sugambri staying behind them to pick off stragglers.

'The Chatti are free to follow us, if you have the stomach for it,' I told Adgandestrius as I met with the kings and their thanes as well as the prefects of the auxiliaries who had joined us to discuss the disposition of the tribes, as while herding Varus northwest it was vital to ensure that he passed between the marsh and the Kalk Riese.

The Chatti king spat at my feet, sneering; behind him his followers bristled and gripped their sword hilts, ready to support their king should the insult be deemed intolerable. 'The Chatti will not be found wanting; we will fight if and when you force Varus to the killing ground. There you will see just what the Chatti have the stomach for. After that, Erminatz, we will have an accounting and I think it will be you who will be found wanting: wanting of manners.'

I raised my hands in a conciliatory gesture. 'If you are promising to fight, Adgandestrius, then I apologise for my manners or lack of them. Forgive me so that we may draw swords together in a common cause.'

We locked glares and a tension ran between us, neither saying a word, as all those around remained silent, ready for violence; but violence did not break out, as Adgandestrius knew that he could not refuse the apology made in front of so many men of high status united in their enmity towards Rome – whatever he thought of me personally. He slowly relaxed, nodding his head in agreement as his lips beneath his beard cracked into a smile that did not reach his eyes. 'We will fight together, Erminatz, and let that be an end to it.'

'Then the Chatti will join the Sugambri and drive the column from the rear.'

'We will do so because we choose to, not because you have ordered us to.'

'Then it is a good choice.' Satisfied that I would get no more from him I turned to the rest of the kings. 'We will catch up with their rear units in an hour or so and then we will spend the rest of the day wearing down what's left of their morale. Keep at them constantly: missile volleys and lightning attacks. They must never feel safe so that the fear grows in the hearts of the common legionary. Then, when it's dark, Engilram will lead us to the Kalk Riese. The Bructeri, Cherusci, Chatti and Sugambri will take position on the hill itself whilst the Marsi and the Chauci will cut off any possibility of retreat so that we will have them completely at our mercy and we shall withhold.'

'What about preventing them from going forward?' Engilram asked.

'That is down to you, my friend. Send all the warriors you can spare ahead by the shortest route to the Teutoburg Pass and prepare the ground. The pass must be blocked; fell as many trees as you can between your Chalk Giant and the swamp to make the way impassable. Have another party take our store of javelins and arrows with them so that we have sufficient weaponry there waiting for us. We will fall on the column just before they reach the barrier; they will try and move forward quickly to escape us and find the way obstructed. At this point they will realise that they have walked into a well-laid trap and the fear that we've built up within their hearts will overflow as they see that there is neither a way forward nor back and they have been brought to the place of their death. As they despair we'll reap their lives and not one will escape; not one.' I looked around the group and there was no sign of dissent, even Adgandestrius stroked his beard and hoomed his agreement along with the rest; I now knew that I had won all these proud men over to my will and with them I could strike the greatest blow for our Fatherland, the land of All Men. Our failure to finish the business on the first day was now behind us for we could all see how Varus would be trapped in the shadow of the Chalk Giant, and with nowhere to go and demoralised troops he would stand no chance. 'So, my friends, go now and lead your men well and may the gods of our land help us to rid ourselves of the invader.'

But the gods of our land include Loki; he tricks and deceives for his own amusement and that day he played a jest that nearly cost our land its freedom. The abandoned camp, itself a huge affair – almost half a mile square – lay in our path as we followed the Roman trail. I had paid it no mind; why should I have as it was just an empty marching camp bereft of its inhabitants and containing now just the smouldering remains of the fires set by our attack the previous night? I gave no orders to avoid it and as the tribes moved forward they passed to either side and saw that the gates were open; and what lay within was too much to resist, as Varus knew it would be when Loki inspired him to such a trick: he had abandoned his baggage and had concealed his action by using the cover of our fire attack to set his own wagons alight.

Within the four walls the camp remained intact: rows of leather tents still stood as if the eight men sharing each one were yet asleep within. Through them swarmed our men, my men, out of control as they swooped down on the plunder of three legions. And I cursed Varus and Loki in equal measure for I realised that the two cavalry alae that had covered each side of the camp as Varus led his men out were placed there for a dual purpose: they were not just for fending off any foray that we may have attempted; they were also there to obscure our line of sight so that we would not notice that the baggage train was not a part of the column but, rather, had remained within the camp as a smouldering wreck of wagons. In one move Varus had speeded up his advance unencumbered by the slow baggage train that would delay our moving on until it had been picked through and every item of value appropriated. Only what could be carried on the backs of mules had been taken; anything requiring wheeled transport had been forsaken.

Varus had played me for a fool.

What could I do? I was helpless in the face of the greed of men who have little and desire to better themselves in any way that they can. And there was much to take as it was not the baggage of an army on campaign, travelling light; no, this was the baggage of an army on its way from its summer quarters to its winter home, an army that was taking everything it owned with it. That was the mark of how desperate Varus must have felt if he and his men were prepared to leave all that loot behind. All that to buy them the time to link up with me – or so they thought – in the northwest so that together we could put down a rebellion that did not exist. He must have calculated that once victorious he would be able to reclaim much of what had been lost from the defeated tribes; either the original items or in kind. Whatever had gone through his mind his ploy had worked and I looked in impotent rage at the unrestrained marauding of my six tribes, unleashed on the treasure of an army.

Through the camp they swooped, taking all that they could find, weighing themselves down with plunder. It was not just the heavy leather tents or the amphorae of wine or bushels of grain, it was the mills to grind that grain; it was the quarter-masters' stores of armour, military sandals, tunics, cloaks, blankets and weaponry, some of which had survived the fires, as well as the remains of the butchered carcasses of the draft-oxen.

And then there was the pay chest buried beneath the praetorium.

This one sacrifice was enough to guarantee that I had no chance of moving my army forward until every scrap of ground had been searched. Varus had been very cunning: the chest had been buried in an obvious manner so that it would be discovered; and it was not even full. Most of the tribesmen, however, couldn't see that it had been left as bait, to tempt them into thinking that there could be more – which, of course, there wasn't. But no one can talk sense into a man in the grip of greed.

'I've had some of our warriors secure the praetorium,' Vulferam said, breaking into my misery as, above, the Thunderer, as if in disgust at his children's behaviour, cracked open the skies with a reverberating strike and rain flooded through the resulting rent. Almost three hours had passed since the looting began and there was no sign of it abating.

I was momentarily confused and then managed to focus. 'And the tent's contents?'

'All gone; it seems as if Varus was only too happy to let everyone else abandon their belongings but his have been packed up and taken.'

Thumelicatz held up his hand. 'And that was so, Aius, was it not?' He gestured at the rich furnishings and lavish silverware that adorned what had once been Varus' command tent.

Aius inclined his head in agreement. 'Indeed, master, he had all this loaded onto mules.'

'And what was everyone else allowed to take?'

'We had been issued with four days' rations and could take whatever we could load onto our contubernium's mule, which was why every eight-man tent-party had chosen to leave their tent and grain-mill behind so as to get as many personal possessions on the beast as possible – much good it did us.'

Thumelicatz smiled in satisfaction. 'Yes, we've been finding coins along the battle's path ever since and will, no doubt, carry on doing so for many years to come.'

'But at the time we thought that the general was doing the right thing and that without the baggage train slowing us down we would escape the rebels' pursuit and soon join forces with Arminius ... I'm sorry, master, Erminatz, and then, once clear of the Wald we would be able to stand and fight on open ground.'

'And then victory would have been yours,' Thumelicatz scoffed.

'Of course, master; that's what we all believed because it had always been so: no barbarians could defeat three Roman legions head-on, and your father understood that because he had decided to ambush the column rather than face it.'

Thumelicatz's fist slammed into the old slave's face, cracking his head back with a surprised cry. 'Don't assume to know what my father did or didn't understand, slave. Your role is to read his words and answer my questions, not to make suppositions that you cannot possibly support.'

The street-fighter made to intervene but was restrained by the two brothers.

Aius hung his head, his hands holding his face as blood dripped through the fingers from a misshapen nose. 'I apologise, master,' he whispered, his voice shaking with pain, 'I spoke out of turn.'

Tiburtius looked on impassively, giving no clue as to his feelings on the treatment of his fellow slave.

'Get on with the reading,' Thumelicatz said before turning back to his guests. 'As you can see, there is still some spirit left in him even after thirty-three years of slavery.'

None of the Romans ventured their opinions on the condition of one who had been of the foremost in his legion.

Aius wiped away the blood with the back of his hand and then dried it on his tunic before picking up the scroll again.

An empty Praetorian tent was of little use to me but I thanked Vulferam nonetheless because it would be expected of me, by all my warriors, to take that as a prize, otherwise I would lose face in their eyes should one of the kings claim Varus' property for his own; having just gained control of the army I could not afford to lose it over a matter of principle.

Then, through the chaos of the looting, I saw the man I needed to speak to most urgently if the situation was not to be lost. 'Engilram!' I bellowed over the cacophony of greed. 'Engilram!'

The old king heard me and made his way over to where I stood.

'Engilram, please tell me that you, at least, have some control of your men.'

Engilram looked grave but his words brought me relief. 'Two hundred I've sent on ahead with the promise of more silver than they would have scavenged from the ruins of the camp; they left a couple of hours ago. It'll cost me dearly but it was the only way to tear them away from the looting.'

I squeezed his shoulder, my heart thumping with relief, and looked into his eyes with mine full of gratitude. 'It will be made up to you by double what you're forced to pay, my friend. Because of you we still have the chance to finish this thing properly.'

'I know, Erminatz; but we'll need to hurry; if Varus sets a good pace he'll arrive at the Kalk Riese tomorrow afternoon. We have to leave soon in order to be able to skirt around him and be waiting when he arrives.'

And that was the reality that I had already confronted in my head but did not know how to overcome: not only were we far behind the Roman column now but we were also burdened down with plunder. There was no way that I could see of us being able to travel fast enough or stealthily enough to be able to get in position to crush the column without them being aware of our presence. There was nothing else to do other than wait for the frenzy to be over and then address the army as a whole and appeal to them to leave their loot for the time being in order that a greater victory could be gained.

Perhaps I had a use for Varus' praetorium after all. I turned to Vulferam. 'Have Varus' tent packed away and brought to me.'

Vulferam nodded and went off to fulfil my wishes as I stood, watching the continued looting, waiting with little patience.

I had to wait for another precious hour before the warriors, by mutual consent, decided that the camp had been picked bare and there were no other pay chests buried within its walls. I called upon the kings to muster their tribes on the ground to its north and prepared to regain the initiative by leading by example.

'Brothers, fellow sons of All Men,' I shouted from the improvised dais before the assembled tribes standing in the steady rain, 'we have been fortunate in that we have enriched ourselves without any great struggle. Each of us has some prize or other; some of great worth, and others less so.' I punched a fist into the air. 'Let us cheer our good fortune!'

This was uncontroversial and produced a roar from the assembly as they celebrated their luck. For many heartbeats I led them in the celebration until I judged that they were ready for what I had to say. I stretched my arms out wide, palms down, and hushed almost thirty thousand men who now wanted to listen to me.

'Fortune has favoured us, but it has done so at a price.'

I paused to let them wonder what the price could be and, judging by the faces of those nearest to me, it was not obvious to them.

'The price is that we have been diverted from our real task, the reason that we have come on this venture. And it was planned that it should be thus, planned by our enemy; Rome has tricked us.'

Again I paused to let that sink in and for each man to begin to feel outrage at being duped even if they did not comprehend just how.

'This booty that we all hold was always going to be ours; but in having it now, having it early, it is missing a vital ingredient: it is not covered in the blood of the former owners. No, my brothers, we've been cheated; all this should have come to us over the dead bodies of Varus and his legions. And where is Varus? Where are his legions? Can you see their bodies lying limp on the ground? No, my brothers! No, you cannot! You cannot because they are miles from here and their hearts still beat and their limbs are still intact. They are still alive on Germanic soil; our soil; the soil of our Fatherland where All Men should dwell in freedom!'

This sent them into cries of indignation as they realised that what I had said was the truth and that they had been blinded by greed that had been provoked by their enemy. Now, shamed, their indignation began to turn to anger.

'But it is not too late, my brothers; it is just half a day since they left this place; we can still catch them. We can still kill them, all of them!'

The howl that erupted from the combined tribes drowned anything they had produced previously; it was a howl for blood, for vengeance and for honour.

Now I had them. 'We must make haste, my brothers, if we are to catch them; we must leave immediately and we must travel fast and light.' I turned to Vulferam, standing beneath me, next to the dais. 'Vulferam, bring me my share of the booty.'

As a dozen or so of my Cherusci heaved and manhandled the packed Praetorian tent to the front of the dais I stood, looking at it, making a show of scratching my head and rubbing my chin as if I was very deep in thought.

When finally the huge bundle was in position, I looked up at my audience; they quietened to hear me. 'But how will I travel fast and light, my brothers, if I am weighed down with my share of the booty? Should I give it to others so that they take the burden whilst I rush to avenge my pride? But what about the pride of those others? No, my brothers; I shall not ask others to make such a sacrifice; I shall, instead, abandon my booty and leave it here and I shall ask the wounded, those who will not be able to keep up the pace that we shall surely need, to look after it until such time as I can return to reclaim it. Thus I shall stand a chance of catching Varus and his legions. Who will follow me and do likewise?'

None now could, in honour, fail to do as I had; the field was soon covered in discarded loot as the wounded of each tribe were brought out to look after their compatriots' share.

Now we were ready; now the chase could begin.

*

Along the trampled trail I raced at the head of the Cherusci
with my father and uncle at my heels; rain and low-hanging
branches whipped into my face and my boots slipped in the
churned mud but I still managed to keep up the pace. Behind
me the six tribes followed, every man chastened by the way
Varus had exploited their inner greed by his ruse and each
determined in his desire to catch the Roman column and
punish it for bringing such shame.

Never letting our speed slacken to less than a jog and
sometimes breaking into a full run, we pursued our quarry and
within three hours had started to come across the stragglers;
some singularly and some in small groups. It did not matter
for they died the same way: in a rush of iron as we sped past,
not even bothering to slow our pace as we sliced the life out
of them, their eyes staring in final terror at the flood of warriors
tearing through the rain. More and more we met the closer
we drew to the rearguard of the Nineteenth Legion and none
escaped our wrath. Those that tried to flee found nowhere to
go as our frontage, by this time, was so spread out that there
was no way around us and their exhaustion precluded fleeing
before us. Mercy they could not expect and they knew it so
none pleaded for his life, relieved to have a swift death rather
than be subjected to our fires; some made a stand and some
just went down under our blades to be trampled beneath our
ever moving feet.

On we went through semi-open hilly ground, a mixture of
farmland and wood, given over to agriculture and coppicing,
but on this day deserted in the wake of three legions. Soon the
hills began to close up and the husbanded land became less

frequent as the forest began, once again, to hold sway. Our pace lessened but I did not mind as I knew that what affected us adversely was even harder for thousands of close-order infantry marching in column.

And then, as the sun started to make its way down to the western horizon, we saw them; we saw the rear ranks of the Nineteenth Legion, which were, by my estimation, at least a mile and a half from the vanguard at the front of the reduced column. Such was our joy that we cheered and bellowed our praise to the gods of our Fatherland so that the legionaries heard us and cried out in fear, warning the ranks ahead of them that they had not escaped the terror that chased them. And so it was without the element of surprise that we plunged our blades into the rear cohort of the Nineteenth.

Along their left side we swarmed, hacking and stabbing with sword and spear; but despite our numbers and the intensity of our hatred, their superior discipline held them intact as they locked shields and, with blades flashing between the gaps, edged forward, the rear ranks stepping backwards as they fought us off. Up the column we went but found their defence solid; here and there a less-experienced legionary let down his guard and fell beneath a flurry of blows but always his comrade next to him would take his place, so that there forever seemed to be a wall of wood and leather that we could not get past.

By now the following tribes had caught up with us and began flowing to either side of the column, the Chauci and the Marsi to the right and the Bructeri joining us on the left. I ordered my Cherusci to disengage and we melted into the forest along with the Bructeri, to make our way, unseen, up the column in order that the fear of being surrounded by an invisible enemy would start to gnaw at the guts of every man under each of the three

Eagles that were our prey; for total demoralisation now had to
be the objective of the next few hours until dusk and then on
through the night. It was to that end that I met with Engilram
of the Bructeri as we drew level with the head of the column.

'How far to the Kalk Riese?' I asked the old king.

Engilram ran his fingers through his beard. 'Assuming that
they will stop for the night in a couple of hours, I think they
should arrive soon after noon tomorrow.'

'We shall keep pressing them; missile volleys to disrupt them
followed by short raids as their defences are in disarray. And
try to bring back some prisoners.'

And so it was, as Varus' men slogged along the track,
ankle-deep in mud, keeping eight abreast, their shields in
hand ready to defend themselves, we swooped down on them
from the cover of the rain-swathed forest to either side of the
column; lightning raids, deadly and demoralising, ever picking
a different target and ever leaving a trail of corpses so that the
cohorts following behind would have to stare into the vacant
eyes of the dead. When we could we grabbed screaming men
from their formation and bundled them back up the hill. No
respite did we give them and nor did the Chauci and the
Marsi operating on the other side, so that the air was always
filled with the screams of the maimed and the dying and every
man in the column would expect it to be their turn for death
soon, constantly looking with trepidation over their shoulders,
peering into the shadows beneath the dripping canopy ever
driven on by the Chatti and Sugambri at the column's tail so
that no rest was possible and there was no time to tend wounds.
The best medicine a wounded man could hope for became
the sword, for none wanted to fall into our hands alive, as they
all knew of our fires and our skill at administering a lingering

death and had seen how we had plucked prisoners from their ranks. And I had given orders that there should be no quick death for those taken alive and I hoped that many would be so taken, for I had plans for them that night; plans that Lucius would have approved of had he been in my place.

As dusk approached, the head of the column came to a rounded hill at a place that Engilram told me was called the Feldenfelt because of the stony nature of the ground; and it was here that the training of the legions was seen to full advantage. The auxiliary cavalry formed a protective screen, riding down any attempted attack aimed at disrupting the manoeuvring of the Seventeenth Legion as they split down the middle with four files heading left and four right around the hill so that before we had time to react the entire hill was surrounded by a cordon of legionaries four deep. Two legionaries stood guard for every two men digging and in less than an hour the hill was surrounded by a four-foot-deep ditch with waist-high breastwork. It was into this defensive position that the battered Eighteenth and the, by now, severely mauled Nineteenth Legion marched. Interspersed with them were what remained of their camp-followers, their numbers even more depleted than the legions as we had not differentiated between soldiers and civilians; all had to die and an unarmed woman or child is easier to kill than an armoured legionary.

And so Varus managed to bring his men to rest for the night on the day that he had very nearly managed to slip from my grasp. Although his losses were not nearly as dramatic as the previous couple of days, they had still been considerable and that evening fewer than nine thousand men made camp in the rain-sodden open, less than half the number that he had originally set out with.

'And how did the men feel as they shared a cold and joyless meal that evening, Aius, on that stony ground?' Thumelicatz asked, interrupting the aged slave.

'Most of us had given up hope,' Aius replied without any need for reflection. 'We had prayed to all the gods that the abandoning of the baggage would buy us the time to escape, but when the tribes caught back up with us we knew that they would never let us go. It was then that many of the senior officers, the legates and auxiliary prefects, began to question Varus' strategy. There was a meeting at the top of the hill where we had placed our birds and before long the voices were loud enough for us to overhear.

'"He will be there at the edge of the forest and together we will move on into the open country and crush the rebellion," Varus shouted at the group of red-cloaked officers surrounding him.

'"Stop fooling yourself, Varus!" Vala Numonius, the prefect of the Gallic auxiliary cavalry, thundered back. "He won't be there because he's already here." He pointed out into the night. "He's always been here; it's him who has done this. Arminius has betrayed us and would see us all dead if we carry on going north-west in a column. Hour after hour he'll wear us down, taking lives until there are none left to take. We need to get to the next piece of open ground and form for battle and see if the barbarians are willing to take us head-on or whether they'll just slink back to their hovels."

'Varus replied: "They'll do neither; they'll skirt around us, sweep Arminius aside and join the rebellion and before we know it the whole of the north will be lost."

'"There is no rebellion! Not in the north, anyway. The rebellion is here and we are in the centre of it and if we don't act we will be the victims of it. Arminius is false."

'"Arminius saved my life!" Varus said. "Why would he do that and then go on to betray me?"

'"For that very reason: to betray you. Who better to lead you into a trap than the man you trust with your very life? Look at you: you're blinded to his duplicity because of the debt you owe him and that's what he's played on all along; that's what's going to get us all killed and you must by now know it to be the case."

'This seemed to get through to Varus and he turned to stare out into the night with the look of a man who has just accepted what he always knew, deep down, to be the truth but had previously been unable to countenance. It was then he saw his folly and it was at that moment that the screaming started again out in the night but ever coming closer. Now we knew there would be no quarter and that we either found a place to turn and fight or we would die far from home. We had started to despair.'

'And you, Tiburtius?' Thumelicatz asked. 'Had you begun to despair? Could you ever see yourself walking in the streets of Rome again?'

'Rome?' The former Eagle-bearer of the Nineteenth Legion looked into the mid-distance as if trying to picture the city he had not seen for more than half his life. 'Rome? Yes, master, by then I think that the image of Rome had begun to fade in my mind. And as the screaming came nearer the fear grew within us all for we knew to expect horror. But we did not expect the scale of the horror. Out from the darkness surrounding our makeshift camp on the hill, scores of piercing screams came from every direction. Closer they came and the lads tensed and braced themselves for a night attack. Although it was not an attack in the conventional sense of the word it had the same effect on our morale as if it had been a successful breaching of our lines.

'Then they appeared through the darkness, wraithlike shadows bearing burdens between them; screaming, writhing burdens that they heaved towards us before fleeing back into the night. Some of the lads – the few who had a pila left – hurled their weapons after them but I don't think any damage was done other than to deplete our store of missiles. The shadows disappeared but the screaming did not stop. We ran forward and hauled the burdens up the hill, but it wasn't as easy as we thought it would be for they were very difficult to get a grip of as they were slimed in gore and wriggled like landed eels, all the time shrieking shriller than a harpy; and it was no wonder that they did as they were but blood-splattered hulks, just torsos and heads, their extremities removed. Their arms and legs had been hacked off and the small stumps left had been daubed in pitch to stop the bleeding, as had the gash that marked the place where once their genitalia had hung. The screams were inarticulate as there was nothing left in their mouths with which to form words, and even if there had been they were unable to see to whom they should direct their anguish as their eye-sockets were a bloody ruin of mush.

'A collective moan of despair rose over the camp almost drowning out the agony of the maimed. What could we do with our comrades left so broken and incomplete? Each scream, each waggle of a ghastly stump, each writhe of an agonised torso instilled fear and terror within us and we all knew that were we to be one of those blinded monstrosities on the ground we would be begging for an end; within moments the screaming had stopped as swords pierced the hulks and exploded their racing hearts. It was then that we directed our rage at the unseen foe in the night and bellowed our hatred, as impotent as it was deep, at the hidden fiends who could inflict such cruelty on our comrades. But no reply came from the dark and many of our men had tears of frustration trailing down their faces; in their exhaustion due to lack of sleep and continuous traipsing through mud, they were unable to control their emotions, and were unmanned, sinking to their knees and tearing at their hair.

'Varus saw the state of the rump of his army and the effect the dismembering of the prisoners had had upon them and he must have then realised that it was all due to his being duped by Erminatz; the responsibility rested on his shoulders and his alone for he had been warned and he had ignored those warnings. He saw around him not three mighty legions and their auxiliaries but a collection of demoralised, terrified and drained men who happened to be wearing the uniform of Rome. He had led them and it was he who had brought them to this. With the promise of linking up with Erminatz taken from him, now that he had grasped the reality of the situation, he could see no attainable objective, no way forward or back; he could see nothing but death, for it was death besieging us on that stony hill, and he knew the fate that death had in store for him at the hands of his one-time friend, Erminatz, would be worse than the now-motionless hulks that littered the perimeter of the camp.'

CHAPTER XIII

'THEIR ONLY OPTION now was to continue to run in the same direction, even though he knew that Erminatz wasn't there, as that was the quickest way out of the forest,' Thumelicatz mused as Aius went about the tent lighting lamps against the fading of the day. 'What he didn't know was that to leave the Teutoburg Wald he had to negotiate the Teutoburg Pass. Tiburtius, take it from dawn on the fourth day.'

Squinting in the light of the newly lit lamps the old slave took a few moments to find the right place.

'They're on the move,' Siegimeri, my father, said as we and the kings of all the tribes peered from the forest; the first rays of the sun touched the leaden sky from beneath, slashing its undulations with deep red.

I remember it for in Cheruscian lore a red sky in the morning is a warning from the Thunderer of his intent to swing his hammer that day; the sight of it warmed my heart because with his aid I knew that we would sweep Rome from his lands in but a few hours.

I watched the bedraggled cohorts form up within their makeshift fortifications on the hill in the field of stone and then march northwest in a column that was now less than half as long as it had been four days earlier: no more than fifteen hundred paces, not even a Roman mile. 'Keep all the tribes moving,' I said to the kings around me, 'so that the column doesn't deviate from its path; as we near the Chalk Giant we shall move ahead of them and be waiting. There the ground will turn the same colour as the sky and that place will be forever sacred, scattered with the bones of the unburied foe.' Even Adgandestrius muttered into his beard his approval of the sentiment as we disbanded and returned to our waiting men who had all slept and broken their fasts well.

We were ready for the final day.

And so was the Thunderer; before the sun had even reached a hand's breadth above the horizon Donar's hammer crashed and again split the heavens asunder and water cascaded down. But we sons of All Men were not weighed down by equipment that grows sodden; once a cloak and a pair of breeks are wet that is that. The Romans, however, had leather shield coverings and leather bags hanging from their marching yokes and they grew heavy with the rain of four days so that the exhausted troops bearing them suffered even more under the strain. The stragglers, and there were many, were being either slaughtered or rounded up for our fires by the time the last element of the column was just half a mile from the hill. Chains of them, roped about the neck, were led away for the celebrations that would follow our victory; and of victory I now had no doubt for it was obvious that, if they were going to head for open ground and then turn and fight us, they had to get through the Teutoburg Pass, and the pass, thanks to Engilram, was now closed.

As the morning drew on, the rain showed no signs of abating; the terrain became more jagged and the forest thicker so that the progress of the Roman column slowed to a crawl. Their pioneers, protected by auxiliary Gauls dismounted for the task, struggled to clear a passage for the column, felling trees and bridging rivers that were, by now, high and fast. But our men kept at them, pelting them with javelins and arrows, many of which got past the shields of the covering auxiliaries, so that their numbers dwindled and progress became even slower. With the main part of the column at a virtual standstill, the remaining legionaries of the Seventeenth, Eighteenth and Nineteenth legions were able to bring their shields to bear far easier and their defence became more effective; nothing was more harmful to our cause than our intended victims gaining some hope.

'Stop the attacks on the pioneers and the vanguard, Vulferam,' I ordered as it became clear to me what was needed.

Vulferam looked at me, not understanding.

'We have to let them speed up,' I explained, 'so that they are more disordered; we can't pierce their defences when they're stationary.'

'Then how will we deal with them when we get them to the killing ground? They'll be stationary there.'

I smiled at him. 'You'll see; trust me. There're less than four miles to go now to the ambush site; I'm going to go forward with half our men. You stay here and keep tearing at them as they move off. I'll see you in the shadow of the Chalk Giant.'

And so I left him and, taking half of the Cherusci with me, slipped through the trees out of sight of the Roman column to join Engilram and his Bructeri warriors waiting at the place chosen for the deaths of so many Romans: the Teutoburg Pass where the forest meets the marsh. Anxious as I was to reach the site, I went ahead, leaving my men in the charge of my father.

'As you can see, the Chalk Giant funnels the pass ever closer to the marsh,' Engilram said, as we stood in the teeming rain behind a rough, earthen wall, looking down onto the open ground, mainly pasture, at the base of the Chalk Giant; at its southeastern end, where the column would appear, it was four hundred paces wide, but it gradually narrowed until the mouth of the pass, beyond which lay the open ground where the legions could turn and face us, was little more than a hundred. He pointed beyond it to what looked like a huge area of heathland that went north as far as the eye could see. 'That is the marsh, and treacherous marsh at that, especially after all this rain. There is no escape through that unless you have the luck and cunning of Loki. A few may get across it but most will be sucked under.' He then diverted my attention northwest to the narrow far end of the diminishing pass and the trees beyond. 'My men have cut down much of that wood so that the trunks will impede anyone trying to escape the pass in that direction. I've also put five hundred of my men there to defend the barricade should they make a concerted effort to break out.'

I nodded in approval. 'Well done, my friend; and what of the other matter?'

'It's all in hand, come.'

Engilram led me diagonally up the hill, so that we soon lost sight of the pasture through the trees; after a few hundred paces there was a scene that filled me with glee: carts, scores of them and each covered with an ox-hide sheet to protect the contents from the endless rain. He pulled one back to reveal hundreds of javelins. 'They were hastily made but they will do the job. I estimate that there are five hundred or more in each cart.'

I tried to count the carts.

'Over sixty,' Engilram said, reading my thoughts. 'We have something between thirty-five and forty thousand missiles to hurl at them.'

I grinned at the old king of the Bructeri. 'That should do it.'

'I hope so. I've placed my nephew in charge of distributing them as the warriors arrive; each man will have four until they run out, and then they will hide behind that earthen wall we were at so that they won't be seen. The first volley will come as a complete surprise.'

This was what I had wanted to hear; Engilram had not let me down: the way to neutralise the Roman shield wall, before it had time to be deployed, was in position. As my men arrived they were given their javelins and went on to join the Bructeri warriors at the wall in the trees, about ten paces from the bottom of the hill. Crouching there in their hundreds they were invisible from the open ground. The rest stayed further up the hill, in the trees, ready to charge down once the ambush was sprung. I calculated that we had in the region of five thousand warriors on the Chalk Giant with more arriving all the time as the column drew closer. Soon the Chatti and Sugambri came in, having yielded their place at the rear of the column to the Marsi and the Chauci who would be the ones to block off any possible retreat from the killing ground, now lush green with pasture fed by rain but soon to be turned crimson by the blood of men who should not be there.

And so we waited as the shouts and screams from within the forest grew closer for there were still warriors harrying the column, keeping their fear up by killing and maiming as well as taking many prisoners.

Closer came the sound of bloodshed and we waited in silence, each warrior knowing that surprise would be worth many more deaths than if the legions were expecting a javelin-storm. Louder it became until finally the head of the column appeared through the trees at the far end of the open pasture. Immediately they speeded up, almost jogging across the long, uncropped grass. Behind them more emerged, the remnants of the first cohort of the Seventeenth all breaking into a quick march. Suddenly the whole pasture was filling up with legionaries desperate to use the open ground to perhaps pull away from their tormentors, if only for a little while, to gain some respite. On they came and when the head of the Seventeenth was level with me, in my position halfway along the open ground, the Eighteenth's Eagle appeared from the woods. Cavalry, who had been dismounted as they were worse than useless in the confined space of the forest, now remounted, and began to canter forward, down either side of the column. I watched, hardly daring to breath, as the doomed legions advanced. Soon the Eagle of the Nineteenth was visible and the space of the column had greatly increased, which, in turn, meant that their order was not so tight; ranks were starting to draw apart from one another. Despite the bellowing of centurions and optios to keep a solid formation, the legionaries' natural fear of what was pursuing them caused them to ignore the shouts and beatings of vine canes.

As the middle cohorts of the Eighteenth Legion drew level with me I pulled down the mask on my helm, muttered a quick prayer to the Thunderer and, leaping to my feet, pulled back my throwing arm to hurl a javelin high into the air. By the time it reached the apex of its flight it was one of thousands cast at the Roman formation and as it slammed through the top of a helm, downing a legionary like a wet sack, the second volley had already been launched and the warriors hiding further up the slope had charged forward and were coming up to us. And so I vaulted the wall; letting loose another javelin and, crying the war cry of our Cheruscian fathers, I led my people forward.

Joy flowed through me as, at last, the opportunity to rid our Fatherland of the men from the south had arrived. There they were, a mere fifty paces away from us, disordered and dying under a hail of javelins that had turned the already slate grey sky the colour of dusk. Ten thousand missiles fell on them in the first ten heartbeats of the ambush and ten thousand fell in the next ten; three thousand lives were reaped in that short time, depleting their numbers by almost a third.

The surprise with which we had ambushed them was complete; just when they thought they had the chance to pull away, just when they were concentrating on what was in front of them, we screamed out of the forest to their left, teeth bared in hatred, death in our eyes: the men of the north, the product of their worst nightmares, manifesting out of the dark northern forest so close to them. Down, the javelin hail continued to storm, felling men as they struggled to raise their sodden shields above their heads; but the endless rain had taken its toll, and the glue that bound the layers of wood together had started to fail, causing the shields to disintegrate under the multiple impacts. And so we raced from the wall, hurling our missiles directly at the column so that the flankers, already disordered from losing formation as they sped across the open ground, were thumped back, impaled, for they could not deploy their shield wall in time so far were they from one another. My last javelin slashed through a centurion's eye, exploding out of the back of his transverse-plumed helmet, arching him back, shrieking, his sword flying into the air; around him his men wavered as their officer clattered to the ground to expel his last few moaned breaths. Before their optio could shout some order into his men we slammed into them, our swords whirring above our heads, our spines curved back, ready for the downwards blow; and so

they came, almost together, blades slashing down, cleaving flesh
and bone or spraying plumes of sparks as they scraped across
armour. Slamming the boss of my shield forward, knocking
the wind from a hysterical youth, I took off his sword arm in
a spray of blood, casting him shrieking to the ground to be
slashed by the warriors following me.

All along the length of the column we tore into them with
javelins hurtling over our heads to rip into the rear ranks; here
and there the line buckled, like a writhing snake, but in the
main it held firm; the six thousand legionaries still standing did
not just wash away under the full force of our tide of hatred.
However terrified they were, however surprised and disordered,
they managed to stagger a few steps back and then, by the sheer
will-power produced by the instinct to survive, they planted
their feet firm and the shields started to lock together. But still
the warriors kept flooding down the hill, piling in behind us
adding their weight to the scrimmage, and I saw, with horror,
just what a calamity it would be if the ambush turned into
a shoving match with a Roman war machine. 'Back! Back!'
I shouted, pushing at the man behind me. 'Back for another
charge!' I barged back, physically pulling those around me after
me; away we stepped from them like a wave receding to either
side as the message to disengage was passed along. Warily the
Romans watched us, breathing deeply, gore-spattered, but their
formation still intact, just. We pulled back almost to our wall
and readied ourselves to charge again, although this time, we
knew, they would be expecting us.

But then something happened that changed the situation;
from behind the Roman lines a *lituus* sounded, high and shrill,
and I knew the call, it was for cavalry to retreat. Every one of
the legionaries also knew that call and those that could turned

to see the remainder of the cavalry under Vala Numonius fleeing northwest, towards the barrier of cut-down trees. They were deserting and a great moan erupted from their erstwhile comrades on foot; and as despair settled on the enemy I led my warriors forward again.

Thumelicatz leant forward in his chair towards his Roman guests. 'Vala Numonius a coward? Well, that's certainly the opinion of your historian Velleius Paterculus.'

The elder brother waved a dismissive hand. 'He had spoken to some of the few who made it back to the empire and they had all said the same thing: Vala deserted.'

'Did he?' Thumelicatz turned to his slaves. 'What do you say?'

A brief glance between them decided that it should be Tiburtius who spoke. 'Varus had assembled his command behind the Eighteenth Legion; we three aquilifers were also there, to keep our birds as safe as possible. He called a meeting of all his senior officers as the Germanic warriors disengaged after the first attack. He knew this was the end. He turned to Vala: "Go," he said, "and take the cavalry with you; make for the Amisia, from there you have a chance of getting home."

"'I'll not, for my honour's sake, desert you," Vala replied.

"'You will," Varus ordered. "What good is it if you die here, because that is certainly what will happen to us. Get out, get back to Rome and tell the Emperor what happened so that he might avenge me and my men. Go, my friend, and tell them I was duped." He put his hand on his cavalry commander's shoulder and squeezed it. There was a moment between the two men before Vala nodded once and then turned away. Varus then looked at his remaining officers and spoke. "Gentlemen, for us who remain there are three choices: to surrender to barbarians and we know what that would mean for us, or to die fighting but run the risk of capture and the same torment as if we surrendered. Or we take matters into our own hands." He paused and looked at the face of each man; only one seemed to disagree.

"'I'm for surrender," Ennius, the camp prefect of the Eighteenth, said. "If we lay down our arms now, and prevent any more blood-shed, then Arminius will surely grant us free passage back to the Rhenus."

'Varus laughed in the man's face as a cavalry lituus sounded and hoofs pounded off. "How did a coward get so high in rank? Of course Arminius won't spare you or any here. I can see that and so I choose death at my own hand."

'That was the only option for him now and it was in this frame of mind that he approached the three Eagles that we held aloft still, and with an expression vacant of the pride that normally resided upon his face he unstrapped his breastplate and laid it on the ground. Most of his senior officers came to support him in his final moments, they too readying themselves to escape the fires and blades of the rebel tribes. I and the two other Eagle-bearers stood beneath our birds as the command of the three legions knelt before them, swords in hand, the blades aimed just below their bottom ribs on the left side of their chests. Without a word, Varus pitched forward so that the hilt of his sword rammed against the ground, stopping it dead as the momentum of his body forced the tip up under his rib and into his heart that had no more appetite for life. His breath burst from his lungs but no cry of pain passed his lips as the bloodied point ripped through his shoulder blade and his body twitched in the spasm of death before resting still. Within a few moments of his passing, his officers had followed him on the road to the Ferryman and the Seventeenth, Eighteenth and Nineteenth legions had lost their high command just at the time when they needed it most. The war cries of the tribes were raised again and we knew that even if we could resist them a second time it was a certainty that we would not be able to do so a third.'

Thumelicatz smiled. 'So, Romans, you see now that Vala was not a coward and actually it was Ennius who comes out the worst from my slave's recollection. However, Varus doesn't come out well either. There is never a right time to die but there is certainly a wrong one; and Varus most definitely chose the wrong one. His staff had already been depleted by him sending many officers back to Rome on leave and now he led a large proportion of the remainder in a useless suicide. He killed himself through fear of what would happen to him if he were captured, not to save his honour; it was the suicide of a coward. Up until that point it was still just possible for the Romans to retrieve the situation. My father's original objective had been to annihilate the column in one day, as he knew that if he was to leave it wounded but intact it would always be able to run for open ground and turn and face the combined tribes; my father did not deceive himself, he knew who would come out best in such an encounter.

'And here they were, in the pass on open ground; confined ground, unlike what lay beyond the mouth of the pass, granted, but nevertheless reasonably open and with the remainder of his men having survived a charge and still just about in good order. As Tiburtius said: it was what his senior officers had advised the previous night, it was the only sensible thing to do and yet rather than take that decision to try to fight in that place and have a chance of extracting half of his men from Germania he kills himself and condemns three legions to death, for there was no one senior enough left who would command the confidence of so many terrified men. The cavalry's seeming desertion, the suicide of their commander and so many of their officers spelt an end to whatever small reserves of hope and good morale the legionaries had left; and then, when a new force appeared in the wood through which Vala was trying to flee, cutting him and his men down, their demoralisation was complete. They were surrounded by warriors on three sides and had an impenetrable marsh, made worse by so much heavy rain, to their backs. Carry on, Tiburtius.'

Tiburtius looked down at where his finger still rested on the manuscript.

And as we crashed into them a second time we felt less resistance; the cavalry's flight had had a profound effect upon the legionaries. Their despair was palpable and they fell back beneath the weight of our blades and the impact of our spear heads. On we hacked, as another, final, full volley of javelins hissed above us and clattered into the rear ranks, many of whom were, by now, desperately trying to dig a makeshift wall in the ridiculous hope that it might shield them from our wrath. Back we ground them, thinning them out, wearing them down. To my right the Chatti were pushing the Nineteenth Legion hard with the Marsi and Chauci taking it from behind; this was the weakest of the three legions having received much punishment as the rearguard. To my left the Bructeri hammered at the Seventeenth whilst the Sugambri roved about behind us charging here and there where gaps appeared. Soon we had pushed them back to their pathetic wall. But this structure caused many to lose their lives as they tried to leap over it in the face of our relentless blades. A mule, already in panic, rushed it and twisted as it jumped to land on its neck, snapping it; it was dead before its back legs hit the ground. Other mules bucked and ran amok, braying ceaselessly, causing havoc in the already fragile formation as the legionaries scrambled over the impediment that had been constructed behind them by their own comrades. Over they tumbled, exposing their backs to us and receiving wounds of dishonour as my warriors targeted the buttocks, laughing in their fury. Although many did not make it back over the wall more than a few did to strengthen the lines manning it. And so we paused and pulled back again to ready ourselves for what would be the final assault on the remnants of the three legions crouching behind their makeshift breastwork.

A stillness fell over the field as if all present were pausing for breath and for a couple of moments the only sounds were the moans of the wounded dampened by the incessant rain.

'Arminius!' a voice shouted from behind the Roman lines. 'Arminius!'

There was a stirring amongst the legionaries and through them came an officer whom I recognised surrounded by a hundred or so rankers. 'Ennius, are you come to beg for a swift death?'

'I come to beg for our lives, Arminius; we offer to lay down our arms in return for safe passage to the Rhenus.'

The base lack of dignity in this plea dumbfounded me for an instant and seemed to insult the honour of many of the legionaries as there came shouts of outrage from many of them.

'What of Roman honour?' I demanded. 'Even if I were to let you go how could you ever face your countrymen again?'

'Let us worry about that when we are west of the Rhenus.'

Again, more shouts of outrage greeted this remark.

'It would seem that you are in the minority, Ennius. But if you want to surrender, you are more than welcome to, although I can assure you that you will not be going west. Some of you will die in our fires and the rest will remain in servitude for the remainder of your miserable lives. Come now and take your chance or stay there and prepare to die with your honour intact.'

To my surprise, Ennius came forward with most of the rankers that accompanied him to the derision of every other Roman still breathing. As he neared me I raised my mask and spat at his feet. 'Take him away,' I ordered Vulferam, 'and guard him well; he shall be the first to burn.'

Ennius fell to his knees. 'Arminius, for the friendship that there was once between us, spare me.'

I refused to look him in the eye. 'There can be no friendship with a coward such as you.'

This, strange to relate, was greeted by some cheers from the Roman line and I felt nothing but respect for those who were about to die because they were willing to die with honour. I lifted my sword and saluted them as Ennius was dragged, pleading, away; to my surprise, many raised their weapons and saluted back.

The time had now come to end it once and for all; down my blade flashed and from the depths of my being came the war cry of the Cherusci, echoed by my followers. The other tribes roared their own challenges as the once-powerful soldiers of Rome crouched, grim and silent, behind their last defence.

Donar's hammer fell; its sparks streaked across the heavy sky a couple of heartbeats before the Thunderer deafened us and we charged.

Our sodden cloaks and hair billowed behind us as we ran, pointing our weapons at the enemy, and baying for their blood as lightning cracked again above. Javelins, retrieved from the field, came flying back at us but we were too many for them to make much impact. For every warrior punched back there were two more behind him ready to take his place knowing that our gods were showing us favour.

The legionaries braced as we neared them, sprinting our hardest. With a strained effort I pushed off with my left foot and, punching my right foot on the top of the makeshift wall, hurled myself onto the shields of the men behind it. I crashed onto the leather-faced wood, kicking with all my might as I brought my sword clanging down onto the helmet before me, cleaving it open. The sodden, weakened shields fell apart with the weight of my attack and the warriors to either side of me piled in with the same commitment and we were over; we had used their wall against them, exploiting its height to leap down on the men cowering behind in the churned mud.

Now there was to be no respite, now we would show no pity, now we would massacre at will. My blade blurred through the air, droplets of gore tracing its path through streaking rain, to hew through the neck of a second ranker whose scream was cut with the severing of his windpipe. Such was the intensity of our charge and such was the surprise that our daring to leap the wall had caused, that the will to resist the attack was sapped and men who just a few moments earlier had been jeering those who had surrendered for their cowardice now displayed the same weakness: they turned and ran.

All along the line, the will of the legions was broken, as broken as the shield wall that we had hurled ourselves onto, and pandemonium ensued as the sons of All Men slew without mercy those who had tried to take their land and their freedom from them.

And as I reaped lives, ahead of me I saw my objective: the Eagles. Still they stood aloft, presiding over the carnage. With a brutality that surpassed all my other actions in the past few days, I hacked and slashed my way towards them with my warriors about me as the deluge diluted the blood spraying over our forearms and faces. Through the last rank we sliced to see the Eagles surrounded by a guard, some two hundred strong; but that did not daunt us for we knew that soon we would be many more as the cohesion of the legions disintegrated. I did not stop but hurtled on towards the grim men who were about to offer up their lives whilst protecting the sacred symbols given to them by Augustus himself. We converged on them as, behind us, great slaughter was wrought; and then above, as if in approval of our actions, the Thunderer swung his hammer again with a prodigious crash that shook the earth beneath our feet as we raced across it. Buoyed by such a sign of divine favour we felt no fear, just joy as we crunched into the wall of shields. The deadly blades of Rome's killing machine flashed in and out of the gaps severing the life-threads of many of those around me. But somehow I was spared, my sword, streaming with thinned blood, keeping me safe as it ate its way through the iron and flesh betwixt me and my prize. And then I saw that there were only two Eagles still standing and cursed the man who had beaten me to the honour of being the first to capture the ultimate symbol of Roman oppression. But on I worked, nonetheless, teeth now gritted, muscles protesting at every step or swing of my sword arm, closer and closer as the Eagle guard was thinned down by systematic slaughter.

'So where were you, Aius?' Thumelicatz asked. 'For it was you who had disappeared; my father had not been beaten to his prize after all.'

The slave lowered his head. 'I tried to save the Eagle of the Seventeenth, but I failed. I had seen your father carving his way towards where we three Eagle-bearers stood and it was obvious what his intentions were. I knew that all was lost and that the reality was that we were soon to be despatched. My only thought was for the safety of my bird; my life was worthless if I couldn't keep it from enemy hands. There was only one direction in which I stood a chance, so I pulled my bird off its pole, wrapped it in my cloak and ran towards the marsh. All around me my comrades were trying to flee, all dignity had gone but I felt I could at least restore a small fraction of it if I could get away and take the bird back across the Rhenus; if that wasn't to be possible then I would sink it into the marsh.'

'But you did neither of those things,' Thumelicatz said, his voice betraying scorn, 'did you, Aius?'

'No, master, I did not. I tried to cross the marsh but the constant rain had made the ground glutinous; my feet were sucked under and, before I had gone more than ten paces in, I was stuck and sinking. Then from behind me I heard a shout. I froze for I knew that voice; I had heard it many times before: it was the voice of Erminatz. I turned and there he was, a thing of horror, blood splattered all over him and streaming off him in rivulets, surrounded by warriors, two of whom held the other legions' birds. "Marcus Aius, bring me that Eagle, and I shall spare you the fire," he shouted at me. I struggled to move forward because there was no way that I would voluntarily hand my bird over to the enemy. He saw that I was making no attempt to comply with his wishes and so sent two of his warriors after me. They knew the ways of the marsh; rather than walk they crawled. I panicked and tried to sink the Eagle in the marsh but they were on me quickly; they retrieved it and hauled me out to become Erminatz's prisoner, and because I had not submitted I knew I was destined for the fires of their gods.'

'And you, Tiburtius?' the younger brother asked, his expression one of interest not scorn, 'how did you survive the capture of your Eagle?'

Thumelicatz nodded at his slave as he looked for permission to speak.

'They flew at us through the rain, ripping into the first and second centuries of the Eighteenth's first cohort that were meant to protect us; but nothing could keep us safe from the fury that finally approached after four days of grinding us down. We were lost. Aius had disappeared and as I turned to Graptus, the aquilifer of the Eighteenth, next to me, he drew his sword and, without pausing, rammed it into his own throat. His legs buckled and his fist, clamped about his bird's pole, slid down its length as the life fled from him, taking his honour with it. The Eagle of the Eighteenth fell forward into the mud as fire seared through my thigh; I looked down to see the haft of a javelin shaking in the meat of my left leg and felt myself tip to the side as the limb collapsed. Instinctively I grabbed at the wound with both hands and then, realising what I'd done, reached back up and caught the bird's pole. In desperation I tried to support myself with the Eagle but I reacted too late and down I went, splayed in the mud, some of it slopping into my eyes. As I wiped them clear all I could see before me were the trousers and leather boots of our enemy leaping over the bodies of my comrades and racing towards me. I struggled for my sword so that I could go the same way as Graptus and keep my honour intact but, as I attempted to get to my knees to draw it, a crack to the left side of my head sent me to oblivion. When I woke up—'

'That's far enough,' Thumelicatz interrupted, 'we'll deal with what happened when you woke up in its place.' His smile did not reach his eyes as he turned to the Romans. 'My father had captured the Eagles of three legions and in the next hour was to take all the rest of the legions' standards: all the cohorts, the centuries as well as the images of the Emperor and the legions' emblems. He also took over a thousand men prisoner including twenty-four centurions, nine tribunes, another prefect of the camp and, of course, my two slaves here. In addition to them were around three hundred women and children and fifty or so muleteers who were all that was left of the baggage train. If more than a couple of hundred managed to get through our lines or the marsh, I would be surprised. As the enemy wounded were despatched and left where they lay, we harvested the testicles of the fallen along with their chain-mail, swords and any other useful items – although not the newly introduced segmented armour that a few had been issued with as it was of no use to us. Our dead were collected along with their weapons to be borne in honour back to their wives and mothers for cleansing and burial. Soon riders began to come in from all the communities that had pleaded for Varus to leave a garrison: they had all been massacred as well as any merchant or official still on our soil. The Roman occupation of Germania Magna, in the space of four days, now consisted of a few score fugitives, or so we thought. But there was one thing that did not go to plan and we shall hear of that after Tiburtius tells us what he first heard and then saw as he regained consciousness.'

CHAPTER XIIII

'"THIS'LL STOP YOU hissing, you little viper", was what I awoke to,' Tiburtius said, his voice flat, devoid of emotion. 'It was followed by a pleading wail that transformed into a spluttering gurgle; I opened my eyes to see Marcellus Acilius, the thick-stripe military tribune of my legion, naked and spewing blood as his tongue was held before him. Tears streamed from his eyes, tears of pain, rage and sorrow, as well as shame for shedding them, for all these emotions must have been going through the young lad's head as he realised that he would never talk again in the unlikely event that he would live beyond this day. But it was obvious that he would not survive for he was an officer and they were being singled out for special treatment. The lad stared in horror at the needle and twine that had replaced his tongue, now discarded in the mud before him. His head was held back and his jaw clamped shut as his hands, bound behind his back, struggled for their freedom; but, no, he was secure. And it was as a helpless, tongueless victim that he endured the needle passing through his bottom lip and then on into the top one; the twine was pulled tight and knotted before the needle pierced again. Stitch after stitch, each one taut and precise, was applied until the lad's mouth was sewed up as tight as a wineskin and he struggled to breathe through blood-choked nostrils. They then cut off his testicles.

'It was in that condition that they took him to the fires.

'Another young tribune from my legion, Caldus Caelius, in his terror as he watched his castrated colleague writhe in the flames, brought the chain that manacled his wrists down so hard upon his head that his skull cracked open and he died almost instantaneously.

'It wasn't until much later that I found out that we were on the top of the hill that they call the Chalk Giant; the very place that we are now. This clearing and the ancient oak is a sacred place in Germanic lore; they had placed all the captured standards about the oak and had built fires at intervals around the clearing's perimeter; next to each was an altar. Priestesses, shrill and fell, shrieked invocations to the gods of this land as priests despatched victims on the slab, taking their heads to hang from the branches around the clearing's edge and from the oak at its centre. These were the lucky ones; or, rather, the second luckiest group – the luckiest had been those who had fallen in the four days of battle. For myself I would have taken the knife on the altar had I had a choice of that or the fire. The fire was something that I had heard tell of but had never witnessed. The fire is truly dreadful. They build a wicker cage in the shape of a man and force their victim within. He is then hoist, screaming, on a pulley system until his cage is many feet above the flames, which are then stoked so that the heat builds, not enough to set fire to the wicker, which has been thoroughly soaked in water, but enough to burn the skin. The victim slowly broils, screeching in agony, begging for mercy; but there will be none for why should they be reprieved from being given to the gods in thanks for such a victory? I watched the young lad being hauled into his wicker man, no sound emitting from his sewn-up mouth other than deep growls in his throat as his nostrils bubbled with bloody mucus. Up he went and over the fire he was placed and I watched and watched as his feet slowly melted and the skin up his legs withered and charred; his, well, his …' Tiburtius paused, shaking his head at the recollection. 'His … just shrivelled. It was at this point that his agony was such that his desire to scream ripped his lips apart and it was with a jagged mouth that he implored Jupiter to save him.

'But Jupiter was not there in that dark forest that day; nor will he ever come here. Jupiter is Rome's god, the god of the city. Here in the north, in the forests of Germania, other gods hold sway and they show no mercy for the Southern Man who prefers ordered vineyards, orchards and fields centred round urban communities with regular markets, temples and courts with officials who've the power to tax and to sit in judgement. The gods of Germania don't understand that way of life, loving, instead, their sons, the sons of All Men, who dwell in freedom in the dark woods, worshipping in groves and telling tales of the forest, glorifying that which to the Southern Man represents nothing but fear.'

'And it is not only the Germanic people,' Thumelicatz pointed out, 'it's all the people of the north, Britannia included, as you will find out if I help you to get what you're looking for.' The sight of the Romans looking uneasily at each other amused him, although he did not let it show; he knew, however, that he had spoken the truth. 'But enough of the Southern Man's fear of the forest that we northerners so love; Aius, read of his fear of the fires.'

Aius cleared his throat as if he was trying to put off for as long as possible the reading of the next passage. Eventually he had no option but to commence.

The joy that welled within me grew as each new sacrifice screamed in the fires and each new head was hung from a branch. The sacred oak, at the centre of the clearing, was now festooned with offerings to our gods and the fires sizzled with fat. None of the officers had met their deaths well, above the flames, pleading and screaming with no concern for their dignity; but this suited my intention for I had a mind to keep two of the prisoners for the purposes of this memoir and I needed a way to bind them to me for ever. I called for the two captured Eagle-bearers to be brought before me and enjoyed the sight of these once-proud men kneeling in the mud.

'You've seen our fires and you know what awaits you both, don't you?' I said.

They kept their eyes to the ground and did not respond.

'Don't you!' I shouted.

'I do,' the Eagle-bearer of the Seventeenth, Marcus Aius, answered; his voice was quiet and he kept his eyes averted.

'As do I,' his comrade from the Nineteenth, Gaius Tiburtius, confirmed.

'And what would you do to avoid that fate?'

They shared a glance.

'Anything, master,' Aius said, causing me to sneer at how subservient he had become in just a matter of hours. 'We lost our honour with our Eagles; we should have died protecting them.'

'I have no interest in your motives, things of no worth. Just tell me this: if I were to give you a choice between the fires and staying alive to serve me and my family for the rest of your days, sworn never to try to escape, never to kill yourselves, which would you choose?'

Again they shared a glance; this time it was Tiburtius who spoke: 'We will serve you, master.'

I looked down at them in disgust and then kicked each in the chest so they fell onto their backs in the mud. 'I'll tell you what my decision is in due course,' I said, walking off, knowing perfectly well that I would let them live to make a record of my life and my hatred of their kind.

'That is always my favourite part,' Thusnelda commented from the shadows of the tent. 'Watching a Roman read aloud of his humiliation at the hand of my husband warms my heart for all the pain that Rome has caused me. Things of no worth; how true. Yet, I've never known anyone go willingly to the fires and would not like to judge what I would do in the same position. But, be that as it may, it was at this point that I remember joining Erminatz's story. He had seen me before, as he has mentioned, when I arrived at his father's house with my father, the traitor Segestes.' She paused to spit on the ground. 'I, however, had not seen him, or if I had, I hadn't noticed him. But victory and power are the greatest aphrodisiacs and when I arrived at this place, with my mother, in the aftermath of the battle to come and beg for my father's life, I saw him for the first time and it jolted my heart, such was the authority that he emitted in the wake of his victory. He was walking away from two Romans whom he had just kicked to the ground and our eyes met; although I was engaged to another I knew in that moment that I must have him and him alone.

'I said to my mother: "I will beg Erminatz for my father's life; I think I can appeal to him in a different way."

'"You may well be right, child," she answered. "Erminatz has as little love for me as he does for Segestes."

'Leaving my mother standing just inside the clearing, I approached Erminatz, my heart pounding, and stood before him with my head held high, praying that I wasn't shaking or showing any other outward sign of crotch-wetting desire; had he asked me to, I would have lain on my back and opened my legs for him then and there amidst the fires and sacrifice. But that was not to be our first conversation. "My lord, Erminatz," I said, holding his gaze and melting internally in the beauty of his eyes. "I come—"

"'For your father's life?" he said, guessing my purpose; his look was intense but at that time I didn't know, nor did I even dare to hope, that this was because he felt the exact same way as me.

"'Indeed, my lord," I replied. "I know that he has tried to betray you and—"

'He interrupted again, surprising me. "You may have it, take him with you."

'I stared at him, astounded for a moment.

'He laughed and the sound of it blocked out the screams of the men being sacrificed; it was not an unkind laugh but, rather, a joyful one: a laugh that quickened my already racing heart and made me want to sing and dance, even in that place of death. It was music to me and I knew that he would always make me happy if I could only have him and not Adgandestrius to whom I was betrothed. "But you must do something for me in return, Thusnelda," he added.

"'Anything," I replied, meaning it.

'Again he laughed. "Be careful what you promise, Thusnelda."

'I smiled. "I always am."

"'Then this is what I wish ... " But no, it would be best to hear this from Erminatz's side; carry on, Aius.'

'I always am,' she said.

It was at that moment that I knew she felt the same way and after so much death my whole being was light. 'Then, Thusnelda, promise me this: keep with your plans until I ask you to change them.' I stared deep into the wells of blue that had so captivated me and for a moment we shared a conspiratorial smile: she had understood and had made me the happiest of men. I turned and, finding Vulferam, said: 'Release the traitor, Segestes, into the hands of his daughter.'

Walking away, past the oak at the centre of the clearing, I descended the hill back to the scene of the slaughter for I had one last thing to do as I awaited news from Aldhard. Taking my helmet, I detached the mask and dug a hole in the blood-soaked ground; I would never again hide my barbarian features, as Lucius had joked when he had given it to me. I was now free of Rome and no longer needed to conceal my true feelings for her. I buried Lucius' gift in the field of Rome's defeat in order to sever, finally, all ties with the hated invader. I had not avenged my murdered friend and I knew that I would never be able to do so and I prayed to his shade that he would forgive my failing as I covered over the mask. A warmth, growing within me, told me that he understood and I knew that although he did not approve of my achievement he could not but admire the grandness of the gesture.

I smiled to myself at the memory of Lucius as I saw Aldhard approach with four warriors carrying a body between them; my happiness increased because I knew that he had been successful in the task that I had given him. 'Where did you find him?'

Aldhard looked down at the body, hawked and spat at it. 'They had tried to bury it under the carcass of a mule.'

'Kneel it down and pull its arms back,' I ordered the warriors carrying it as I drew my sword. They let the legs slump to the ground and then pulled the wrists, dragging the arms back so that the corpse knelt with its chest on its knees and its head hanging forward.

With the ingrained anger of years of enforced exile I swung my sword and it sang through the air to sever the head of Publius Quinctilius Varus, the first and last Roman Governor of Germania Magna, the man whose life I had saved. 'Have it preserved in cedar sap, Aldhard, and then I want you to take it personally to Maroboduus of the Marcomanni; tell him that I sent this in token of good faith. If he will watch over the Danuvius frontier while I do the same with the Rhenus frontier then together we shall keep Germania free; but to stay free we must be united. If we fight amongst ourselves then Rome will take advantage of our disunity and force herself upon us again. Tell him, Aldhard, that what I desire is a united Greater Germania.'

'With you as its king,' a scornful voice said from behind me before Aldhard could reply.

'No, Adgandestrius,' I responded, turning to face the Chatti king, 'with whomever we decide to set up over us all as king.'

'There was no talk of this before; you specifically said that you were not trying to rule over us.'

'I am not trying to do that, Adgandestrius; what I'm trying to achieve is to keep Germania safe, its culture, its language, its law, its gods, all of it so that there is a Germanic future in conjunction with the Latin one.'

'But if you were asked to be king of a united Germania you would accept, wouldn't you?'

I could not deny it and yet I could not admit it; I turned to Aldhard. 'Go! And meet me in the Harzland in two moons with his answer.'

'Yes, my lord.'

'You see, Erminatz, you have already got people calling you "my lord",' Adgandestrius observed as Aldhard went off, carrying Varus' head by an ear. 'And when they start doing that it's just a small step to you actually becoming their lord and that is something that I cannot and will not countenance. We have done our share of the fighting and therefore I'm now taking my warriors home before any of them get the impression that you're their lord and not me.' He stared at me with a burning hatred that I returned in full, despising him for his obvious willingness to put personal ambition before the good of our Fatherland and yet understanding it as it was the way of our people and had always been thus.

We held each other's gaze with such intensity that I almost started when Engilram came up unnoticed and said: 'Erminatz, there's news from my people to the south of the Teutoburg Wald: they've failed to destroy the Roman garrison at Aliso.'

'Aliso,' Thumelicatz mused, staring up at the ceiling and stretching his legs before him. 'What a double-edged sword that was.'

'What do you mean?' the elder brother scoffed. 'Aliso was the one thing that gave us a modicum of pride during the whole calamity. Lucius Caedicius, the primus pilus of the Eighteenth Legion who had been put in command of the garrison of Aliso on the River Lupia, defied your father and eventually got his people out of Germania. That is surely a single-edged sword, one that cuts only Arminius.'

Thumelicatz muttered something to his slaves before turning back to his Roman guests. 'You're right on the face of it, Roman: Caedicius did save his garrison as well as many of the Roman civilians who had sought shelter with it. And yes, it could be seen to be a blow for my father's prestige, but it was one that he was actually quite grateful for because it bought him time and gave him an excuse that politically he desperately needed.'

'An excuse?' the younger brother exclaimed. 'What did he need an excuse for as far as his countrymen were concerned?'

'That is what we shall see in this next passage. Tiburtius, from where I just told you.'

It was exactly one whole moon since I had struck Varus' head from his shoulders and my Cherusci and the Bructeri had been encamped around the wooden walls of Aliso for twenty of those days. Despite my pleading with them to stay and finish completely what we had started, the other tribes had dispersed to their homelands taking with them the plunder they had earned and the trophies that we had captured, amongst them the three Eagles and the three legion emblems that I had allotted to the tribes in secret, along with the cohort standards, so that none knew what the others had received.

The weather had relented and grown milder but there were still enough rain bursts to make our billets less than comfortable. The total strength of the two tribes was less than four thousand, for many of the warriors had returned to their families, content with the victory they had achieved and ready to boast of their part in it around the fires as the nights drew in.

With such depleted numbers we had tried many assaults on the walls but each had been as unsuccessful as the last. It was as I was contemplating the reason for the failure of the latest attack that screaming erupted from within the fortress, before, a few moments later, the gates opened and a group of thirty or so warriors were herded out, wailing and holding their arms in the air showing the pitch-daubed stumps that now adorned them in place of hands. On they ran, past the lines of Roman heads impaled on stakes, reminders to the besieged of what awaited them, and into our camp, staring in horror at the mutilations that would blight the remainder of their lives.

After their stumps had been bound and the trauma they had endured had diminished enough so that they were capable of coherent speech my father and I questioned them as to the state of things within the Roman garrison.

'They have food enough to hold out until the relief force arrives,' the eldest of the group told me, unable to tear his eyes from the horror at the end of his arms. 'Caedicius, the commander, took us around the storerooms to show us how well stocked they were with grain, salted pork and cabbage in addition to a well that produces plenty of fresh water.'

'How's their morale?' I asked.

'Good; they aren't hungry, they have women and they've kept their discipline. Their talk is of the relief force, which they say is imminent; no one is despairing or planning for death and even the score or so of fugitives that made it out of the Teutoburg Wald are in reasonable spirits, especially after Caedicius allowed them to wield the cleavers that took our hands in vengeance for their fallen comrades.'

My father looked at me, concerned. 'If they get help then they'd have a fair chance of making it back to the Rhenus.'

I contemplated the point for a few moments. 'Would that be such a bad thing?'

'It would give them a small measure of victory after such a heavy defeat.'

'I know; would that be such a bad thing?'

He frowned, not understanding my train of thought.

'I mean, if they feel that they have salvaged some honour, however small, they may be less inclined to come straight back to try to avenge Varus, especially after the survivors start telling their tales of defeat in the Teutoburg Wald. They're very superstitious, the Romans, and they are not enamoured of forests; the fear of them will grow as the tales of our savagery get exaggerated in the retelling. It may well buy us some time before the inevitable attempt at retribution; time to unite and organise ourselves.'

'Are you suggesting that we let them go?'

'I'm suggesting that when the relief force arrives we use it to our advantage for that reason and for another: they will probably come in sufficient strength to fend us and the Bructeri off, so why waste good men's lives trying to stop the inevitable? If I had been able to keep the alliance together then it would be a different story: we could have withdrawn and then fallen upon them on their way back to the Rhenus just as we did with Varus; but now I can use this reverse as an example of what happens if every tribe just thinks about its own interests. This could be good for us, Father, very good indeed.'

And so we left a token force besieging the fortress and withdrew a mile or so west and waited for the Romans to make their move.

It was not a long wait. The weather once again played its part in my story in the form of another display of the Thunderer's power. The night sky cracked with the beating of Donar's hammer and rain fell in a curtain thicker than at any time in the previous month. Men hunkered down under whatever shelter they could find and waited for the God's wrath to abate. Such was the intensity of the storm that it was not until the third outpost was passed that the Roman escape was noticed; they had crept out under the cover of the weather. I offered a prayer of thanks to the Thunderer and the promise of some Roman blood for providing me with a way of letting the garrison go without their suspecting it. I roused my warriors and they began to work themselves up into a battle frenzy as the ranks of legionaries marched on, with the civilians in their midst, covered by the filthy night. And then we heard horns in the distance sounding the signal for a double-quick march, the sound of the relief force approaching. As the end of the escaping column left the fortress I allowed my men to tear at it but only enough for Caedicius to think that he'd had a narrow escape and that had it not been for the relief force's timely arrival he would not have made it out at all. After we had reaped a hundred lives or so I slowly pulled my men back so that we lost contact and the Romans disappeared west into the downpour. That the horns sounding the relief force's arrival were in fact the garrison's own horns playing a clever ruse was something that I didn't find out until later and it added to my enjoyment of the trick, as Caedicius would have genuinely felt that he had outwitted me and so never for one moment would he have thought that it was him who had been made a fool of.

With the departure of Caedicius and his garrison, the last living free Roman left our land and it was time for me to prepare for what I knew would come; I hadn't spent all those years amongst the Romans without getting to know them: vengeance would come as sure as death follows life. The questions were: how long would we have to wait and, when it did come, how would we resist it?

It was time for us to decide how we would use our freedom: fighting amongst ourselves or preparing to repulse Rome when she came for revenge. It was with these questions going through my mind that I disbanded my army and returned to the Harzland to await Aldhard and his message from Maroboduus; he arrived two days after my return and his news did not bode well for the future of Germania.

'Maroboduus seems to think that he can use Varus' defeat to gain a better deal with Rome,' Aldhard told me as we sat, shortly after his arrival, at board in my longhouse, next to a blazing fire; he drained his horn of ale and refilled it. Covered in the dirt of travel he had come direct from the lands of the Marcomanni and had refused a chance to clean himself up before imparting his news.

I cut a hunk from a smoked cheese and passed it to him. 'By promising not to raid across the Danuvius whilst Rome strikes over the Rhenus?'

Aldhard bit into his cheese and asked through a full mouth: 'How did you know?'

'Because it's what I would've done if I were him and were thinking just about my position and not about Germania as a whole. Rome would very happily sign a peace treaty with him now on extremely good terms – he probably won't even have to pay any tribute at all – in order that they can release a couple of legions from the Danuvius garrison to come north to join the Rhenus legions when they come for their revenge.'

'That's exactly what he's negotiating at the moment with Tiberius; he's sent Varus' head on to Augustus in Rome to show his good faith and his disapproval of your actions. I was surprised to be allowed to live, so keen he seems to be at becoming Rome's best friend.'

'For the time being. As soon as Rome's attention is on us here in the north he'll allow his people to raid for cattle and slaves across the river. I was expecting better of him: I was hoping for an alliance or at the very least a promise to keep the Danuvius legions busy for the next few years.' I slammed the palm of my hand down onto the table. 'The conniving bastard!'

'You said it was what you would have done in the circumstances.'

'*Would have done*; it's what any of the kings of any of the tribes *would have done* before we'd had such a total victory; but now with the Fatherland free of the invader surely it would be better to ensure that it stays free, rather than making it easier for Rome to come back in. It's the short-sightedness of Maroboduus' policy that angers me: if Rome can retake the lands up to the Albis then his lands in Bojohaemum will also be threatened.'

'So what do we do? Send an embassy to him and hope to change his mind?'

'It'll be too late for that; the treaty would have been negotiated by now and will probably be signed in the spring.' I paused for thought, pouring myself and Aldhard more ale from the jug. 'I suppose that what this does tell us is there will be no punitive raid next year.'

'What makes you say that?'

'If the treaty isn't signed until next spring at the earliest, then they won't be able to risk moving any of the garrison legions until the summer, which would mean that they wouldn't be on the Rhenus until autumn; too late for a campaign next year. Perhaps Maroboduus has done us a favour after all by allowing Rome to gather her strength before she attacks us; gathering takes time and that time we can use to prepare ourselves. Have messages sent to all the kings of the north inviting them to the Kalk Riese on midsummer's day next year; there we shall decide our fate.'

But before I met with the kings I had some ...

'The perennial problem of the Germanic peoples,' Thumelicatz said, cutting Tiburtius off. 'The inability to cooperate. Your capacity to do so is what makes you Romans so formidable. It's worth remembering that you are made up of Romans, Etruscans, Campanians, Samnites ...'

'Sabines,' the younger brother added.

'Indeed. And many more tribes from Italia and yet the world sees only Romans.'

'We fought many wars to enable that to come about,' the elder brother pointed out.

'True, but one hundred and thirty years ago your Latin allies fought a war against you for the right to have your citizenship, to be like you; imagine: fighting your enemy in order to be assimilated by him! I can't picture the Chatti fighting the Cherusci for the honour of becoming a part of our tribe. To unite the tribes, so that we would think of ourselves as All Men, was my father's dream and he died knowing that was an impossible goal; and I have learnt from him the sad truth of the matter and do not share that dream.' He turned to Thusnelda. 'But I've interrupted just before your part of the story, Mother; I apologise. Tiburtius, continue from where you left off.'

But before I met with the kings I had some unfinished business to take care of.

It was only natural, as kin to Segestes, that my father and I should be present at the wedding ceremony of his daughter, no matter what had passed between us; so when

Adgandestrius came to the Harzland to claim his bride, the following spring, just before the time of the Ice Gods, I made sure that I was there. What I planned was audacious in the extreme, another grand gesture that Lucius would have been proud of, and it would confirm Adgandestrius and Segestes as my enemies for ever.

Adgandestrius rode into the Harzland with two hundred of his warriors; they were in a celebratory mood with garlands tied to their spear tips and helms and adorning their horses' bridles. Our people cheered them in as they climbed deeper into the range of hills that was the heart of the Cherusci homeland and all seemed to be well between the two tribes united in victory over Rome. The last time the Chatti had come this way in such great numbers was the raid on our people the year before my return; now they came in friend-ship – or so they thought.

Adgandestrius, as was his due as king of the Chatti, was received by my father and was feasted in his longhouse along with his retinue; because of our mutual antipathy we were seated at different ends of the high table and managed only to exchange a brief nod of acknowledgement throughout the night. The following afternoon, after spending the morning sleeping off the inevitable hangover, Adgandestrius led his men southeast to Segestes' settlement; my father and I followed, along with our households, a couple of hours behind.

Now, I had not seen Segestes since Thusnelda had begged for his release in the clearing at the summit of the Kalk Riese; he had refused all offers of a reconciliation from my father and uncle, Inguiomer, throwing their generosity back in their faces despite the fact that it was him who had tried to betray us to Varus and would have happily seen us executed. He had not even invited us to the wedding, a fact that expressed itself in his greeting of my father.

'You have a nerve to show up at the wedding of my daughter!' Segestes shouted as he saw us riding through the gates of his settlement.

My father waited until he had dismounted before replying: 'As king of the Cherusci, I have a right to go where I please in this land. And do you know why that is, Segestes?'

My father's cousin scowled, but could not deny the truth of what my father had implied. 'Because it is now free of the Romans?'

'Bravo, Cousin; but had you had your way, my son would have been crucified as a traitor to Rome and we would still be a province. But today we shall put all of that behind us and celebrate.' He stood in front of Segestes and opened his arms to him.

There was complete silence around the compound as the two men regarded one another.

Grudgingly, Segestes moved forward and submitted himself to his cousin's embrace; his people and ours cheered as they thumped each other on the back. Inguiomer too embraced the errant cousin and then it was my turn. I slipped from my horse and approached the man who had tried to betray me to Varus just a few months ago.

Segestes backed away as I neared him. 'This I cannot do.'

I smiled, cold and with narrowed eyes. 'Are you afraid that your friends in Rome may hear of your embracing the architect of their defeat?'

'You are not welcome here, Erminatz; for whatever reasons you might wish to think of, you are not welcome at the marriage of my daughter.'

'Don't concern yourself on that account, Segestes; I'll not be here for the wedding. I shall take some refreshment and then leave, seeing as my reception has been less than courteous. You have not grown so ill-mannered as to refuse food and drink to a traveller, have you?'

The look on his face suggested that he would have liked to have refused me but could not be seen to do so before so many people. 'Take what you wish and then leave.'

'Thank you for that kind offer, Segestes; I shall take full advantage of it, you can be assured.'

The feast had been set up outside Segestes' longhouse, on many tables surrounding the oak at the centre of the settlement; its branches had been decorated with ribbons that hung to the ground and smoke from the fire pits, roasting game whole, swirled up about it. Everywhere the atmosphere was that of a holiday: children played in the warm sun as their parents sat around drinking, talking and laughing, waiting for the food to be ready and the feast to begin – the ceremony would only take place once all had eaten and drunk their fill so that the couple would not have to retire to the marriage bed on an empty stomach. Warriors competed in tests of strength, wrestling or lifting huge stones over their heads, whilst slaves went to and fro preparing the fare for their betters. A group of musicians with pipes and lyres struck up a merry tune and the youth of the village began a series of complicated dance steps beneath the oak whilst holding onto the ribbons flowing from it.

I walked around, savouring this Germanic idyll, reflecting on how I was just about to ruin it and set myself on a path that would mean that there could never be friendship between the Chatti and the Cherusci again; however, seeing as that friendship was also impossible whilst Adgandestrius remained alive it seemed to me that there was nothing to lose and everything to gain in what I planned.

And so I walked into Segestes' longhouse.

Thumelicatz held up his hand. 'Mother, I think it would be appropriate for you to continue, for this is your entrance.'

Thusnelda came forward from the shadow. 'I remember it so well; I was being dressed by my mother and the better-born maidens of the settlement at the far end of my father's longhouse. My spirits were low as there was only a matter of hours before the ceremony would take place and it looked as if, despite what he had said on the Kalk Riese, Erminatz was not going to be able to change my plans. I fidgeted as my ladies tried to fasten my dress and plait my hair, threading flowers through the tresses; and then a shadow appeared in the doorway and my heart leapt, Erminatz had come for me. My mother shouted at him to leave, no men were allowed in the longhouse as the bride was being readied, and he did so without saying a word; but his very presence was enough for me to know what he expected of me.

'I now rushed, helping to tie my girdle and stepping into my slippers, so eager was I to put the mean-spirited Adgandestrius behind me. My father had arranged the marriage in the hope that he could persuade the Chatti into a far more pro-Roman policy, one I would be ashamed of and ashamed to have been a tool in bringing it about. How could he think that my virginity could be used to buy our subjugation? But he was always a weak man who worshipped strength in others because he could find little in himself.

'Happy with my appearance, I almost skipped outside to find that the feast was ready and my father was waiting for me.

'"Today you will make me proud," he said, stepping back and admiring my hair.

'"I hope so, Father," I replied and I really meant it for I did hope that he would someday understand that I did the right thing.

'I took his arm and he led me to the table of honour at the head of the feast. Here he placed me to his left whilst Adgandestrius took the seat to his right. We sat and broke bread and my father proposed many toasts to us and our happiness, but if he really was concerned about that then perhaps he should have consulted me in my choice for a husband. After many horns had been drunk, my father suddenly stared ahead of him and then pointed at Erminatz who was seated far down the tables. "What are you still doing here?" he roared, getting to his feet and spilling his drinking horn over his lap. "I thought you said you would leave after you had taken some refreshment."

'Erminatz looked unperturbed at this outburst; all conversation stopped and he became the centre of attention. He deliberately finished the mouthful that he was chewing and then washed it down with a long, slow slug of ale. Wiping his mouth on the back of his hand he stood, stepping back over the bench, and said: "I still haven't finished taking my refreshment, Segestes, but seeing as you seem so anxious for me to be gone I shall show more grace than you have in throwing me out, by complying with your wishes. However, there is one more piece of refreshment that I wish to take." He raised an arm and a rider appeared leading a horse. As it drew near, Erminatz jumped into the empty saddle and kicked the horse forward in a walk to come to a stop in front of the high table.

'Erminatz looked down at Adgandestrius and said: "Tell me, how would it feel for your woman to always be thinking of another each time you bed her?"

'Adgandestrius returned the look, hatred in his eyes. "You should know, Erminatz."

'He replied: "I don't; but I am going to do you a favour and ensure that you will never have that humiliation; although why I should help you is beyond me." With a quick glance in my direction, Erminatz eased his horse side-on to the table.

'I reacted immediately, pushing myself up from my seat and clambering onto the table. "I choose Erminatz!" I shouted as I leapt behind him, my legs astride the mount and my arms about his waist. "Let no one here say that I did not go of my own volition."

'My love swung his horse around as uproar broke out; he pushed it into a gallop with Aldhard, the second rider, following us. Before anyone could react we were through the gates and heading like the wind to the northwest. I held onto the man to whom I planned to dedicate the rest of my life and laughed at his audacity; and he laughed too for we were together for the first time and hoped that it would be this way for ever.

'However, we were not bargaining for the wickedness of kin.'

CHAPTER XV

'THE WICKEDNESS OF kin,' Thumelicatz ruminated, each syllable stretched and stressed. 'How our lives have been blighted by the wickedness of kin, eh, Mother? Betrayed to Germanicus by your own father and given to Rome whilst pregnant with Erminatz's child in revenge for him taking you away on the day you were due to marry Adgandestrius. Segestes even travelled to Rome two years later as a guest of Tiberius to watch his own daughter and grandson – me, born in captivity – being paraded as trophies in Germanicus' Triumph. What wickedness to gloat at your own daughter's misfortune that you have brought about because of your hatred for your cousin's son and now son-in-law. And then to ... but no, that comes at the end of my father's story; we mustn't skip that far ahead. But my father's narrative does jump; it jumps four years to the year before my mother's betrayal. Aius will read.'

Happiness is not a commodity that's easy to come by in our world and although we wanted no one else other than each other we were not destined to be together for long. I still pray that one day we will be reunited and I shall meet the son I have never seen, a gift to replace our daughter who was stillborn in the second year of our marriage; but that is, perhaps, for another day.

My supposition that there would be at least a year before any retaliation proved correct; Tiberius raided across the Rhenus two years after Varus' defeat. However, instead of the weather influencing my story at this point another factor came into play: age. Augustus was ageing and fading; he recalled his heir, Tiberius, to Rome and decreed that the empire should have its border on the Rhenus and go no further. It seemed that we had won and our freedom was now guaranteed, which was just as well seeing as the meeting of the kings that I had called at the Kalk Riese had proved inconclusive since none were willing to accept me as the leader of a united Germania and a suitable alternative acceptable to all could not be found; but Augustus' decree meant that the need for unity had disappeared. Rome, theoretically, was never going to come back so therefore we were free to return to our old ways. And for three more years that's what we did.

The mutiny of the Rhenus legions on Tiberius' ascension further fed our sense of security and so it came as a shock when the news broke in October of that same year that the lands of the Marsi had been ravaged by the new Roman general in the north, my old acquaintance, Germanicus. Thousands had been put to the sword and the Eagle of the Nineteenth had been recovered. The speed of the campaign had been breathtaking and had caught all by surprise; but its timing was the one thing that was in our favour, if we could mobilise. October can be a harsh month on the northern plain along the line of the Lupia and there was a good chance that we could fall on Germanicus' army as it retreated to its base on the west bank of the Rhenus; a second Teutoburg Wald was possible.

I sent messages to all the kings, begging them to come to the Lupia and set off with as many of my warriors as I could muster in the short time that I had. With less than three hundred men – but with the promise of more to come – I came to the fort of Aliso in the southern lands of the Bructeri to find that what we had left in ruins had been rebuilt. There was no one there to meet me other than Engilram with four thousand of his men; four half-strength legions and the similar amount of auxiliaries faced us. But battle was not on Germanicus' mind as the weather had closed in and the ground was sodden, winter was nigh and he was withdrawing; a paltry force such as ours was not worth the few lives that it would have taken to defeat us and so he pulled back along the road knowing I was powerless to stop him.

'No one else will come,' Engilram said as we watched the last cohort disappear from sight. 'The Marsi are too battered and the rest of the northern tribes are worried about giving you another victory over Rome.'

I looked at him, incredulous. 'Giving *me* another victory? Surely it's giving *us* another victory?'

'That's not how Adgandestrius sees it; he's the one who's been working against you, making the others fear your ambition.'

'The short-sighted, mean-minded—'

'Aggrieved and humiliated proud man,' Engilram interrupted. 'You were wrong to take Thusnelda from him in such a public way.'

'Right or wrong, surely the chance of spilling Roman blood outweighs his anger at me?'

'You know that can never be true. But there'll be other occasions in the next few years; Germanicus will be back again and that reality will focus a few of the more pragmatic kings. You may well get some unity then; in the meantime my warriors will harry them all the way to the Rhenus just to let them know that we still have teeth.'

I thanked the old king of the Bructeri and, cursing the perfidy of Adgandestrius, returned to the Harzland.

But the gods have a way of bringing a proud man around, for the next year it was the Chatti who were the target; but I was elsewhere.

'My father, Segestes, came to our settlement after the summer solstice whilst Erminatz was away,' Thusnelda said, silencing Aius with a sharp hand gesture. 'He came under a branch of truce, saying that he wanted to talk with me. I thought nothing of it as I hadn't spoken with him since that day Erminatz stole me from under his nose four years previously. He and his escort were allowed through the gates; there were few warriors around as most were accompanying my husband as he went about the thanes who had some sympathy for my father's pro-Roman stance, trying to dissuade them of their opinion; and that is what he took advantage of.

'"You want to talk to me, Father," I said as he came through the door of our longhouse with two of his warriors behind him.

'"No, bitch, there's nothing to say," he retorted. His two men grabbed me, hitting me across the back of the head, and hauled me, semi-conscious, from the house. Outside the rest of his men had formed a cordon; I was slung across a horse and before I could gather my senses we had ridden down the few warriors who had tried to block the gate and were away back to his settlement that had been recently strengthened judging by the work that had been done on the palisade.

'For half a moon I was kept prisoner, locked in a storeroom, and it was with the passing of that moon that I realised that I was pregnant again and I wept. But the tears did not last for long for, when I woke the following morning, my love had come for me;

from my prison I could see naught but I could hear: from all angles came the sound of shouting. We were surrounded and under siege.' Thusnelda nodded to Aius. 'Take it from that point.'

Aius scanned down the scroll.

I grabbed the kneeling captive's hair, yanking it back, and then prised out his left eye with the tip of my dagger. I waited until his screams subsided. 'I'll ask you one more time: where is she being kept?'

'In a storeroom at the back of the main longhouse.'

I looked in his one remaining eye and could see that he was telling the truth; I gestured to Aldhard to let him grip his sword so that he would gain Walhalla dying with a weapon in his hand, then slit his throat and let him slump to the ground. 'Aldhard, we'll dig a ditch all the way around the settlement; no one comes in or out until I have Thusnelda back.'

He looked at me not understanding. 'But who will do the digging?'

'My warriors.'

'You can't ask them to do slaves' work; they'll never countenance it. They're here to fight not dig.'

And that was just the problem: our men were too proud to be able to bring themselves to conduct a siege in an efficient manner; for them a siege was just lying around outside the gates waiting for the enemy to come out and challenge them to single combat or, as with Aliso, hurling themselves at the walls in a vain attempt to scale them. But I couldn't afford to do that, not with Thusnelda within those walls.

And so we were at stalemate; no one came in or out during the day but at night supplies were always getting through and the besieged showed no sign of weakening, not even by the middle of September when Germanicus' army appeared from the west. With fewer than two thousand men I could not stand against him; it was with tears of impotent rage that I ordered our withdrawal and watched from a distant hill as a party left the settlement and joined the Roman ranks. My wife was now a prisoner of Germanicus and I did not know how to get her back. But, as I said, the gods have a way of bringing a proud man around and it was the loss of Thusnelda that brought Adgandestrius to me.

'They have ravaged my lands, burnt my chief town of Mattium, killed thousands of my people and I want revenge,' he told me soon after he arrived in the Harzland, with barely five hundred warriors, a few days after Germanicus had left – unfought.

'And why do you come to me, you who have done all within your power to stop me uniting an army against Rome?'

'Because the thing that divided us is gone and is now in Rome's hands.'

'Thusnelda?'

'Yes, neither of us have her now; you want her back and I am grateful to her because had Segestes not called Germanicus to his aid to relieve your siege and help him escape, I would most certainly be dead; such was the prize that Segestes offered that Germanicus dropped everything to come for Thusnelda and we were down to our last few days of food and water trapped in some caves in the south of our lands. Because of her capture we have lived. For the present, let us put what is gone behind us and unite our forces.'

I looked at my enemy and although I could see no trace of friendship in his eyes I knew that his intention was honest; for the time being we could be allies. I took him into an embrace. 'We will muster the tribes at Aliso again. We shall try to do what we did in the Teutoburg Wald, something that we could have done last year had ... well, never mind what we could have done last year because we will do it this year. We will make them pay as they attempt the passage of the—

'The Long Bridges,' the street-fighter cut in. 'I was there with the Fifth Alaudae.'

Thumelicatz looked pleased at the admission. 'Tell us then, Roman; and I'll have my slaves take notes so that the narrative can be fleshed out, as my father didn't leave that detailed an account.'

The street-fighter rubbed one of his cauliflower ears and collected his thoughts for a few moments. 'Well, the year before had been a fraught summer because Tiberius had refused our demands that military service be reduced from twenty years, and five in reserve, back down to sixteen years in the legions and then four years as a reserve; none of the lads was best pleased when the news came through and so we refused to take the oath to the new Emperor. We wanted Germanicus to be emperor; him we loved, whereas Tiberius was dour and distant; but he refused and eventually shamed us into backing down. Once we were back under military discipline, with hardly any warning, he had a bridge built and we crossed the Rhenus into the lands of the Marsi with the more rebellious cohorts of Germania Inferior's four legions. Germanicus reckoned it best if we take out our frustration on the Germanic tribes rather than each other, and he was probably right. So, we were back in the land of fear and forest and unable to complain about it, as we had only just submitted to his will and couldn't mutiny a second time without the consequences being far harsher than just handing over the ringleaders for execution.

'But it seemed that it would not be a repeat of the disaster of five years previously as we caught the population unawares; we ripped through them, burning every homestead and slaughtering all the inhabitants, regardless of sex or age, who we could find. A few of the lads, a very few, who had made it out of Germania after Varus and had been drafted into the Alaudae – you can imagine the thoroughness with which they took to the task, if you take my meaning? Well, after about twenty days of laying waste to anything we came across, the Eagle of the Nineteenth was uncovered and Germanicus felt that would conclude proceedings for that season very nicely and so we headed back to the fortress of Aliso, which had been rebuilt by auxiliaries whilst we'd been off enjoying ourselves, in order to pick up the military road back to the Rhenus and a well-earned rest for the winter. And so we did and had a fine winter of it. The following spring we came east again, this time to give the Chatti a good taste of our iron, and they didn't like it, that much was for sure. We burnt Mattium, killing or enslaving most of the inhabitants, before chasing the rump of the Chatti army south to a series of caves, high in some cliffs, that they'd fortified so that they were almost impossible to break into; but just as we were about to starve them out Germanicus suddenly lifted the siege and we raced northeast. When we saw why we could understand it.' He looked at Thusnelda. 'You were a beautiful young woman and we knew that you would be a great loss for Arminius and a trophy for Germanicus. By that time the season was coming to an end. Germanicus took two of the legions back to the empire by ship, sailing up the Amisia and then out into the Northern Sea – but that's another story – us along with the Second, Fourteenth and

Twentieth were to go back with his number two, Caecina, along the military road following the Lupia.

'But it didn't prove to be quite so straightforward; things never are in Germania.

'"Shit!" my mate Sextus said as we paraded in front of the camp on the morning of our departure. "That don't look good, Magnus, not good at all."

'Now, Sextus isn't the brightest of the bunch – indeed, of any given bunch there's a fair probability that he will be the least bright – but this time he was absolutely right: it didn't look good at all. "Shit indeed, mate," I said, sucking the wind through my teeth. "There're a fuck of a lot of them." And there were; thousands, or so it seemed, lining the crest of a hill a couple of miles to the east of us and looking hungry for some Roman blood. "And we're two hundred miles and twenty bridges from the Rhenus."

'Sextus screwed up his face in the way that he always does on the very rare occasions that he attempts arithmetic. "That's a bridge every seven miles," he guessed eventually.

'"Something like that, Sextus, my old son, something like that."

'"And who gave you permission to have an opinion, soldier!" Servius, our optio, screamed, from behind me, into my ear. "Any more talking in the ranks and the only opinion you'll be having is how much the cane bruises on your back hurt with every shovel-load of shit I have you move from one side of the latrine ditch to the other, and then back again."

'Sextus and I snapped to attention and pulled on our most earnest military expressions, staring intently somewhere in the middle distance. But Servius' ire was distracted by a communal groan of anguish from the entire parade of four, almost full-strength, legions, as if we was all being buggered for the first time. To our left, across the river, in the hills that followed it west, thousands more of the hairy bastards ... er, my apologies, noble Germanic warriors appeared and, at some signal unseen, both groups gave a low roar of wicked intent: a nasty sound to say the least, but very chilling when you know you've got at least a ten-day march ahead of you with those bastards snapping at you all the time and then running away sharpish every time we turn to offer them a decent toe to toe to be settled by whose got the sharpest iron and the biggest balls.

'Anyway, the blow-boys started rumbling away on their *cornua*, standards got waved and then dipped or raised depending on what series of oaths each primus centurion of the cohort roared. Our cohort standard leant left and then dipped once as the cornua rumbled a downwards call; the centurion of our century, Carrinas Balbillus, or the arse-widener as he was affectionately known, due to the novel usage he would put his vine cane to when he felt that a simple beating was not sufficient punishment, politely asked us to turn about and retreat one hundred paces. Once we had done that he requested us to be so kind as to form column. We were facing west; we were not going to offer battle but, rather, make a run for it. From where we were, in the Fifth Alaudae, ninth cohort, seventh century, it was impossible to tell what was going on, but rumour swiftly made it through the ranks that all four legions were forming a hollow square with the baggage in the middle and that we were the left-hand side with the First Germanica at the front, the Twenty-first Rapax on the right and the Twentieth watching our arses, something, Servius observed in a rare display of wit, they should be very good at given their habit of hiding behind us every time a rumble threatened.

'Mars alone knows how long it took to sort ourselves out but eventually the centurions and optios decided that they had shouted at us enough for the present and we were all in the right place. Out to our flank we could see a couple of the Gallic auxiliary cohorts forming up defensively as if an attack were coming in from a previously unseen source whilst two of the Hispanic light cavalry alae swirled around either flank, no doubt wishing to dissuade the Germanic bastards from trying to claim a few Gallic heads – we all know they hate a Gaul as much as a Gaul hates a German, but a Gaul in the uniform of Rome is a sight so provoking to them that they would trample their own grandmothers to get at such an offensive thing. As you can imagine, we were quite happy to let them sort it out by themselves, if it meant we could just get on with our marching in peace and quiet; eventually, after more rumbling of cornua and dipping of standards, the arse-widener, with the utmost consideration for our sensibilities, suggested that we might like to move forward at the convenient pace of double-quick march. We, of course, were only too willing to oblige him so kindly had been his entreaty, and with our equipment yokes over our shoulders but our shields in hand and not slung behind us, we happily yomped off west.

'But Germania is not a place renowned for giving us Romans an easy go of it and they have some very anti-Roman gods, one of whom, Donar, seemed to have it in for us in a particularly spiteful way. He has a hammer, I believe, and it was at the same instant that we broke into a quick trot that he brought his hammer down on whatever he brings it down upon and the clouds burst with a rumble that put to shame all the efforts of the blow-boys during our recent manoeuvring. Down it pissed and the wind gusted so that the rain washed by in sheets and swirls, driving into our eyes and through our chainmail – our cohort hadn't yet been issued with the new segmented armour– so that before we'd gone a mile we were all about as miserable as the arse-widener liked us to be, and it showed in the glee on his face as he gave us playful taps with his cane to help us along the way.

'Out to our left the rain partially covered the running battle that the Gauls were having with their friends, but with the help of the Hispanic cavalry and a couple of reinforcement cohorts of Aquitanians they seemed to be holding off any attempt at making a meal of our testicles.' The street-fighter paused and scowled at Thumelicatz's jar. 'That just ain't natural.' Shaking his head he continued: 'Anyhow, on we went, gritting our teeth as the miles mounted up, each one harder than the last and, bearing in mind that we were four legions in a hollow square, which was, in fact, a rectangle two hundred paces across and over a mile long, following a road that was only ten paces wide very few of us had any firm footing. Where we were in the exalted heights of the seventh century of the ninth cohort, by the time we got to any given piece of mud a few hundred other lads had been there before so the going weren't at all good, if you take my meaning, not like a nice canter around the track of the Circus Maximus back in Rome. And then, of course, there was the small matter of the bridges, which only the transport could use seeing as they were on the road; the rest of us had to cross the rivers in whatever way we could, up to our necks often enough, and if we weren't cold when we splashed in then we certainly were as we scrambled up the opposite bank.

'On we yomped, our lungs bursting and our throats on fire, despite the rain, with hardly any of the lads able to at least make a quip, which mightily annoyed the arse-widener as the only excuse he had for savaging us was imagined slacking; but no one was going to slack when the choice was between physical torment under the loving strokes of Balbillus' cane or to be entertained by a nice bunch of lads who are very keen on warming your toes on a cold day above one of their fires.

'"Halt!" the arse-widener shouted just as I thought that a fire might not be so bad a thing after all. I came out of the nightmare that I'd been subjected to for however long to find that we were all standing still and were now being invited to knock up a marching camp for thirty thousand men.

'Well, we ain't never worked so hard so quickly; although each spade-full of earth seemed to be twice the weight it normally was due to the excessive amount of water it contained, we had very soon dug two and a half miles of four-foot-deep ditch and piled the earth up around it in a four-foot-high breastwork. As we worked, the auxiliaries kept the tribes at bay, covering us in long screens on both flanks of the column; but despite their efforts they couldn't push the bastards back far enough into the forest to either side in order that we could cut the extra wood we needed for the palisade. As a lot of the stakes we carried with us had been lost, the ditch and breastwork were all that we had to shelter behind. But at least we had our tents and were soon taking our cheerless cold meals inside them, grateful to be out of the rain for a short while at least. And it *was* a short while for after just two hours the arse-widener slams his cane down on the tops of our tents and suggests that we might like to join the tenth cohort in spending the next couple of hours manning the perimeter so that the rest of the legion could sleep safe and sound tucked up in their bedding-rolls knowing that we were watching over them like concerned mother hens. Obviously we told the arse-widener that nothing would give us more pleasure and he and Servius showed their gratitude by thrashing us into position next to the eighth century.

'And it weren't nice, not one bit, because the auxiliaries had withdrawn into the camp so that there was nothing to prevent the blood-lusting bastards from coming right up to the ditch and throwing the javelins at us; and they did just that again and again. I had Sextus on my left and on my right this Greek, Cassandros, who had just been transferred into the Fifth from an eastern legion and had brought all those nasty eastern habits with him. We peered into the downpour and through it we could just see the shadow of a mass of men; forward they came, running towards us, halooing and ululating and making all sorts of ghastly sounds. We hunkered down behind our shields, resting on the top of the breastwork. "Brace yourself, Sextus, my lovely," I muttered as I felt my arsehole clench tight enough to strangle an inquisitive rat. "I don't think they're coming to deliver our break-fast and enquire whether or not we slept well."

'My mate frowned. "That would be stupid because it ain't breakfast time yet and they're the ones who are keeping us awake."

'"Never mind, Sextus, never mind."

'"He's not that bright, is he?" Cassandros observed.

'"He never claimed to be," I replied.

'Any further discussion on the subject was curtailed by an influx of javelins. They thumped into our shields all along the line, hollow and resounding, like hail on ox-hide drums. I don't know how many stuck themselves into my shield but by the time the hairy bastards had started to fling themselves across our nice ditch it felt extremely unwieldy and there was nothing I could do about it.

'Now, when you first join the legions you're made to attack a wooden post with a wooden sword day after day for months, when you're not doing twenty mile route-marches in full kit, that is; well, no one really understands just why the drill-masters favour such a seemingly pointless exercise until the first time you

have to make your iron bite. And so it was that night, my blade
punching through the gap between mine and Sextus' shields,
stabbing faces and chests as the Germanic tribesmen tried to
climb over the breastwork, sometimes using the javelins in our
shields as handholds, hauling themselves up and forcing us to
pull hard on our grips so our protection wouldn't be pulled
down. Blood spurted from severed arteries and rough-hewn
stumps as we worked our blades; now it was automatic, second
nature and the hours at the post made sense and the cursing of
the drill-masters now seemed like music our strokes could keep
time to. Stab, twist, left, right, pull, stab again, all of us in a line,
two deep, with the arse-widener at our centre, howling his hatred
at the unwashed barbarians for having the cheek to try to break
into his camp as he sent warrior after warrior to whatever the
Germanic afterlife consists of in payment for such effrontery.
Behind us, Servius, with his optio's rod held to the backs of the
second rankers to keep our line straight and also to dissuade any
one from thinking that it might just be more comfortable back in
the tent, yelled insults at us to keep us cheerful as we flung them
back, dead, dying on top of the growing pile in the ditch. And
that was just the problem: the more we killed the shallower was
the ditch and the easier it became for them to scale the breastwork. I felt my shield being tugged at, hard, and had to squeeze
the grip for all I was worth for it not to be ripped away; a quick
glance down and I saw fingers wrapped around its rim. With a
sideways jerk of the wrist my blade cleaned them off, their former
owner's screams lost in the din, and I felt the pressure release on
my shield as, in the corner of my eye, something flashed towards
me. Instinctively I raised my shield and blocked, with the top
rim, a spear thrust aimed right at my eyes; but the move opened
a gap between the breastwork and the bottom rim. I felt the air

punched out of me and looked down to see a spear point rammed into my stomach. I cracked my shield back down onto it and, to my relief, it shifted; the thrust hadn't been enough to break through the chainmail. However, by now I was starting to get cross, as was Sextus and Cassandros to either side; in fact the whole century was not in the best of moods and, much to Balbillus' glee, we bellowed our defiance and took as many lives as we could before they slunk back off into the pissing rain.

'Now, the trouble with Germans is that if one German does something then all the other buggers have to do the same thing so that they won't seem to be deemed lesser men; and so when we beat off that attack that wasn't the end of it, far from it. Back they came but this time it was fresh ones who'd been sitting out the last effort and now wished to show their beaten comrades how it really should be done. We swapped ranks so that Sextus, Cassandros and me just had to do some pushing whilst holding our shields over the men in front. Only the arse-widener seemed happy to stay in the front rank and we were all happy to see him there in the hope that some barbarian would do us a favour but, contrary as they are, none of them did. By the time we were relieved a couple of hours later he was covered in blood and in fine fettle, having piled up a nice big mound of dead in front of his section of the breastwork, and was more than ready to shout us to sleep. Sleep, however, was not the easiest thing to come by as the raids persisted throughout the night and air was constantly filled with the screams of the maimed and the dying so that they almost drowned out the blow-boys' reveille an hour before dawn. Down the camp came, tents loaded onto each tent-party's mule and the bigger items, like the grain-mill and the arse-widener's tent, loaded onto the century's cart that also carried the carroballista. The auxiliaries formed up again to shield us whilst we were bawled into the correct order of march, but for some reason the tribes held off, preferring instead to watch us from a distance and jeer and favour us with the sight of their arses as we moved off.

'It wasn't until the rear of the column had gone a couple of miles that we realised what they were waiting for: they had been busy overnight and soon our feet began to sink further into the mud and then the mud became very liquid until we were walking through an endless puddle that gradually deepened to ankle-height and then knee-height. The bastards had spent the night, when they weren't attacking us, damming the next couple of rivers so that the flood-plain between them lived up to its name. Needless to say we were by now really struggling and even Sextus, who could wrestle down an ox, was having trouble moving forward and the column's pace was reduced to no more than a shuffle as the carts were constantly getting stuck. Then that cunt Donar crashed his hammer down and, just when the arse-widener thought that we couldn't be more miserable, more water came tipping from above and its arrival heralded a new series of attacks on the auxiliaries. But this time with the water level so high the cavalry couldn't protect their flanks nearly so effectively and it weren't long before the first Gallic cohort broke, turning and splashing back towards us in the main column; and then the rest of them turned and the hairy-arsed savages came tearing after them, felling them as they ran, and having a good laugh about it as nothing pleases them more than the sight of a dead Gaul. Even the cavalry were ravaged as the horses weren't willing to move fast through the water and shied when pushed, so that many of the riders abandoned their mounts to try and make a quicker getaway.

'With the cover swept away we were open to attack but a toe to toe was not what they had in mind. The javelins fell down on us almost as thickly as the rain and, by now, the image of what had happened to Varus was in all our thoughts for we had heard the four-day battle being recounted many a time and there was not a man in that army who didn't fear its repeat. And that's what looked to be happening. Helpless we were as the lethal rain fell, volley after volley down onto our upturned shields, many a missile getting through, such was our disorder; and we were unable to return the favour as all our efforts were concentrated on protecting ourselves and trying to move forward and, besides, we hadn't been resupplied with pila due to the chaos of the previous night. The few archers we had tried to hold the savages off but they were so small in number that they hardly made any difference as the Germans would just back off when they saw them coming and concentrate their efforts elsewhere.

'For hours we waded forward, only leaving our dead behind; those unlucky enough to be too wounded to carry on gratefully accepted into their hearts the sword of their comrade rather than be left behind for the fires. But the dead soon caught up with us again as the savages took their heads and hurled them into our midst and we raged at our impotence, not being able to avenge the mutilation of our fallen.

'The day dragged on and our hunger grew as we could not stop to eat and, besides, there was no way that we could make a fire in the middle of what had become a huge lake. Even when we finally made it onto dryer ground, in other words ground that was just a quagmire rather than being submerged, we knew that there would be no pausing. So we chewed on whatever scraps we could find in our kit, wishing that we could make use of the eleven days' rations that we were each carrying because the order hadn't come through to break them out.

'We made it across another river, one that hadn't been dammed, and found ourselves on more open ground. The blow-boys started doing their thing and it wasn't long before the arse-widener was politely requesting that we start digging our share of the ditch for the night's camp. That camp was no better than the previous night's and our misery did not let up and neither did the savages, although we were so knackered that no matter how many wounded were screaming their agony to the gods we slept as soon as we had finished our shift at the breast-work. Even Balbillus showed us a bit of consideration and didn't bellow at us for a full four hours.

'"I don't think I can make it through the day," Cassandros muttered as the bellowing started again soon after reveille and we were trying to make a mush of cold flour and ground chick-peas.

'"Well, it's a choice between going on, falling on your sword or warming your toes in the fires," I said, none too helpfully, "and personally I'll take the first option as I don't like fire and I'd rather avoid the serious bollocking that I'd get from the arse-widener for killing myself without permission."

'Cassandros grumbled a complaint although acknowledging the truth of the matter whilst Sextus looked painfully confused as he tried to work out how the arse-widener could chase him into the afterlife; he was still working on the problem when we had, once again, formed up and the order to advance in double time was sounded by our legion's blow-boys.

'Now, I don't know what happened because in those days I didn't query anything; I just followed the last bellowed order unquestioningly to make life easier and to avoid Balbillus demonstrating on me, for all to see, how he got his nickname. And my guess is that the arse-widener himself didn't know how it occurred; but occur it did and it was nearly the end of us all.

'Off we went, moaning as much as we dared about being asked to set off at such a pace on a virtually empty stomach and getting no sympathy from the arse-widener other than some encouraging taps with his vine cane. We pressed on, thinking that we were all doing the right thing, over the gradually drying ground as Donar had obviously decided to have a lie-in that day, and we had nothing worse to contend with than a strong, cold, northerly wind that would have caused us considerable misery in our damp clothes had we not been fortunate enough to be sweating with the exertion of jogging in full kit.

'However, it seemed that no one was paying attention to what the rest of the army was doing for they were certainly not doing the same thing as us – except for the Twenty-first on the left flank, that is, who were doubling away with enthusiasm. The First and the Fourteenth, however, had taken it upon themselves to have a far more leisurely start to the day and were strolling along as if they were on a country ramble with their sweethearts. Well, it didn't take long before the inevitable happened and we and the Twenty-first outpaced the rest of the column exposing the baggage train, and if there is one thing that a German enjoys more than fucking a dead Gaul it's an exposed baggage train; and this one was irresistible. Out of the morning mist they came, hallooing and—'

'My father's account of this is worth hearing at this point,' Thumelicatz interjected. He looked over at his two slaves, who had been scrupulously taking notes; they put the styli down on the desk. 'You can collate your notes later and I'll decide what to add to my father's account. Aius, read from the eleventh scroll, from the moment that Erminatz sees the exposed baggage. Tiburtius, refresh the lamps and candles.'

After a few moments Aius had found his place and began to read as Tiburtius went around the tent tending the lit candles and lamps.

How such an order had been given I couldn't understand; it was madness to me but it was happening and it was an opportunity that I could not pass up: here was my chance to split the Roman column in two, right through the middle and then deal with each half piecemeal. Here was my chance to achieve an even more crushing victory than at the Chalk Giant. I was standing with my father and his household warriors at the head of the Cherusci, to the north of the Roman formation; without hesitation, I raised my sword and cried to the gods our war cry, praising them and reviling our foes. Forward I sprinted, my sword held in both hands over my right shoulder and my eyes fixed upon the junction of the baggage train and the Fourteenth Legion, at the rear of the hollow square not more than four hundred paces distant. My warriors followed gladly, seeing their chance of blood and booty, as before us, the command of the Fourteenth suddenly spotted the danger. But they were advancing in line, five cohorts abreast and two deep now that the ground was more open, so as to seal the fourth wall of the square, but the side walls had now disappeared; with no time to manoeuvre and turn and face us head-on, the best they could do was to halt and turn at right angles, switching their line into a column. At the moment they did so the Chatti and the Bructeri charged from the south and the Chauci joined in behind us.

The panic in the Roman ranks was evident, even at two hundred paces out, as they tried to face both attacks: files became entangled with one another as contradictory orders came in as to which way to turn and so their cohesion began to suffer. The baggage train began to scatter as the drivers all tried to catch up either with the two legions that had so inexplicably left them exposed or the legion closest to them either to their front or rear. But they didn't make it to safety; our charge went home. Almost four thousand of my warriors hit the Fourteenth in its disorganised flank and then spilled into the rear of the baggage train. Their disorganisation meant that they were unable to launch a timed volley of pila and it was with the loss of very few casualties that we pressed our charge home.

Swiping my sword from over my right shoulder I cleaved my way through the haphazardly formed front rank, sending one and a half heads spinning up into the air, bloodying all around, as, to either side, my father's household warriors broke the shield wall in many places and began fighting in the way they know best: as individuals. Through them we tore, causing mayhem and mortality, as the ranks and files split and the united war machine became no more than a collection of terrified, unsupported soldiery.

But even in so dire a situation the Roman army can still pull itself together through the discipline instilled into the men over years of training and, more especially, through the professionalism of the centuriate. By the time we had carved apart the first two cohorts on the flank the more central ones had rallied, the centurions realising that not to do so would spell death for them all. We hit their shield wall as a wave hits a cliff and, before long, I realised that it was as far as we would get; to waste my men's lives in trying to crack a nut that we had never cracked before was a futile aim and, besides, most of the baggage was still there for the plucking. And so the drivers died in droves and bolting mules were brought down with spears as if we were on a hunting trip on a day sacred to one of the gods and for the second time we captured the baggage of an entire army. As we plundered, the three leading legions ran west whilst the Fourteenth closed up and, making its own hollow square, pushed on past us leaving their dead in piles on the bloody ground. I was happy to let them go because I knew that there would be other opportunities to take them in the next few days that it would take them to reach the Rhenus; soon they would be no more and Tiberius, like his predecessor Augustus, would also have legions to mourn.

But it was not to be. Once again it was my family that thwarted me but this time it was not Segestes, now safely in Rome; the man was even closer to me. It was the following morning, as the warriors of the five tribes roused themselves with the leaden heads of men who've drunk far too much wine when their normal fare is ale, that I stood with my father, Inguiomer, Adgandestrius and Engilram, watching the Romans break camp. They had built it on open, flat ground about three miles from where we had looted their baggage train; once we had taken everything of value, enslaved the women and children and then sacrificed all the prisoners in thanks to the beneficence of the gods, we followed them. We had made our camp to the east so that they could carry on their journey west in the morning and hopefully make a similar mistake. I knew that their morale was shaky as there had been uproar in the camp during the night and yet we hadn't gone anywhere near it.

'Yes,' Thumelicatz said, halting the narration and looking at the street-fighter, 'I've always wondered what that was about; perhaps you could enlighten me?'

The street-fighter ran his hand through his hair, shaking his head in regret. 'It weren't our finest hour, that's for sure. It was a horse had got loose and then the slaves trying to recapture it spooked the thing so that it ran amok through the Twenty-first's section of the camp – not that it was really a proper camp as we'd almost all lost our tents. Well, as you can imagine, the lads were very edgy after what they'd been through the previous few days and a lot of them thought that the perimeter had been breached and, I'm sorry to say, many of them panicked. As there were hardly any tents there were no tent-lines and, therefore, very little order so the panic quickly spread as many of the lads tried to get out of the west-facing gate, the one furthest from the enemy. Well, Caecina had been wounded the day before, his horse had been shot from under him, and so he was confined to his bed and unable to do anything to help calm the lads and explain that they were spooked by a spooked horse and shame them into going back to whatever bit of muddy ground they had been fortunate enough to have been given. So, inevitably there was quite a scrimmage at the gate when the duty centurion refused to open it and it weren't until the legate of the Twenty-first, whose name escapes me, came along and shamed the frightened ladies into accepting the reality of the situation that things began to calm down. By the time they had all dispersed there were eight bodies lying on the ground; all of them had been trampled to death. If I remember rightly I heard that the legate was so ashamed of his men that he punished all those who'd been involved with exclusion from the camp for a whole year. This meant that they weren't allowed the protection and support of their comrades at night and had to make do as best they could on the outside. None of them made it through that year.'

Thumelicatz smiled in the lamplight, his teeth glowing softly through his beard. 'How gratifying to hear that Rome's finest were running scared of a horse by this time; my father would have been most amused, no doubt. But I think amusement was the last thing on his mind that morning. Aius, read on.'

But, to my surprise, Caecina decided not to run but offered battle with his demoralised army instead. I looked at his position and laughed. 'If he thinks that we would be stupid enough to come and face him head-on when all we have to do is wait for an opportune moment to take apart his flanks and then eat into the rump of his column, then he's mad.'

But it soon transpired that I was in a minority of one with this opinion. Inguiomer, my own uncle, spat on the ground. 'You've spent too much time away from your homeland, Erminatz; you've lost a real sense of Germanic pride, Cheruscian pride. Shall we really carry on sneaking around, taking our enemy in the back and the side, trying to drown him and doing just about everything other than face him like the sons of All Men should be proud to do. He's offering battle; are we so womanish to refuse?'

I stared at him in disbelief. 'You're as mad as Caecina. Have you learnt nothing about fighting the Romans? Take them from the side, take them in ambush, rain javelin volleys down on their formations, snip at them here and there and you negate their power; but take them from the front, head on, toe to toe, and they will always win, even against ten times their number. Always!'

'Not this time they won't, Erminatz; they're tired, hungry and dispirited; we will triumph and it will be a triumph of men and not the sneaking ambush of the Teutoburg Pass. This will be a victory of which we can boast with our heads held high. To refuse him now will be to be thought of as lesser men and our women will taunt us.'

My father put a hand on my shoulder. 'He's right, my son: we need to show our people that we can defeat our enemy as men and not just sneak-thieves. To rule, one needs respect and that can only be gained in honest combat. That tired, hungry and demoralised army is our chance and we must take it.'

As I looked around the faces of the kings and their thanes behind I could see that this argument had convinced them and I cursed, inwardly, the pride of the Germanic male that makes him do things that are totally illogical. But at that moment I remembered that they had never had the benefit of an education from Lucius Caesar; I would never be able to dissuade them from their suicidal course. It was pointless to argue. 'Very well, we will take his offer, and may the blood of the warriors we lose today weigh heavy on your heads for there will be much.'

I wanted none of it and yet what option did I have but to fight at the head of my tribe alongside my father and uncle? Our horns sounded and from all about our warriors began to form up in their clan groups and then into their tribes; ale was passed around and they drank themselves some courage as before us Caecina – or so I thought at the time as I was unaware of his injury – completed his disposition. Four legions, albeit all of them under-strength, and almost the same number of auxiliaries, confronted us and our numbers were not much more than theirs. It was a foolhardy decision and now that it had been made nobody could go back on it without losing face. It was with a grim smile that I reflected that a Germanic warrior would rather lose life than face.

And so we moved forward, our men jeering and shouting whilst swigging from skins of ale and captured wine, all the while boasting of their feats and urging their comrades on to great deeds. Closer we got to the Roman line, three legions wide, each three cohorts deep, with the fourth in reserve and supported on the flanks by auxiliary Gauls, Aquitainians and some Iberians, and with light cavalry swirling beyond them, and it did not move; in fact it did not make a sound. Silent they stood there, waiting; and I knew that with every step we took towards them their confidence would grow for this was going to be the way of fighting that they knew best and they were looking forward, with relish, to repaying the indignities we had heaped upon them over the last few days. And so, filled with foreboding, I led the charge.

'What did it look like, this charge?' Thumelicatz enquired, with genuine interest.

'Like any other charge of screaming barbarians,' the street-fighter replied, refilling his cup. 'We hadn't had much sleep and it had been so long since we'd had a hot meal that the last thing we fancied was a toe to toe but we knew that would be our best chance of getting back to the Rhenus. So we stood and none of us uttered a word, not even the arse-widener; even he neglected to growl at us as the massed attack came on. I felt Sextus to my right and Cassandros on my left shoulder; around us our mates were breathing deeply, gulping in the air that they knew, from previous experience, would soon be in short supply. The palm of my right hand was sticky as I gripped the first of my two pila, ready for the order; I glanced down at my left forearm, the muscles bulging as I held my shield firmly to the front, the second pilum grasped in the same hand, and I recalled the shock of the impact of all the other head-on charges I'd faced. But no matter how many times you've watched, over the rim of your shield, a mass of sweaty savages, howling for your blood, scrambling over one another to be the first to try and take your head off, it don't make it any easier. You could smell the piss from some of the less-experienced lads and I hoped for their sake that the arse-widener wouldn't know the culprits as that was one of his pet hates: pissing on your own ground makes it slipperier and he tended to give a good demonstration of the difference between slippery and dry with his cane afterwards – if the culprit was alive, that was.

'The cornua rumbled and the arse-widener roared; we stamped forward with our left feet and pulled our right arms back and then, with another roared command, we hurled our pila. Without looking at the results of our handiwork we hefted our second missile into our throwing hands and before four heartbeats had passed they were hurtling at a lower trajectory at the screaming hatred just twenty paces away and we already had our swords drawn. It's a lovely sight, a pilum volley hitting home; scores of the bastards went down, blood spraying and slopping as faces were pulped and chests were skewered. They came down in scores, they did, and each one would trip at least one of the arse-holes behind him. But casualties have never stopped a barbarian charge in my experience. "Brace yourselves, you worthless cunts!" the arse-widener bellowed encouragingly. "Your play-mates have arrived. Shoulders down!"

'It's easy: weight on the left foot, left shoulder hard on the back of your shield, the top of which is just at eye height, and you feel the shield of the man behind press against your back adding to your weight along with all the other lads in your file. Bearded, long-haired and tattooed, they were a hideous sight as they closed. And then, crash, no more time for thought; they hit you at full pelt and it's then about timing. Up and forward went our front rank shields, punching the shield bosses onto their chests and blocking the downward slashes of swords or the overarm thrusts of spears with the rims; an instant later you ram your blade through the gap, pray for flesh, and it was there. Right and left I twisted my wrist, just as I had been shown on my first day of training. Blood sprayed up my arm and I pulled it back, feeling the suction of the wound pulling on my blade as, next to me, Sextus began to howl like an unnatural thing as he slammed with his shield and punched with his sword. All along our line we heaved and grunted, hardly ever looking over our rims, as a spear thrust could be the last thing you ever see, working our blades and bosses and not giving a fuck about anything other than keeping our formation for we knew that a solid wall of Roman heavy infantry supported by the weight of the seven ranks behind is the safest place to be in a battle – unless you're sitting on a horse directing matters from the rear, that is.

'Now, I was just one soldier in a century somewhere towards the centre of our line so I have no idea what happened, but within the time it takes to fuck a couple of whores, the whole hairy bunch of them were running away leaving the ground carpeted with as many dead and dying as you could wave a sword at. I ain't ever seen so many after such a comparatively brief ruckus; thousands of them there were, with hundreds more trying to crawl away. On the flanks, the Gallic auxiliaries were following up the rout, enjoying their favourite pastime of sticking Germans, whilst the cavalry swirled around their flanks hefting javelin after javelin into them bringing more down in droves. A lovely sight it was, that's for sure.

'"Don't you fucking dare move, pig-swill," the arse-widener suggested, the wild grin on his face and the magnitude of his roar indicating that he was thoroughly enjoying himself, "until I tell you to!"

'But he was wasting his breath as none of us fancied chasing the bastards, let the auxiliaries do that, we reasoned, and we were happy to watch them do so. For about an hour we stood there, reeking of piss and shit, pleased to be doing nothing. And then the blow-boys started up, but it weren't the cornicerns, it was the *buccinators*; we were on the march. Gradually the army peeled away and carried on westwards …'

'And my father watched it go, unable to do anything to stop it,' Thumelicatz said. 'Covered in blood that was more Germanic than Latin, he watched you go as Inguiomer lay on the ground next to him slowly bleeding out through the gaping rent in his belly. I remember this passage almost word for word. "As I watched the legions leave the field, one by one, I looked down at the man who had, through pride, squandered our chance of victory and could not bring myself to blame him as he lay dying: he had acted in the correct way to the Germanic manner of thinking and, however much I hated Rome, that day had shown me just how much Rome had influenced my thinking, how much I was a part of them despite myself. I turned to my father who held his brother's hand. 'We've let them escape now and there is no way that we can stop them; so now they'll be back next spring and more of our people will have to die.' My father shrugged, tears trickled into his beard. 'Let them come and then perhaps we will do it your way.' But that would not happen as I knew, watching the rear-guard disappear into the west, that we would never be given the opportunity to harry a Roman army on the march again; it was over unless a miracle occurred. But a miracle did occur in the form of a woman on a bridge."'

The street-fighter frowned. 'You mean the elder Agrippina, Germanicus' wife?'

'Not me, but my father, yes,' Thumelicatz replied, 'and he was right. What happened when you reached the Rhenus?'

'Well, we was knackered; five days since the battle and not a sign of the savages but we were only too happy to go as fast as we could; even the arse-widener seemed content with our progress. The evening of the fifth day we came to the bridge that we'd built to cross the river and on it, at its eastern end, stood a woman. As we got closer we saw it was Agrippina and as we began to cross the rumour flew down the column that the prefect of Castra Vetera had panicked when he had heard that we were under attack as we made our way west along the Road of the Long Bridges and assumed that we would be defeated and that Germania Inferior would be over-run unless he demolished the bridge. But Agrippina refused to let him and stood on it for days holding her newborn daughter of the same name in her arms; as we paraded past her we cheered her for she had saved us from being marooned on the other side, becoming easy prey as we tried to board whatever ships that could be sent to pick us up. How we loved her for what she did.'

'Of course you did,' Thumelicatz agreed. 'But imagine what effect that love of the Rhenus legions for the wife of a general, who was already seen as a dangerous rival, affected the mind of the Emperor brooding in Rome. Imagine the jealousy and fear it inspired when it came to the ears of Tiberius.'

CHAPTER XVI

'IT WAS THE end of Roman ambitions east of the Rhenus,' Thumelicatz asserted in answer to his rhetorical question.

'But we came back the following year,' the street-fighter pointed out, once again draining his cup, 'and defeated Arminius twice.'

'But did you? Did you really?'

'I know we did; I was there and I left a good many of my mates lying on the banks of the Visurgis.'

Thumelicatz pushed the flagon of beer across the table. 'I don't question that; my point is that what seemed like a victory to you and Germanicus was in fact the final factor that created the miracle my father had prayed for.'

The elder brother scoffed. 'A miracle born out of his defeat! I find that unlikely.'

'And yet it was so; read from just before the meeting of the brothers, Tiburtius.'

The former aquilifer cleared his throat as he unrolled the last remaining scroll on the desk.

Chlodochar, my younger brother, had returned with Germanicus' army the year after the Battle of the Long Bridges; the thought of it made me feel sick: my own blood fighting on the side of our foes. And yet, he was not the first of my family to betray the Fatherland: Segestes, my father's cousin, had done far worse to me personally in that he had handed over my pregnant wife to the enemy, and she had since given birth to a son that she had named Thumelicatz – a good Germanic name. But despite his grievous treachery, Segestes' offence seemed nothing in comparison to actually being prepared to bear arms against one's own tribe. There was no doubt that Chlodochar was prepared to do that and that's what revolted me even though since my last meeting with him in Rome before my return to Germania I had always known I would face him across the battlefield. However, regardless of this, when Germanicus' army sailed down the Amisia and then marched east to the Visurgis, once again offering us battle, I felt it my duty to talk to the renegade.

We waited for them on the eastern side, on a flood-plain sacred to the Goddess Idis. I stood on the bank and watched the cohorts arrive; behind me were twenty-five thousand warriors from three tribes with the will to fight in the open; a will that I was again unable to counter with cogent argument and so, therefore, had to bow to. My hope was to tempt Germanicus into a crossing and hit him as he did so; but I knew the chances of this would be small as he was far too canny a commander to allow himself to be attacked during such a sensitive manoeuvre. Soon I saw his command tent being erected and I shouted across to the centurion commanding a century of archers lining the bank, asking if Germanicus himself was there. He asked me my name and when he heard the answer he immediately despatched a messenger; it was not long until I saw a familiar figure striding towards the west bank.

'Do you still persist in your treachery, Arminius?' Germanicus shouted across the fifty paces of river that separated us.

I laughed at his Roman arrogance and, to my surprise, he shared my amusement.

'I know you think me to be a stupid and bull-headed Roman who doesn't understand your true motivation, Arminius; but you're wrong. I understand you entirely and know that you consider yourself a Germanic patriot and not a traitor to Rome; isn't that so, Erminatz?'

The use of my Germanic name startled me but I was interested by his admission that not everything should be seen through Roman eyes. 'That's what I always have been although I was forced to bury it deep within whilst I remained, nominally at least, in Rome's service.'

'And when you had the chance to leave, shall we say, that service, you took it. And, I will admit, Erminatz, you took it well: three legions destroyed and the greatest military force in the West humiliated. We taught you well, or, rather, my late brother-in-law, Lucius, did; he was always one for the grand gesture and what a grand gesture the Teutoburg Wald was. Even if I kill every one of you tomorrow or the next day, which I fully intend to do, I will never wipe out the memory of it nor get close to avenging it fully, such was its magnitude. I salute you, Erminatz, and wish you to know that if there were a way that I could conclude a friendly treaty with you I would. But Tiberius would never allow it. There will be no peace until you are dead. However, you will be pleased to hear that Tiberius has refused an offer by a person unnamed to poison you, stating that that is not the Roman way of dealing with our enemies and I fully applaud that sentiment. You will die by the blade, Erminatz, and it will be soon and hopefully wielded by my hand; only then can we make an honourable peace. I wish you well in what remains of your life.'

As he turned to go, I shouted after him, 'Before we meet on the field, Germanicus, I would be grateful if I could speak with my brother – if he is with you, of course.'

Germanicus looked over his shoulder. 'He's here, he never leaves my side like the true friend he has always been. He's risen in rank since you last saw him; he is now a prefect commanding an auxiliary cohort, a Germanic cohort.'

I shrugged because this was nothing new; the Batavians and the Ubii had always served Rome and even since Varus' defeat the Frisii and a couple of other tribes had once again started to serve in the auxiliaries.

'You may shrug, Erminatz; but this is not an auxiliary cohort recruited from the usual tribes.' He smiled, and even at that distance I could see that it was a smile of a man about to impart an astonishing piece of knowledge. 'Your brother commands the new Chauci cohort.'

My surprise must have registered even at that distance.

'Yes; and if they do well in the coming battle then I will allow them a prefect of their own tribe and your brother will become the prefect of the newly formed Cherusci cohort. And that will happen, Erminatz, after you are dead and the Cherusci have been defeated. But let's not speak of that again; I shall send for your brother and he can tell you how it will be. May your gods go with you, one-time friend.'

With that, he left me and I never saw him again. I didn't have long to contemplate his words until my brother arrived and when he did it was his appearance that shocked me. I turned to my bodyguards and dismissed them and then requested the centurion to remove his archers so that my brother and I could talk in private; or at least as privately as one could shouting across fifty paces of river.

Once we were alone I looked at my brother for a while, shaking my head at his disfigurement. 'How did you lose your eye, Chlodochar?'

Spurning his mother tongue, he replied in Latin. 'Against the Marsi, last year; a spent slingshot crushed it.'

I was not impressed; I continued the Cheruscian dialect. 'So you took part in that shameful massacre, did you?'

'It was justified punishment for the outrage they helped to perpetrate in the Teutoburg Wald; and seeing as you were the architect of that outrage you can consider yourself responsible for what happened to the Marsi.'

I was not going to let myself be drawn into this specious line of argument. 'I hope you got well rewarded for slaughtering women and children and sacrificing half of your sight.'

But Chlodochar chose not to hear the sarcasm in my voice. 'Apart from the fact that I am now a prefect of auxiliaries and therefore get paid very handsomely, as you would know, Arminius, I've the right to wear a military crown in Rome and have been awarded various other donatives, including this gold necklace from the hands of Germanicus himself.'

I scoffed at such vanity. 'Cheap trinkets as a poor reward for servitude, Chlodochar.'

'Servitude! How can I be a slave when I command my own cohort in the greatest army known to man? Look at Rome's power, Arminius, look how long the Emperor's arm is that he can reach you here. Tomorrow you will die along with thousands of our tribe; but it doesn't have to be that way. Throw yourself at the mercy of Tiberius, he may well be magnanimous; it's Rome's policy to always show clemency to those who surrender, as opposed to treating those who don't with the ruthlessness they deserve. You know this to be true, Arminius; if it were not then explain why Thusnelda and your son are being treated as friends of Rome and not enemies. Why, they have even been given into my custody and live in my household.'

'Then return them to me if you have any honour! It is here, in the liberty of our ancestral Fatherland, under the care of Germanic gods, that my son should be brought up, not in some renegade's family. It is here, Chlodochar, that you should be; how long is it since you saw our mother? She grieves for you and longs for you to return so that she can face the rest of the tribe without feeling the shame of your betrayal. And what of our sister, Chlodochar, do you not think of her, ever?'

I saw my brother pause in thought and realised that he had been away for so long that he had even forgotten that he had a sister.

'Yes,' he said as if he delved deep into the past. 'How is Erminhild?'

'She's dead, Chlodochar! Dead these ten years past and you never bothered to find out, did you? No, you didn't because we're all dead to you; you've betrayed your kinsmen, your tribe; in fact, you have betrayed your entire race and are nothing more than a slave without honour. Chlodochar, the toad wallowing in the slime of subservience.'

This proved too much for Chlodochar to bear and he screamed for his horse and weapons to be brought to him. Hating him more, at that moment, than I had ever hated anyone in my life before, I laughed at the futility of his gesture, seeing that there were fifty paces of river between us. 'If you want to swim it with your mount then you're welcome to try; but I warn you, Chlodochar, I won't give you the privilege of single combat with me, I'll pick you off with an arrow before you're even halfway.'

This infuriated him even more and he had to be dragged away by a tribune, all the while shouting threats at me.

'We'll settle it tomorrow,' I called after him, 'if you can cross this river in the face of an army waiting for you to scramble up the far bank.'

And, of course, being a Roman army and being commanded by one of their greatest generals, they could and they did.

It was during the night that they set their plans in motion and, as I dictate them now, a few years later, I still feel admiration for Germanicus and will admit to feeling sorrow when I heard of his death, poisoned out in the East, ostensibly at the instigation of a jealous Tiberius.

We woke to a pale dawn, damp with dew and swathed in a river mist that clung to trees and rolled on the water's surface. The opposite bank was only intermittently visible; what could be seen through the swirling trails were a couple of cohorts of auxiliary infantry and one auxiliary cavalry ala that were forming up on the west bank.

'Batavians,' I said to Aldhard as we sat on horses and squinted to make out their standards. 'They're going to try and swim the river.'

'Let them try,' Aldhard said with a grin, 'they'll be dead before—'

Screams, flattened by the mist but still audible enough to make out the pain within them, cut in from the north; Aldhard and I shared a brief look and then urged our mounts in the direction of the noise. All around, our camp, which had already been rousing from sleep, now broke into frenetic action, each man convinced that we were under attack by the full Roman force that had somehow crossed in silence during the night. Again I cursed the ill-discipline of my people as leaders of clans and war bands tried to outdo each other in rushing to where they assumed the enemy to be.

'Stop!' I shouted as we rode through what was boiling up into chaos. 'Hold your positions!' But I might just as well have tried to get them to dance a jig for all the good my shouting did. They began to swarm to the north, thousands of them, and there was nothing I could do to stop them. And then, through the mist to the south of us came the spectral shapes of horses; those warriors nearest them turned and with mighty war cries raced towards the new foe who promptly wheeled and disappeared into the mist. But this did not deter the warriors pursuing them and I watched in despair as hundreds of them were enveloped by the miasma that I knew would contain their deaths. There was nothing that I could do for I realised that, at that very moment, the Batavians were resting their shields on their inflated water-skins, to give them buoyancy, and were on their way across the river. Renowned for their ability to swim in full armour, they would be across in a couple of hundred heartbeats in numbers enough to form a bridgehead.

I looked to the far bank and a soft breeze cleared my view for a few moments, long enough for my fears to be realised; there were men and horses in the water and boats being launched behind them. But these boats were not all just transports; no, they were more than that, they were also barges already linked together ready to span the Visurgis and construct a pontoon bridge across it. And my army had been split in two by a couple of small night crossings. I looked to the south and knew that it was pointless trying to rally the warriors who had chased the horsemen in that direction; those that survived to make their way back to the main body would find the Batavians in their path and would doubtless perish or flee. So north was my only option; north I went to try to pull my army back into some sort of disciplined unit rather than an unruly ensemble of glory-hunters, with no idea of how to act as a coherent force, bent on pursuing Germanicus' feint. My advantage had been ripped from my hands and now there was no way that I would be able to fall on Germanicus as he crossed; I had yielded the east bank unfought and had been made to look a fool. Now I knew that the only hope we had was to form up with our rear protected by the thick wood that traced the northern edge of Idis' plain, with our right flank protected by the river and our left flank secured in the hills that rose a mile to the east of the river; in these hills I placed the bulk of the Cherusci warriors leaving the plain manned by the other tribes. And so, with a prayer in our hearts that the Goddess would hold her hands over us as we faced the might of Rome, we waited for Germanicus to come to us.

But what power can a Goddess of little renown have over eight legions and their auxiliaries? As the sun rose and the mist cleared we could see rank after rank of them marching across the four pontoon bridges that had sprung, seemingly, out of nowhere, screened by cohorts of auxiliaries. The entire army was over by the eighth hour, but instead of offering battle Germanicus decided, rather, to build a camp and rest his men.

At this moment anyone with any sense would have chosen to wait until darkness and then withdraw. I, however, had to stay and face the superior force, for to retreat would be seen as the act of a coward and my life would be forfeit. That would achieve nothing as the Germanic army would remain to be slaughtered under the generalship of another.

So we stayed, sleeping out in the open under the multitude of stars that crammed the sky above our land for what would be, I suspected, the last time for many of us.

In an attempt to avert the inevitable that night, I tried a stratagem born more of desperation than of logic. With a small bodyguard, I rode through the darkness to within hailing distance of the Roman camp and had Vulferam, because I knew that my voice would be recognised, try to tempt the legionaries into desertion. It was farcical—

'And it was insulting,' the street-fighter interrupted. 'We heard this voice coming out of the night offering us one hundred sesterces a day as well as land and a Germanic wife if we would let down our mates and desert.' He paused to hawk and then spit on the wooden floor. '"Bollocks!" we shouted back. "We're going to take your land and steal your women anyway; why should we throw away our honour to get what is already within our grasp?" Well, as you can imagine, the lads got themselves pretty worked up over this and really began to look forward to the battle on the morrow, thinking of ways that they would avenge the insult on the first hairy-arsed savage that they came across.' The street-fighter paused to grin at his companions. 'It was a massive error of judgement on Arminius' part seeing as before that we was all for getting home as quickly as possible as we wasn't at all enamoured of the idea of proceeding any further east; but this had got us going and Germanicus heard our change of mood because he disguised himself as a common grunt and went around the camp during the night listening to our conversations.

'Well, when the reveille sounded an hour before dawn most of us was already up and shoving our faces in our breakfast bowls, that's how anxious we were to be at it. We almost had to be held back as we paraded in our cohorts and the gates were opened – it was a far cry from the Battle of the Long Bridges, that's for sure. Anyway, we formed up opposite this mass of grunting barbarians and Germanicus treated us to one of his rousing speeches saying that it was further to go back to the Rhenus than it was to go on to the Albis but there would be no fighting beyond it if we won today and asserted the authority of Rome once again in this province. Needless to say, we were right up for that so we cheered and cheered him until we was hoarse. When eventually we stopped we could hear our enemies cheering and we wondered just what Arminius had said to them to make them feel that confident in the face of line upon line of very pissed-off, heavily armoured infantry. Not that we really needed to know, it was just curiosity that soon faded as the blow-boys began to do what they like best and the arse-widener, who was just two places away from me, the other side of Cassandros, started to get so excited that he was slavering and rolling his eyes as he suggested, in the tenderest of tones, that we might like to advance towards a mass of warriors who had nothing but our demises in their minds. I think we rather shocked him when it became apparent that there was nothing that we would like better at that moment and that his vine stick wouldn't need to be wiped clean in the near future.

'Forward we went with the auxiliary Gallic and Germanic cohorts in the first line, supported by the archers, and us, the Fifth, a part of the second line with three other legions and then another four legions in the third line; the whole formation was supported by swirling cavalry – mainly Batavians, Gauls and Hispanic, as well as a few Illyrians – on our right flank to keep all the bastards up in the hills from charging down and doing us some serious damage. If we thought that we were already as enthusiastic as it's possible to be when limbering up for a day's killing then the sight of eight Eagles, the same number as our legions, flying over our heads towards the massed sweaties before us made us boil over with enthusiasm. Indeed, some of the lads swore afterwards that they had seen tears of joy roll down the arse-widener's face as he bellowed at us to stop behaving like a gaggle of Mesopotamian bum-boys, pull our communal thumb out of our communal arsehole and start acting like Roman legionaries ready to deal out righteous slaughter to anyone who entertains a malicious thought towards Rome and her beloved Emperor.

'As the auxiliaries came into contact with the forward masses of the Germanic horde there was a huge shout from off to our right and the hills began to look as if they were crawling with thousands of gigantic ants, so alive they were with warriors rushing down at us trying to take us in the flank. This brought even more joy to the arse-widener's heart as we, the Fifth Alaudae, were on the right flank of the second line and our cohort, the ninth, was on the right flank of the legion; but what brought pure joy to Balbillus' heart was that our century, his century, was on the extreme flank of the cohort and so all that hate-filled charge was coming directly at us. The blow-boys rumbled away and standards began dipping this way and that as our legate issued orders for us to turn and face the incoming; the arse-widener and Servius screamed abuse at us and, without pausing or even slowing our pace, we turned when the charge was still a couple of hundred paces out. But there were no orders to stand and receive the enemy, it seemed that we were expected just to stroll on as if we was spending a pleasant afternoon in the gardens of Lucullus; and who were we to question it? So on we went as the cavalry began to get very excited and thundered off in a huge looping manoeuvre that seemed to be aimed at taking the bastards coming towards us in the rear. Well, it goes without saying that we were grateful for all the help that we could get and it was with the sure knowledge that we'd be fighting an enemy that was soon to be surrounded that the arse-widener, his voice cracking with the emotion of it all, suggested that we might like to throw our pila, which we did willingly and followed that with a second volley before drawing our swords in preparation for engaging in the arse-widener's second favourite pursuit of trying to get as much blood and shit on his sandals as possible.

'In they came, whooping and halooing and already splattered in blood from the casualties rightfully caused by our pila volleys. With swords and spears waving, hair flying, covered in their strange tattoos and led by a big bastard in an auxiliary's captured chainmail, they closed with us. With unconcealed glee, the arse-widener bawled that the big bastard was his as they roared into our shield wall with a velocity that made us stagger and feel grateful for each of the seven ranks behind us pushing into our backs. Straining with my left arm to keep my shield upright and with Sextus growling like a rabid dog to my right, I slammed the point of the gladius forward and felt it snag on chainmail. I ducked below my shield rim as I sensed a blow coming down from above; sparks flew into my eyes as iron scraped iron and thunderous noise crammed my ears. Again I stabbed and this time I split a ring and punctured flesh, not deeply but enough to feel my opponent step back. Sextus bellowed like a rutting boar, battering at a young warrior's shield, as Cassandros hurled unpleasant Greek at his opponent who screeched back in their foul tongue.

'Then, over all this noise, rose a clamour of hate and clashing weapons so intense that men on both sides turned to see the cause; it was a fearsome sight: the arse-widener and the big bastard had squared up to each other and such was their ferocity that they had created their own little arena a couple of paces across and seemed to tower above everyone. With savagery that comes from a deep love of violence they laid into one another, hurling their bodies forward and raining down the fiercest cuts and thrusts. Round they went in their own private dance of death and no one dared interfere; in fact, I seem to remember that all combat close to them stopped for a few moments as we marvelled at the violence of it. But we soon remembered what we was meant to be about and iron again slashed through the air; I was one of the quickest to refocus and with a backhanded cut I opened the throat of the man opposite me. The big bastard glanced to his left as my victim sank to his knees and screamed at the sight, giving the arse-widener the fleeting instant he needed to cut low at his thigh but he mistimed the stroke and caught the hem of the chainmail tunic; hatred overflowed in the big bastard and, with a roar that deafened and movement that blurred, his sword arm flew around and down and the arse-widener's transverse plume parted as the blade split his helm and skull to wedge itself in his upper teeth. I swear the last expression in the arse-widener's eyes was exaltation as they looked their fading last at the man who had stolen their light.

'Now, say what you like about the arse-widener, and we often did, but he was our centurion and to see him cut down by some bearded barbarian got the lads well and truly worked up, me included. I threw myself forward at the nearest enemy, a grizzled grey-beard, and crashed my sword fist into his face, shattering teeth, before ramming my shield rim up under his jaw, crushing his windpipe, as Cassandros, next to me, downed another of the big bastard's bodyguards with a slash to the thigh; I finished the job with my blade in his eye, leaving the way clear for me to fly at the huge brute, shield first. Punching the boss into his chest, as he struggled to wrench his blade from the ruins of the arse-widener's head, I took the wind from him, following it up with straight thrust to the throat that he all but dodged so that the point rammed through his chainmail and into his shoulder, jagging on the bone. He staggered back, almost pulling my sword from my grasp, his eyes rolling and blood pulsing from the wound. I tried to get at him again but Sextus had the same idea and we collided as hands grabbed the big bastard and hauled him away from us and other warriors took his place; but our blood was up and we ripped into them with nothing but vengeance in our hearts for the arse-widener and all the indignities that had been thrown at us every time we had crossed the Rhenus into this land of strange gods and dark forest.

'How long it went on for after that, I don't know, not long it seemed; and what happened, I've no idea as we could see very little in our confined little corner of the battlefield. All I knew was the ease with which we beat them back after the big bastard was wounded was surprising. But beat them back we did, back into our cavalry that had slammed into their rear, and before we knew it they were running and we were following them up killing at will, revelling in the exhilaration of the greatest sensation a soldier can have.'

'I think I can answer how long the fight went on for before the rout,' Thumelicatz interjected, looking at the street-fighter with a real interest. He took the scroll from Tiburtius and after taking a few moments to find the right place began to read:

I screamed my protests but they fell on deaf ears; no one would let me go forward to avenge him. Aldhard, tears flowing down his face, held me firm along with others who were no more than a blur. Rigid, I gave in and watched as the attack at first faltered and then, with the inevitability that comes with the wavering of ill-disciplined troops, broke. But the repulse of our flank's attack in itself would not have been the end of the matter had the centre at least tried to stand – but it did not. Within a couple of hundred heartbeats, for reasons that have never become clear to me because all those who took part in it are too ashamed to countenance even its mention, let alone engage in discussion over its causes, the main bulk of the Germanic army broke, without giving battle, into two columns; one fled north into the wood and the other made for the hills. But in flight the back is exposed and thousands were cut down with dishonourable wounds, carpeting the path of their shameful retreat with dead.

I grieved for my men and I grieved for my father as I felt Aldhard pull me back, his tears still flowing for his loss; I knew that I should go with him and, forgetting my grief for the time being, try to rally my army to the north at the final line of defence that I could think of. I looked back to where my father and Vulferam had fallen, both now under the feet of the enemy, and then winced at the pain from the wound in my shoulder and cursed the ugly little legionary who had so effectively avenged his centurion whom I had killed.

Thumelicatz again stared at the street-fighter. 'So, it was but a few hundred heartbeats, that's the answer to your question as to how long it went on after you wounded the big bastard, as you call him; but that is supremely uninteresting compared to the life-threads woven by the Norns. That you should be a part of this group come to seek my help – you of all people – shows me that I was right to meet with you and that the gods have some deeper scheme to which I am not a party. However, it has confirmed my decision to help you. Why else would the gods send to me the ugly little legionary who avenged his centurion by killing my grandfather, Siegimeri, my kinsman, Vulferam, and wounding my father, Erminatz?'

CHAPTER XVII

'I SPIKED ARMINIUS?' The street-fighter could not conceal his pride. 'Who would have thought it?' He looked at the younger brother. 'What do you think of that, sir?'

'Somehow, after all we've heard, the coincidence doesn't surprise me, what with my father escorting the young Arminius to Rome and then giving us his knife to return to the son he never met. It seems that we're all in some way woven into his tale.'

Thumelicatz nodded in slow agreement. 'Yes, that's the way of the gods. But further than that, the wound did more than just hurt Erminatz: it prevented him from functioning at his best as his army was chased north to a ridge that the Angrivarii had built along the southern border of their territory on the east bank of the Visurgis. It was here that he had thought to make a stand and, perhaps, had it been successful and he had beaten Germanicus back then things would have been different. But it was not to be and that wound was a major reason why it failed: it meant that my father did not organise the defence with his normal energy. Thus, the final factor that wove the miracle was put in place: Germanicus' second victory in as many days was too much for Tiberius' jealousy to bear when it came to his ears not long after and, afraid of Germanicus' rising star and the power that his wife, Agrippina, had over the troops on the Rhenus, he recalled him, ostensibly to celebrate his triumph. Germanicus pleaded to be allowed one more year to campaign, but was refused; that year, had he been granted it, would have been all he needed to finish the job and pull Germania Magna back into the empire.

'Rome withdrew and we fell to fighting amongst ourselves. My father fought a war with Maroboduus of the Marcomanni but failed to break through the natural defences of Bojohaemum and it ended as an insignificant sideshow that had no bearing on history whatsoever; as did all the other wars between the tribes that were fought.

'And so, with our land secure and our freedom to do as we wished returned to us, my father, realising that he would never unite all the tribes under his rule and pose a threat to Rome, was content to take Siegimeri's place as king of the Cherusci and spend much of his time dictating his story to his two slaves. What we have heard is barely a third of it, but it has been enough and now, seeing as I have the manuscript, I shall read the last lines he dictated. "As I contemplate Chlodochar's message and Segestes' guarantee of my safe passage, for his daughter's sake, I know them to be false. And yet how can I not go if there is the smallest chance that I might be wrong and my brother really is returning my wife and son to my side? But if they really are false and they mean to kill me, then, with my long-dead friend, Lucius, in mind, I shall give them the grandest of gestures."' Thumelicatz looked at Thusnelda. 'Where were you, Mother? Did Flavus bring you back to this land, because he certainly didn't bring me?'

Thusnelda spat. 'He was false and we have dealt him just retribution. No, it was merely a way of snaring Erminatz; his love for me meant that he could but go.'

'So, tell our guests what happened,' Thumelicatz ordered the two slaves.

It was Aius who spoke first. 'It was so obvious a trap that there seemed a good chance that it was genuine; who would believe that they could ensnare the great Erminatz with such a simple device? And so he went and took us with him to act as witnesses should he be betrayed. We travelled to the arranged meeting place on the banks of a small tributary of the Rhenus and there he ordered us to conceal ourselves and watch the proceedings. And so, shivering in the dawn, because it was the time of the Ice Gods, we watched from a distance as two men approached our master.'

Tiburtius interrupted. 'There weren't just two men; behind them were a dozen or so warriors and, although they looked to be Germanic, it was evident that they had been equipped in the empire. However, they held back as Erminatz approached the two men. "Chlodochar, Segestes," my master called as they neared each other, "where are my wife and son?" They made no reply.'

Aius took up the tale from Tiburtius who was visibly upset by recalling the memory. 'It was now that our master knew that what he had hoped against hope for was not to be and at that point he lost his will to carry on. Walking forward, he opened his arms, a sword held in one hand, exposing his chest to his brother and kinsman. "I do not run from traitors," he shouted, "nor will I demean myself by fighting them. The coward strikes down the man who refuses to defend himself and the cursed murder their own kin. I call down Donar's curse upon you, Flavus and Segestes, and I seal that curse with my own blood." And with a cry to the gods for vengeance in this life or the next he allowed them to strike him down with a weapon in his hand so that he would attain Walhalla.'

'The grandest of gestures, I think you'll agree,' Thumelicatz said. 'When life has no value left to you then sacrifice it to curse your enemies; his mother also understood that too. Tell us the end, slaves.'

Aius began. 'When they had gone we crept from our hiding place and took our master's body back to his mother; we told her that it was her youngest son who bore the responsibility for her eldest son's death.'

Tiburtius finished. 'She saw to Erminatz's funeral rites, laid a curse woven with much magic on her youngest son and his descendants hereafter and then, to seal it with her own blood, threw herself on the pyre.'

No one spoke as the two old men finished and began rolling up the scrolls and replacing them in their cases, their eyes never leaving the work on the desk in front of them.

Thumelicatz looked thoughtfully into his beer cup. 'My father was a great man and it is my loss that I never met him.' His eyes flicked up and bored into the Romans one by one. 'But I've not had you sit here with me and listen to his story just so that I can wallow in a bit of self-pity afterwards. I wanted you to hear it so that you can understand my motives in what I shall do next; I intend to go against everything that my father stood for.'

The elder brother's face grew intense. 'Does that mean you can tell us where the Eagle is hidden?'

Thumelicatz could sense the desperate hope behind the question. 'I can tell you which tribe it is with, that is easy; the Chauci on the coast to the north of here have it, but how and where they've hidden it only they would know. But I'll do more than that; I will actively help you find it.'

'Why would you do that?'

'My father tried to make himself king of a Greater Germania, uniting all the tribes under one leader. Imagine the power he would have had if he'd succeeded. He would perhaps have had the strength to take Gaul; but would he have had the strength to hold it? I don't think so; not yet, while Rome is so strong. But that was his dream, it's not mine. I look far into the future to a time when Rome starts its inevitable decline as all empires have done before. For the present I see the idea of a Greater Germania as a threat to all the constituent tribes. It is the potential cause for a hundred years of war with Rome; a war that, for the next few generations, we don't have the manpower to win.

'So I do not desire to be the leader of a united Germanic people but there are many of my countrymen who suspect that I do. Some actively encourage me by sending messages of support but others are jealous of me and would see my death as furthering their own ambitions. But I just want to be left in peace to live, in the manner that was denied me all my youth, to live as a Cherusci in a free Germania. I want nothing of Rome, neither vengeance nor justice. We've freed ourselves from her once; it would be foolish to put ourselves in the position where we have to fight for our freedom again.

'However, Rome will always want her Eagle back and while it's on our soil she will continually come looking for it. The Chauci will not give it up and why should they; but their keeping it puts us all at risk. I want you to take it, Romans; take and use it for your invasion and leave us in peace. So I'll help you steal it and the tribes will learn that I helped Rome and they will no longer want me to become – or fear me becoming – an image of my father.'

'Won't the Chauci see that as a declaration of war against them?' the younger brother asked.

'They would if there weren't other circumstances involved. You see, in my position I get to hear things: I know that Rome collects tribute from many of the tribes in Germania and I also know that recently Publius Gabinius, the Governor of Germania

Inferior, has been demanding ships from the coastal tribes instead of gold. Now, the Chauci's neighbours, the Frisii, are very fond of their ships and I heard that to avoid handing too many of them over they sold the secret of where the last Eagle is to—'

'Publius Gabinius!'

'Exactly. So the Chauci are going to lose their Eagle soon but if we can get it before Publius Gabinius arrives with a Roman army then many Chauci lives will be saved.'

'How far is it?'

'Thirty miles east of here is the Visurgis River; that takes us all the way to the Chauci's lands on the northern coast. We'll be there the day after tomorrow if we go by boat.'

Thumelicatz held his mother's hands and looked into her eyes; he had divested himself of Varus' uniform and wore a simple tunic and trousers. The flame of the single tallow candle burning in the tent played on Thusnelda's pupils; tears fell down her cheeks. From outside came the muffled noise of men striking camp as dawn edged over the eastern horizon.

'This morning is colder than yesterday,' Thusnelda whispered. 'The Ice Gods will be here tomorrow; that has always been a time of ill-omen for our family. Can you not wait three days until they have gone back under the ground?'

Thumelicatz put a hand on the back of her neck and drew her towards him; he kissed her forehead. 'No, Mother; this must be done now in order to save lives. Besides, I've already spoken with Romans and worn the uniform of one of their governors. Donar has not struck me yet and if he does hold me to my oath he'll strike me down whether the Ice Gods are roaming the earth or not.'

'Their chill will add bitterness to his wrath.'

'No, Mother, it will make no difference; what does the Thunderer care for the Ice Gods?'

Aldhard stepped into the tent. 'The Romans are almost ready, my lord; we should go soon if we want to be at the river by mid-morning.'

'I'll be with you shortly.'

Aldhard bowed his head and withdrew.

Thumelicatz looked back to his mother. 'Do you remember the tales you used to tell me when I was young?'

'Every one of them.'

'If I don't return then compose one about me. Tell how I braved the wrath of the Thunderer to keep our land, the land of All Men, free until we have the strength to take on Rome and beat her.' He kissed her again as the tears continued to trickle unevenly down her age-lined face; he turned and left her behind him.

At mid-morning the column rode into the dilapidated remains of a small, Roman military river port, uncared for since the final withdrawal of the legions back across the Rhenus twenty-five years previously. Although the roofs of most of the single-storey barrack buildings and warehouses were still reasonably intact, their brick walls were being eaten into by dense, dark ivy and other climbing plants. Barn swallows swooped in and out of open windows, whose shutters had long since rotted away, constructing their mud nests in the eaves of the deserted build-ings. A pack of wild dogs, which seemed to be the only other inhabitants, trailed the column as they made their way along a grass-tufted, paved street down to the river.

'My people didn't burn this port because my father felt that it was of some strategic use,' Thumelicatz explained. 'He made it a supply depot from where he could provision his forces quickly using the river, but after his murder it was abandoned to rot.'

'Why?' the younger brother asked. 'It could still be extremely useful to you.'

'Yeah, you would have thought so; but the problem would be: who would stock it and who would guard it?' the street-fighter pointed out. 'I imagine there would be a lot of competition for the latter but very few volunteers for the former.'

Thumelicatz laughed. 'I'm afraid that you have understood my countrymen all too well. No clan chief is going to give up his grain and salted meat to be guarded by men from another clan, even though they are all Cherusci. My father had the strength to make them do it but since he's gone they've returned to the old ways of bickering amongst themselves and only ever uniting in the face of an external threat from another tribe.'

'It makes you realise just how close we were to subduing the whole province,' the patrician said as they passed a crumbling brick-built temple. 'To have built all this so deep into Germania shows that we must have been pretty confident of remaining here.'

'It was confidence or rather overconfidence that was Varus' problem.'

The street-fighter scowled. 'Arrogance more like; yet another pompous arsehole.'

Any more opinions the Romans may have had were pushed aside as they passed between a line of storehouses and onto the riverside quay. Before them, each tied to a wooden jetty, were four sleek boats; long with fat bellies and high prows and sterns with a single mast amidships and benches for fifteen rowers on each side.

'We live in longhouses and we sail in longboats,' Thumelicatz quipped. 'We Germans think that it's quite a good joke.'

None of the Romans shared his amusement; instead their expressions were all similar: confusion.

'What's the matter?'

The patrician turned to him. 'Horses, Thumelicus, that's what the matter is. How do we take our horses with us?'

'You don't. The horses are the price for the boats.'

'Then how do we get back across the Rhenus?'

'You'll get home by sailing on out to the sea and then follow the coast west. Your Batavians can handle this sort of boat, they're good seamen.'

'But good seamanship won't protect us against storms,' the street-fighter muttered. 'Last time Germanicus sailed back to Gaul he lost half his fleet in the Northern Sea. Some of the poor buggers were even driven ashore in Britannia.'

'Then you'll be there, ready and waiting, when the invasion fleet finally arrives.'

The elder brother looked sourly at Thumelicatz. 'Is that another Germanic joke, because I didn't find that one particularly funny either?'

'No, merely an observation. But that's the deal: horses for boats and you'll be in the Chauci's lands tomorrow.'

The Romans pulled their horses closer, talking in hushed tones.

'There's Rome for you,' Thumelicatz observed to Aldhard. 'Just wanting to take and unwilling to give anything in return.'

'What if they don't agree?'

'They will; they have to. The prize is too great for them, ultimately, to worry overmuch about a few horses; they just can't bear letting go of anything. Have the horses put into one of the warehouses and leave a man to look after them until we return.'

The younger brother looked over to Thumelicatz. 'It's a deal.'

'But what about my horses?' the patrician asked through clenched teeth. 'It takes months to train them and—'

'And you'll do as you're told, prefect,' the younger brother snapped before turning back to Thumelicatz again. 'But we keep the saddles and bridles.'

'Agreed.' Thumelicatz smiled to himself, and, as the Romans dismounted, whispered out of the corner of his mouth: 'What did I tell you?'

'He really doesn't want to give up his horse,' Aldhard observed seeing the street-fighter remain stubbornly in the saddle.

His expression solemn, Thumelicatz turned to Aldhard. 'The one that looks like a street-fighter—'

Aldhard held up his hand, interrupting him. 'I know; he killed my father and your grandfather as well as wounding Erminatz. I heard; I listened to the whole story and strangely enough I wasn't surprised. I knew that it was more than just a coincidence. Your father's life was spun in a way that it still resounds here on this Middle-Earth even as he feasts in Walhalla.'

Slipping from his horse, Thumelicatz stepped into a boat. 'The story of Erminatz's deeds and their effect upon the Roman empire and Germania will go down through the centuries; of that I am in no doubt.'

A thin, freezing mist draped both banks the following morning, as they made their way north on the second day of their journey; the Ice Gods had passed that night. In the wake of their progress through Germania, the flat land to either side of the river was carpeted in their frost; their chilled breath, biting into his flesh, made Thumelicatz uncomfortably aware of their proximity and the adverse portents they had always brought for his family. He shivered and touched the hammer amulet that hung on a leather thong around his neck, praying to Donar for his forgiveness but knowing that, whether it would be manifest or not, he had to continue on his path for his father's sake.

The sweat of the Batavian auxiliaries heaving upon the oars permeated the chilled air, already melancholic with their ponderous, deep-noted song that blended with that of the oarsmen in the following boats.

'What do you feel, Aldhard, now there has been some time to think about it, knowing that he was the ugly little legionary who killed your father?' Thumelicatz asked, looking at the street-fighter standing with his companions in the stern of the ship behind him.

Aldhard shrugged. 'It was battle and from his account he did it with honour. I cannot in truth hold him to blame for what happened in a fair fight; as neither can you for his taking your grandfather's life.'

'No, I can't. If anything we should be grateful to him for his wounding of my father and making him less than effective at the Battle of the Angrivarii Ridge. Germanicus claimed the easy victory that could be argued to be the final factor that caused Tiberius to recall him. We might be looking at the unknowing saviour of Germania.'

Aldhard grinned. 'Or we might be looking at just an ugly little legionary.'

Thumelicatz joined in his cousin's amusement. 'That too but what a strange whim of the Norns to weave him into my life; it can only mean that this was meant to be the course of action that I should take.' A cry from the lookout in the bow of the ship as it rounded a bend in the river took his attention; a mile distant the eastern bank was filled with ships disgorging troops. Thumelicatz's face hardened. 'It looks as if Publius Gabinius has

come for the Eagle; we had better make haste if we want to get it.'
He turned to the helmsman. 'We'll land here; take us in.'

'That's the Chauci's main township,' Thumelicatz whispered,
pointing to a large settlement about a mile away, built along a low
ridge; the only high land in an otherwise flat and dismal landscape still swathed in a light mist. To the northwest of it, six
cohorts of auxiliary infantry formed up, in a line across frosted
farmland, shielding a legion deploying from column to battle
order behind it. Before the Roman force was a massed formation
of Chauci, growing all the time as men rushed in from the
surrounding areas, answering the booming, warning calls of
horns that echoed all around and off into the distance. 'Their
sacred groves are in the woods to the east, the Eagle will be in one
of those.'

'This could be a welcome diversion for us,' the younger
brother suggested, his breath steaming.

The street-fighter grinned. 'First bit of luck we've had; it looks
like they're all going to have plenty to keep them occupied for a
while.'

The elder brother looked equally pleased. 'We should get
going before we freeze our bollocks off; if we skirt around to the
south the mist will obscure us and we should be able to reach that
woodland undetected.'

Thumelicatz was not so sure. 'It's not ideal; the Chauci will
know why they've come and will either be moving the Eagle or
sending a large force to defend it.'

The younger brother blew into his chilled hands. 'Then we
should do this as fast as possible. It's a mile back to the boats and
a mile and a half to that woodland; with luck we could be on the
river within an hour.' As he spoke a group of mounted warriors

emerged from the Chauci ranks and rode slowly towards the Roman line; one held a branch in full leaf in the air.

Thumelicatz smiled. 'They're going to parley, that may give us more time; let's get moving.'

The Romans moved back into the copse where their Batavian auxiliaries waited as Aldhard crouched down next to Thumelicatz. 'Do you still mean to go through with this, my lord? It makes no difference now which Romans get to the Eagle first, ours or the legion; Chauci blood will still be spilled. Your actions cannot stop that now; we could just leave.'

'We could; but would that guarantee that they would find it? The Chauci hide them well. I need to be sure that it's found so I must go on. I've seen the path that has been woven for me, Aldhard, and, like my father, I must dare to follow it.'

Thumelicatz and Aldhard led the Romans and their auxiliaries at a fast jog across the flat terrain; to the north the two armies were mainly obscured by the freezing mist but it was thinning all the time as the sun climbed higher. Every now and then it lifted slightly and figures could be seen; but they were still stationary.

A huge shout rose up after they had covered nearly a mile.

'The Norns are preparing to cut many a man's life-thread,' Aldhard said as the Chauci began to hammer their swords against their shields, roaring their defiance at the invaders.

Thumelicatz increased his speed. 'The Chauci are brave but they cannot withstand a legion for too long.'

They broke into a run, splashing through an icy stream, brown with the filth discharged from the Chauci's settlement, and pressed on, keeping well to the south of the ridge.

Roman cornua started their low rumbling calls, signalling orders throughout the cohorts; these were countered by the blaring of Chauci horns used more to intimidate the enemy than to inform comrades.

More bellows and war cries filled the air until there came the unmistakeable screeches and ululations of a Germanic charge. As Thumelicatz led them into the wood the first clashes of iron against iron and the dull thumps of shields taking blows resonated in the air; they were soon followed by the shrieks of the wounded and the dying.

Thumelicatz turned to the younger brother. 'The first grove is due east, about four hundred paces away.'

They ran on, following a weaving path, deeper into the wood, occasionally having to hurdle the fallen branch of an oak or beech. Behind them the Batavian decurions were struggling to keep their turmae in some sort of semblance of a two-abreast column but were losing the fight, their men being unused to acting as infantry.

He started to slow; behind him the auxiliaries' officers signalled their men to fan out into a line. They carried on, crouching low, taking care with their steps, easing forward through the trees, javelins at the ready. 'It's straight ahead,' Thumelicatz whispered as he signalled a halt.

Before them, through the light haze of the wood shaded from sunlight by the thick canopy, the atmosphere was brighter where the sun shone down directly onto the thinning mist. The faint sounds of the battle could be heard far off, but nearer at hand the only sound to disturb the peace was birdsong. Thumelicatz crept forward; the two brothers and the street-fighter followed him having given orders for the auxiliaries to wait.

As they came closer to the grove the mist became more translucent revealing a clearing with four ancient oaks at its heart; in the middle of these, resting on two large flattened stones, was a slab of grey granite next to which was piled a mound of wood. Above it dangled a cage, swinging gently, made of thick wicker, the exact shape of, but slightly larger than, a crucified man.

The street-fighter spat and clenched his right thumb in his fingers, muttering to himself.

The younger brother crouched next to Thumelicatz. 'There's no one in it, I can see light coming though the gaps. Thumelicus, what do you think?'

'There doesn't seem to be anyone around; if the Eagle's here it'll be close to the altar, but the lack of guards makes it seem unlikely.' He walked out into the clearing, Aldhard and his men to either side of him; the three Romans followed, nervously poking the earth with their javelins, fearful of stakes concealed in hidden pits.

A search of the altar and the surrounding area proved fruitless. They looked for signs of the ground being disturbed, searched the wood pile and checked for crevices in the trees.

'Our Roman friends seem fearful of the wicker man,' Thumelicatz whispered to Aldhard, noticing the nervous glances at the ominous construction swaying gently above them.

'As well they might; I've watched many a Roman shriek his last in honour of the gods.'

'It's not here,' Thumelicatz concluded eventually. 'We should move on to the next one about half a mile north of here.'

Thumelicatz and his men led the way accompanied by a turma, split up into pairs, scouting to either flank; the rest of the Romans followed behind just visible in the ever-thinning mist. The ringing cacophony of battle had escalated but had drawn no closer as they moved onwards. The fresh scents of damp vegetation, musty leaf-mulch rising from underfoot adding a tang to the clean bracing air, invigorated Thumelicatz; the smells of his homeland were in stark contrast to the swamps around Ravenna where he had spent so much of his life. A gentle neigh from up ahead stopped him dead; he raised a hand and went down onto one knee. The two brothers joined him.

'Sacred horses,' Thumelicatz whispered, pointing through a gap in the trees.

The second clearing was larger than the first and this time had a small grove of elm trees in its midst. Surrounding these was a henge of rough wooden columns, ten feet high and a pace apart; each had a skull placed upon its top. Four tethered white horses grazed on the lush grass around the circle. Three heads, one fresh and the other two decomposing, hung from the branches of the grove above a wooden altar.

After waiting for a few heartbeats it became apparent that, again, there was no one else around. The horses looked up at them curiously as they moved towards the grove and then resumed cropping the grass once satisfied that the intruders neither posed a threat nor possessed any equine treats.

Thumelicatz led the Romans between two of the wooden columns and into the grove; scattered around on the ground were more heads in various advanced states of decomposition. Clumps of hair tied to branches above showed where they had hung until decay had eaten away the scalp and they had fallen free.

'Who were these men, Thumelicus?' the younger brother asked

'Slaves probably; or sometimes a warrior from another tribe captured in a skirmish; any man who is taken prisoner will know what he can expect.' Thumelicatz indicated towards the altar; the wood was ingrained with dried blood.

'Very lovely,' the street-fighter muttered, prodding the ground with a javelin looking for signs of something being recently buried. 'I suppose your gods lap it up.'

'Our gods have kept us free so, yes, they must appreciate human sacrifice.'

'Free to fight each other,' the elder brother scoffed, checking the underside of the altar for anything attached beneath it.

'That is the way of all men: your biggest enemy is closest at hand until foreign invasion makes that enemy your most valuable ally. But come, it's not here; there's one more grove to try to the east.'

They made their way deeper into the forest; here the mist remained in patches, clinging to ferns and low branches. Although they were travelling away from the battle the noise of it seemed to be growing. Thumelicatz ignored it and the muttering of the Romans behind him and pressed on at a crouch concentrating his senses ahead of him. A murmur floated through the air; he signalled for silence and crouched down.

'What is it?' the younger brother whispered, squatting down next to him.

Thumelicatz cocked his ear and pointed ahead. Faintly through the mist, voices could be heard, talking quietly. 'They're no more than a hundred paces away, which means that they must be guarding the grove; I think we're in luck.'

The Roman nodded and gave orders for a scout to go on ahead; moments later a Batavian crept forward into the mist.

Thumelicatz left the Romans to plan their attack and moved over to Aldhard and his men. 'This is not your concern; you don't have to fight alongside these men.'

'Will you fight with them, my lord?' Aldhard asked.

'Yes, although I've no wish to shed Chauci blood. However, I've led these Romans here to reclaim their Eagle and I cannot in honour stand by and watch while they risk their lives for something that will benefit me and my people far more than it will benefit them.'

'Then we fight with you.'

Thumelicatz placed his hand on Aldhard's shoulder. 'So be it, my friend.' With a nod to the other men he turned and rejoined the Romans.

Not long later the scout reappeared. 'Fifty, maybe sixty,' he said in Latin with a heavy accent.

The younger brother looked relieved. 'Thank you, trooper.' He turned back to the patrician. 'Nothing we can't manage. Get going, we'll give you a count of five hundred to circle around them.'

'These men will give no quarter,' Thumelicatz warned the patrician as he left with half the Batavian force. 'They've sworn to protect the Eagle with their lives.'

'If it's there,' the street-fighter muttered.

'Oh it's there all right; why else would they be guarding this grove and not the other two?'

'Fair point.'

The elder brother got to his feet. 'Come on then, up and at them.'

The clearing came in and out of view as a light breeze got up and started playing with the mist. The Chauci warriors could be occasionally seen standing to the northeast of the grove of twenty or so trees of mixed species.

'Donar, sharpen our swords and give us victory,' Thumelicatz mumbled, clutching the hammer amulet around his neck. 'With this Eagle we shall rid our Fatherland of Rome for ever.'

'And you're welcome to it,' the street-fighter added.

Thumelicatz ignored the insult.

All along the line, men were going through their pre-combat rituals, checking weapons, tightening straps and muttering prayers to their guardian gods.

'Right, let's get this done,' the younger brother said, signalling left and right for his men to move out.

Almost sixty men in two lines crept forward towards the edge of the clearing; ahead of them the Chauci talked amongst themselves, sharpening their swords and spear points on stones or flexing their muscles, suspecting nothing as the noise of the battle still raged.

The younger brother raised his arm, took a deep breath, looking left then right and then flung it forward. As one, the Batavians screamed their battle cry and then pelted out of the trees towards their enemy, shield to shield with javelins at the ready.

Taken completely by surprise the Chauci struggled to form up into two lines, their captains bellowing at them and shoving them into position as the low-trajectory javelin volley hit hard, tearing through the gaps in the incomplete shield wall. Screams filled the clearing as a dozen and more warriors were punched off their feet with the slender, bloodied tips of javelins protruding from their backs.

Thumelicatz and his men surged forward on the Batavians' left flank, whipping their long swords from their scabbards and forming a small wedge with Thumelicatz at its head.

Keeping in good formation the Batavians hit the disorganised Chauci in unison, cracking their shield bosses, with explosive force, up into faces whilst thrusting low with their swords at fleshy groins and bellies, harvesting the slimy, grey contents within. In a couple of places a wall had been formed and these warriors fought back with the ferocity of desperate men, jabbing their long spears over the shield rims at their onrushing foe with such strength that, with the momentum of the charge, their tips cracked through the chainmail, to lodge half a thumb's length in a few screaming Batavians' chests; not deep enough to kill outright but painful enough to incapacitate whilst a killing blow was administered.

With a fleet, downwards slash of his sword, Thumelicatz sliced into the shoulder, splintering the collar-bone, of a wide-eyed, snarling man, whilst blocking his counter blow with an upwards thrust of his shield. Blood exploded from the deep wound, slopping over the man's beard as he raised his head to the sky, lips curled back and mouth wide, issuing a scream that would summon the Valkyries. Using the weight of the howling man's body as it slumped to the ground, Thumelicatz wrenched his sword free from the shattered bone as Aldhard, to his right, ducked underneath a wild slash, driving the tip of his sword with an explosive punch, up into the exposed neck of the perpetrator.

Slamming his shield hard to the left, Thumelicatz cracked a skull as he exploded over his writhing victim, punching his sword-weighted fist forward, shattering the teeth of the next warrior in his path, ripping the skin from his knuckles. Ignoring the pain, he sliced his blade left, clean through the warrior's right wrist as he tried to slash his sword down; with a surge of crimson, the hand fell, still clutching the sword as the arm carried on its descent, spewing blood from the fresh stump as yet unnoticed over the agony of the warrior's ruined mouth. The man's eyes rolled as he caught sight of his shortened arm flashing through the air; he screamed, spraying Thumelicatz with a fine red mist and shards of bloodied teeth. With a violent jerk, Thumelicatz brought his knee up to slam into the man's testicles, doubling him over and the scream abruptly changed into a deep growl as the wind grated out of his body; a sharp downward crack of Thumelicatz's sword hilt punched a hole in the back of his head and he crumpled down

Suddenly a shockwave rippled through the whole melee; the encircling force of auxiliaries had struck the Chauci in the rear. It was now just a matter of time. The Batavians pressed their advantage as the dwindling Chauci retaliated with ever-diminishing force until the last one slid to the churned grass with brains spilling out of what was left of his skull.

'Halt and re-form!' someone cried as the two opposing Batavian forces met either side of a ridge of mainly Chauci dead and moaning wounded. The officers bawled their wide-eyed, panting men back and into lines before they could do their own comrades any harm whilst under the influence of the rush of combat.

Thumelicatz looked at his sword arm; it was streaked with blood.

'We should get searching,' the young brother said, taking deep gulps of air.

Thumelicatz nodded and ordered Aldhard and his four men to follow him as he turned towards the grove.

The grove consisted of about two dozen trees of a variety of types that had been planted by man many years ago. Thumelicatz strode through them to a stone altar at the grove's dark centre between an ancient holly and a venerable yew.

The altar was bare.

The Romans joined him; Thumelicatz looked at them in puzzlement. 'There's no sign of the Eagle here.' He kicked at the mossy ground but it was solid and showed no signs of recent disturbance.

'What about in the surrounding trees?' the elder brother asked.

After a futile search Thumelicatz shook his head. 'It's not here.'

'But you said it would be,' the younger brother almost shouted in his frustration.

'That doesn't mean it has to be; perhaps they moved it deeper into their lands.'

'Then why were they guarding this grove?'

'I don't know.'

'Perhaps they just wanted us to think it was here,' the street-fighter suggested, 'after all, fifty or so men aren't going to stop determined people getting the Eagle, but it would be enough to convince people to look in the wrong place.'

The younger brother frowned. 'So where could they have hidden it?'

'I don't know, perhaps we should ask one of their wounded.'

'They won't talk no matter what you threaten them with,' Thumelicatz stated.

'What about the prospect of a nasty time in that wicker man back at the first clearing? That might—'

'Of course!' the younger brother exclaimed, looking at the street-fighter. 'You're right. They were trying to draw attention away from where they had hidden it by guarding the wrong grove. It's in the first grove; we checked everywhere but we didn't look inside the wicker man as it seemed to be empty because light was shining through it and because it was so chilling to look at we wanted to avoid it. But how come it was swinging when there was no wind? Because they had just finished hanging it up when we arrived! We must have just missed them. It's in there.'

The elder brother smacked himself on the back of the head. 'Of course, how stupid. I almost said that would be a good place to hide it as a joke.'

'Would that have been funny?' Thumelicatz asked; he had never understood Roman humour.

'Not really.'

'Good, I thought not. We should go.'

Thumelicatz led them southwest along the side of the triangle they had not yet travelled. The raucous sounds of battle growing ever closer, away to his right, gave even more of a sense of urgency to the final sprint.

After a lung-tearing run of almost a mile they entered the first clearing from the opposite side. The wicker man was still visible hanging over the altar at the centre of the four oaks that made up the small grove. Thumelicatz ran over to it and stopped, looking up at the chilling artefact.

'Can you see it?' the younger brother asked, stopping next to him.

'No, I can't make out anything inside it; we need to get it down.'

'We should be very careful.'

'Do you really think that I don't know what sort of traps could be protecting this?' Thumelicatz turned to Aldhard. 'Hrulfstan's the lightest; get him up into the trees to spring the traps.'

Using their clasped hands as steps, Aldhard and his men immediately began to hoist the lightest of their number up onto the lowest branch in the grove. 'Move away from the altar,' Thumelicatz advised the Romans.

They stepped back, looking up nervously as the leaves above them started to rustle and the wicker man began to twist and sway as the man ascended higher.

Thumelicatz glanced at the swinging man. 'Careful, Hrulfstan, don't shake the branches so much.' The pace of the climb slowed and the wicker man's movement lessened.

A cry of alarm followed by the creaking of straining ropes caused Thumelicatz to jump back. 'Get down!'

The strained creaking grew; two huge logs, sharpened to points at either end, swung down from the treetops, lengthways, arcing through the clearing so that at their lowest point they were chest high, passing just either side of the altar. The creaking rose in tone and volume as the logs swung through to their zenith, straining at the hemp ropes, pausing for a heartbeat at the extreme of their pendulum, before reversing their direction.

As they flashed back through the clearing it became apparent that they were not independent but, rather, joined by a thin iron blade at their centre that passed between the top of the altar and the feet of the wicker man. 'That was designed to slice anyone in half who tried to take the man down.'

'Nice lot, these Germans,' the street-fighter growled, as the logs swung back through with lessening force.

'And you think you Romans are nicer because you crucify people or throw them to the wild beasts?' Thumelicatz asked, getting to his feet.

'Another fair point.'

'Aldhard, cut the ropes.'

The swinging lessened; Aldhard grabbed the logs and stilled them. His men began sawing through the ropes with their swords; they did so cautiously stepping back quickly as they cut each one, looking nervously up at the trees, but no more traps sprung from the heights.

'Can you see any more ropes up there, Hrulfstan?' Thumelicatz shouted.

'Just the rope for the wicker man, my lord.'

'He can't see any more ropes up there other than the one supporting the wicker man,' Thumelicatz translated for the Romans, 'we should be safe to approach it.' He climbed onto the altar and stood up so that his head was knee-height to the wicker man. 'They're made so that they can open, for obvious reasons,' he said examining the thick wickerwork. 'This one opens along either side; we'll have to get it down.' He drew his sword and stood on tiptoe; the end of the blade just reached the rope that hung dead-centre between all four trees disappearing into a thin mist that still clung to their dark, upper reaches. He started to saw; two of his men came to stand either side of the altar to catch the wicker man as it fell. The rope thrummed as the sharp edge worked its way through it.

Thumelicatz sawed harder as the strands of the rope sprang back, one by one, until there were only a couple left. He looked down at his men, checking that they were ready to catch and then worked his blade for the final cut. The rope parted; the loose end flew up into the trees and the wicker man fell, its feet landing with a crunch on the altar. His men grabbed the legs, preventing it from toppling in any direction as a faint metallic ring sounded from above. Thumelicatz thought for an instant and then turned his head up towards the noise as the sun broke through the mist; his eyes and mouth opened in alarm as flashes of burnished iron dropped out of the canopy like lightning bolts. 'Donar!' he shouted at the sky.

Two swords plummeted down from above.

A blade entered his throat at an exact perpendicular, slicing its way down through the internal organs until it came to a jarring halt on the base of the pelvis. The second hit the altar, bending and rebounding with a thunderous roll. Thumelicatz shuddered; his eyes focused in disbelief at the hilt just before them protruding from his mouth, like some cross perched upon a hill of execution. Blood flowed freely around it, trickling into his beard. He knew that his oath had not been cancelled. His legs started to buckle; a grating gargling sound exploded from his throat and blood slopped onto the pommel and the twine attached to it, leading up into the mist-shrouded branches. He fell against the wicker man, pushing it back off the altar, its centre of gravity being too high for the shocked men holding it to support it. Leaving an arced trail of blood globules marking his descent, Thumelicatz fell with it, crashing onto its chest as they hit the ground and then bouncing up slightly, owing to the springiness of the branches woven together. As he thumped back down a second time the wicker man broke open; a bundle wrapped in soft leather rolled out. His eyes began to mist over, white and swirling; as the younger brother picked up the bundle, he could see that it was heavy; it was the Eagle, he knew it.

Thumelicatz looked at the younger brother holding the Eagle and felt triumph as the life seeped from him; Rome had her prize and she would use it to lead her armies away to the north. Rome was about to make her greatest mistake. Germania, the land of All Men, the land his father had liberated from the conquest-hungry empire, was safe for generations. Safe to breed warriors, safe to grow strong, safe to wait until the time was ripe for Germania's tribes to burst out from their dark forests and crush the hated empire.

The white mist thickened and Thumelicatz knew that he would soon meet his father, Erminatz, for the first time; he would be able to stand tall in his presence, look him in the eye and revel in the fact that between them, father and son, they had ensured a Germanic future for the West. With a final effort he grasped the hilt of the sword to ensure that Walhalla awaited him.

The mist became complete and all was white; white as the frost of the Ice Gods.

AUTHOR'S NOTE

This work of historical fiction is based upon the writings of Tacitus, Suetonius, Cassius Dio, Josephus and Velleius Paterculus.

Thumelicus was born in Rome and was forced to become a gladiator. Tacitus says that he will tell us of his fate at the appropriate time; the fact he never does points to it being part of the missing text, either 30–31 or 37–47, thus giving me the freedom to have him still alive at the time of the story.

As a hostage in Rome, Arminius would, more than likely, have lived in Drusus' house as it had been to him that Siegimeri had surrendered and given his pledge. Because of this I have felt free to have him be a part of the elite society of Rome and to be befriended by Lucius Caesar. Lucius' excessive character is my fiction but not out of the question.

Arminius was given equestrian rank by Augustus.

Gaius Caesar did go on a mission to Parthia to conclude a treaty with Phraates V; there is nothing to suggest that Lucius went with him, although Sejanus did go as one of the tribunes. Phraates was the son of Musa, a hetaira who had been given, illegally, by Augustus to Phraates IV as part of his negotiations for the return of the Eagles lost at Carrhae. Josephus tells us that she married her son but that was too much for the Parthians and they were overthrown.

Lucius died in suspicious circumstances in Massalia in AD 2; Sejanus being a part of his entourage is my fiction. Gaius did die two years later forcing Augustus to recall Tiberius – coincidence?

Tiberius was planning a mass invasion of the Marcomanni in AD 6, planning to push all the way to Maroboden, modern-day Prague, when news of the Pannonian revolt came through. He spent the next couple of years suppressing the revolt and Arminius served with him as auxiliary cavalry prefect. Varus being present for the invasion of Bojohaemum was my fiction.

The Battle of the Teutoburg Wald I have based mainly on Cassius Dio's account of the four-day fight, which happened pretty much as described. The tribes did join in, one by one, and there was a terrible downpour. With the fantastic work that Major Tony Clunn did to identify the site of the final day at the Teutoburg Pass, it's now possible to walk much of the ground – and I highly recommend a trip to the museum if you are ever that way. Paterculus tells us of Eggius' surrender, Vala's flight with the cavalry and Caedicius holding out at Aliso.

Strabo is the only writer to preserve Thusnelda's name although it is Tacitus who tells us that Arminius abducted her whilst she was engaged to another; that it was Adgandestrius is my fiction.

Tacitus gives us good accounts of Germanicus' campaigns and I have based my narrative mainly on them. For those of you who wish to read more on the subject, I can recommend *Rome's Greatest Defeat*, by Adrian Murdoch.

Arminius and Flavus did have a conversation across the river before the Battle of Idistavisus and Flavus did end up losing his temper. Arminius was wounded before the final battle at the Angrivarii Ridge and that was blamed for his less than lustrous defence. Tiberius did recall Germanicus before the re-conquest was complete, ostensibly to celebrate his triumph but, more probably, because he was jealous of Germanicus' success.

Arminius was killed by a kinsman; whether it was Flavus and

Segestes we do not know but I felt that they seemed to be the appropriate two to do the deed.

Publius Gabinius did retrieve the Eagle of the Seventeenth in AD 41. To find out how he gets it you'll just have to read *Rome's Fallen Eagle*!

Although this is a stand-alone novel it is connected with *Rome's Fallen Eagle* in that I conceived the idea for writing the story of Arminius' life when Vespasian meets Thumelicus in that book. Both books therefore share a couple of chapters although they are told from different points of view, Thumelicus' and Vespasian's. I hope, dear reader, that you will forgive me for repeating myself.

ACKNOWLEDGEMENTS

I would like, as always, to thank my agent, Ian Drury, at Sheil Land Associates; I wrote this book over four summers and the encouragement he gave me in the third of those summers when I was in the depths of writer's despair was invaluable. My thanks also go to Gaia Banks and Melissa Mahi in the foreign rights department. My best wishes for you in your new job, Melissa.

Thank you to everyone at Atlantic/Corvus, especially Sara O'Keeffe and Will Atkinson and their continued support for my books. Also thanks to Louise Cullen, Alison Davies and Lucy Howkins, to name but a few, for all their work on my behalf.

Thanks again to Tamsin Shelton for doing such a thorough copy edit and wheedling out all those little gremlins that my eyes just can't see.

Finally, thank you to the two people who always come along with me for the ride: you, dear reader, and my lovely wife, Anja.

VESPASIAN

If you loved *Arminius*, why not look out for Robert Fabbri's *Vespasian* series, available now in print and e-book...

Tribune of Rome is the first instalment in the *Vespasian* series

AD 26: Sixteen-year-old Vespasian leaves his family farm for Rome, to find a patron and join the army. But he discovers a city in turmoil and an Empire on the brink. The aging emperor Tiberius is in seclusion on Capri, leaving Rome in the iron grip of Sejanus, commander of the Praetorian Guard whose spies are everywhere. Vespasian is out of his depth, making dangerous enemies (and dangerous friends – like the young Caligula) and soon finds himself ensnared in a conspiracy against Tiberius.

Vespasian flees the city to take up his position as tribune in an unfashionable legion on the Balkan frontier. Unblooded and inexperienced, he must lead his men in savage battle with hostile mountain tribes. But there is no escaping the politics of Rome. Somehow, he must survive long enough to uncover the identity of the traitors behind the growing revolt...